Hoshi and the Red City Circuit

Dora M. Raymaker

ARGA
WARGA
PRESS

Weird Books for Weird People

Argawarga Press is an imprint of Autonomous Press that publishes weird fantasy, science fiction, and horror.

Autonomous Press is an independent publisher focusing on works about neurodivergence, queerness, and the various ways they can intersect with each other and with other aspects of identity and lived experience. We are a partnership including writers, poets, artists, musicians, community scholars, and professors. Each partner takes on a share of the work of managing the press and production, and all of our workers are co-owners.

ISBN: 978-1-945955-12-9

Cover art by Dora M. Raymaker.

ACKNOWLEDGEMENTS

This book exists because Margaret Donsbach Tomlinson let me into her writing group; I thank her and Steve Theme for the early edits, encouragements, and willingness to share the wisdom of their craft. I thank Sheila Thieme for proclaiming herself my first fan and showing me I could make something loved. I thank Ralph Savarese for support in all the ways as we worked together on his book *See it Feelingly*, and for pointing me at Autonomous Press. I thank Andrew Reichart for the incredible edits and the manifestation of publication. And you, too, Muse, for ever always.

CHAPTER 1

I woke, blood trickling from my nose and the dreams of the city tangled in my sweat-damp hair.

There's a bug in my programming. Or maybe it's my hardware. Either way, as I'd slept in the supposed-safety of my bed, the city's entire fleet of vidfeeds had routed straight to my visual cortex: lovers and liars, a babe being born and an old man dying, thieves in black alleys and a plan to break the windows of the Federal Housing Authority—in a city of eighteen mil that's too much information for even me to process. So here I was, shuddering and sobbing, bleeding into my pillow. Again.

Despite the unpleasantness, whatever had downloaded in my sleep could save my life. Thus one of the reasons I never try to fix the bug.

I opened my eyes.

Outside my cathedral window, the jagged skyline of Red City reached for crimson clouds. I traced the graceful spiral of the Arts and Culture Building, the triple towers of the 100 Worlds Trade Union joined by their series of sky-bridges, the prickly quills of the Red City Reporter, the dip of Lan Qui Park all the way down to Landing and Marcie Bay. I loved Red City. Loved every street corner and sky-lift, every tree in every park, every rumbling tube beneath her crust. I loved her, even when she hurt me.

I sniffled into my pillow and dragged myself out of bed. I needed to get to my Private Investigator's office in East of Central if I wanted to catch a new case. I'd gotten the Zander thing wrapped two days ago and that was two days too long without a puzzle.

But four cups of espresso later and feeling no better, I had to concede: not even a puzzle could improve this day. I scrapped the leaving-the-apartment plan and blocked all incoming com transmissions with a thought through my hardware. I sat on the floor instead, fingers twined in the plush carpet, and watched daylight colorize the skyline to the drumbeat of my headache.

BANG BANG BANG!

"Hoshi Archer!"

The voice of Inspector Cassandra Sorreno resounded through the door as she pounded in time to the throb of my temples. She wasn't large, but she sounded large, especially when she was annoyed with me.

Sorreno had been my primary sponsor back when the Red City Police Department owned me as a code-breaker, before Integration Law had passed and I got my private investigator job. I liked her, but I didn't want to let her in. I was still under a lot of scrutiny and if I were her I'd be convinced I'd been on an all-night bender, or worse. I couldn't tell her the truth either; I wasn't supposed to be able to see through the city's sensors even when I was awake.

"Hoshi! Open up!" BANG BANG BANG!

I sent a mental command at the door, yanked a dust-colored throw over my shoulders to hide my underpants and bra, and wiped the blood off my face with the corner of the throw.

Sorreno entered, stocky and brown and dressed in brown, her hair coiled in a zillion tiny braids. She wasn't pretty but her presence filled the room. The brown bag under her arm smelled of teriyaki and mangoes. She glared at my empty studio as though hunting for clues. "You look like hell, Hoshi."

"Sorry, Sir, too many hours at the code and a bit of bad sleep." Wasn't a lie. But it didn't justify hiding under a blanket in my underwear at noon either. I ran my fingers through my hair. Trying to look presentable had to count for something, right?

"I brought you some solid food." Sorreno searched for somewhere to set the bag. I find furniture perplexing. I don't even have a desk at my PI's office because, well, what would I put on it? All my stuff's in my head, as evidenced by the pale blue shine of my quantum processor, my navis, beneath the skin of my forehead: the mark of my caste.

"Thanks. Um." I also find social graces perplexing. I wasn't supposed to interact with Sorreno in my underwear. But I also wasn't supposed to tell her bluntly that I needed to put on clothes. And I also wasn't supposed to walk away without saying anything. So I swayed uncertainly, trying to dredge up some lesson I'd learned in Socialization and coming up null.

Sorreno was helpful, as always. "Oh for Kripke's sake Hoshi, go put on some clothes!"

She let me wash, dress, eat (indeed, teriyaki yakisoba and mango with sticky rice), and pull myself as together as I was going to get before she dropped her bombs.

"I need you at the RCPD on consult. I've got three Operators dead. One of them was Claudia Foucault, I think you knew her?"

Knew her, Claudia, knew—knew her. Claudia, lavender and soap, the smell of her hair as I pressed her head to my lips and her arms wrapping around my waist, no—*NO*. The programming that would have moved my body into a visible reaction couldn't process the shock, frozen, for three seconds, in place, even breath, stop breathing. Surely Sorreno had no idea how close Claudia and I had been or she would have been more delicate in how she'd put that. Shock slid toward grief and rage, heat rising in my cheeks, and I bit back the feelings and stuffed them as far from my heart as I could get with the deftness of life-long practice. *Forget Claudia.*

Sorreno wasn't done ruining my terrible day. "You're coming with me to the station. And while we're there, stay away from Martin. He's dropping hints he has something on you. Don't give him any fodder."

Perfect. If there was such a thing as an arch-nemesis in real life, Martin would be mine.

Sorreno made a snap-snap "follow-me" gesture with her fingers.

Technically, I didn't have to go. I'm a free citizen these days, Hoshi Marie Archer, Private Investigator. Among the first of the Operator caste in Red

City to be granted a job that didn't involve programming quantum computers. In the first cohort of those with power over their own lives.

Realistically, I wasn't as free as the Integration Office led people to believe. There was the fact that I owed Sorreno a lifetime of favors; the fact that I had to abide by an unknowable number of conditions and rules, both official and unofficial, often contradictory; the fact that I cared about Red City more than myself (that's the danger of spending too much time tangled in her sensors); the fact that I'd just learned my ex was dead—

I re-swallowed my feelings, buttoned my black bolero jacket over a white blouse, slipped my steel-tipped boots over the most comfortable black slacks I owned, and braced myself for The World Outside My Apartment.

It wasn't as bad as I'd feared. Most of the night's information overflow had jammed itself into the pits of my subconscious, where there was room for it to writhe and process far from my conscious functioning.

It wasn't great either. Sorreno handed me a wad of tissues as my nose started to bleed again. I saw a sensor cam on the side of the building at the corner of Ship's Way and Xavior, where we descended to the tube, and I gave it a dirty look.

♦ ♦ ♦

The Red City Police Department was not one of my favorite buildings in the city. Black, seemingly windowless, and shaped like five boxes with rounded edges stacked precariously atop each other, its receipt of an architecture award did not make it any less of an eyesore. What did make it less of an eyesore—to my eyes at least—was the RCPD sigil, its corporate symbol, shining from all four sides. The backdrop was a shield, like all law enforcement corps. But within the shield was the city seal: a Valkyrie with one foot in the fields and one foot in the sea, fierce and noble. In her hand, a trident aligned with the bird-shaped constellation Cleo, its middle tine pointed at

Sol. Below her shone the city's motto: "She flies on her own wings between the stars." The seal was supposed to represent commerce, but to me the Valkyrie of Red City was an emissary, a bridger-of-worlds.

Sorreno thoughtfully brought me into the RCPD building through an unmarked, unremarkable employee entrance, sparing me the chaos of the public lobby.

She punched the lift button for the third sub-basement and I felt less spared of anything. The only things on that level were the department's quantum stationary systems and the morgue. Since I could access the stationaries from anywhere with an idle thought, we must be headed to the other place.

"Hoshi!"

Dr. Angel Smith grinned up from a gurney I took care not to look down at. She was small, cute, blond, freckled, and looked about a decade younger than her actual mid-30's. I liked Angel. A lot. As much as I hated the morgue. I tweaked my sensory programming to block my sense of smell.

Angel's grin wobbled and fell as she processed through *Yay, Hoshi!* and into *Ugh, Hoshi hates the morgue.* She frowned. "So sorry you had to come down here."

"It's okay." I hugged myself and wished I could cut the rest of my senses too.

"We're here about case number 88975b." Sorreno took a white-knuckled hold of the triangular sleeve of my bolero, as though to keep me from falling.

Well, there was some precedent for falling. I'd only worked with code at the RCPD, and there were reasons corpses weren't on my PI list of services. The two previous times I'd visited the morgue for anything besides hooking up with Angel hadn't gone well.

"Of course, Sir." Angel blinked at a 3V, and I heard the clicking of latches releasing on cabinets. Click. Click. Click. Three bodies.

Sorreno tugged me by the sleeve to the closest one, watching me with awkward intensity. The fingers of her other hand wrapped around the fused glass locket at her neck, fidgeting the way she always did when nervous. Family heirloom, she'd told me once. She'd not told me what was inside. "Ready?"

I sent a silent prayer to the Trinity of Signal, Encoding, and Noise that it wouldn't be Claudia and nodded. Signal help me if seeing her makes my feelings bubble back to the surface. Sorreno slid out the body pan.

The good news: it wasn't Claudia.

The bad news: it was someone else I knew.

I spun a one-eighty and fixated on the cream-colored mortar between the polished stone floor tiles, tracing the thin lines with my eyes. Waiting for the pre-faint speckles to either overtake me or subside.

"Hoshi?" Sorreno's hand on my shoulder.

"I'm—I'm okay," the words came as an automated response from my linguistics programming rather than anything volitional, or even honest. I swallowed. "I know her. Her name is Nessa Mason."

I'd only seen her face once in the flesh. But I have perfect recall via my memory index and facial recognition programs to identify people even if their skin had been...altered. Nessa and I had run into each other in a Cryptos Soup 'n Sub. I'd become desperate for lunch during the Endless Boring Stakeout of Endless Boredom of '09. She was a regular. I wouldn't have spoken to her—or even noticed her—if she hadn't been wearing a gem-studded clockwork bee pin that I recognized.

Because in the Mem, the informationsphere, I knew her pretty well. In the Mem Nessa went by the name Bees, presented as a jet-black hermaphrodite in a yellow duster, and had an identical bee pin programmed onto the duster's lapel. Her trademark in both worlds. I wouldn't call Nessa a friend, but I would call her a regular acquaintance. She was owned by 100 Worlds Music Corporation where she worked in big-time advertising, programming primo promo feeds. She was also the hottest coder of illegal pornware in Red City. Which, as far as illegal things went, wasn't high on my list of concerns, but Sorreno might disagree. So I said simply, "I had lunch with her once."

Sorreno grunted.

Maybe Nessa's moonlighting in pornware would matter. Maybe not. I walked a fine line with the denizens of the Red City underworld and didn't want to piss off anyone left of legal without a really good reason. I braced for a visual scan of the body and turned back around.

Nessa had been painted entirely—eyelids, lips, ears, every millimeter of skin—with vibrant designs of exacting complexity. Structured lattices folded into fractals which dissolved into chaotic haze before becoming lucid again, whorls and weaves and explosions of geometries and colors and patterns: quantum code. Or, what code would look like if it only used visuals instead of a full sensory space, and its multi-dimensionality was flattened to cover the surface of human skin. Rather like a flat map of a planetary sphere, unfolded into that funny jagged shape, without the smell of dirt or the feel of the wind, frozen in rotation. I fell into its curious mathematics, matrices too incomplete to resolve into meaning, yet hinting there was meaning, given the right key. Which distanced me enough from the fact that this was once a person to snapshot the image into my memory index for recall. Angel turned the body so I could see it all.

The skin of Nessa's forehead had been slashed; someone had removed her navis. I twitched beneath Sorreno's grip and pointed.

"We don't know where her navis is. Yet," Sorreno answered.

I wanted to ask a million questions, but the faint-feeling started stalking me again, so I grimly gestured for the next cabinet.

The next one was Claudia. I couldn't think about that yet, about her. Had to stick to business. I snapshotted the ghastly pseudo-code, the slashed forehead, and moved on.

The last corpse I did not recognize. But it was another young woman from my caste, painted and mutilated like the other two. Her tag identified her as "Jane Doe." Which, considering how tight the city is about registering my people with fifty different agencies, fingerprinting, retinal printing, chipping, pattern scanning, and cataloging us seventy-five ways to Lastday, meant she was illegal, a rone.

So what do a half-legit half-pornware programmer, an ultra-conservative do-gooder, and a rone have in common? Other than the same make-up artist?

On that note, I did my usual passing-out-in-the-morgue thing.

◆   ◆   ◆

I woke in Sorreno's office to the sound of her voice at a height of hissing annoyance. I didn't move.

"Of course I brought Hoshi in on this, who else do we have? Martin? I need the code on those bodies broken."

"That would be fine if all she was going to do was break the code. But she's not. She's going to go out there and play Thelma Savvy, Girl Detective. She's not under oath anymore, Cassy, and she was slippery even when she was. And I think you underestimate the severity of her impairments." The second voice belonged to Inspector Rolland Zi from Vice, who I did not like. Zi is Op-o-phobic, and openly and vocally anti-Integration. Plus, he's corrupt as a bad memory slip that's been dipped in acid and sunk to the bottom of Marcie Bay.

"She took just as strict an oath to get her PI license. And I don't know what you mean about slippery; Hoshi was an exemplary employee, and she's been an exemplary consultant." Sorreno stretched the truth there, but I did always do a good job. "We've no one else skilled enough on staff, and no one else I trust enough civilian-side. And if she finds out something useful besides the meaning of that code, I don't see how it's a problem. And it's my case." Punchy emphasis on that last sentence.

"Well, she's going down, Cassy. Martin's really found something on her this time. And you don't want to be connected to her when it breaks. It's not going to look good for the Department." I imagined Zi's bushy black eyebrows and greasy round face wrinkling with feigned concern.

"You let me worry about that."

Most of that was Zi's routine anti-Operator and anti-Hoshi griping, but the comment about Martin had me concerned. No one took seriously Martin's attempts to catch me red-handed in something unsavory, certainly not someone like the Director of Vice. Particularly not *the* Director of Vice, given that Martin was an Operator and Zi never listens to anything Operators say. After I heard Zi leave, I waited seven minutes and twenty-three seconds before pretending to wake.

"Here, have some water. How are you feeling?" Sorreno handed me a cheap degradable cornstarch cup that was already disintegrating from the water.

"I'm okay. I'm good." I sat and sniffed back a fresh trickle of nosebleed.

"Sorry to make you do that, but—"

"It's okay. If you'd tried to show me pictures I would've asked you to take me down in person anyway." Quantum code is a surprisingly subjective business for mathematics. Cameras, machines of any kind, can't focus on it right; it must be experienced with human senses. Which is the whole point; when computers can process virtually infinite calculations simultaneously, the irrationality of human thought is the only way to create effective encryption. And nothing is more irrational than the idioglossias—the private, internal, and unique languages—of my people. I sipped my water.

Sorreno's office reflected the hard-working chaos of a competent civil servant with four times more work than anyone, no matter how competent, could manage. Two of the walls were encrusted with holosheets and digipages; the third, an over-erased board with little boxes sketched around things labeled "do not erase" and a square centimeter of clear space just left of center. A 3Vplate with its little black dataslip box spanned her desk, the same old awful one I'd begged her to replace for years. It's got a flaw that causes the holography to cycle too slowly. Sorreno's non-Operator eyes can't see the flicker, but it makes me batty.

The front of her desk and office door sport silver plaques:

Inspector Cassandra Sorreno, Director

Miscellaneous Physical Crimes Division, Red City Police Department

Due to the miscellany, I guess, she ends up with unclassifiable cases that bridge between my world and hers. I suspect the main reason she lobbied so strongly for my Integration job was it gave her more leeway to send me across cultural lines. I can travel into the Operator community where she can't go. Not to minimize our personal relationship, but people have complex motives.

Theoretically, because I'm an Operator, I'm not supposed to understand most of them.

Realistically, I have unique insights into motivation because I'm not blinded by the same assumptions normals make.

Practically, I had a lot of work to do before I would get anywhere near understanding motivation with respect to Sorreno's Strange Case #88975b. Starting with factoring what the point of the crime was in the first place. Was it to kill the women? To steal their navi? To make awful art? Did the code mean anything? I didn't even know yet if it was murder; dead just meant dead and did not alone imply method or motive. That's what forensics were for.

"...in the file," Sorreno was saying.

I blinked and shivered. "Sorry, Sir, could you start that again?"

"The forensics. They're in the case file. And you're not to share that information. Given yesterday's fistfight with Councilor Kang over housing limits, the last thing we need is mainfeed coverage of weird Operator deaths. There'll be another backlash, and another fistfight, and then the mobs again like last month, and Kang, Popov, and the rest will use the whole mess to request a repeal of Integration Law, like they always do. I mean it, Hoshi." She shot me an angry-mother look. Then she opened her mouth, closed it, shifted. Movements uncharacteristically indecisive for Sorreno. She sighed. "Three women, all Operator caste, between twenty-five and thirty-two years of age, all within the past few weeks.... Hoshi, just—" She stopped.

"Just what, Sir?"

She jerked and turned on me with such intensity I couldn't bear it and had to look away, her voice shrill with implication, "Three Operators your age, Hoshi! Your age!"

Holy Trinity, Sorreno thought I was on the Next Victim List!

She looked away, now aloof. "Just.... Just be careful."

I sat motionless, cutting the programming that would have moved my flesh into an expression. My thoughts got tangled in my feelings, making my linguistics slow to figure a response. And when it came, it came stuttering and strange. "Well. Deep. Uh... Well, well better get back to work. I."

On the way out, I glimpsed Martin Ho lurking behind a gunmetal-gray cubicle wall near the lift, his close-set blue eyes tracking me. He tugged on his straight, white-blond hair, the way he does when concentrating extra hard.

I couldn't help it. I hadn't left the house with much self-control and nothing had happened to improve the situation. I opened a channel in the Mem and shot Martin a message on his work frequency with a total disrespect for any level of protocol. "Mr. Ho. Didn't they teach you in Socialization that it's not polite to stare?"

Martin clamped off his channel, bared his teeth, and vanished back into Cubeland.

Okay, that was probably unwise. But I wasn't going to find out if the Sword of Martin was really hanging over my head by doing nothing.

True, I played along the edges of legality, but never had I done anything outright against the law. Well, besides the stuff with the city sensors and the RCPD access codes, but—

I took the sonic tube straight home.

I really needed to process.

CHAPTER 2

The next morning I stood at my window, as I do every day, tracing the skyline of Central with a fingertip. The peaks and domes and points, and the graceful spiral of the Arts and Culture Building, and the triple towers of the 100 Worlds Trade Union joined by their series of sky-bridges, and the prickly quills of the Red City Reporter, and—I've recited a litany to the major buildings in Red City since I was six. The diamond-shine off Marcie Bay and her strands of boats and piers twinkled through the opening made by Lan Qui Park. Morning fog obscured the water further out, but in a few hours I'd see the blue-green of the Beryl Sea all the way to the horizon.

That window is why I rent this apartment. It's more than twice my height and arched like an ancient cathedral. One pane. No flaws. No reflection. A perfect view of the terrible city before me, within me.

Between my mind and my machine, the programs I'd started last night ran and information churned, using the meat of my brain as swap and storage. No matter how advanced our materials technology gets, nothing compares to the brain for sheer memory capacity. I'd erected a partition between my consciousness and the programs, but my thoughts were sloggy with so many extra processes running in the background. I rely on my navis' hardware just as much as it relies on my wet-memory.

All Worlds Medical Association has the following to say about me and my people:

> *K-Syndrome is the result of defects in multiple areas of the "K-Region" of the human genome, as identified early 22nd. cen. by Dr. Wilton Karl. Due to the epistatic relationships between affected genes and the rest of the genome, multiple pathologies*

result.

1) Verbal-sequential IQ at least three standard deviations below visual-associative IQ (Parenti Scale)

2) Abnormal sensory processing, including perceived intensity, attentional capacity, and integration of sensory stimuli

3) Impairments in motor-sequencing required to carry out complex tasks such as speech

Additional pathologies may occur.

Due to the complexity of the epistatic interactions between defective and healthy genes, the possibility of cure is excluded. However, symptoms are generally relieved by early intervention and socialization training coupled with life-long medication/assistive technology.

But what the official medical description doesn't include are these additional facts:

1) Our visual-associative IQs are by definition at least a standard deviation higher than a non-Operator's.

2) Our sensory processing gives us preternatural capacity for detailed observation.

3) Our "assistive technology" is really the most powerful machine ever created. And, not despite but because of our "defects," only we can use it.

During the Marston Debates four years ago, the main arguments against

Integration Law were that we were so stupid we'd never survive our autonomy, and that we were so enhanced we'd put the normals out of work and create an employment crisis. Luckily the voters of Red City found both arguments, if not as ironic, as least as ridiculous as I did. Narrowly, anyway.

So here I was today, working consult as a free woman and having trouble finding the sleeves in my shirt because I was sacrificing sensory integration and motor controls to work out complex case data. A girl's gotta prioritize.

I can take in a lot more information than I can understand. So I sort it all with seekers and filters to get it down to a size my consciousness can manage. None of the data would be understandable for at least a day, so I'd do some legwork first.

I dressed for disreputableness in a tunic of burned-out data slips that shimmered like a fish's scales and a necklace of kinetic art studded with black-and-white gems. When visible tech is taboo (reminds the normals of pariahs like me), data slips and clockworks sadly pass for edgy. Plus the art was made by Nessa's bee pin tinker Kelvin; a sympathetic connection for those who believe in that sort of magic. And Nessa's bee pin tinker was the first stop on my to do list. Lastly, I added my requisite boots and bolero.

After two shots of espresso to help with the sloggy, I hopped the sonic tube to Shirring Point, infoseeking. Trusting the city's convoluted wisdom more than logic, flowing with the current of her Signal.

Gory details of the case and Martin-threats aside, I love nothing better than a ridiculously perplexing puzzle. Except a walk through Red City's streets.

Brine blew from the sea as I came above ground at Port Street and Ship's Way, and crossed toward the water. Shirring Point juts into Marcie Bay, long and narrow, separated from the Landing District by an archway of twisted metal and colored glass. Shirring is where most crimes and most innovations in the city are born, courtesy of law enforcement's abandonment of the area in hopes its depravity will remain contained. The usual urban planning tactic.

Shirring enforces its own.

Within, Frontal Market hummed with streamers and glitter and the click and whirl of gears and the shouts of barter like a fairy market from a fantasy holo, and I grinned, working my hair back into a messy braid. Music blew on the breeze off Marcie Bay. My steel-toed boots clicked on the blackstone cobble of the oldest street in Red City, built just after the Cleopatra landed at the tip of Shirring to start the first settlement outside Sol's system. I loved this part of town. I loved every part of town, but this part I loved for both its history and its chaos.

I worked my way through Frontal Market with zen-like abandonment of desire and a blind faith that if I wandered long enough I'd find my destination. The booth configuration changes constantly and no one's got a map. The sensor cams in Shirring had been smashed ages ago, as had any hotspots or citizen ID readers; people walked invisible here.

Eventually I heard a clockwork ticking and the tinkling of chimes in the rising westward sea wind. A holosign on its last legs flickered above the sun-faded blue and orange awning: Hi-Five Tinker and Repair. Kelvin looked sun-faded too, hair the color and consistency of dry straw, blue eyes bleached, and face white with the zinc sun-block he applies to maintain his near-albino pallor. He polished something small and shiny with a black cloth and smiled without looking up. "Hi Hoshi." He has 360 vision via a clever arrangement of mirrors, as well as a reputation that deters thieves.

We've also known each other since we were ten. For all I knew he could smell me. He wasn't an Operator, but the people who choose to be tinkers feel like kin. They work with macro-machines and program the old-fashioned way, in pull-stops and plain-text and other archaic mumbo I don't understand.

"Hi Kel. Here's for you." I pulled a handful of tiny metal parts and bits of broken jewelry from the pockets of my bolero. I collect them for him, things found underfoot or flowing toward a gutter in the evening rain.

He split a gap-toothed grin and snatched the treasure like a raven after sparkle, pushing his creepy tinker's lenses down to inspect the objects with eyes gone nightmare-size. "I say gal, 20 c's I'll give ye for the lot of 'em!"

"Apply it to me tab, good sir!" I replied with an equally affected accent. We'd been play-acting roles for decades; my scavenged parts are given in friendship, as are the tinker's toys he gifts me.

Kelvin secreted the trash into the cabinets beneath the counter and I pushed a clear space between bins of knick-knacks to plant my elbows and get serious. "I need some help, Kel."

He frowned at my worried face. "What's up? That bitch Mai Chandra at Integration getting you down again?"

"Urg, yeah. She's always getting me down. Do you do personality repairs?" I wanted to shade that with a laugh but wasn't feeling amused enough for my programming to supply it. "No, I need help with crime stuff. Know Nessa Mason?"

"Yeah, sure. Bees! I made her bee pin, you know." A happy grin.

"Yeah. I know."

Intel number one: Kelvin, who knows everything that happens on the upper layers of the underworld, didn't know Nessa was dead. Which eliminated syndicate activities from the motivation-for-murder list. The spectacular nature of these deaths would've been more public if they had been intended to make a gangland point. So much for the easiest answer. "Heard any slop on Nessa lately?" I asked.

Kelvin pulled over the swivel stool from the part-strewn back counter. My auditory filters chose that moment to go down—part of the same bug, I've always suspected, that causes sensorfeed to invade my sleep—and I winced as the metal legs screamed across the cobbles. Amping down my hearing, I focused in a directed angle toward Kelvin. The chatter of barter faded and I heard the soft smack of Marcie Bay slapping against the breakwater beyond the marketplace. Kelvin settled on the stool. "Not really, why? You're not going after pornware now, are you, Officer Archer?"

"I'll go after pornware right after the brain removal."

"So what is it then?"

I was too slow with everything running in the background to turn off the programming that manages my facial expressions in time. I winced and Kelvin saw it.

"Hoshi, is Nessa in trouble?"

Torn about Sorreno's warning to keep mum on the case, I thought about the strangeness of the paintings and asked instead, "What about anything akimbo from the Cantors or the NuVuDoo folk, the people who talk to the élan vitals?"

Kelvin's breathing changed and he shoved the tinker's lenses out of his face. Deadpan: "You know I don't get mixed up in alien business."

Intel number two: Something was akimbo with the people who communicated with the élan vitals, the creatures that lived in the electromagnetic. Something that made even Avidly-Apathetic-re.-Aliens Kelvin feel afraid. Which kept human sacrifice on the motivation list—I didn't know much about the creatures, but I did know they could be attracted by ritualistic acts, and some of them liked blood or extreme emotions. Much less of an easy answer than the syndicate would have been.

"Trinity, what's got you all torqued up about the Cantors and Santeros?" I asked, but a customer interrupted with a blocky machine to fix.

While Kelvin worked, the man gossiped, good as live feed from a vid cam. People will slop almost anything to Kel's homely face, making him my traditional first stop for random intel. Plus, it's an excuse to visit him. Four years ago, after getting beat nearly to death by riot cops for defending an Operator during the Moondust Rebellion in Central District, Kelvin had entered Shirring Point and never come out. I always felt a little guilty because I'm not sure he would have been so sympathetic toward the protesters had he not been my friend.

After the man left, Kelvin turned back to me. "I haven't heard anything

about Nessa in weeks. As far as I know she's still churning out those custom
com chips. Can't you just, you know, contact her direct in the Mem?"

I scanned the area before leaning in close. Curse Sorreno's orders. Kel
wouldn't know an important detail without context to hook it on, and he
wasn't likely to slop the intel without knowing the stakes either. "She's dead,
Kel. Nessa. I'm trying to factor it."

Kelvin's pale face went long, and he exhaled and bowed his head. "I'm
sorry, Hoshi. I've heard you speak of her more than once."

"I'm sorry too. And yeah, she wasn't a friend like you're a friend, but she
was one of my own. Know anything that can help?"

Kelvin closed his eyes and I let time pass, listening to the slosh of the bay,
the awking of the sea birds, the muffled clatter of commerce.

"One thing. Maybe helpful," Kelvin finally said. "Nessa started doing
business out of Husson District recently, a place called the Velvet Glove. You
know about that?"

"I know the Glove, yeah, high class. But no, I didn't know Nessa was
distributing there. What are you thinking?"

Kelvin's eyes flickered to check his mirrors before answering quietly.
"The folks at the Glove...they're not like the syndicate here in Shirring.
They've got ties back here—you know, everyone tithes to Regina in the end—
but they run a different op uptown. Some nasty drug stuff. Some powerful
people. Powerful as Regina and not Devoted to her. I figured Nessa was in
with them because they have access to a higher crust of clientele, but you never
know. It's all I can think of. For now. Interesting?"

"Mm... maybe." On one hand, Nessa had worked her way up in the
advertising world quickly and efficiently; no reason why she wouldn't work
her way up in the underworld the same way. On the other hand, Nessa
would've come into contact with unusual people at the Glove, people who ran
far outside any circles I touched—or wanted to touch. "It's worth exploring.
Thanks."

I still wanted to know what had him so nervous about the Cantors and Santeros, but he'd already evaded twice and I didn't want to lean further. I get my intel more by pulling than by pushing. And I had other sources.

We chatted about silly stuff, laughing to dispel the tension. If Kelvin had been a young female Operator I might have slopped more facts about the case and told him to watch his back. But I respected Sorreno enough to keep quiet about the details; she was right about the political implications of the evidence.

All three women had died of massive intracerebral hemorrhage when their navi were ripped from their heads by brute force. All of the evidence suggested they were alive and conscious up to that point. Our hardware is, of course, removable for upgrades and repairs. But the hundreds of thousands of tiny needles connecting our brains to the machine through the pores of our skulls only retract with a willful command. Which made it extra disturbing that the women were conscious at the time of their deaths. Why would they, seemingly, let themselves be killed?

They showed no other signs of ill use. No bruising, no chafing, no evidence of struggle, and none of the stress-and-fear chemicals expected in murder victims. But then, their blood alcohol levels at time of death approached a stupefying .2. Angel's report listed the culprit as 2500c a bottle, top-of-the-line vintage, Cassiopeian red whiskey, mixed with a crude home-brew distilled from beckerwood that produces hallucinations along with its hundred-proof whammy. Their blood also contained trace amounts of nyquolium-quadrolate, a drug that inhibits an Operator's ability to visualize code. One possible explanation for why, if the women were conscious, they had not sent the command to safely remove their hardware.

They had been painted before they died.

All three women were dumped within two days of death into the refuse bins outside the Integration Office kitchen, and found by the sanitation worker who pushes the bins down the hall to the reclaimer. No sensor footage explained how the bodies got there. A month ago, when a bunch of Operators were murdered in the bombing at Club Blue, it had sparked city-wide protests uncomfortably reminiscent of the prelude to the not-too-far-distant bad-old-riot days. Add this week's friction over the Inclusion Act and housing limits, and the city couldn't seem to cool down. The Integration Office is Controversy Incarnate even without the addition of corpses.

I know. I go to the Integration Office weekly (or the IO, an acronym Operators use with irony since it's more a singularity of Kafkaesque bureaucracy than anything capable of "Input/Output"). My time there passes like this:

Integration Officer Mai Chandra: Have you been working as a PI exclusively?

Hoshi: Yes, ma'am.

MC: Have you been keeping away from illicit substances, illegal activities, and unethical actions?

H: Yes, ma'am.

MC: Have you had at least eight solid meals this week and spent at least 96 hours away from your berth?

H: Yes, ma'am.

MC: Have you socialized with at least four individuals who are not Operators in face-to-face interactions over the last eight days?

H: Yes, ma'am.

MC: What did you do on Secondday last week, between noon and four?

It goes on like that, twenty minutes just like that, every eight days, for the rest of my working life—or until Integration Law either gets repealed or amended. Trinity, being on parole would be easier!

The IO: its poorly-conceptualized implementation the only thing supporters and opponents of Integration Law agree on. As the Red City Reporter dubbed it, "an equal-opportunity loathing."

Anyway, Sorreno's case file didn't include anything else particular to the

Integration Office or caste frictions. It did include a lot more wacky weirdness and glaring gaps. Like...

The hand-made paint used for the pseudo-code contained charred human bones, blood, feces, shells from Broadway Beach, crushed blackstone, and tzaddium—the nearly-noiseless element that makes large scale quantum computing possible and Operators identifiable from afar. The iridescent pale blue of the tzaddium on our navi is what shows through our skin.

The forehead slashing on the victims had been done by an easily-procured under-the-counter Maverick sonic blade 550. Untraceable, illegal, and everywhere.

Not a single enlightening fiber, fleck of dirt, or scrap of DNA to be found. The DNA of the charred human bones linked back to no one. Probably Black Market, procured off-orbital.

The blood and feces belonged to the victims themselves, as did the tzaddium. Every Operator, including me, keeps a small stock of tzaddium around in case we need to repair, upgrade, or generally tinker with our hardware. Given that we Ops are treated like live firearms, possession of tzaddium is tightly controlled. A unique marker in the liquid metal makes our navi—and our spare tzaddium—always traceable back to the owner.

The ritualistic nature of the painting and the navis removal suggested a serial job.

Or, someone trying to get the attention of, or communicate with, an élan vital. Like when the ambassador from Callisto visited Red City last year and made a show of setting up a compass rose made of compasses and star ship dimension drives to call the élan Strange Navigator. That had been pretty weird; I still couldn't work out if the creature looked more like a silver woman or a bunch of tentacles. And she's one of the more human-looking aliens.

Anyway, the ritualistic nature could also suggest an elaborate hate crime or incendiary political statement since the bodies were found at the IO.

Or a combo of any number of those unsavory options.

No wonder Sorreno's fingers had barely left her locket as she discussed the case!

A lot would depend on what I pulled from the paintings. If it wasn't really code, then the hate crime option remained in play. If it turned out to be true-code, it meant one of my kind was responsible in some way for the painting. Hate crime less likely—unless we had an Efram Caper, working the other side.

Which segued nicely into where I was headed next, out of the domain of my friend and into the lair of my enemy. Off to spy on the Sea Witch.

CHAPTER 3

I pushed through the fractal-painted doors of the Julia Set Saloon. The Julia is the oldest Operator establishment in Red City. And, mostly by virtue of its location deep in the heart of Shirring Point, the most disreputable.

Well, I shouldn't down-spin the Julia. Given that I was grinning at Blinker behind the counter and ordering "the usual!" clearly I found something redeeming about it.

Blinker isn't an Operator (technically Integration Law allows any occupation; realistically no Op would be allowed to choose "bartender"). But he is always there, as single-minded as one of us. I hear he even sleeps in the back, in little three-and-four-hour shifts on a bed of lorrie feathers. The Julia's bartenders have always been remarkable. Maybe if I'm ever bored I'll make a history docu about the Julia. Or not—I'd be shot by the syndicate or something worse long before it reached the public feeds. The Julia was prime turf for Operator-related black market deals.

Blinker nodded and smiled and started my black-trance espresso, while I turned away from the bar to get a lay of the clientele.

My people are idiosyncratic, mathematically trained if not always inclined, and have a wicked sense of humor. The place was less club and more encrustation of half a century of variations, puns, and artistic reinterpretations of the function $J(f)$—the Julia set fractal. I pushed the delicately curving, self-repeating leaves of the botany experiment "Creeping Julia" out of my face and read a new poem projecting on the floor at my feet that led with, "Julia, don't leave me in the Fatou Dust." The Julia Set was filled with Julia Sets, fittingly and satisfyingly fractal in itself.

I heard the whoosh of my espresso hitting the wooden surface of the bar, and I reached back, my hand finding the warm comfort of the cup.

Eighteen people, all Operators, sat mostly in pairs or threes. The usual mish-mash of styles and types from the messy kid with the food stains to the haute couture lady looking like she'd stepped straight off a runway in the Diamond District: my people forever unified by our lack of uniformity. This early in the day there wasn't much going on.

But the Sea Witch was always here around now. The Sea Witch being the street name of Luzzie Vai, the narrow man in the corner, his skin so covered with living tattoos no one knew its natural color. His cosmetically-altered earlobes stuck out in bony horns, and his greasy chartreuse hair had been worked through with gears and mini-bots that clicked and spun, making his head seem home to a swarm of insects. He wouldn't be able to set one foot outside Shirring Point without being arrested for half a dozen or more illegal mods. And that's not counting the fact that he's an undocumented Operator, a rone. The blue of his navis shimmered beneath the shifting shapes across his forehead.

Luzzie Vai. To some a hero. To me, and plenty of others, a traitor.

I took my espresso in one shot, my eyes fixed on Luzzie. Luzzie the Sea Witch is who an Operator goes to when they want to play at being a normal— or when they want to disappear. He deals in new identities—which is impossible business, implying he functions at a high level of scary-smart. But that's not what bothers me. He's also the number one supplier of nyquolium-quadrolate to my people—the exotic drug Angel had found in the victims' blood.

NQ is nasty business. For 99 percent of the population it's just a mild empathogen, increasing feelings of connection and communication with others. But for Ops it gives us the ability to function without our tech, to remove our machines and superficially pass as normals. The stuff increases verbal and motor processing, allows an Operator to ignore sensory overload, and gives a massive rush on top of all that. It's the only way to effectively hide what we are.

I sympathize. I do. After all, three years ago it was illegal for me to work as a PI. Even now, the Integration Office doesn't approve everyone's application, and rejected Ops look for other routes to their dream jobs. Routes that inevitably led to Luzzie's table. And yeah, I'm not keen on being sneered at for walking down the street, either. But NQ addiction isn't the way. It's just a more chemically lethal form of bondage. The normals don't like it either; they're more comfortable identifying us by the shine of our foreheads. Not even Luzzie's tattoos could hide the shine of his. Luzzie destroyed other Ops for his gain, and that spelled betrayal to me.

I settled on the fractal-painted bar stool. I had a clear sight on Luz but he didn't have much of a view of me due to the position of the Creeping Julia. Without sensor cams, this was the next best thing, and I was here to watch him. Among other things.

"Hey Blinker," I said, "pass me a 3V projection plate?"

I heard a plunk as Blinker set the thin rectangular plate behind me and I half-turned, stealing bandwidth from a few background programs on the way. I needed the resources to split my consciousness between Blinker and my eye-line on Luzzie.

Places like the Julia always keep plates around so Operators can communicate with non-Op staff without the awkwardness of speech. I pulled the image of Jane Doe from my memory index, ran a simple transform to remove the paint and restore her amber skin tone, and fixed her wounds. Then I opened a channel to the plate and shoved the image through.

Jane Doe's face, fine-boned and healthy, rotated above the plate. "Seen her around, Blinker?"

The barkeep came close to the image and squinted, pushing stringy black hair out of his eyes, as though proximity would increase the likelihood of identification. He stared at the image for two minutes forty-eight seconds. Occasionally, he gestured with his finger for me to rotate the projection.

"Can you make her cheeks a little fuller?"

An easy 3-D transform.

"Uh... Mouth a little wider. Just a little! And her hair, yeah, put some curl, some frizz in it, you know, like Carmen had." Carmen being Blinker's predecessor as Strangely Obsessive Barkeep to the Julia.

I obliged. We went through a few more minor tweaks, the kind that come cheap at a black market surgery—just enough to fool pattern recognition programs, not enough to fool anyone's mom.

Blinker pulled back, wagging his finger in triumph. "Yup, I seen her. That one." He pointed to the altered face revolving over the plate.

"How long ago, Blinker?" No one knows why he's called Blinker, but everyone knows not to call him Blink. He was a great guy unless someone did something he didn't like. Then he introduced them to the array of illegal hardwired weaponry in his forearms where his bones used to be. Running a business this deep in Shirring Point's cesspit of crime and creativity required a lot of tough and a touch of crazy.

"I'd say maybe a month. Came in here all the time for a while. Then—" he shrugged and made a blowing sound through his teeth.

I was so excited I shook. Jane Doe, you're about to be identified!

I wasn't done though. Thank the Trinity that Blinker likes me.

"You know her? She ever say anything interesting?"

The barkeep looked me over through his long, soft eyelashes. "You want another black-trance, Hoshi?"

When Blinker came back to me with the cup, I leaned in close. I'm small enough that "lean in close" means climbing half-way onto the counter. I braced for the discomfort of eye contact and caught Blinker's startlingly green eyes in my own brown ones. "She's dead," I said. "I think someone's killed her. Bad for business?" I dug my nails into my palms, feeling like Blinker's eyes were yanking my soul out through my pupils.

The effort was worth it. I saw the barkeep process through shock, disbelief, anger, and then grim protectiveness. This was news to Blinker; strike two for syndicate involvement.

The reason people like Blinker help me and protect me even though I'm wrapped up in the RCPD is because they know I'm more interested in justice than I am in the law. I'd done my share of protecting Shirring Point over the years.

"Bad for business." Blinker nodded, breaking the painful eye-gaze and fussing with the bottles behind the bar.

I exhaled and sipped my second shot more carefully. Out of the corner of my eye, I kept the visual feed on Luzzie, recording into my memory index. He sleazed with a customer, a sapped-out slip of a thing with limp yellow hair and shaking hands. Looked in her mid to late twenties; for all I knew the next entry on the Victim List. Luz and I would have a talk about that soon, both of us in the Mem where we could express ourselves properly.

After my cup was empty and cold, Blinker got back to me. "Yeah. The girl. She wasn't from around here. Not sure where she was from, but it wasn't Cassiopeia Prime or Phoenix Station. Somewhere other than the Cadmus system. One of those who comes hoping for Integration Law to give 'em a new life, but doesn't get shit. You know how it goes. Spent a lot of time with the Witch." Blinker shrugged toward Luzzie.

I frowned sadly at my empty cup.

"There was something else too," Blinker leaned close. His face was blank and his voice came out a little high. "Last time I saw her, she radiated the Sha Chi. Like she was gettin' in heavy with some ugly spirits, kinda creatures no one wants to invoke, you kish what I mean? I almost asked her to leave. Bad for business."

The idea that something could make a worse vibe than Luzzie was truly disturbing. I knew Sha Chi, negative or harmful energy, from my studies of the city. A lot of the major buildings had been designed to enable the flow of Sheng Chi, or positive energy. Not that anyone believed in pre-Revolution religions anymore, but Feng Shui facilitated a pleasing aesthetic. I was pretty sure Blinker wasn't talking about Feng Shui aesthetics though. "You mean energy like from the telempathic field of an élan vital? A negative or harmful telempathic field? From which one? Can you be more specific?"

"No." Blinker's dangerous deadpan killed even my curiosity.

"Thanks." I pushed my empty cup toward him with my fingertips. He took it and refilled it from a coffee machine that looked more like a medieval alchemist's lab than restaurant equipment.

I knew about the existence of the élan vitals in the electromagnetic like anyone who'd seen a mainfeed in the past six years. Hard to miss mega-star Caran Watts announcing to the galaxy with utmost theatrics that we weren't, after all, alone. The élan vitals had brushed against our world—and us against theirs—since the first shaman, but it had taken until recently for either of us to realize the other was real. Now they palled around with Callisto's Cantors like we were long-lost cousins, and the NuVuDoo Santeros who had refused to let go of spiritualism got a big "I told you so." None of that, however, made the creatures any less mysterious—or less skin-crawly—to most people. Most people weren't Cantors or Santeros. Life was complicated enough without worrying about invisible beings, and what use were they to me anyway? I'd never met an élan vital.

Ambivalence re. élans aside, I didn't like the thought of people or places radiating Sha Chi. Made me think of dangerous alleys and tragic tube accidents. And murder.

I put the thought away for now. Now was for adding information, not for factoring it.

I settled in for an afternoon of recording Luzzie during business hours.

Sometime pre-dusk, Luzzie shook hands with a straight-cut man and left the club. Blinker was busy squaring things with the evening band, and I swiped my thumb over the credit plate to pay for my million cups of joe and left too.

I had one more stop in Shirring before I hit home, and that stop had gotten a lot more important since both Kelvin and Blinker had alluded to the alien.

I turned into the sequin-and-shell-encrusted facade of the Shirring branch of Madame Shane's NuVuDoo Supply and made for the reading room. While I never knock the utility of a skilled Tarot reading, I wasn't here for the cards.

A curtain of red and blue beads interspersed with white ornne shells and a machete bathed in rum signaled the current reader as one of Ogun's. Apparently, like the Cantor's public ritual with the compasses and dimdrives, such trappings facilitated resonance between a Santero and an élan vital, made human-alien communication possible. The privacy holo above the curtain was dark, so I stepped through the beads into a scented swirl of cigar smoke and plum blossoms to see my dear friend Lillie's pretty face smiling from her nimbus of frizzy brown hair.

Lillie's smile dropped as she recognized me.

Hissing, teeth bared, she leapt over the small round table between us, Tarot cards spilling everywhere.

"Archer put your bow away, do not make us all to pay!" she howled in her Scary Voice, the one that comes out in an inhuman multi-frequency that I've never—despite extensive research into the physiology of the human throat—been able to explain.

I paused, stunned, just long enough for her fingernails to swipe centimeters from my face, before I turned tail and fled.

Physical fighter I am not.

Holy Trinity, what had I done to make my good friend want to maim me?

I reached the exit and looked back but she was still coming, spitting wrath like a Fury between the shelves of colored candles and dried stuff in jars, knocking over a barrel of token-coins. My feet hit the street as she whistled at me in multi-frequency, "Stay away! Stay away! Stay away!"

I stopped looking and kept moving till I reached the northern seawall, and halted, breathless, peering down into the blue-green sparkling clarity of

Marcie Bay. Lillie wasn't behind me anymore. A brassfish stared up with its round yellow eye, shivered, and disappeared.

♦   ♦   ♦

It's almost twenty kilometers from the tip of Shirring Point to my studio in the Hill District. I decided to walk home and stop for dinner (my tenth solid meal this week, take that, Integration Officer Mai Chandra!) because walking through the city, touching her with my feet and drinking her with my senses, helps me think.

I wondered if Kel's fear at the mention of Cantors and Santeros meant he'd gotten the same treatment I had from Lillie. Lillie had called me by name, *Archer put your bow away, do not make us all to pay.* Did she mean my work on the case? But how would she have even known what I was working on? Did she learn it from Ogun? Why would the élans know or care? I felt terrible and I didn't know why.

Plus, I really needed to talk to Lillie about the ritualistic flavor of the case. Sorreno would put consultants on it, but I didn't trust a one of them. The mainstream priests in the city had worked extra hard to kill Integration Law. Not all élan vitals were keen on civil rights for humans. I'd be more inclined to believe the consultants were behind the deaths than able to provide an unbiased opinion on them.

At least I had learned three important facts: the syndicate wasn't involved but bad Chi was, where to look next with respect to Nessa, and the contours of Jane Doe's real face. Not that any of those items made me less uneasy.

By the time I reached the outskirts of my neighborhood the sun had set and the evening rain had been falling for half an hour. Refreshing for the first six minutes fifteen seconds, now I was soggy and cold and rueful about my decision to walk. As if to make sure I was as chilled and despondent on inside as well as on the out, the mainfeed projecting from the side of Lancy Tower ecl to consider the Inclusion Act as an amendment to Integration Law. It seemed like simple logic that one couldn't have an "Office of Operator Affairs" without any Operators involved in its administration, but there was only so much change the city would bear at once. "Not time yet," the 'feed commented. "It's only been four years since Callisto's Revolution and the Great Apology made us reconsider Operator autonomy. We still don't understand the danger posed by the aliens. We still don't know how to safely integrate the Operators. Not yet time." But when would it be time? When the city erupted in bloody pro-versus anti-Operator riots again, like it did during Callisto's Revolution?

I put my head down and shuffled onward, just wanting to reach P Street and home and have quiet time to process everything I'd learned today so I could wake up tomorrow bright and early and chock-full-o-insight.

Three shapes rushed me, darkness given life. Two in the front and one behind.

The two in front were faster, and I put my arms in front of my face. Sorreno's warning and flashes of Claudia's dead breasts and the cold, lifeless eyes of Jane Doe flickered with my own self laid out on the morgue body-pan, Sorreno staring down at me, pissed off that I hadn't solved the case, and I wondered whether I'd be killed before or after they tore my navis out of my head.

These thoughts rode in with the adrenaline tide, and I made a muffled, grunting sound as one of the guys (or maybe gals—they were head-to-foot covered in baggy black so I couldn't even tell their sex by the tilt of their hips) caught both my wrists and held them together so tightly tendons ground against bone.

A knife jutted into my eye-line.

I didn't know what the one behind was doing but it couldn't be good.

I tried to open a channel out but instead of seeing the crackling tunnel of energy, I saw only the static of Noise. One of them had a jammer.

I wanted to shout for help but terror overrode my linguistics, leaving me speechless. Would they draw morbid pseudo-code all over my naked body before they killed me? If I survived, somehow, what details could I remember to report to Sorreno? Everything was recording into my memory index but it would only be accessible for playback if I remained alive—

"K-dromer retard scum!" the one with the knife spat at me. "Why don't I cut that precious processor out of your head, see how smart you are then."

He punched me in the gut and I collapsed in toward the center of pain, crashing to my knees, my wrists still prisoner of the other goon's crushing grip. The one behind me grabbed my hair and pulled. My face pointed up into the acid yellow lights and the rain. The knife came down, tracing a symbol across my cheek.

Then the adrenaline cleared enough fear so I could find one of those self-defense programs I'd had to download years ago as part of my RCPD training but never used. I ran the programming and let it take over most of my motor functions, my body a puppet to its reflexes. The loss of control would have been terrifying if I hadn't passed beyond terror into the cold detachment of survival.

My hands were free; I didn't know how.

My elbows flew back, jammed into the guy behind me.

Knife came forward; I ducked back, then clocked knife-guy in the face. I'm not big and I'm not strong, but I did get him by surprise and he stumbled away from me.

Miscalculation: the guy behind me also had a knife. A bigger one. He drove it straight toward the middle of my back.

Which was a big mistake.

I don't just wear the bolero jacket because it's cute. I wear it because it's made of the best indestructible nano-cloth credit can buy. Pretty much the only things that'll destroy it are acid, extreme temperatures, and time. The impact knocked me down onto my hands and knees but it also drove the goon's hand all the way down the blade of his own knife and he dropped it, howling in the rain.

I took advantage of the chaos to shut off as much as I could of my sense of pain and pelt away into the awful night before they realized I didn't have any real fighting abilities, just a few predictable, puppeted, easily parried moves.

I didn't stop running until my breath got so ragged I started to hyperventilate. By then I was one block from my apartment. I don't remember making it inside.

It took almost twenty minutes for my heart to stop pounding and for me to realize my hands were covered in a thin film of my own blood.

In the bathroom I stripped down and inspected the damage: knees and hands torn up, wrists bruised, I wasn't going to be moving well come morning. Across my left cheek the guy with the knife had carved a bright red "K." K for K-Syndrome. K-dromer. Retard. Oh yes, and scum as well. Apparently he thought I wasn't marked enough already on the surface by the blue shine of my forehead—or more deeply by the markers in my DNA.

I started giggling and fell wetly to the white tiled floor, smearing it with rainwater and blood. I never thought I'd be happy to be the victim of nothing more than a good old-fashioned hate crime. The wound was ugly and jagged and logically I knew I should care about that, but emotionally any caring was wiped out by the joy of being alive. I was alive!

I didn't bother reporting what had happened to the RCPD. I could find the perps through the city sensors and lead officers right to them, but even if I brought the goons in myself and locked them in a jail cell personally, nothing would come of it besides pissing off the hate-gang so much they'd triple their efforts.

That's the reality for us Operators, even now; there's rarely any choice but to take the punches.

Thank the Trinity a few scars was all I got.

Tonight anyway.

CHAPTER 4

I woke whimpering at bruised wrists and ribs. My face ached beneath the kilo of antibiotic cream and sealits and synthskin I'd plastered over it.

I opened my eyes, and through the window the skyline transfixed me with molten dawn. The city whispered, below the aches, below the surface of sleep, telling me I'd netted important information yesterday. Processed data waited in my machine memory for inspection. Today was a good day to work in the Mem. I didn't want to feel my body anyway.

I rolled gingerly onto my back and told my berth to plug me in.

As far as Operators go, I'm pretty tame. I play by Socialization rules, I run all the right language, sensory, and motor programs not to creep out the normals too badly, and I take an unusual amount of interest in things one can touch with one's hands. Hence Reason Number One why I was in the first batch of Ops allowed an Integration job. I've had to be conservative to counter the controversy of my birth. Which is Reason Number Two I was selected—the public loves an "overcoming adversity" story, and I was, in a way, a peace offering in the struggle between the castes that had taken my parents as casualties. A living token of The Great Apology following the revelation that our enslavement had been founded on a lie.

On the other hand, I am what I am—a highly-classed Operator born of the illegal mating of two other highly-classed Operators—and not even a back-alley-beating, or executing my parents for having me, can make me ashamed of that. For example, why bother with the time consuming untidiness of the human metabolism when I had an option? My berth is the usual Operator's rigging—a self-contained life-support system capable of food, waste, and muscle stimulation for up to eight days at a shot (though theoretically one isn't supposed to use it longer than two because it's bad for the innards). No one takes a break when deep in the code, and that's probably the only Operator lifestyle choice normals approve of. They want us spending all our time maintaining their technology so we don't get big ideas about superfluous stuff, like civil rights. Just because they feel bad about the slavery doesn't mean the normals want anything to change. Sorreno's comment about solid food hadn't been a sarcastic quip. I do either take-out or tubes.

I closed my eyes on the window in my studio and opened them to the window in my imagination. The city spread before me in its perfect dawn detail through the cathedral arch, but the walls of the apartment were gone. The blank blackness of my mental workspace contained only the window, the crackling blue spark of a channel out, and a vague sense of up and down. The window is where I access my memory, both meat and machine. The spark is the link between my hardware and the city's micro and radio networks; through it I access the Mem. Not a "virtual" reality, but an actual reality, one made of electromagnetic signal, information encoding, and the occasional degradation of noise. A reality made by centuries of my people's thoughts.

Every Operator sees these things differently, but we all see them: personal memory, transmission flow, data pools, trace wakes—the underlying architecture of the Mem. Ultimately it's just information flowing through the airwaves or jammed into memory matrices. We create programs in our own unique idioglossias. Then we encode the programs of our idio with a lingua franca, a bridge language, so others can understand them (unless we're working encryption, which requires a key in idio). I don't know how Martin, or Luzzie, or any other Operator experiences true-code. We only share the franca.

Theoretically, one must present one's self in an officially-sanctioned franca to transit Memspace. The presentation broadcasts who we are, and records our movements in a wake that can be traced.

Realistically, well, that's the other reason I don't try to fix the bug that occasionally rains a hell of sensor data into my sleeping unconscious. I have invisible access to all the sensors in Red City. No franca needed. No Hoshi-mind detected. No wake to trace.

Through the crackling blue channel I leapt and slipped into the city's sensory organs, the rush of power and the crush of insignificance that comes of seeing all and touching nothing, of existing both as an immortal city and an inconsequential human psyche, the mingling of these extremes in an alchemy of egoless panic that resolves, explosively, into peace.

Awake, in control of the incoming transmissions, I am the eyes, the ears, the IR and magnetic feelers of a great beast, sleeping and exquisitely alive.

Stillness came as signal passed through me. Far too much signal to process safely, but I wasn't trying; reading the transmissions wasn't the point. Lillie uses a meditation routine with a candle and a mantra. This is my version. I claim my gods as the Trinity of Signal, Encoding, and Noise on government forms, but sometimes I think should claim Red City as my divinity instead.

Refreshed and ready to face the data, I pulled back into my workspace and turned to the imaginary window to check on yesterday's programs. The transforms on the pseudo-code wouldn't be ready for days still, but most of the rest had finished. The identification of Jane Doe headed my to do list. Today I'd get further working within the system than outside of it.

I embodied my presentation, which looks like me, steel-toed boots and bolero and all. It feels like me too; a presentation processes sensations the same way a body does, at least as far as a brain is concerned.

Through the window, reaching into imaginary Marcie Bay, my fingers dug under the water where I'd stashed Jane Doe's original face. I pulled the visualization into my workspace, expanded it, and set it on a slow rotate, enhancing the resolution. Then I compressed it into a little wadded up cube and rode the stream out to Cassiopeia Prime Law Enforcement Agency, the local branch of the LEA, Memside.

Stepping out of the crackling blue flow into the Cassiopeia Prime LEA public pool feels like transitioning from fresh air off the bay to the gates of a bureaucratic level of a barbaric hell. No scents were programmed here, but I smelled sulfur nonetheless. Franca presents the informationspace as a towering black windowless edifice emblazoned with the screaming eagle, claws outstretched, barbed beak open, swooping in for the kill. The Law Enforcement Agency sigil is supposed to make citizens feel protected, but mostly it makes me feel like dinner. Gotta love inter-planetary Big Government and, like it or not, Cassiopeia Prime is part of the New Organization of Federal Banking Worlds and under the jurisdiction of the LEA.

Like the relationship between Operators and normals, the relationship between the RCPD and the local branch of the LEA is one of resentful interdependence—on a good day. The RCPD cursed the rules and red tape of its overseer while the LEA stepped all over the RCPD's jurisdiction. And yet, the LEA kept necessary peace between corporations and managed the complexities of interstellar citizenship while the RCPD understood the curves of Red City. There were forty-three other routes I could take to Jane Doe's identity, but this was the only one that wouldn't risk my PI license.

So I walked across the mirror-smooth ruddy-colored floor of the information pool and up to the revolving door between the screaming eagle's claws, sticking out like ketchup on a white shirt amongst the flat, faceless, generic francas of non-Ops. Those would be people like Sorreno, accessing the LEA by manipulating holicons with their eyes over a 3Vplate in a hotspot instead of direct-interfacing like me. Operators comprise only one percent of the population, but here the ratio of Op to non-Op was closer to one in ten, with the non-Op franca bland to the point of ignorable. The auras of Operator emotives—colorful and creatively programmed to complement each unique presentation—showed relief as the pressure of being surrounded by normals lifted, just a little bit. My own aura, a dust of color that kicks up from around my boots, included.

I waited for a spot in one of the entry queues and slipped into the building.

Inside, desks and lines and non-Op francas in the uniforms of LEA workers filled a space experienced as Very Large. Essentially, the same chaotic mess civilians see just inside any law enforcement building flesh-side. Luckily, I didn't have to deal with the mess Memside either.

I stepped away from the chaos of people reporting crimes and barking demands, over to a door marked "Official Bypass" in terse, formal lettering. I walked through the door without opening it. The sensation of walking through a solid-seeming door, even if it's just in the imagination, is more disturbing than it sounds; I've never factored why the Op had chosen to program it that way. Maybe they'd just run out of time to finish the job. That door—and the four others I stepped through on my way to Records—contained pattern filters designed to keep civilians out. As I approached each one, the various law enforcement credentials embedded in my franca were scanned. Hoshi Archer, PI, on special assignment from Inspector Cassandra Sorreno, RCPD, please-let-her-through.

The other thing I could get in trouble for, besides the city sensors, is possession of the RCPD access codes. However, unlike the sensor access, this could get Sorreno in trouble too. Because she'd just sort of "forgotten" to rescind my RCPD access codes when I'd left the Department. And I had just sort of "forgotten" to remind her. She's aware of our mutual memory lapse, but it saves us both seven hells of red tape and time. We agree on silence over the codes like we agree on silence over my less savory contacts.

I reached Records thinking as usual how I'd become a caged animal if I had to work in this space. The ceiling was too close, the lighting too bright, and there was nothing interesting to look at. The kind of Memspace designed to get people in and out as fast as possible.

The lady at the Records desk I queued to was a non-Op, but dolled up to look like an individual for those of us who find francas as real as flesh and bone. Her brown eyes were painted in the style of the latest fad, and a complicated network of ribbons and bows wove through her blond hair. A line of similar desks spanned the space, eighty in all. Behind the desks, small channels out to other Memspaces pulsed blue. Behind me, the wall was lined with tiny drawers, each marked with unique colors, shapes, and numbers. The more sophisticated programs get, the more human beings you have to add to the security mix in these highly restricted areas, to make sure data exchange runs human-to-human.

"Hello, Citizen ID Records, how may I help you?" the Records Lady asked, her blond non-descriptiveness and utter lack of emotive programming creepier to me than a shapeless pink blob would have been.

"Hoshi Archer, PI, here on RCPD business for Inspector Cassandra Sorreno." If she'd been one of my people she'd have been able to read my patterns the way the doors had, but the rules here were to talk politely to the normals not shove data in their faces. In her office, the Records clerk would be experiencing my response as a simulated voice through ear phones or speakers.

"Category and I/O?" Records Lady prompted, my identity checking out.

"Direct search, simple. Three-D visual facial pattern input, public identity output."

She held out a little tray.

I plopped the cube of compressed Jane-Doe-face into the tray, memorizing the colors and symbols on the shallow box.

The tray disappeared through the flow behind the desk.

I turned to the drawers where I'd receive my results, seeking the one that matched the symbols on the tray, my fists stuffed into the pockets of my bolero, and split my consciousness. Didn't want to waste time waiting.

Thread of consciousness #1: Flowing back to home.

Thread of consciousness #2: Waiting at LEA Records.

Most of me manifested back in my workspace, digging into the city of my memory through the imaginary window. I began pulling out disparate-seeming bits and pieces that had processed from my various searches and surveillances the past day.

Back in the LEA Records department on Thread #2, I noticed Martin Ho second-in-line four desks down. Well, that was interesting. There was one person in front of him, and one behind. Both non-Ops.

Not necessarily remarkable, but definitely out of character for Martin. Something so mundane as a Records search he'd surely delegate to a poor intern.

I squinted at him, factoring a way to be sneaky. He hadn't noticed me, else he'd be glaring in my direction.

It's not easy business to intercept official citizen ID data while standing in a big urban branch of the largest law enforcement agency in inhabited space. So I split my consciousness again, pulling some awareness out of Thread #1 to redistribute my focus.

Thread of consciousness #3: Walking over to Martin's line and queuing up behind him. Hoping he wouldn't notice, counting on his tendency to run more threads than he could manage in an attempt to impress Sorreno or Inspector Zi or one of the other RCPD directors he takes orders from. I had maybe thirty seconds to come up with another search query to justify my presence in line.

The first guy in the queue finished up and went to his drawer to await output.

I clocked nanosecs. As Martin gave his identity to the Records desk, I took a mental breath, grateful the person between us was non-Op and therefore wouldn't notice the brief shift in queue I was about to create.

Martin does not present how he looks in the flesh. His franca is an almost comical puffed-up super-hero version of himself with huge muscles and very white teeth. He's an obsessive fan of the Doctor Planet series, and there's more than a touch of Doctor Planet's facial features and rippling rust-colored cape to Martin Ho's appearance. I told him once, that presentation's got to go if you want any respect. But he just scoffed at me. What do I know, everything just comes easily to me in his mind. Luck, not effort or skill.

But it took all three for me to get the timing on my next move just right.

I ran the subroutine for a smile, not worrying about the fact my emotional programming didn't back it up, and shifted forward in the queue, grabbing the edge of Martin's ridiculous cape as he leaned in to give his search category and I/O criteria.

Martin said, "..., comprehensive. Mai Chandra, input. Public and private activity records, output."

I shut my emotives off on that Thread fast as possible as Martin turned toward me, the tug on his cape as solid as if it had happened in the flesh. His own emotives read surprise and then anger with a tinge of fear, which is exactly what he would have seen reflected in me had I been a nanosec slower in hiding it.

Mai Chandra: my Integration Officer. The person holding the power over whether I remained free under Integration Law.

Ohshit.

Oh shit oh shit oh shit. For benefit of anyone watching I exclaimed loudly, "Martin! What a coincidence! How have you been?"

Martin stuck his overly square jaw in the air and sniffed, his special Hoshi-glare now in effect. "She's not going to be able to cover for you anymore. I know what you've been up to with the Roccini Boys."

"You do?" By Purity of Signal, who were the Roccini Boys?

But Martin had already stomped off to his drawer. I ducked back into my place in the queue, now having only about ten seconds to figure a query. My mind choked on a thousand very unpleasant reasons why Martin Ho, who really did think he had something on me, was pulling records on my Integration Officer. Who did Martin mean by "she"—Mai? Did Martin think Mai Chandra was covering something up for me? Or was he referring to Sorreno? Who were the Roccini Boys and what had I been up to with them? I have perfect recall; I'd remember if I'd ever met anyone called the Roccini

Boys!

"Hello, Citizen ID Records, how may I help you?"

I gave my credentials again, trying to think fast. Nothing came. I banished thoughts of the Roccini Boys and cleared my mind by picturing the Red City skyline.

"Category and I/O?"

I smiled at the Records Guy, who couldn't see me do it—to him I looked like a string of numbers and not a fully realized smiling franca—and let the city make the next move. Let it give me something from the information overflow the other night. Words fell from my unconscious into Memspace. I communicated to the clerk, "Purchase search, comprehensive, bound by last six months to current. Bill's Ragtime input. Citizen ID list, detail level three, output."

Thread #3 of my consciousness went to wait by the new drawer while Thread #2 received the results of Jane Doe's identity in the franca of a sealed envelope.

Bill's Ragtime? I'd never heard of it. At least not consciously. No more than I'd heard of the Roccini Boys.

I flowed Thread #2 back to home to merge with Thread #1 and waited for output on Thread #3.

And every one of my bits of consciousness worried over what Martin Ho wanted with records on Integration Officer Mai Chandra. The very person I would be making my weekly report to tomorrow, and needing to answer all of her questions just right, or I'd lose my freedom and my job.

CHAPTER 5

Hours later I commed Sorreno, my imagination so full of the case I could barely picture her address. I told Sorreno that Jane Doe's name was Aysha Ayres. She'd been born on Mars twenty-seven years ago, Earth Standard. That made her twenty-four by local time. She had worked for AlphaMarc Corp, low-level maintenance programming environmental systems for single-person housing units. Five months ago, she'd spent most of her credit on a one-way to Cassiopeia Prime. She'd stayed at the Nelson Hostel in the Husson District for almost two months, then vanished. Presumably into the murk and glitter of Shirring Point.

Sorreno is the kind of person who likes to talk through her thinking, so I told her these things even though she could see them in my report.

"Well, that's the sort of story you'd expect to have an unhappy ending," Sorreno said sadly.

"Said" meaning subvocalized into her com. For all that implanted technology reminds normals distastefully of Operators, the com unit remains ever-popular. Operators can't use them; subvocalizing requires a bunch of complicated, error-prone programming in our navi, at which point why not just have the navis transmit the communication directly and correctly? Flip-spin being we have visualization and associative abilities they don't, which is why they can't use a navis either. Telephone version-dot-million, or quantum computer that gives me super-human powers of information processing, hm... I'll take my lot any day.

"Aysha's story doesn't help me make a pattern between the three victims yet," I frowned. From Sorreno's perspective, I was a voice in her ear as her com stimulated her cochlear nerves. She couldn't hear the frown.

"No, but we'll find a pattern. This is good work Hoshi. I didn't expect an ident on the Jane Doe so soon. What else do you have?"

From my perspective, I was sitting cross-legged in my once-empty workspace in the Mem, surrounded by the chaos of the case. Four-hundred and seventy-eight objects in full sensory crowded around me, above me, below me. Dozens of uninstantiated variables in the mathematics of crime floated among the concrete facts of the case, represented as blue-black cubes waiting to be filled and fleshed with explanations. Some items were linked by thin silver lines, but not many; my mind still held an incomplete tapestry. Images as yet unconnected:

The IO sanitation worker walks to the cafeteria bins.

Luzzie Vai exchanges something with a crooked cop from Vice.

A recording shows NQ binding and breaking down with the receptors in cell walls.

Ambassador Morgan gives a speech about the current state of human/élan relations.

An Operator is beaten unconscious behind an Always-C, stripped and painted with an inversion of the Cassiopeian Union. The wall is painted "Reals Rule Reality."

Mainfeed coverage comments on the relationship between the IO and the Inclusion Act controversy. The wall of the IO is painted "Ops are not the Enemy / Make good on your Apology!"

The graceful curve of an antique bottle of Cassiopeian red whiskey glows a reminder that I need to finish hunting down the particular vintage that was fed to the victims....

Notes and unsorted data appeared as paper boxes tagged with colors and flavors, easy for me to identify in the idiosyncrasy of my own thoughts with a brief taste. A brown, bitter box of vague musings on city-wide drug networks; a sweet wine-colored box leading to Nessa's pornware business; a secret box hidden in the corner marked "Claudia" which I didn't dare to touch. Hundreds more. I could barely see the window to my memory through the mess, meaning I'd crammed about as much as I could into my consciousness without losing it all.

"Hoshi? What else do you have?" Sorreno's words came at me disembodied; she wasn't giving me any vid along with the audio in her transmit today.

"What else do I have?" I echoed Sorreno's question, and it made me laugh. How could I share with her the fantastic mess I was looking at, tasting, feeling, smelling, hearing! But that's not what she wanted to know. "Okay. Here's what else I have. The syndicate isn't responsible for the deaths. At least not directly."

"No? What makes you say that?"

"The right people haven't heard about them," I touched small images of Kelvin and Blinker lightly with my fingertips, both of whom had more signal on Black Market movements in the city than your average mobster; Kel by virtue of gossip and Blinker from... well, Blinker's role at the Julia Set Saloon was complicated.

Sorreno gave the subvocalized version of a grunt.

"Also," I pulled over the bottle of whisky and inspected its contents. "I got some tracking on the whiskey. Only fifty bottles of that vintage ever made, and I could account for forty-eight of them. Of those forty-eight, I could rule out all but ten as previously consumed or still uncorked. Mostly the latter." I was forgetting something. Oh, "Give a thanks to Angel for excruciatingly complete Hoshi-level detail on the chemical analysis." (Which reminded me, I needed to contact Angel for a dinner date.)

"The list of twelve bottles you couldn't account for—they're in your report?"

"Yes, Sir."

Sorreno grunted again. She grunted a lot more subvoca than out loud. I imagined her scribbling reminders on a digipage on her desk: deploy officers re. whiskey. She didn't ask me how I knew this time, which is good, because a fair amount of the answer was "illicit spying through sensor cams."

"That's a stand-out point, actually," I added.

"What is?"

"Well," I brightened the image of the whisky bottle, "so much was tidied up, untraceable. The bodies scrubbed clean, anything identifiable their own, I still haven't figured how they were placed at the IO without anyone seeing, all so careful. So then why use a vintage of Cassiopeian red so rare I can track it like that?" My imaginary fingers snapped. Because they made an imaginary noise, Sorreno heard it.

"What's so special about that vintage?"

"Um... everything? It's the tenth batch of Cassiopeian red ever made, the year the settlers first planted carmine rye on the Oba Plains. It's the third rarest and highest priced in existence."

Sorreno made a whistling sound. "Interesting. There must have been something that made the risk worth it to the perp. Or the perp wanted the whisky to be traced."

"Or—" I wasn't sure if I was ready to propose what I was about to propose.

"What?"

Too late. "Um. Just a thought. Probably not right."

"Your wrongs are closer to right than most people's rights. Out with it Hoshi."

"There are some other explanations for why everything is so tidy besides a really careful or manipulative perp." I tapped a variable representing "lack of expected forensic evidence" and another one holding information on the chemicals found in the victims' blood. "According to Angel's report, the victims didn't have enough NQ in their bodies to have prevented a life-or-death command to their navi. And I don't know of anything besides NQ that could have stopped them. Could be it wasn't murder but some weird alien ritual or something. Maybe they were trying to call some élans and things went wrong? Or maybe they willingly sacrificed themselves?"

"They ripped out their own navi and carried themselves to the IO refuse bins?" I imagined Sorreno's eyebrow arching.

"No, of course not. But the rest of it." I shrugged. "Told you, probably not right."

"No, no, I shouldn't be so quick. It's certainly consistent with the ritualistic flavor of the evidence, as well as the lack of signs of struggle. The more we learn about the aliens the less we know, and the less we know the stupider we act. It's a path to keep open." Sorreno paused for twenty-eight seconds and I waited, resisting the urge to slip into the sensor cam in her office and spy on her. Then she asked, cautiously, "What's your sense for urgency, Hoshi?"

I hadn't thought about that yet (bad investigator!) so I had to factor an answer, touching variables quickly to put the pieces together. "Claudia turned up dead two weeks ago, Nessa one week ago, and Aysha three days ago. If there was a true pattern for halving the time between deaths, there would have been a bit more time between Nessa and Aysha, so it's not that. On the other hand, the deaths weren't exactly far apart. Either there's a series going on and I don't have enough data points to factor yet, or it's random but close-together. Need another data point to tell more, but hope we don't get one of course." I blinked, done.

"Plain language, Hoshi, please."

"Sorry, Sir. High probability of another one within the next week, but I can't say for sure when. I don't think we've seen the last of it."

"Why do you say that?"

I shook my head. Then I remembered Sorreno couldn't see me. "I don't know well enough to put it into words yet. But the pattern—it feels incomplete."

"That's okay. This is good, Hoshi, really good. I've got something for you too." Sorreno's voice sounded strained and I imagined her fingers around her locket. "I sent Gibbons and Gorski out to follow up with the Integration

Office worker who found the bodies. They found evidence in his purchase history that could link him to the victims; specifically, pigments. The same used in the paints. It's enough to bring him in, but I told them to wait because it's not enough to hold him, and I don't want to spook him. We've got him under manual surveillance for now."

"Anything interesting in the interview?"

"I'll put the recording in the case file for you tomorrow, but it was pretty bland. The worker described his usual routine, that he found the bodies because of the smell, and he commed security the moment he found them. Everything checks with what was recorded by the Integration Office sensors. He paints as a hobby, has since he was a child."

"His name is Samo Oro, right? From the case file?"

"Don't you go talk to him, Hoshi!"

"I won't! I just want to run some searches. You know, troll the public data pools. Maybe I can learn something for you."

"Okay. I mean it, though, no interviewing him on your own."

Right. Hoshi does the underworld and Mem. Sorreno does everyone and everything else. So hard to remember the rules when following clues! "Anything else for me, Sir?"

"Not yet. Keep up the great work."

A colorful storefront in my internal landscape caught my eye. "Wait, I have a question."

A hiss of static dirtied the connection as she put a white noise filter over the com channel for forty-nine seconds. Then, "Yes?" her tone ran rushed, irritated. Not at me. Someone had come into her office? Someone she didn't like? Someone who made her angry and nervous?

I reminded myself I wasn't investigating Sorreno. "Does Bill's Ragtime mean anything to you? It's a clothing shop in the Husson District."

Sorreno had her tone back under control. "No. Should it? Why?"

I shook my head. "No real reason. Random wondering. Not sure it's related."

"Anything else?"

"No, Sir. Thank you."

"We'll talk again tomorrow Hoshi."

"Okay."

"Okay."

"Okay." I can never figure how to end a com transmission. With another Operator, we have explicit protocols to cue when a conversation is done. So much more civilized.

"Good bye Hoshi." Sorreno helpfully cut the connection.

I sat quietly, surveying all 478 of my variables. There are levels to how I see case data. I'd spent the past twelve hours shifting between the levels, working. Digging into the tiny details, forming discrete variables on everything from the blueprints for the Integration Office to the exact chemical composition of the mind-altering compounds Angel found in the victims' blood. Forming connections, like between Aysha and Luzzie Vai, or, more tenuously, between the NQ found in the victims and Vai. I'd zoomed out and looked at the whole from a distance, seeing no patterns yet, just the expected malformed mess of the early stages of investigation. Patterns would come though eventually. Solutions would form after that. But later. Later.

I added Sorreno's information about the interview to Samo Oro's floating portrait and drew a thin line between him and the palette holding the information on the paints. Then I took a step all the way back for a bird's-eye on the whole, greater than any sum of parts or substance of patterns. Etching the whole into the bones of my subconscious.

Solution is equal parts inspection and incubation. It was time to let ideas sort beneath the surface of thought.

I folded up large regions of my workspace and compressed them into higher-order pointers I could retrieve and unfold to view the details. I pushed the compressed bundles out the window, storing them in my memory. When

I was done, colored and flavored shapes stacked neatly, each connected by a gossamer thread to the city, easy to tug on and pull out whatever I wanted. This cleared room in my consciousness for more personal business.

I reached through the window to my memory, avoiding the strands, and into a building on L street in the Hill District, not far from my studio: Martin Ho's residence. From it, I pulled the past day and a half of sensorfeed surveillance on Martin and started filtering through.

Martin and I had known each other for ten years. And this wasn't the first time I'd surveilled him. Not much changes with Martin. First I filtered out anything I'd seen him do before. No use watching him brush his teeth after lunch or go for his evening walk yet again. What remained were about twenty-two hours. At 4x speed, that was still longer than I wanted to spend scanning Martin-footage, so I filtered out any time he'd spent focused fully in the Mem. And was left with twelve remaining hours.

I settled in to watch the Martin Show.

Martin Ho isn't a bad person. He's just a small and lazy person. The kind who wants to know things without learning them, to get kudos without doing anything, and to be given gifts without making any sacrifices. And don't bother trying to point this out to him either; in his eyes, he is not a failure but a victim of favoritism. He'd been working the RCPD code-breaker job several years before I was assigned, and yet I got promoted to senior only a year after I started. Even though—and I'm first to say it—Martin is a better programmer than I.

"If you want promo you have to be willing to do the hard stuff," I'd told him.

"If you want promo you have to be cute little brown-nosing Hoshi," he'd whined.

It didn't matter what either of us thought, though; choices don't exist when you're owned. You do the work you're told to do or have your navis removed and get sent to a Farm. My title became Senior Operator and his remained Associate Operator. He didn't report to me, but I had to divvy out assignments in our little department of three because our keepers didn't understand them well enough to order us about.

That was when I started noticing small acts of sabotage.

Martin is smart enough to hide his actions from others.

He is not smart enough to hide his actions from me.

I knew Martin was behind many-a-rumor and supposed mistake I'd made. Unfortunately, my primary means of knowing this was via sensor cam surveillance, meaning I couldn't call him on it publicly. Fortunately, it's easy enough to block the blows when I'm watching them get set up. Time and again I thwarted Martin's attempts to get me in trouble. He went through greater and greater contortions of lies and setups trying to get past my parries. Neither of us said a word: he'd be punished for doing it, and I'd be punished for how I knew he was doing it.

When I left the Department, Martin finally got his promo and became Senior Operator of the RCPD Code-Breaker Section by sheer weight of years and whining. Sal VanEryk, the third member of our section, remained happy as ever to keep his thirty year status quo as low-man on the pole, and instead of getting a replacement for me they started assigning kids on learning-trial to save credit. I got out of direct competition with Martin and good riddance. I still keep my eye on the snot, but I'd thought it was safe to relax a little after three years.

Apparently not.

Though whatever tricks he was up to now, they were new ones.

I paused feed from the RCPD on an image of Inspector Rolland Zi from Vice perched on the end of Martin's berth at work, doing the mental equivalent of narrowing my eyes. Since when were Martin and Zi so chummy? Martin took plenty of orders from Vice, but Zi was notorious for sending underlings to communicate with Operators. He didn't want to sully his reputation for being so Op-o-phobic he couldn't bear to be in the same room as one of us. If I didn't have the evidence in front of me, I wouldn't have believed Zi capable of even occupying the same room as Operator equipment like a berth, let alone resting his left butt cheek on its malleable surface.

Unfortunately, the cams in the RCPD employee cubes were vid only, no sound, only there to capture the action if a perp went wild in the offices. The angle didn't give me enough lip-view to reconstruct the conversation either.

Fortunately, Martin was holding a 3V projection plate and the camera could see the holo above it. The holo was a recording from a camera in the corner of a ceiling. I could tell by the fact I'd looked through that same lens countless times that it was the corner of the ceiling at Long Shore Lassie's, a mixed bar in the Pier District. I'd looked through it countless times because I rather liked going to Long Shore Lassie's—or the LSL as its regulars called it— on my time off. The LSL is comprised of equal parts smelly fishermen off the Bay and technophiles, from Operators to tinkers to garden variety weekend tech-taboo transgressors. There's a funny solidarity between the coarse fishermen and the technologically outcaste. Maybe being, for different reasons, the undesirables of our segregated worlds.

Anyway, the LSL didn't serve espresso, but it did serve a cup of joe so thick and black it might as well be, and there wasn't a thing I didn't love about the dark, bustling place. Including the wall of window in the back that showed the thick of Red City's working piers.

Martin's 3Vplate showed a man in a long, tan coat and a peculiar wide-brimmed hat with a floppy top—stand-out gear that screams low-level gangster. The man's back was to the sensorcam, and all I could see were the edges of a cheek and nose and thick brown hair bristling from beneath the hat. The fingers of his hand cupped a tumbler filled with the ruddy shimmer of Cassiopeian red whiskey.

I reached into my recent memories of the bar.

Over Martin's 3Vplate, the man leaned forward, bending toward his drink.

Revealing—lo and behold!—to his right, me.

Me, sitting there, drinking my joe, innocent as could be.

My memories spit out the event, recursively: the camera-eye whose point of view I now simultaneously viewed over Martin's 3V, the cup, the counter, the scent of coffee, liquor, and sea.

The footage was recent: last week.

The man moved back and fidgeted, and I fidgeted a little too, and we both interacted separately with the barkeep. But from the angle of the feed, it looked for all like Hat Man and I were having a chummy conversation.

Which of course we were not.

What are you up to Martin?

I know you're a little shit, but even you wouldn't get friendly with Inspector Zi, the man who routinely makes public statements like "Operators have no souls" and "Integration Law is humanity's death warrant." Not even to take a jab at me.

Martin and Inspector Zi.

Martin looking up records on my Integration Officer Mai Chandra and viewing circumstantial vids of me with suspicious looking types (the Roccini Boys?).

Sorreno's warning to me about Martin having something on me.

Zi's warning to Sorreno about not wanting to be near me when that something came to light.

I set the footage of Martin and Zi on a loop and split my consciousness. Thread #1 rewatched the feed. Thread #2 worked on magnifying the holo over the 3V plate, trying to clarify the man's profile—a man I had noticed so little I couldn't even find him in my memory index. And Thread #3 created images for each of the known elements in the Martin Mystery. Instantiated variables by giving them concrete portraits of the players: Martin, Zi, hat-man at the bar. Added links between objects. Created new variables for unanswered questions.

I made an image of myself, and connected my portrait by silver threads to both the Martin Mystery and to the stack of colored pointers into Sorreno's case variables.

I sent some automated seeker programs out to comb the public pools for mention of the Roccini Boys, and set a sustained query loose on my memory index for images fitting the patterns I pulled from the man at LSL.

Started working my levels.

At some point, I shifted from work into sleep.

CHAPTER 6

Alarm programming from my navis propelled me to consciousness in a flush of adrenaline. I may be unashamed of what I am, but I'm no fool either. The last thing I needed was to miss my weekly appointment with Integration Officer Mai Chandra because I'd stayed up too late in the Mem. Especially since she had become an Object of Investigation in the Martin Ho mystery. I sent the command to my berth to let me go, and the tubes released.

My eyes opened to dawn over Red City. I loved her still, beatings and hate crimes and small-minded vindictive RCPD code-breakers and all.

After the silhouette of the skyline became a collage of earth-tones and greens with a splash of blue-violet from the lapis-paneled buildings, I dressed for respectability in a snappy white blouse and flared black-and-tan pinstriped pants that covered the knee-high tops of my boots. I ran my fingers over the back of my bolero before I put it on; no evidence of the recent brutality. On the jacket anyway. Thirty hours of bed rest had been more healing than a day of mountain climbing would have been, but I was still a mess. Nothing much could be done about that but time and a mouthful of lies.

I took the tube to Central and limped across Telecon Plaza to the Integration Office building. Otherwise tan and boring, after three years the IO still sported a colorful skirt of both pro- and anti-Integration "concerned citizens" rotating around their lunch breaks. Neither side wanted to appear to have caved to the opposition. Of course fist fights over housing limits, lack of Operator representation, and random club bombings helped keep the conflict fresh. On the west side, holo projections flared with "Ops are not the Enemy / Make good on your Apology!" "Nothing About Us Without Us!" and "Red City Housing Rights NOW!" On the east side: "Keep Red City REAL!" "Safety First / Hobble All Ops!" and "No Crime No Apology!" It was just the die-hards now though; most of the action had moved to the Office of Operator Affairs in protest of lack of representation. Between the picketers and the pathway, a spattering of yawning RCPD riot guards slumped in the stupefaction of routine. I remember when there were thousands on each side, not a few dozen, and the LEA had provided supplemental guards.

The cross-fire of accolades and insults hit me as I approached the building, happy, at least, that each week fewer protesters called me by name. My face wasn't on the mainfeeds anymore with the rest of the first-emancipated cohort, and public memory fades fast. There had been a time, though, when any Operator entering the IO had to do so with armed guards. I kept my head down, hair over my face, and hands stuffed in my pockets all the way to room 301 where Mai Chandra presided.

I closed the door to the barren little office and slumped into the chair opposite Chandra's desk. Sweat tickled the bridge of my nose but I wasn't sure if it was from pain I couldn't filter out with programming, or from how nervous she makes me.

The first thing Chandra said to me, naturally, was "What happened to you?"

Synthskin and makeup can only go so far. My face was puffy and bruised and I couldn't move normally in any direction. But I wasn't about to say anything that could possibly land me back in Operator-only housing without my window, or back in a job that wasn't my choice. The protesters may have gotten bored with the Integration Office, but I couldn't afford let down my guard. "I fell."

"On what?"

"On stairs."

"Oh Hoshi, do you need help?" The corners of Mai's eyes cracked crinkle-concern, but their centers only reflected my swollen face.

"No, I'm all right. I'm fine. I did first aid."

"Because—you know—I can get you in to see a doctor."

"Really, I'm fine."

"Okay. I trust you." Mai Chandra smiled. "Aside from falling down stairs, how have you been, Hoshi?"

I took a painful deep breath, wishing I knew if Mai was friend or foe. One of the first things I'd learned as both an Operator and an orphan was never trust a smile on a social worker. "I've been very well, ma'am. I'm doing a new consulting job for Inspector Sorreno."

"That's always good to hear, Hoshi, very good to hear." Her tone and demeanor communicated the same detachment she'd always shown for me. Mai Chandra was an exercise in outer simplicity and inner obfuscation. Her clothing fell in straight, pressed lines, solid colors; today a pale gray blouse and dark navy pants. Her hair was straight and black as mine, but cut short at an angle with the bottom forming tiny saw-toothed triangles so precise they left me wondering if she got a professional trim every morning. Her past was as ambiguous as her demeanor, always average at everything, almost overlooked; I'd found hints in various data that she may have been ill-treated by her parents, but nobody came out and said it, so maybe I was imagining things. The most notable thing about her was a run for Director of Integration Services five years ago, back when the office was new. She'd been fast forgotten by the city after she'd come in third in that election, though she still made frustrated comments to me about how she would be doing things better. What "better" meant she failed to specify; no surprise she'd lost the election. Red City likes a concrete platform from its poli-folk, even if it's just to snark against.

Mai and I had practically the same conversation every week. One full of unspoken questions and nearly-hostile nuances, glazed over with paternalistic saccharine. One where I was constantly unsure if my answers would allow me to keep my apartment and private investigator's office or plunge me right back into slavery under pretense of "for your own good." Still, when Martin had said, *She's not going to be able to cover for you anymore*, he might have meant Mai was protecting me; I had to stay open to possibilities. She had been instrumental in getting me my PI's office in East of Central, even though the landlord hadn't wanted me there. She'd kept quiet about half a dozen things that could have gotten me into trouble, like that week I failed at cooking. She'd defended me more than once when others had put me down or gotten in my way. All things considered, I had no idea what truths lay beneath her immutable angles.

"How is the case going?"

"Very well."

"What's it about?" A simple question.

"I'm sorry ma'am, I'm not at liberty to discuss the details of the case." The complex answer to the real question of whether I was too stupid or gullible to remember my ethics or oaths when prompted to betray them.

"I watch the mainfeed you know, and I always wonder—is that one of Hoshi's cases? What about that kidnapping one, that would be exciting!"

"I'm sorry. I can't discuss it."

"Or maybe that robbery at the Crimson, the 'feed said the only way security could've been overridden is if an Operator worked the job."

"I'm sorry ma'am. I'm not allowed to talk about my cases." Typically she only tried to catch me up on this point once per session, but today she wouldn't let it go.

"You know, there's been an awful lot of crime in City Central lately, especially around Cleopatra Square. It's a shame, so close to the RCPD too. Have you been looking into that?"

"Officer Chandra. I cannot discuss my cases. I'm sorry." Holy Trinity, give it a rest lady!

Mai smiled vaguely without warmth, coolness, or other information, and finally settled into our usual script. "Of course. I'm just worried about our city. I often walk through Cleopatra Square. So tell me, have you been working as a PI exclusively?"

"Yes ma'am."

"Have you been keeping away from illicit substances, illegal activities, and unethical actions?"

"Yes ma'am."

"Have you had at least eight solid meals this week and spent at least ninety-six hours out of bed?"

"Yes ma'am. Ten meals this week."

The interview went on in its usual way. I mostly tuned out, scanning the room in hopes of finding what, I didn't know—a big holographic arrow pointing toward an envelope marked "CLUE" would've been nice. But Mai Chandra kept her office as plain and starched as her wardrobe. Finally we got to the last "do you need anything" question.

"No ma'am. Thank you for your time and concern."

"No problem. You're doing great. Just remember, I want you to succeed; I work for you. If something's bothering you, if something bad has happened, you tell me and we'll work it out. You and I—we're a team." Her precisely-painted lips twitched in maybe a smile or maybe a nervous tic.

Yeah. Right. Like I'd ask anyone at the IO for anything. One of the tenets of Integration Law was Independence, which in theory meant control of one's life and decisions, but in practice meant don't show any weakness or it will become a reason to land a body back into slavery. I saw it happen to Ghe Garver in my own first cohort, six months after we were emancipated. He'd confessed to having trouble keeping his apartment tidy and asked his Integration Officer for help. She'd run an inspection and flagged his quarters unsanitary. "Some of you won't be able to make the transition, that's just the nature of your disabilities," she'd told him as she took away half his rights. "Don't worry, you've still got your voting privilege and all of the other stuff, even if you live in Operator housing." But Ghe didn't care about any of that— he'd just wanted the graphic design job. Of course no one had offered him a housekeeper. Freedom for normals meant the ability to make choices: freedom for Operators only meant the ability to make the choices normals wanted you to make.

I stood for the post-meeting hand-shaking and fake-smiling.

That's when I saw it, when my angle changed.

At Mai's feet, slumped against the side of her chair, an orange bag stamped on the side with curvy letters: Bill's Ragtime.

Well.

What do you know about that.

Maybe this Bill's Ragtime thing—whatever it was—had to do with the Martin Mystery rather than Sorreno's case? I shifted my focus into the Mem and tugged on the cord to the purchase histories from Bill's Ragtime I'd gotten yesterday from Records. Created a silver thread between it and the pile of Martin-data that remained in an untidy mess on the other end of my imagination, just so I wouldn't lose the thought.

"Hoshi?"

"Oh, sorry. I was thinking," I gave my best slightly-embarrassed absent-minded smile. Hoped it read properly.

"What were you thinking about?"

"Something occurred to me about a case."

"Oh? What?"

"I'm sorry ma'am, you know I can't discuss the details of my cases."

Mai's angles shifted into an unreadable semi-smile and she put her hand on my arm, which I hated. "That's good Hoshi. You're doing great. We make a good team."

There were a hundred actions I wanted to take at this moment to learn what was inside that bag, but I needed to stay focused. The murder of female Operators—possibly myself included—being a higher priority than whatever Martin and/or Mai was up to. It was time for the second item on my agenda at the IO. Since it was lunch time, what else would a super-responsible, really well-adjusted, totally-integrated Operator do besides drop everything and eat a nice, solid meal among plenty of normies at the conveniently located Integration Office cafeteria?

I slipped my consciousness into the area sensors as I limped toward the unfortunate scent of industrial food. I got pretty wobbly running so many threads and seeing so many perspectives at once, but my bruised everything made it seem like the slowness and sometimes-staggers were due to the injuries. Six vid cams, two in the cafeteria, one in the kitchen, one in the back hall where the refuse bins lived, and two outside where the closed and locked mouth of the reclaimer lurked, ready to consume as much waste as anyone could throw into it. Two city-run credit plates for paying for food. One motion sensor and one infra sensor mounted around the back door. After numerous attempts to burn down the IO, sensor security around the outside entrances had gotten pretty extreme.

Something that didn't make sense, assuming Samo Oro was your typical killer or clean-up crewman: All Oro would have needed to do to hide the crime was dump the bins. The reclaimer sucks everything into the city's waste treatment facilities deep underground to be sorted and re-processed into useful materials. The lids of the bins were closed, the bodies hidden. But instead of just letting the evidence slip invisibly into the reclaimer, Oro had lifted the lids in full sensor view, inspected the contents (capturing a fine portrait of himself with the corpses in the eyes of the sensor cams), and commed the RCPD.

So regardless of Oro's role (or lack thereof), someone definitely wanted those bodies found. And they definitely wanted them found here, at the Integration Office. Anyone who could fake out the sensors—particularly these sensors—well enough to leave the bodies without being seen would've had their pick of drop spots in the city.

Fake out the sensor.

Fake out...

I pulled my consciousness back to a single focus in the flesh to concentrate on purchasing lunch. The menu projected behind the counter cycled too slowly and glowed too brightly, the flicker and contrast making it impossible for me to read. I tried to adjust my visual sensory filters to no avail, and wondered why they hadn't tried a little harder to make the cafeteria accessible to Operator sensitivities given the function of the building. "Vegetarian special," I muttered to the person behind the steaming piles of foodstuffs, hoping something on the menu approximated such a thing.

Heaps of greasy noodles with too few greens plopped onto a plate by way of a dour-faced man, and I moved the plate to my tray, resisting the urge to drop the starchy mess as the weight invoked screaming wrist-pain.

Sliding the tray down, I passed my thumb over the credit plate and made a beeline for a particular table. I'd decided where to sit earlier when I'd peered through the cafeteria vids.

There was a blind spot in this room. Not a big one, but it was there. And I was sitting in the middle of it. Now you see Hoshi; now you don't.

Blind spots aren't a big deal. A moving target doesn't stay in them for long, after all. So even a well-monitored room typically has a few. Especially when people aren't that worried about tracking particular areas. Like the wall of the cafeteria and the corner of the refuse bins in the back hall. Because, of course, anyone accessing the area from the main cafeteria entrance, the back hall, or the kitchen—the only ways in—had already been captured on vid a zillion times long before they reached the blind spot.

I looked up from the lightly hovering camera above my head, toying with the pleasant vertigo of being both inside its sight and seeing it from the outside at the same time. Through its eye I saw the second cafeteria sensor; a lens hovering high in the far corner and monitoring the doorway in from the main hall.

Casually, I rocked back in my cheap siliplas chair until the front legs left the ground and the molded backrest THUNKed against the wall.

THUNK.

I did it again.

THUNK.

Then a few more times because the sound made me happy THUNK THUNK THUN—

Then I remembered where I was. A non-Op stared at me disapprovingly from the next table over. I ran a routine for a sheepish grin I didn't feel and bent toward my food.

The wall was hollow under the blind spot.

Not The Answer, and not unusual given the plaster construction of the place, but it was the start of an answer as to how the bodies could have gotten to the dumpsters.

I tugged the cord pointing into the Integration Office in my imagination, and through my memory window reeled in the blueprints for the building, unfolding them in my workspace. Then I pulled out all the information from the IO sensor cams that had processed while I'd made my ill-fated trip to Shirring two days ago. In the cafeteria, I tried to remember to look like I was eating. I wasn't doing particularly well at that, so I hoped Mai wouldn't walk in.

No one had tampered with the data from the IO sensors. Given my relationship with sensor cam data in general and those sensorcams in particular (what else am I going to do bored in the cafeteria?), I was even more sure of that than Sorreno's official RCPD forensics team. And I'd already been through every normal route to the refuse bins in simulation yesterday, and not a one of them would enable someone to sneak in with bodies undetected. Unless the route could get short-circuited. By, say, part of it being walked between the walls.

The blueprints didn't show anything about hidden corridors of course, but theoretically it was possible as they also didn't show any piping, environmental controls, or other doodads to get in the way. Modern walls, particularly in industrial buildings, were built thick to accommodate the ubiquitous technology that ran through everything unseen. In fact, someone could get all the way from the—

I opened a channel to the Mem and signaled Sorreno's com.

"I'm in the middle of something Hoshi, can it wait?"

"Data coming at you. Important. Where do you want it? Your eyes only." I loved saying that.

"Stick it in my secure 'Immediate' bin, the one you describe as looking like a brick with three X's through it? Top of the queue."

"On its way."

I should double-check the tube maps to be sure, but I knew Red City better than her civil engineers. Someone could get from the tunnels of Telecon Plaza tube station into the walls of the Integration Office and all the way to the blind spot I was sitting in without ever crossing a sensor's path. Between this spot and the very top-tippy corner of the closest refuse bin, if someone (say a sanitation worker) had pushed it into just the right position, a person could be invisible all the way through.

On top of the package of maps and theories I dropped off to Sorreno, I stuck a note: "Have the Ops in forensics check the sensor feeds from Telecon Plaza tube station for tampering."

Satisfied to my toes, I finally allowed myself a quick break to eat my lunch. The small victory made even the cafeteria food taste delicious.

◆   ◆   ◆

It took three very slowly consumed cups of weak coffee (no espresso in this uncivilized place) post-noodles for my last bit of business to show up. That being one Samo Oro who worked the morning shift, making his last rounds before going home. I'd seen him through various sensor footage but I needed more than eyes. Nothing remarkable about Oro's appearance—a little on the small side, brownish, plain. Wearing a light blue jumpsuit uniform with the IO sigil—a pair of linked ovals—on the left breast pocket. Isn't that what people always say about killers after they're caught? "But he was so ordinary looking!"

I never understood why that should come as a surprise. Statistically speaking, there's no reason for a killer to look more remarkable than any other person pulled from a crowd. It would be more surprising if the killer didn't look ordinary.

At just the right moment, I stood with my tray and made toward the bus buckets dazedly, as though concentrating in the Mem rather instead of on where I was going.

A wet smack and a piercing jar through my bruised ribs.

I looked up into Samo Oro's ordinary face as my lunch dripped an extraordinary mess down his chest. He smelled faintly of cleaning solutions and dust as I focused in on details, experiencing the encounter to the fullest to get the memory solidly in my index for replay.

"Oops! Careful there! You okay? Here, let me help," Oro bent to pick up the pieces, pulling a soft gray rag out of his pocket and mopping at the slippery pile of greasy noodles I'd left on my plate just for this event.

I dropped just enough linguistics to fail at smooth communication. "I wasn't—I'm so. Sorry. I am."

"No worries, really. Leave it. It's my job," he smiled at me.

Later tubing down to Shirring Point, I replayed the encounter from my memory index seventeen times. No reactions from Oro beyond surprise at the impact and a mild desire to help, tempered with the expected degree of weariness for someone nearing the end of their shift. If Samo Oro was responsible for the deaths in any way, it definitely wasn't because he hated Operators.

Hey! It's not as if I went and talked to him! I'd merely bumped into him. On accident. Yeah.

CHAPTER 7

Halfway to Shirring Point I stopped at an Always-C for pain meds. It's a myth that we Ops can just turn on and off any physical sensation we want with programming; some stuff in the nervous system is just too complicated to control. And other stuff is just too dangerous to control. I didn't like the risk of further damage med-numbing would create either—sure, a person could drug up enough to walk on two broken legs, but is that really going to help them heal? But there were more important things right now than tending my bruises.

More important things like a second try at a conversation with Lillie about the élan vitals. Or possibly someone less attack-y at the Shirring branch of Madame Shane's NuVuDoo Supply. But I really wanted to talk to Lillie. Her screams as she chased me off played back with the pain of perfect recall, *Archer put your bow away, do not make us all to pay!*

I still had no idea why she'd yelled it. I'd hoped something in my preliminary analysis of the case variables would have given me a clue but I remained as confused as I'd been fleeing Lillie's alien-fueled wrath.

Which meant I still had no reason to connect whatever was akimbo with the Shirring NuVuDoo crowd to the victims in Sorreno's case—but no reason not to connect them either. Forensics suggested something ritualistic about the crime. Particularly considering the extreme risk of using such a distinctive vintage of whiskey. The average killer doesn't waste a 1200c bottle of Cassiopeian red on a trio of dead girls unless they've either got a whiskey fetish or are involved in weird rituals to communicate with élan vitals. Or want it to look like they're involved in weird rituals to communicate with élan vitals. I wouldn't know without better intel—intel I didn't trust from Sorreno's consultants who all held anti-Integration views. Which is why I'd gone to visit

Lillie in the first place.

The beads across the reading room doorway at the Shirring Madame Shane's were blue and silver, twined with pearls and pieces of polished glass. Veronica's colors, not Lillie's. That made for equal parts disappointment and relief as I minced to the edge of the sales counter and tried to catch the attention of Blu Lou.

NuVuDoo had been one of the most popular spiritual paths for generations, and it had gotten extra-popular now that science had explained why ritual acts sometimes produced real results. Rituals invoked a specific mood that would make the people doing them visible or attractive to one of the alien creatures. Once attracted, the élan would generate a magnetic field around the person and more actively align frequencies, like a sentient magnetic resonance imager. If the person and the élan became aligned enough to start amplifying each other—they called it resonance, for obvious reasons—communication became possible. Plus the creatures could manipulate light and radio waves and zap people with lightning and such. This could get dangerous and weird when resonance happened with large groups instead of a single Santera. Horrible things like the massacres on the Jovian moons—and wonderful things like the success of the Operator Rights Movement that lead to my Integration job today. I was a little hazy on all the mechanics of resonance though I'd lived through its results; the mechanics hadn't come up in relation to either a case or the City yet so I'd no reason to study them. Like most Operators, my interests range deep but narrow.

Lack of insider-status on the whole talks-with-aliens thing aside, the Shirring NuVuDoo folks always treated me with a suspect amount of friendliness, awarding me the same deference as their own Santeros—while also smirking and exchanging obscure looks over my head without letting me in on the secret. They don't realize what it's like to be spoken about instead of being spoken to. When I'd asked Lillie about the deference and the looks, she'd only said it was because of my relationship with the City, and avoided elaboration. I avoided further pressing since the topic of my relationship with Red City could lead to the topic of the city sensors and the overload of images in my sleep, which, no matter how dear a friend Lillie was, she didn't need to know about.

Who knows, maybe Lillie and her people were onto something with me and the city. According to the Cantors on Callisto, who have been dealing with the aliens for ages, important places can attract élan vitals. If the moons of Jupiter could have spirits, why not Red City? Except that it would seem, given my obsession with all-things-Red-City, I would have heard about it. Not all celestial bodies have an élan vital that likes to bathe in their EM fields.

Blu Lou stood fantastically tall and broad with the kind of blue-black skin one rarely saw in these days of racial homogenization. He wore a floor-length lapis and silver dress, and an animatronic necklace comprised of links of Möbius shapes that twined around themselves in restless infinities. My vision is hypersensitive enough so even in the dim light I could tell they were pseudo-fractal: larger links comprised of smaller links, down to a third level, each size the same twining Möbius shapes. Kelvin's fine work; I'd recognize it anywhere. Lou had been a professional fighter before one of the élans decided he should be a Santero instead. He'd kept both his workout routine and his fighting name after becoming a priest. Definitely who I wanted next to me most days. But today I imagined him flattening me with his beefy pinky like a cartoon mouse.

Lou didn't try to smush me. Or scratch my eyes out. Or chase me out of the store screaming obscure rhymes in eerie inhuman multi-frequency.

He did let me know I was not welcome.

"Lady Hoshi," Lou stood with stiff formality, his hands hidden by the thick, scarred wood of the counter. The features of his face made his Chinese and European ancestry clear in a way his black skin did not. "Lady Hoshi, with due respect, this is not a wise time for you to visit." At least he didn't ask what happened to my face.

I played the Socially Clueless Operator card and pretended I didn't catch the hint. "Lou, why is Lillie mad at me? I don't know what I did!"

Lou's beautiful eyes tugged down with his frown. "I do not speak for Santera Lilliana Redwing. Her voice is not my voice; her god is not my god. Perhaps you should wait a while and then, months from this moment, ask her. Now is not a wise time to visit."

Lou was being deliberately stiff and formal. Keeping me out. So I offered a way in. I took a deep breath, steeled myself for the discomfort, and looked Blu Lou straight in the eyes. This time not because I wanted to monitor pupil dilation, but because I wanted him to believe my sincerity. And I was sincere. Just had to give off the right non-Op signals so he'd kish the weight of what I had to say. I pulled myself tall as I could and adjusted my linguistics to mimic his formal speech patterns and vocal inflections. That's what they teach in Socialization for establishing rapport, and it seemed to work on normals most of the time. I took a wild guess as to what was upsetting the Santeros. "Santero Bohai Lousi Liang. I, Lady Hoshi Archer, do not believe my friends responsible for murder. Please, let me help my friends prove it."

Even for me, the connection was more of a grav-assisted pole vault of intuition than a leap, but that's how the few pieces of the puzzle I had associated together, so that's what I played.

And was rewarded by Blu Lou growling low in his throat, his eyes glancing furtively to the sides, and his enormous hands grabbing my upper arms and dragging (lifting?) me behind the counter and into the back stockroom in a single gesture that completed before I was halfway through processing it.

"Shit, Lady Hoshi," Lou dropped me on a tall wooden barrel of who-knew-what in a storage space thick with creepy trinkets and the confusing scentscape of hanging herbs. "If you'd any sense at all, you'd've left Red City when Lillie and Ogun warned you off-orbital."

"Warned me off-orbital? Warned me off!" Now that really spun me. "Coming at me like she was gonna take my eyes out was supposed to suggest an off-world vacation? Wouldn't something more like, 'Hey Hoshi, there's something I need to warn you about, let's discuss it,' been a bit more effective!"

Lou backed up and put his hands out, palms up, as though my anger was a heat that needed shielding. But Trinity! I could be reasoned with!

"I'm a person with the power to make informed decisions about my own life, you know. I'm not some thing to be ordered around like a servo! Not to mention what Lillie said to me is hardly interpretable as 'I'm warning you off-orbital'."

"No, no, Lady Hoshi, please! Listen! She and Ogun are trying to protect the city! To protect you! The gods are not always good with human relations. Sometimes they misunderstand the feedbacks, the resonances."

But I was standing now, two steps toward towering Blu Lou who had won 14 City Series medals in the fights and who stood over twice my weight and moved four times faster than my sadly programmed reflexes, shaking my little fists and yelling—

Okay, maybe people are right about me not having a properly developed danger sense. But this was serious! "I'm trying to solve multiple murders, Lou! Murders with enough of a ritualistic angle your folks could be blamed for them! I don't need protecting, but by the look of it you do."

My out-of-proportion anger spun out as fast as it had spun up, and I sat back down on the barrel but forgot I'd moved forward and plopped too hard on the cold concrete floor instead, impacting with a force that would've made my bruised ribs scream if I hadn't been chock-full of Pain-Ez. My overly associative brain added another tally to why I despise furniture and refuse to put any in my apartment.

Lou had backed up a-ways, hands out defensively, the creases around his eyes gone tight.

"I'm sorry," I mumbled. "You didn't deserve that. I'm just a little stressed." And a little sensitive to people deciding what I should or shouldn't do without asking for my input on the matter—but Lou had no way to understand the calculus of institutionalized oppression. He didn't know how much my meetings with Mai reminded me what little control I had over my own life was granted by someone else. He didn't know how many of my freedoms had been denied under the false aegis of protecting me; he was used to taking freedoms for granted. I had to cut the normals some slack.

"It's okay, Lady Hoshi. You just don't know all of what's been happening with the gods."

I put my face in my hands and rubbed my temples, the roughness of the synthskin reminding me I probably shouldn't do that. Looking back up, "I think it will be safer for everyone if you tell me."

"The gods, they worry Lady Hoshi is poised to bring Sha Chi, terrible danger, to the city," Lou frowned. "Lillie's Ogun already fears you as the enemy."

I wanted to say something really cranky to that, but instead opted for the more diplomatic, "I can't duck, Lou, if I can't see the blow coming."

He unfocused and swayed, looking for all like an Operator who'd gone still accessing something consciousness-intensive in the Mem. If he was communicating with an élan vital, he sort of was. The Mem, after all, was a field of EM signals. The élans communicated by manipulating EM, that's how they managed to talk to humans. Lou snapped out of it and nodded miserably. Sitting cross-legged on the floor in front of me, he took my small brown hands in his huge black ones, and held them. I don't know why he felt the need to touch me, but I let him. Anything to make him comfortable enough to talk.

Lou led with, "Ngao and Ogun disagree about how far things have gone. What do you know of the Dragon's Crossing?"

I ran a quick search through my memory index, and came up null. I shook my head.

Lou scooted back and pulled a few strands of white bead necklaces off a rack, arranging them on the floor. I identified the outline of Red City long before he finished; the jagged spits into Marcie Bay, the crescent of Broadway Beach, the lumpy boundaries of the city limits to the south and even an oval for Lan Qui Park down the center.

I sat still, waiting.

Lou made a meandering criss-cross shape over the city with blue and red beads. An "X" from the northeast top of Shirring Point to the southwest border of Husson, from the northwest curve of Broadway Beach to where Hill met the southeast mountains. "The Left Dragon," he pointed to the blue line, "and the Right Dragon," he pointed to the red. The lines intersected at Cleopatra Square in the center of Lan Qui Park. The bull's-eye middle of the city. I pulled up maps in my head and compared—I hadn't heard the term "Dragon's Crossing," but I had seen that shape before.

Lou rubbed his palms on his knees. "In the beginning, Red City was built to hold its center at the Dragon's Crossing, to maximize the Sheng Chi. City Planners since the Landing have known of these power lines, built around them, placed Lan Qui Park and the laws protecting the city greenspace to make sure the Chi flows smooth and strong and bright."

I found the map I was looking for: a survey of Cassiopeia Prime's geomagnetism. Indeed, natural lines of force flowed in the patterns described by Blu Lou.

Lou took my hands again, holding them over the center of the map where the lines met. "Do you understand the significance of the Dragon's Crossing at Cleopatra Square?"

I wanted to blurt out something about how if there was an élan living around Cassiopeia Prime, it would be attracted to areas of geomagnetic activity, but also wanted to be respectful of Lou's need for religious poetry, so I kept my mouth shut and shook my head.

Lou opened my hands, pressed my palms, one atop the other, into the center of the cross, held them there. I felt a heat, a buzz, like faint electric shock where my palms pressed into the middle of the map. He turned my hands up, folded my fingers into a cup. He whispered, with wonder, "the Dragon's Crossing holds the heart of the city," and then he jerked my hands up and out and I startled, my own heart pounding as Lou loosed a roar and smacked my hands together so hard they smarted beyond the numbness of the Pain-Ez.

My hands plummeted like dead birds as Lou dropped them into my stunned surprise.

"Someone did something very bad to the heart of the city," Lou whispered with scary softness. "Three times now. Very bad energy. Sha Chi. Someone's corrupting the heart of the city."

Three times. Three dead Operators. Click. Click. Click. "What else do you know about the murders?" I asked.

Lou took my hands again. "We felt the Sha Chi. The gods felt it and told us of its heat. We know human sacrifice has awakened something. Murder makes a strong resonance. The essential electric twitch as the nervous system dies, it is a thunder to the gods. If you do it right, it makes them like you better. We know someone will be looking for who to blame, and at first it will be us. But that is not what scares us. The blame will not last. The corruption will. The corruption can sway the thoughts, the actions of the city-whole, just as human-corrupted élans recently swayed us to the brink of genocide. We must protect against the completion of the circuit."

"Murder isn't something one does 'right,' Lou." I choked on a bit of bile. "You mean someone's trying to communicate with an élan? Which one?"

"I think you'd better leave Red City."

"Come on, I'm not the bad guy."

"We must protect against the completion of the circuit."

"Talk plain Lou, I'm not one of you. I don't understand your religious words." Then I thought of Kelvin and Blinker's frightened faces, and my own hurt over Lillie's behavior toward me, and I pulled my hands away from Lou and scowled, "And neither do most of the people in Shirring Point. You're scaring the neighborhood, Lou. You need to speak plain."

Lou's face made a shape that meant I'd said the wrong thing. I watched his eyes flick to the shine across my forehead and adjust his reaction. It's true, I do use the perception of Operators as social cripples for specific effect. But then, sometimes, I do genuinely screw up, and when I do, I never understand why.

"Ah, Lady Hoshi. Things in the messy world of people and ideas are not so simple as your science and your Operator mathematics," Lou sighed and caught my hands again to squeeze briefly, but he had closed up.

"What aren't you telling me, Lou?"

His back was to me now, but his creepy laugh made me glad I couldn't see his face. "Go back to your safe apartment in the Hill District, and to your little PI office East of Central, and to the umbral worlds you wander in the Thin Electrick of your Mem, and let the Santeros take care of the problem. Better, get out of Red City. Put your bow away before you make us all to pay."

I slammed myself on the top of my head with both fists. "You are exasperating me, Lou! I have access to law enforcement resources, and it would help everyone if we worked together."

"I am chosen of Ngao, the Shield. I am protecting Lady Hoshi of the City from harming that which she loves."

"You are taking the advice of aliens who—by their own admission—have no idea what it's like to be human let alone what it's like to live in Red City. You're impeding justice!"

"I am doing what I must."

Arg! Well, this interview was over. And probably for the best since I had a date to make and a long uptown tube ride to travel. Straight up the Right Dragon's tail. "Will you talk to Lillie for me? Please? Ask her to com me, just do that? She's my friend Lou. I don't like bad energy—Sha Chi—between us."

Lou turned to face me and lowered his shoulders a little. "All right. I will talk to Lillie for you. I will not advise her, but I will relay the message." He led me out of the storeroom and to the door of the shop without further word.

But as I turned the knob to exit, he caught the triangular sleeve of my bolero and pulled his face close to mine. "Lady Hoshi, please be careful. Those who attacked you—who cut your face—it was part of the shape of things to come. I do not know why, but they cut you for a reason, a part of the attack on Red City's heart. Remember, you are a symbol in the city. Symbols, like murder, have power, are a way to call the élan vitals. In three years the public has not forgotten you were among the first to be emancipated. You have power to sway ideas. If you won't leave—and you should leave—be careful. Be safe."

I opened my mouth to speak, but my thoughts and feelings were too surprised and confused for my linguistics to figure what to say. By the time I got my act together to move at all, let alone use speech, Blu Lou had vanished into the Tarot room. The "IN PROGRESS" holo winked on above the curtain of blue and silver.

Outside the shop, my boots clicked on the blackstone cobbles, and I was unsure if I felt anger or fear, and for whom I felt them. It was hard to factor what in Blu Lou's intel was meant to be taken literally and what was the poetry of the Santeros' story-telling-way of understanding the world, but there was a reality behind even the poetry. The gods and spirits were really élan vitals, sorcery a pretty word for resonance—but there was a poetry behind the reality as well. Such star-spattered unknowns surrounded the creatures with whom we shared the universe. We were like two-dimensional squares trying to understand three-dimensional spheres, when all we could perceive was the single point at which the spheres touched our plane. Another puzzle. Another mystery.

What if the attack two nights ago hadn't been a simple hate crime?

What if someone had wanted me dead, and wanted it to look like a simple hate crime?

I paused in little Bailey Park and rested my injured cheek against the pagoda there, the coolness of the blackstone taking the heat from the wound.

This pagoda had been carved from Red City's bedrock, still attached to the larger mass below. My pulse beat against the polished stone and I thought of how all of Red City was connected by unbroken blackstone deep beneath her soil. I pulled up the geomagnetic maps, but they gave up no secrets.

Sorreno thought I was on the next victim list for whatever had been done to Aysha, Claudia, and Nessa, but I'd instead received a blunt, direct attack with a knife.

Was I part of the pattern of Sorreno's case, or was I part of a larger pattern of manipulation in the city? Or was I part of nothing at all, and this just speculation and distraction?

All the more reason to keep pressing toward the truth.

CHAPTER 8

I was late to meet Angel. There had been a holdup at the Union Street Station—the tube stopped while four plainclothes officers I recognized from Robbery extracted a pair of kids two platforms down. I watched the action through the station's sensors while the people near me grumbled about the lack of proper maintenance on the tunnels and how they wished City Coordinator Cosenza would do something about it. The level of certainty some people have given no verifiable information is amazing.

When I finally got to the warm light of Capelli's Restaurant in the Hill District, Angel was already seated in her high-backed wicker chair like Alice in Wonderland after taking a drink. Considering I'm not much bigger than Angel, the large furniture had similar effect on me. I giggled, as always, and slid into the huge chair opposite her.

Her happy-to-see-you grin faded almost as fast as it had in the morgue. "What happened to you?"

"Op bashers," I shrugged.

"Oh Hoshi! Are you all right? Have you been to a doctor? Do you want me to take a look?"

I shook my head. "I'm fine, really. Just a little scraped and bruised. It could've been worse." And might yet be worse, if Blu Lou was to be believed.

"Have you gone to Sorreno—"

"Nah. I was stupid. Really. I never should've been walking alone down Gayle Street after dark. I never should've been walking along Gayle Street, period. I should've taken the tube or walked home via the Koi Street Exchange. Don't tell anyone, please."

Angel's halo of blond curls and girlish looks jarred with the complexity of her displeasure. "Don't you dare say it was your fault! You should be able to walk anywhere you'd like in Red City. I can't believe those—" she balled up her fists and her face flushed and she looked like she was about to bash something herself.

I wasn't keen to dwell on it, if only because it reminded me how sore I was now that the Pain-Ez was wearing off. "Anyway, sorry I'm late. I was following a lead down in Shirring and on the way back the tube was stoppered-up and munged."

Angel's smile returned like the Red City dawn. "It's only six minutes past the hour, I don't see how that qualifies as late."

"Well, there's bread on the table. There wouldn't be if—"

Angel laughed lightly, "Oh Hoshi, I love seeing you no matter the bread status!"

Her laugh lifted the stress out of me. If Angel didn't want children, we might have tried the dating thing, but I'm not allowed to breed because I'm rated too high a class of Operator—they only encourage those of us with lesser impairments in the range of Class One through Eight to pass on our defective genes. I'm Class Twenty, though you wouldn't know it by how bad I am at programming. I'm not fond of kids anyway, even if someone else supplied my half of the DNA to Angel, and it wouldn't work, no matter how progressive we both are on the mixed-marriage thing. Or maybe these are just the lies I told myself to cover up the fact that I hadn't been on a date with anyone since Claudia and I broke up four years ago. Now Claudia was gone.

The waiter came by and took our orders, and I yanked the wings on the red-and-white checkered origami napkin-crane to unfold it and spread it over my lap. "There's some stuff akimbo in your forensics," I said, my face screwed into a little frown that hurt.

"I'll say!" Angel laughed.

"No, I don't mean the obvious strangeness of the case. I mean..." I pulled a portable 3V plate out of my pocket and unfolded it on the table, shoving aside the salt and pepper shakers and aligning the breadbasket as a privacy screen. I looked through the sensorcam at the back of the restaurant to make sure it couldn't see. Not that anyone but me and Angel were likely to recognize or care about what I was about to display.

Above the plate, I made pictures manifest. The gritty black-and-white of a magnified medical vid zoomed in on blobby receptors attached to a cell wall, a neurotransmitter according to the info scan I'd done. Fluid floated by, blood or brain goo, I had no idea, but a differently-blobby chemical entered the scene to interlock with the receptors, opening them like weird flowers. Numbers scrolled below to indicate elapsed time, somewhere around 10x speed. The receptors furled back up gradually as the chemical dissolved and its effect wore off.

"That's a vid of nyquolium-quadrolate interacting with the cells of a non-Op," I pointed as the feed ran through. "Now compare."

I played a second vid, same grainy medical zoom of receptors on a cell wall, only this time the chemical locked in tightly, held on longer, and dissolved abruptly. The cell shivered and recoiled, spasming in some sort of chemical crisis.

"And that's a vid of NQ interacting with the cells of an Operator." I looked at Angel.

She didn't get it. Well, she got what it was, heaps more than I did given her medical training, but based on when her eyes lit up and when they smoothed over in dull confusion she didn't get why I was showing it to her. She blinked at me, waiting. Good. The last thing I wanted was to find dear Angel at the head of a hate-fueled conspiracy to obstruct justice.

So I supplied a third image, a still one, that looked like the latter stages of the first vid I'd shown, the non-Op vid. "This is from your analysis of the drugs in the victims' bodies. You concluded there were trace amounts of NQ in their systems. You even included this picture. But what's in your report only works for non-Op physiology. There is absolutely no way the tissue sample in your report could have come from an Operator."

Angel's expressive face flashed through a sequence of surprise, disbelief, and near-ah-ha moments, before converging on confusion. "I'm not that shitty at my job, something strange happened here."

Her reaction came as a relief. But not as hard evidence of her innocence. It was dangerous to trust the heart instead of the head.

"You know, I was interrupted in the middle of that tissue analysis. It was your," she grimaced and made little quote marks with her fingers, "'friend,' Martin. He'd come down with a thing from Inspector Zi, a—I think it was a big toe. Or maybe it was a second toe. Anyway, one of those gangland things, the usual. I've no idea why Zi sent Martin down with it and Martin wasn't happy playing courier. But I suppose someone could've—"

"Angel, where were you in the analysis? What had you completed?"

"Well, everything except the last bits. I'd already ID'd the whiskey and the beckerwood brew, done the stats, I had just noted the positive on the NQ and—"

"Who else was in the morgue at the time?"

"Just Jaali and Sorreno. You know, Jaali Henri, the guy who helps with the sanitation. Sorreno was impatient for me to finish up, she'd come down to chivvy me, hurry-it-up, you know how she gets." Angel rolled her eyes; our love of Sorreno notwithstanding, she was often frustrating.

The food came and I banished the images with a thought and folded the 3V plate away. My favorite veggie bouillabaisse, savory and tomato-y, might as well have been a bowl of plaster for all it interested me. "If there was NQ in the victims at the time—"

"Oh there was," Angel set fork to her primavera. "Definitely. I'd gotten that far at least when Martin interrupted me. I just hadn't done any more detailed analysis."

"If there was a more substantial amount of NQ in the victims, they wouldn't have been able to send the command to remove their hardware, even if they were conscious, even if they wanted to."

"I don't know much about NQ Hoshi. It's not a compound I see very often."

I picked bits out of my bread, making small white balls with my fingertips and lining them up in spiral patterns. "Ops who use NQ for years can sometimes access their processors with a lot of pain and effort. But for a casual user, the accelerated verbal processing from the NQ also makes it impossible to form the visualizations needed to operate a navis. That's part of how NQ gets us to us pass as normals, it makes our brains process words like yours does. And why we can use a navis and you can't—because ordinarily we don't process words like you do. It's all scrambled-up sound and color and texture and smell and stuff in here." I tapped my forehead.

"But were they casual users, Hoshi? My gods, if someone messed with my analysis or the evidence, who knows what—"

I shook my head. "They weren't addicts. Trust me." The thought of Control Freak Claudia succumbing to NQ addiction was as preposterous as me growing wings. And Nessa was too productive a programmer to support a habit. Plus both of them had reported to work right up until two days before their bodies were found. Maybe Aysha was a long-time user, I knew so little about her still, but the other two couldn't have been.

"But why that bit of evidence, Hoshi? Of all the things someone could've messed with, why that?"

Sopping up broth with bread, I made myself eat a few bites purely to make processing time for linguistics, to force my very non-linear thoughts into a flat word-based approximation. I tugged some variables into my workspace and stared at them with most of my focus: the black box marked MOTIVE, the faces of the three victims, a shadowy variable that was a place-holder for "identity of killer"....

My mouth finally moved, "If the women could send the signal to their navi to safely disengage the machines from their brains, which the phony forensics strongly imply, then they consented to the forceful, fatal removal of their hardware. A really, really weird suicide, or possibly an accident while attempting some kind of ritual to communicate with an élan vital. Which is what I'd been thinking, right up until I took a closer look at the picture you included with the report. I'd even mentioned the suicide theory to Sorreno."

Angel caught on then, "Ah, but if they couldn't use their processors, then it's simply murder."

"As much as a murder is ever 'simple,' but, yeah. I think whoever munged the evidence—my guess is by swapping the tissue samples—wanted it to look like a bizarrely assisted suicide or an accident."

"That's a solid idea," Angel's forehead wrinkled with seriousness.

"Built on rickety assumptions," I observed.

Angel emitted a humorless laugh. "I'll recheck all my data tomorrow. Make sure nothing else got misreported. I'll check the tissue samples too. Switching the sample would've been the fastest and easiest way to mess me up."

"Sounds like a good idea. Thanks." My tone failed to include enthusiasm. I'd hoped for things to have untangled a bit by today; instead, they'd gotten knottier.

Only one of four people, in a short range of eleven minutes twenty-eight seconds, could have swapped the evidence. That is, if Angel was to be believed about who was in the morgue and when—and right now all I had was her word. The morgue sensorcams covered only the main doors; recordings were made manually by staff, and Angel wasn't recording at the time.

One of four people, including Angel. And Sorreno. I didn't get to rule out people just because I liked them.

Worse yet, whoever was responsible was likely linked to the murders. Because who else would want to do something like that? Four people.

Martin Ho, Senior Operator, code-breaker and unwilling courier.

Jaali Henri, Sanitation Worker Rank B and morgue clean-up crew.

Inspector Cassandra Sorreno, Director of Misc. Physical Crimes and chivvier extraordinaire.

And Dr. Angel Smith, Forensic Specialist Tier One and in-charge gal of autopsies.

Childishly, I hoped Martin was to blame. But, unlike Martin, I made an honest investigation before I made an accusation, so I had to consider the bigger picture.

I pulled a few more details on Jaali out of the RCPD employee contact pool. Jaali Henri, started at the RCPD working biological sanitation twelve years ago. That was a lot of time at an entry job.

I asked Angel, "What do you know about Jaali?"

"Not much. But gods, he's been around forever. Before my time. But why would he—or any of them—have wanted to do it? I mean, unless they were in on the murders."

Yeah. I'd reached that distasteful conclusion too. Motive was gonna be a bitch.

She ate and I brooded, then Angel took a big drink of water and broke the silence with, "Come straight with me Hoshi. Touchy as it is, we would've had this convo via com channel if it had just been about the forensics, and we wouldn't have talked about the case at all if this was just about a dinner date. What else do you want?"

I looked at my half-eaten bouillabaisse. Even with all the linguistics programming and the Socialization it can be hard for me to find an approach to expressing stuff to normals sometimes. "I need you to take me down to Archives so I can look at some old evidence. From a closed case."

Angel blinked; not what she'd been expecting.

She didn't say anything else and I didn't want to get into details yet, so I added, "Just something I think might be related. It's not in the e-archive and you know how I like touching stuff with my hands."

The additional information didn't affect the confused expression on Angel's face, but she shook herself and asked, "Hoshi, why didn't you just come down to the station on your own? You are allowed to enter the building, you know. And you're free to access Archives when you're hired on consult."

"And brave the daytime bustle and all the people who'd wanna talk to me and, 'Oh Hoshi, how are you, why do you look like you got knifed in the face?' No thanks!"

Angel shook her head affectionately. "You are one strange lady Hoshi. That's why I love you so much." She smiled, but with sadness.

"I'm Op," I shrugged off her endearment, then gave a smile of my own, "I'd lose all my cred if I wasn't strange." Then I got distracted by my thoughts again, "Can we go?"

Angel grinned at me like the sun sparking off Marcie Bay, twirled up the last of her primavera and waved to the waiter. "Yeah, sure, just let me get mister over here to come by with the credit plate."

Outside, the evening rain started to fall. Umbrellas blossomed and hats came out of sacks and pockets, automatic gestures for anyone used to the routine of Red City's weather. Unless you were like me and enjoyed getting damp in the evening rain. Only a few folks on the street shared my preference. One of them was also an Operator, and he looked up into the steel-green sky, hands out to catch the drops in his palms, laughing high and clear and without care for the woman with the toddler who pulled her child in closer and scowled. Good for him. I stuck out my tongue to catch a drop.

Evening light turned the pavement greenish-violet. Angel unfurled a petite purple umbrella studded with tiny stars while I focused on a puddle forming under the large leaf of a cello plant. I counted drops, factoring their dynamics. Did they converge on a single inevitable end, following a fixed-point attractor? Or were they ultimately unpredictable, chaotic in nature? I decided it depended on how I looked at it. Each drop behaved chaotically—too many tiny variables involved to clearly determine each exact rivulet's path from cloud to ground—but as a whole, they always filled the same small basin of puddle.

Eyes closed, I filtered auditory until I felt the quiet vibration of the tube running between the M Street and Cambridge stations through the soles of my feet. Feeling the city's structures support, contain, enable her diversity.

I saw Lou's bead-drawn map in my memory and superimposed it over my physical sense of the city, realizing I stood along the tail of the Right Dragon, which happened to follow the Blue Line local northwest from the Hill District to the bay. Had the Blue Line been laid down the path of the planet's magnetic field on purpose?

I needed to be careful though not to jump to conclusions, like the people in the tube earlier. Despite the apparent chaos, there was a logic to this case too, a hidden structure, and I would find it the same way I had found the tunnel beneath my feet. It was all in how I looked at things, like the behavior of the water drops.

I didn't need to be inside sensors to be within the body of the city. I smiled, though no one but me would ever know why.

"...Hoshi?" Angel's hand found mine, lightly pushing.

I sighed and twitched, charged full of the city's life. Eyes open, I saw Angel's golden curls, her intelligent blue eyes. I smiled less secretively, took her hand, and we walked toward the tube entrance three blocks down.

CHAPTER 9

The Archives Division offices turned gloomy after sundown.

While most areas of the RCPD remained bustling no matter when, the fourth sub-basement had emptied of its humanity hours ago. Now only sensor eyes gazed passively into the mausoleum of evidence, without judgment.

Archives' purpose was to store physical evidence related to cases now closed. By Red City law, no evidence, once used in the justice system, could be discarded. Every few years a lackluster movement to get rid of some of the physical stuff reared its head, but ultimately it was more cost-effective to maintain the existing process than to come up with a new one. Not to mention the protests of the officers and consults like me who need to touch things to stimulate the intuition. The subjectivity of the human senses can be useful in more situations than programming.

I wasn't in Archives because of the murder case, though, but because of the Martin thing and the edge of a memory that, had I not been an Operator, I would have long ago forgotten.

Memory indexing scares most non-Ops. Usually, I factor that's because they don't understand how it works. They think we can track everything all the time, like human spy devices. But in order for a memory to get indexed it needs to be consciously experienced. This means that things like dreams, a conversation across a crowded restaurant, visuals we're filtering out with programming—none of these things make it into the index. We can't remember things we weren't aware of any more than normals can.

Other times, the power of memory indexing scares me a little too.

The idea is simple. A program created for the very first navi tags all conscious experiences with identifiers, and then, any time an Op wants to recall anything, they think a simple search with one or more identifier. Calling up the identifier stimulates the place in the brain where the memory is stored. If I wanted to recall the last time I ate teriyaki yakisoba, I'd picture a current date range and a pile of brown noodles and veggies, or the dish's salty, garlicky aroma, and then I'd be replaying the memory of lunch on the floor of my apartment with Sorreno three days ago. If I wanted to recall every memory I had of Kelvin, I could pull them all up and shuffle through them like a deck of cards. Difficulty remembering is really difficulty recalling, after all. The memory index is a recall aid. Simple.

The reality is complex. Perfect recall can be painful; not all memories are ones a person wants to—or even should—remember in detail. The boundaries of what is "consciously experienced" blur too, with subliminal events sometimes getting included in the recall, if not in the index. So there can be surprises—again, not always pleasant—in a memory recalled. And then, of course, there's the fact that just because something is experienced does not make it true. Experience is always a very subjective business.

Operators grow up with perfect recall, so we know how to deal with its various issues. It's not as unpleasant as normals imagine. But it can still be spooky, even for us.

Last night I'd tossed the enhanced image of the behatted man on Martin's projection plate into my memory index, along with the phrase "Roccini Boys." And I'd gotten back a snippet from a mainfeed projection that I didn't fully understand, so I had backed up in my memory to replay the full context surrounding it.

◆　◆　◆

Six years ago.

RCPD cafeteria, food time. No fix on time of day.

The media wall was tuned to the local mainfeed, and my back was to it, my eyes only registering the tray of vegetables and rice enough to shovel the stuff into my mouth. The majority of my consciousness was busy with encryption. Blue hexagons rode roaring slivers of pecan into an oily sonata of rainbows, interrupted only by a densely-woven envelop of variegated loops of logic folding in on themselves to cover the warmth where a key might fit—

Sorreno's officers had confiscated a storage crystal from an industrial-secret smuggling ring or something and I was breaking its locks, figuring the code within. It was particularly complex encryption; I'd been at it for days and the puzzle still hadn't come unstuck. Sweat prickled my nose from the strain of making it through lunch without losing my mindscape. The only reason I was sitting in the cafeteria at all was because someone had poked me awake and forced me downstairs for solids, but my mind was so groggy with code that I couldn't remember how the plate got in front of me.

The mainfeed clucked and flickered on the wall beside me, nothing more than white noise.

"Fuck! Did you see that!"

Words filtering through the cracks of awareness, I shuttered my consciousness to keep them out. If I were to put the blue rectangle over there and the corduroy filter over the tangle of any-loops, what happens to the 8-D matrix of—

"Hoshi!" an elbow in my ribs.

Curse it all to Noise!

I turned slightly, holding the complex coding structures in my head, praying silently to Signal, Encoding, and Noise that I wouldn't need to say anything because if I did I was gonna lose it all.

Officer Kim sat across from me, eyes round as wheels, gaping at the mainfeed. "Isn't that the guy from the case you were working last week? The guy they let go?"

Delicate code structures fragmented and popped like bubbles, and I bit the inside of my lip in frustration so hard it bled. I hated the normies for not understanding what they did to us when they forced us into their world. Why were we always the ones who had to compromise? What gave them the right to decide they were healthy and we were flawed? Cranky and frantic, I tried to salvage what I could, cramming code half in my own idio and half in the original franca into my hard storage. I turned to look behind me where Kim was gaping, because if I didn't appear sociable he'd report my aloof behavior to a higher-up and then I'd have to take supplemental Socialization courses or worse.

The mainfeed was alive with a broadcast of a burning building. The reporter stood in the here-and-now but the footage of the building, which was about 10 seconds long, replayed on a loop. The flames appeared to suck back into the short wood and brick building every time the loop restarted.

"...said arson was the least of the problem. Sources on the scene say the Roccini Gang used the blaze as a distraction to stage the assassination of Councilman Verg Ban two blocks down, where the Councilman was..."

The building in the replay exploded into black destruction as three figures ran from it—figures wearing the same signature long, tan coats and wide-brimmed floppy hats as the man who sat next to me at Long Shore Lassie's last week. The man on Martin's 3Vplate, who it seemed like I'd been talking to.

"No, not my case," I stammered to Officer Kim as the last of my code ghosted through the grasping fingers of my thoughts and was lost. My resentment remained.

"Oh. I thought it was. Isn't Verg Ban the guy who tried to boot you out of the RCPD because of the Upshaw thing? Said you were overstepping Op-Law because you're not allowed to work anything but the code?" Kim continued, oblivious to my black mood.

"Yeah, but..."

Smalltalk and food. A whole day's work shot to chatter and Noise. Bitterness swallowed in the flow of how things are.

Life goes on.

♦   ♦   ♦

It was the sort of unimportant memory no one recalls. Without the assistance of a memory index at any rate. These were the two closed cases I was interested in now: the Verg Ban assassination and the case Officer Kim had referenced when I was too distracted to pay attention.

Because it had been my case, in a peripheral way. I'd failed to find whatever it was the RCPD had been looking for in the code I'd been given to break, and whoever's arrest had hinged on that code had been released, no charges. I didn't know it at the time, but I found out now with a quick glance through RCPD records, that the person I'd indirectly let off was one Hank Roccini—the ringleader of the Roccini Gang (not a one of them whose real name was in fact Roccini). They were a small pseudo-independent group of black marketeers working deep in the Pier District. And, given a few simple 3-D transforms to get a partial profile from Hank Roccini's mug shots, also the guy sitting next to me at the Long Shore Lassie's in Martin's sensor footage.

It didn't take an Operator's talent for associative thinking to see the setup potential in all that.

So I needed to get a better handle on whatever "evidence" was sitting back in the past to fuel my alleged connection to the Roccini Boys. Had I made a mistake in my code-break somehow? Was there anything here that could turn Martin's sensor feed into more than pure circumstance? I can't duck if I can't see the blow coming....

I closed my eyes on the hangar-like two-story warehouse of densely packed metal shelves and long metal tables, and opened a connection on the shortwave to the Archive Division's stationary systems. Stepping through the blue tunnel in my workspace, I flowed into Archives, Memside.

A large room, square, white, plain. A closed book, heavy and thick, rested on a single podium of pale wood at the center. If it had been business hours, I would have seen instead one podium for each person using Archives. I'm not sure how many podiums the Archives stationary can handle at once, but I suspect more than will ever be used. A single stationary processor has more power than eight personal navis systems like mine, though it lacks the storage capacity of a human brain.

I approached the podium, imagined the case number into my palm, and cast it onto the book. With a totally gratuitous whirling sound, pages turned, dense with case numbers stretching back almost two centuries. The pages stopped turning when mine appeared, glowing cold, dull reddish on the creamy paper. The whimsy of the original programmer caused the text to appear literally "hotter" depending on how recently and frequently the evidence had been accessed. I touched the cold-case number and the page turned to show a map with a violet "you are here" dot and an orange "your evidence bin is there" star.

Tearing the map from the book, I switched primary focus back to the physical warehouse. I spread the map over my vision so I could walk through it in fleshspace while monitoring my location Memside.

When I reached the right rack, I dipped back into the Mem and adjusted the lever for "fetch me this evidence bin." In the flesh, I watched the two-story metal boxes reconfigure themselves with the hiss of pistons and the creak of steel. My box dropped within arms' reach and opened.

I pulled out the stuff I found inside and set it all in a jumble on the steel table between the towering shelves of bins. This was the physical evidence from the high-profile arson and assassination case, the incident I'd caught the edge of on the feed in the RCPD cafeteria and never given a second thought to.

For such a big case, there was a small amount of evidence.

The charred, mangled remains of a crude mechanical object which, if I'd ever had reason to study pyro, I'd probably be able to identify as something more nuanced than "the thing that went boom."

A torn piece of tan fabric, hermetically sealed in a clear trace-preserving sheathing.

A pile of holo-stills taken by a bystander at the Verg Ban assassination. They showed someone in a long, tan coat and a wide-brimmed floppy hat angling a sniper-style lite-rifle into the gap made by the crowd as they ran from the exploding building. The rifle clearly protruded from the perp's forearm; illegal implanted firearms tech. The rifle was trained on the esteemed councilman.

Neither Hank Roccini nor his gang had been caught on either the arson or the shooting.

When examined by Red City Medical, not a one of the gang had an illegal implant of any sort, let alone a retractable wrist-style lite-rifle. All of them had solid alibis. The conclusion being that someone had tried to frame the Roccini Gang for the violence.

Dr. Angel Smith had signed off as Medial for the RCPD, as then second-in-command of the Department's Medical Forensics Division.

The case had been handled by Inspector Zi of Vice because of its ties to gang activity.

Closed, but not solved.

And, despite the initial public outrage, forgotten. Ah, the fickleness of the media and the public opinion. As I well knew.

I sighed, irritated by the sparse evidence that inspired nothing. I carefully examined the objects so I'd have them all in my memory index, and put them away. Then I went back to the Archives book to locate and retrieve the evidence for the other case, the one Officer Kim had interrupted me to go on about. I cast the case number into the book on the podium and waited for the unjustifiable dramatics of the whirling pages, tapping my foot. And startled back from the smoking result. What should been a case number as cold as the last one I'd accessed, the characters blazed orange and puffed ash. This case wasn't exactly on fire, but someone had accessed the evidence recently, like in the past few days. I could press that button at the edge of the podium for more info, but it was bad enough I'd fingered the case at all. Best not call any further attention to my interest. I tore out the map and slunk away to the shelves.

The bin for that case, the one I'd actually worked on, was so stuffed full of evidence I had to close my eyes and count to ten before I could sift through the mass of junk without becoming paralyzed by the options.

There were piles of blankets. Each wrapped dozens of small mechanical parts: gears and motors, crude twentieth century style technology. The sort of stuff used in building the most taboo sorts of modern robots—the kind that exposed all of their inner workings. I would guess, had I actually lived in the twentieth century, that this would be analogous to staring at piles of strap-on dildos and photographs of sodomy. Not illegal, but shocking to some. Not to me of course. The whole reason silly taboos against visible technology exist is because normies can't face their dependence on defectives like me. The taboo is just a reaction to the blue visible across the forehead of every Operator. It took a bit of an effort for me not to swipe a few of the parts to give to Kelvin for his tinkering. Premium parts, these were.

Beneath the blankets were two opaque siliplas bags. I pulled one out and opened it gingerly; I don't like reaching into sacks of lumpy darkness, but was too impatient to go back to the Archives index and read the manifest.

I pulled out a small stationary system, a cube about half the size of my head. The shimmer of its tzaddium was hidden behind a shiny red siliplas casing. Several long scrape marks marred one side. I remembered the object now that I had it out; this was the stationary I'd been asked to break the crypto on. The only thing I'd found behind the incongruously impressive security had been personal photos of the suspects with legitimately hired sex workers. Nothing related to contraband robots, a mechanics grift, or the reason why the suspects had been nabbed in the first place—a tip that the mechanics smuggling was just a front for a far more illegal human slave trade. A normie slave trade, that is, Operators being legally traded slaves.

The last object I pulled out with irritation; for all the tons of junk in this box none of it was going to be of any use to me either. Another dead end.

Two-point-four seconds later the significance of the object I was holding hit my awareness. I dropped it, clattering, to the table.

It was a child's toy—a bright yellow box with dancing bears along the sides and a few buttons in the back. The front had a small window, molded for pressing against the eyes and peering in. "My First Film" was writ in jumbly childish letters above the dancing bears.

Theoretically, it was a preschooler's movie-maker, a cheap thing that shot up to ten minutes of poor quality holo and played it back over a tiny 3Vplate inside.

Realistically, these movie-makers were perfect for recording sophisticated encryption filters by the sorts of characters who might want to hide the keys to their shady operations in their little nephew's toy box.

Practically, the RCPD had busted so many people after finding their "My First Film" decoder rings that we'd gotten the city to quietly ban the toys. But back at the time of this case, they had been at their height of popularity; a real criminal fad. The idea that I'd never seen this bit of evidence before no matter how much I cross-referenced my memory index, well—

I ran through the film inside the toy as fast as I could get it photographed with my eyes into memory. The weird wavy lines and complex hatches and crap that looked one step closer to Noise than Signal confirmed that this was an encryption filter. Recording random stuff out of focus plus the device's natural noise created the perfect unreproducible key for non-Ops.

I opened a channel to the red stationary system and smashed through its crypto with breakers I recalled perfectly after all these years, pulling up the stupid sex footage.

Then I dropped my vision past the franca, into my own idio of the coding structures, and shoved the filter over them.

Transformed, the porn became a detailed set of records on deliveries of "product" to multiple Red City destinations, most of which I recognized as deep within the less savory sectors of the black market. Sectors that would have been a lot more interested in human trafficking than in pseudo-legit machine parts.

Hank Roccini shouldn't have been let off.

Why hadn't anyone shown me the filter key!

Or had they, and I was just too distracted at the time to notice it? I raked through my memory index, but couldn't find the awful yellow toy in it anywhere. Another bad thing about perfect recall is that there's no way to know why a memory might be missing—did it not happen? Or was it just below the threshold of consciousness?

Inspector Zi had handled this case too. Zi, who hated all operators in general but me in particular, and who was probably on the payroll of the Roccini Boys himself, along with every other sketchy-but-powerful character in the city. Had Zi made sure I'd missed the key? No one would ever believe my word against his.

Regardless of whose negligence explained my failure to break the code, this wasn't looking good for me. The fact that someone had been through this evidence recently meant that someone else knew I'd failed to report key incriminating evidence against Hank Roccini. If I were to bet at this point, it would be that Martin had decided I was protecting the Roccini Gang. I packed everything back in the bin as though it might cut me, set it back on the shelf, and walked slowly out of Archives.

"Did you get what you needed?" Angel asked, meeting me at the door.

I nodded, thinking miserably of Zi sitting chummily with Martin. "Yeah. But not what I wanted. Let's go home."

Angel sweetly walked me all the way from the tube stop to my apartment.

CHAPTER 10

I told myself I was going to the Rose and Thorn to relax.

More honestly, I was going there to troll for info until I exhausted myself enough to fall asleep sometime this week. Maybe that qualified as relaxing. Maybe not. I could make a strong case either way.

Rose and Thorn is less thick than most Memside Operator clubs; seventy percent of the patrons are usually my people. A real thick place like the Dahlia Den would be one hundred percent Ops. At the Rose and Thorn, the rest are mostly fan-kids—normals who like to interact with us in the Mem, though I'd never factored why. They would be accessing the club from 4V and 5V hotspots, forever distant from true sensory experience. It's not like they can enjoy most of what the club—or the Mem—offers. But who am I to judge? Or even know?

Built in the early colony days of the city and reprogrammed rarely, the Rose and Thorn has an enduring status as most popular Op-club in Red City Public Memspace. Popular because it's easy to get into; its carved imaginary bloodwood doors open regardless of what one's ID patterns contain. The place only boots people who disobey its few and obvious rules:

Don't attract the attention of either Red City or Federal Banking law.

Don't harass others.

Pay your tab, thanks.

The low bar to entry breeds information exchange, and finding pretty much whatever you're looking for. Be that a quiet drink with friends, a local sensory music act, or something a good deal more... specific.

And what was I looking for this night?

Well, I had a list of about 400 things but was happy to take the three I spotted right away: a pair of acquaintances playing a game of vorpal pool; a

Cantor to Zaos sketching bits of gossamer code in the air, as far away from everything else as she could get; and Martin Ho and his cronies and fan-kids, guzzling beer and laughing obnoxiously at the big round table next to the currently-empty sound stage.

I split my consciousness three-way and mingled.

Vorpal Pool Thread:

A variation on the game of pool that could only exist in the Mem, the colored balls of vorpal pool hovered in the three-dimensional oblong of the playing field. I watched Casidy squint at them with orange, slitted eyes, calculating how the balls might react within the complex, invisible vector field in which they floated. Depending on where he tapped the balls with the tip of his electric cue, they could skitter anywhere. There were as many areas of chaotic dynamics as fixed ones in the playing field, and the key to winning was to deduce the physics faster than one's opponent. The game was in its early stage: all of the balls still in play, and scattered too randomly to factor the dynamics by looking at them. But both Casidy and Manny would have discovered a few warps by now.

"Casidy bet me the most boring task on our docket at the spaceport," Manny grinned, emotives reading ruthless pleasure.

Casidy split threads briefly, his willowy man-goat franca appearing next to Manny to quip, "I'm gonna win too. You'll be fixing baggage router bugs into the next millennium, bwa-ha-ha!" while also remaining fixated on the playing field. Then the thread next to Manny vanished as he merged back, staring intently at the floating balls.

"That's what he thinks," Manny smoothed his thick black hair and laughed. "What I think," he leaned in confidentially and scoped the message privately to me, "I think he's about to hit a roamer with the six-ball and take a penalty for sinking my seven!"

"I can't say because I haven't been watching the field, but if he doesn't take his shot soon the timer's gonna blow." I observed the clock above the field as it inched into the red.

"Just like my zen if you keep me in suspense any longer about what you wanna know."

"Who, me?"

Manny's emotives shifted to good-natured teasing, "Hoshi, you never come to chat unless you're trawling for clues. That's why we love you, of course."

"Arg! Caught in the act!" I feigned distress. "So, seriously. I'm wondering if you've heard any slop about Bees lately. Or anything akimbo about me or the city. Or just anything local and weird. I guess I'm just trawling with a really wide net today."

"Ah, look, Casidy's about to make his move. He's shifting from foot to foot, he does that in the flesh you know, right before he does something. I gotta watch the field, and then you should ask Casidy to tell you about the black hole in Red City Public while I take my shot."

Cantor to Zaos Thread:

Cantor Gno presented, from a distance, as a woman glowing softly white. Closer in, the illusion dispelled, her franca an abstraction of glassy layers, slipping and looping in a shifting semblance of woman-form that refused to resolve into any singular shape. The visual made it hard for me to communicate with her, its dazzling ambiguity overwhelming my senses and making me forget what the fuck I was trying to say. But Gno was a Cantor, connected to the folks at the élan embassy on Callisto even though she lived in Red City, and that meant she knew more than pretty much anyone else about the creatures. Unfortunately, she was as impossible to understand as her franca. Something to do with having grown up in space or a cave or something. The Callisto people had never been forthcoming about their origins, at least not to the general public like me.

"Sister Hoshi," Gno greeted me, the code she'd been sketching above the table vanishing. Tendrils of translucent veil-stuff spread toward me as her emotives extended welcome. "Please, sit."

I gave myself nine seconds to get lost in Gno's presentation, hoping to get it out of my system. Then I rested my elbows on the table and looked for a more stable place to fix my vision. That knot in the wood grain would do. "Thanks, Gno. I have a murder case with some ritual-looking evidence and I'm trying to factor if it's got something to do with the élan vitals. Do you have time?"

"I always have time for kindred," the impression of smiles flowed through me like I was really feeling it, not just reading her programming. Followed by the impression of frowns. "But we need to talk about circuits."

Blu Lou's cryptic parting words chilled through me. "We must protect against the completion of the circuit," I whispered.

"Yes, we must," Gno concurred, like I'd any idea what Blue Lou had meant by that.

Gno made an image in her mind visible to me over the table: a diagram of whimsical symbols—cat heads and flower pots, candies and dynamite—laced together with shimmering strands. Despite the whimsy, I recognized it as an old computer circuit diagram, mostly because Kelvin actually used that kind of drawing in his work. Ovals and triangles and cat heads as and-or-not gates. Squiggly resistors and gaping capacitors. Software and hardware, all connected up except for one gate that dangled, disjoint, from the edge of the network.

"A circuit is a lot of things," Gno said. "A machine, mechanical or informational." She snapped the unconnected gate into place and the network lit with whirling numbers, transforming as they passed through each node. The calculation of pi poured out the central gate to splash on the ceiling.

Gno broke the circuit and the numbers stopped flowing.

"A circuit is also a pathway, a journey from here to there." Closing the loop again, a dab of light traced through the nodes and vertices. Instead of processing through the logic gates the circuit made a path, the dab of light choosing the shortest route through the complex connections without repeating a leg, solving the Traveling Salesman problem. I smiled. Poor old Traveling Salesman, such an impossible mathematics problem back in the silicon-chip days, he'd been rendered trivial by the first large-scale quantum processor. It was a cute touch by Gno. But she destroyed the connection as the loop completed and the circuit went dark.

"A circuit," Gno said, "is also power." Eye-shapes flickered beneath her veils. "It is the on-off that pours electricity into our navi, that sets in motion every machine humanity has made, that runs our minds, our bodies. On-off is the difference between light and dark, between being and not being. Having and not having. Power."

I quivered, exhilarated, horrified, as the air became electrified. Gno closed the circuit again and the unit ignited into a fiery blue flame.

Gno wrapped her form around the flaming circuit, subsuming it, consuming it, laughing in multi-frequency. The sound that meant an élan vital had gone into resonance with her, was speaking through her. Was riding her.

I pulled back; imaginary flames don't burn flesh but they can be programmed to hurt just the same. Too late—the fire lapped over me, bringing with it not burning but danger and glee and the buzz of a minor electric shock—the same feeling I'd had when Blu Lou pressed my palms into his map of the Dragon Lines. The touch of an alien creature, probing me, very much alive—

I stood and stumbled out of the fire's reach.

Gno dispelled the imagery. Her franca returned to its soft, white glow, and she made a quiet laugh-purr. A strange sound, but human again. "Power," Gno said. "Power means control. Circuits—whether they are made of tzaddium spread thin across a quantum processor, or made by the connectivity between humans and élans—are always a means of control."

Martin Thread:

It was a rare opportunity. Martin Ho trapped in full view of friends and fan-kids, forced to do anything to save face. Even have a conversation with me. There could be no storming out, no stalking away nor shutting me down. Not unless he wanted to look like he was afraid of little old Hoshi. One thing I can say for Martin, he did always attract an impressive gaggle of friends.

"Hello Martin, having fun?"

"I was until you showed up," his ridiculous rust-colored super-hero cape snapped with irritation.

My own emotives read pleasure while the cronies and fan-kids emitted weak snickers, uncertain how best to back up their favorite super-hero versus semi-notorious me. I smiled and pulled over an imaginary chair from the next table over and sat in it backwards. "Aw, come on, for old time's sake, let's have a drink together. Introduce me to your friends. The next round's on me." I sent my citizen ID at the credit plate, a small tureen in the center of the table, before Martin or anyone could stop me.

The cronies and the fan-kids craned toward Martin for guidance. But he just sighed, resigned, and played it iced. Perfect.

"Maybe I don't wanna remember old times," Martin grumbled sullenly, but even he realized he sounded like a whiner, so he closed his mouth and glared at me and raised his mug. "Congrats on still being a manipulative bitch."

"Ah, you wound me," I held my hands over my heart melodramatically.

"C'mon Martin, I'm not the one who's been snooping around Integration and dredging up circumstantial evidence about me from stale, closed cases."

Vorpal Pool:

"The black hole, yeah." Casidy hadn't sunk Manny's seven-ball but he had hit a roamer. Perturbations in the playing field propagated madly as the roamer dynamic moved through the field, scattering balls every which way. "Black hole is my affectionate name for it anyway. Actually, it's creepy as fuck."

"And 'creepy as fuck' is unlike a black hole exactly how?"

Casidy laughed at me and watched Manny, who watched the field. Manny's index finger tapped a complicated beat on the tip of his electric cue as he concentrated. "Too many hours at the spaceport," Casidy said, "and the black hole jokes run a bit thick. Black holes being places where something goes in but doesn't come out, like the sink-hole dynamic in the vorpal pool field. Or, in more typical usage, the Human Resources Department at the spaceport every time I try to put in for a week's vacation," he grinned. Then frowned, "But no, I found this creepy thing going on in Red City Public earlier today."

"Yeah? Creepy how? And exactly where?"

"It doesn't have a where, exactly, not Memside anyway. But I'm pretty sure it has a where in the flesh. It's— Well, it's hard to describe. Here—" Casidy held his hands together, palms up and open, in the age-old gesture for memory playback.

I fixed my focus above Casidy's hands and he spread them apart, unfolding the image between them. I put my hand out to touch and then I was inside the playback experiencing it from Casidy's point of view—

Cantor to Zaos:

"What's all this circuit business to do with my murder case?" I asked Gno, not quite sitting back down. I still felt like there was static electricity in the air even though that wasn't possible—if only because there wasn't any air.

Gno's inscrutable form shimmered and morphed. "A circuit, a control diagram, is full of feedback. Take the early development of cybernetics: the study of communication and control. How do we understand nonlinear relationships where two things affect each other simultaneously? Feedback." Above the table two spheres appeared, blue light flowing into the red one, red light flowing into the blue one. The more the blue flowed into the red, the brighter the red became; the more the red flowed into the blue, the brighter the blue became.

"Positive feedback," Gno said. "As X increases Y increases; as Y increases X increases, until—"

Both spheres exploded into white light and disappeared.

"The most important thing—perhaps the only important thing—to know about the élan vitals is that we are continuously engaged in feedback with each other. Our species make a circuit. If someone pours hate into an élan, that élan will pour hate back into our world. That's what's almost destroyed both our species during the Revolution and again, more recently, during the Outing. We are an inseparable, nonlinear ecology, both on the personal level of a relationship between a Cantor and an individual élan, and on the universal level of humanity and all the élans that truck with Inhabited Space."

Although Gno had no face and her emotives didn't even seem to be working, her words landed on me like a blanket of doom. And I didn't even know what they meant. "If someone gets murdered it makes the élans deadly too?" I grasped for anything useful.

Martin Ho and Co.:

"Oh-ho! You got something on that bitch finally?" Crony-on-the-Right gave his best try, but Martin's emotives had gone cold and unhappy with my little pronouncement, and I saw him dig Crony-on-the-Right in the ribs.

"What are you on about, Hoshi?" Martin asked quietly, not hiding his rattled emotives.

The beer arrived and I tipped mine in a toast toward him, even though we both knew I'd no intention of drinking it. I hate beer as much as I love espresso. "Congrats, Martin, on Sherlocking another completely untrue thing about me out of your imagination! Seriously, you can't think I have anything at all to do with Hank Roccini. Sitting next to someone at a bar doesn't make them your best bud, does it? I mean, look at you and me sitting here, now, right?"

Martin's presentation scowled, but his emotives read surprise. Emotives are great for making feelings clear, but say nothing about motivation; was Martin surprised I'd figured out what he was trying to pin on me, or was it about something else?

I kept going. "You're wrong about anyone protecting me too. Seriously, who'd want to aid and abet a Hoshi-crime? Half of Red City would love to see me fail; that'd be a great big blow to Integration Law."

The cronies and fan-kids were clearly all baffled. That Martin hadn't shared with them troubled me. Martin likes to brag. For him to keep something brag-able a secret...

Martin shifted in his seat, uncomfortable. Then he laughed a little, in cautious relief. "Is that what you think? Well look at you, Miz Thelma Savvy, Girl Detective. You've got it all figured out."

He hadn't turned off his emotives. He wasn't trying to hide his reactions. I really hadn't hit the bull's eye on his Master Plan, not exactly. But I was close, close enough to make him really nervous. I was on the wrong track somewhere. Where?

"Speaking of unlikely best buds," I decided to play another card and see what it did to Martin's poker face, "what's going on with you and Inspector Zi of 'Operators have no souls' fame? You haven't turned Effram Caper have you Martin, turning on and turning in your own kind?"

Vorpal Pool:

Inside Casidy's memory playback.

Forty eddies past the Orphium Theatre, shoved downstream by data-flow, jetting into Red City Public, the central information nexus of local Memspace, opening—

Millions of people and seeker programs swarmed the daze of floor-level stores and adverts, and the blue-lit portals of official city services beaming from sky-level sectors. Densely packed with colors and sounds and, less often, other sensations, the second biggest Memspace after Earth Public was too chaotic to be useful. Until a mind organized it with a want, a will, a volition of what was sought.

Transported by desire, Cassidy/Hoshi stood beneath the glowing wave-and-bird sigil of the Cassiopeia Prime Indigenous Nature Conservancy, reaching up to touch and flow through the portal—

Resolution on the portal staticked out.

What?

Nothing. Just a momentary glitch, a bubble of data lost in the system.

Reaching up to touch and flow through the portal and—

No, it's something. The rez was off. The edges of the portal weren't fully clear.

Squinting back into Red City Public, shifting vision from franca to idio to see the code, learn where it's broken.

Hoshi's mind-within-Casidy's-memory cannot understand the whirls and shouts and flavors of Casidy's idioglossia. But she can recognize the small black squares where bubbles of data should have been but weren't.

Casidy's mind stepped back, away from the Conservation Agency portal. Took a bigger picture.

Within Red City Public, dispersed so far apart one would only see them if one were looking, were holes in the fabric of Memspace. Information vanished into—where?

That wasn't possible, there was too much system redundancy.

And yet—

I stepped out of Casidy's playback, shaken, shaking, but didn't return the thread to awareness of the Rose and Thorn yet. Casidy would see my franca standing still in the throes of his playback, but I was detached from my presentation entirely, my awareness plunging instead into the transmission lines used by the city sensors, invisibly, omnisciently riding the city's currents. Now that I was aware of them, I felt the missing bubbles of data like tiny slashes in my flesh, so attuned to the city's data networks I wore them like a skin.

Underlying the complex consensual dream of the Mem runs cold, hard physics. Data is transmitted on infrared and micro and radio waves by station and satellite and personal transmitter. Every bubble that flows through the Mem has a physical existence as Signal—is a wave form flowing through the electro-magnetic.

Extremely talented Operators can trace Signal through the Mem to its physical source.

I am not an extremely talented Operator—at least not in that way—but I didn't need to be.

I had the City as my guide, showing me exactly where the signal was flowing in the physical world.

The missing bubbles were all being sucked out of existence and vanishing in the vicinity of the transmission towers and satellites around the center of the city at Cleopatra Square. The very place where the Dragon lines crossed.

"Casidy," I choked, pulling my consciousness back into my franca, "Thank you. Thank you so much. I've got to go."

Cantor to Zaos:

Gno's indistinct form arced with cold menace. "Yes, it is like what happened during the Callisto Revolution. Human-corrupted élans versus Callisto's resonance—it started so far away, but made riots in Red City. If someone gets murdered it makes the élans deadly too—or, more accurately, it makes their interests resonate with the murderer's interests. The more murders, the more alignment. The more the public knows about it and amplifies the alignment, the further the resonance carries. The greater danger you are to the City."

Martin Ho and Co.:

Martin's hands were around my throat so fast I didn't know it until it was too late.

That was the ridiculous thing about Martin's envy of me—he was, in fact, so much better than me at all things related to the Mem. Martin was the faster programmer, faster thinker, faster code-breaker. And faster at blind-siding me with his fingertips pressing hard into the soft, vulnerable flesh of my imaginary neck.

The sensation of suffocation by crushing lines of code is no different from the same happening to the physical body. Martin was crushing the imaginary life out of me. My hands flailed forward, trying to shove him off, trying to squirm away.

The cronies and fan-kids closed in to pull Martin off me, but he clung, savage, emotives burning a hate and rage hotter than the surface of Cadmus.

Gagging, flailing, darkness swarmed over the table as Rose and Thistle bounced us and our terrible, sudden violence out of the Mem.

♦ ♦ ♦

I was home again.

In my workspace, Mem channel closed.

Bounced right out of Rose and Thorn with a "don't come back for a month" tag on my patterns. Which was completely unfair since I hadn't done a cracking thing! It was Martin who attacked me!

What an idiot I'd been not to have simply closed my channel the moment Martin had made his move. Then I would vanished from the Rose and Thorn before the bouncer got me, no harm done. Stupid Hoshi!

What was with all the violence lately? Lillie and her Overly Wrathful Warning, Martin and his Inappropriately Irate Reaction to my mention of Zi, the city itself seeming to consume its own being from the inside in the form of lost Signal, Gno and her dire, epic warnings—

Martin's violence wasn't just inappropriate, it was out of character. Martin schemed and whined and tried to set me up, but he had never made a violent move.

If someone gets murdered it makes the élans' interests resonate with the murderer's interests, Gno had said. Corruption in the heart of the city.

With a shiver, I wondered if Martin's actions were being driven by something other than his dislike of me.

I opened my eyes to see Cepheus' moonrise brushing the black skyline silver.

My thinking was crowded and unclear. Circuits and black holes and élan vitals and violent assaults. One thread in my workspace, the other watching the pale rise of Cassiopeia Prime's second moon Phoenix joining its sister over Central, I shoved the disturbing encounters at Rose and Thorn into their respective case landscapes. The thump of my heart quieted in the safe routine of organizing. But not nearly enough to sleep.

I did something I hadn't done even once since switching to my PI job two years ago—I ran a sedative program, stimulating the parts of my brain that would encourage melatonin production.

Sleep deprivation, after all, wasn't going to solve my cases any faster.

CHAPTER 11

BANG BANG BANG

I hoped for a dream but suspected I was awake and someone was pounding at my studio door.

BANG BANG BANG

"Hoshi Archer!" Sorreno's voice pierced through the wall all the way to the room where I lay on my side, facing the window.

I got only the barest morning skyline fix before the next volley of banging started. Dragging a blanket with me, wrapping it inarticulately around myself, I slogged toward the door while sending the command to open.

"Sorry for the early visit, but I was in your neighborhood and I'm wretched with meetings the rest of the day." Sorreno was in a foul mood, but she wasn't fiddling with her locket in her nervous tell, and her irritation wasn't aimed at me. Which is all that matters when I'm less than a half-step over the threshold of consciousness.

"I swear Hoshi, I'm going to buy you some chairs."

The automation on my programming had me cringing before I could stop it, and Sorreno laughed.

"I'm joking, I'm joking, don't worry! Your blind spot theory checks out." Then she scowled. "And we need to talk about what happened to your face."

I sighed. And avoided. "Espresso?"

Sorreno shook her head.

I ducked into the kitchen alcove to make my morning drink. Yesterday's clothes lay puddled on the bathroom floor, and I threw them on while the coffee brewed.

Five minutes later my hands curled around my mug, its heat filling my core. "Glad the blind spot theory checks."

"Yes. Perp has construction skills, proficiency with a plaster-sealer unit at least. And the forensics Ops found fifty minutes of noise on sensorfeeds from the Telecon Plaza station twelve hours before each of the bodies was found. Perp enters Telecon with a high-quality tunable jammer, vanishes through the maintenance duct just past the south-bound platform, and goes the length of Telecon Plaza underground. Then enters the Integration Office walls via a suspiciously sawed opening in the building's foundation." Sorreno paused to scowl deeply. "That's a lot of effort if you ask me."

Yeah, and a lot of premeditation. And a lot of very well-executed planning. And a lot of creeping doom feeling regarding the fact that reality generally isn't that tidy, so what did it mean? But saying all of that would be stating the obvious to Sorreno, so instead I asked, "I don't suppose anything useful was found between the walls, like some DNA?"

"No."

My mind was as blank as that answer, so I just drank my coffee.

"But it's a good start." Sorreno didn't sound as happy about that good start as she should. In fact, someone who didn't know her well might even regard her pointed lack of enthusiasm as evidence that she was unhappy with my work. But I'd seen that look before whenever a crime fell into the "too tidy" category, that "what are we missing look." I felt the same way.

If someone were really trying to stir up caste tensions by killing Operators, and could travel unseen below Telecon Plaza via some as-yet-unknown magic, why not drop the bodies in the middle of the lawn smack between the dueling protesters? Or, if someone was really trying to hide the bodies, why not leave them hidden in the tunnel? Why would someone want those bodies found, specifically, in the Integration Office cafeteria dumpsters?

I wondered then if there was some symbolic meaning to the dumpsters, something related to the ritualistic nature of the crime. If only Lillie and Lou had been more friendly, or Gno more comprehensible.

Sorreno's heavy breath interrupted my thinking. "We're running simulations now, testing ways someone could have gotten into Telecon Station with the bodies. And rounding up witnesses from the times around when the sensors went static. I also have an update for you on a number of other details."

"Me too. For you. Update." I sat cross-legged on the soft carpet, blowing on the top of my espresso so the aroma curled into my nostrils. "You first."

"I sent Chaucer and Tang out after the exotic whiskey in the victims' blood. Seven of the twelve bottles you didn't ID were found full and corked. Another half-drunk in the possession of the Alcon family up on Mace Hill; we're not particularly suspicious of that one. Another behind the bar of an exclusive club run by the Breaker Society, too full to be our target."

"That's nine. The other three?"

"Yes. We still haven't placed the last two bottles, but number ten is interesting. Know of Madame Bosco?"

I perked up, and not because of the coffee. Three days ago, at the start of this puzzle, Kelvin had told me Nessa might have been entangled with the syndicate at the Velvet Glove. Madame Bosco figured prominently in that pseudo-legal establishment. If Nessa'd been running her pornware out of the Glove, she would've had contact with Bosco.

Sorreno took my perking up for a yes and continued, "Bosco claims she'd kept a bottle locked up in the Velvet Glove's safe for 'special events'. But someone stole it."

"Someone stole from the Black Widow of Carmine Street? Brave, that!"

"If you believe her."

"Do you?"

"I checked records with Theft. True to what she told Chaucer and Tang, Bosco reported the whiskey stolen to the RCPD three weeks ago."

"Right before the murders started."

"Right-o. The fact Bosco reported the theft to the RCPD instead of having her own enforcers deal with it has me wondering how she's involved."

"Not because she's trying to cover up abetting murder; she's got better ways to do that. These murders anyway."

"Then it probably means the officers she reported it to are on her payroll. The whole RCPD's coming apart at the seams these days." Sorreno's voice ran heavy with the disgust she felt for crooked cops.

But the politics of corruption didn't interest me right now; my thinking had soared a light year down a different path. "None of that matters. What matters is that one is the bottle we're looking for."

"There are still two more bot—"

"No. That's the one. That's the bottle we're looking for."

"What makes you so sure?"

I shook my head. I didn't want to tell her, not yet, about Nessa's side business in pornware. And I didn't want to tell her about Kelvin ever, because I didn't want the RCPD visiting his tinker shop looking for intel. That would be the best way to ensure people stopped slopping their gossip to him. Plus, unlike me, Kel had no fondness for Red City's finest. If I'd been beaten nearly to death by cops I'd feel the same way. "Client confidentiality, sorry," I shook my head and lied, distracted by a thread I spilt off to explore the sensor landscape in and around the Velvet Glove.

Sorreno didn't look pleased, but she didn't push. "Well, Theft is collaborating with us on Bosco's missing whiskey and we're still hunting for the last two bottles."

"Good. Very good. The bottle could lead us to the perp. Did Angel tell you about the problem with the switched evidence—"

Sorreno's face went red and her lips went white and her hand went to her locket and I didn't need to finish my question. "That's one of my meetings. Regarding the analysis, Angel wanted me to tell you that you were right. The blood sample was switched. The victims in reality had much more than trace NQ in them at time of death, and would not have been able to send the command to disengage their hardware. Fortunately, the NQ was the only thing that ended up analyzed in error. Everything else Angel'd finished before the... the thing with the evidence."

I wanted to ask how the investigation for that might be going, but Sorreno's legendary temper was barely dammed. Plus she knew as well as I did that she, herself, was a suspect in the affair. I let her change the topic.

"I also ran a consult with some religious experts on how the various elements of the crime could function in a ritual context."

I scoffed, loudly, before I could damp the reaction. Any mainstream consultant the RCPD hired was going to be as anti-Integration as Zi. I didn't trust a one of them on a case that involved Operators and public opinion.

"Something you want to tell me Hoshi?" Sorreno always sat across from me dragon-style, her knees bent under her. She'd been in a hurry, or maybe distracted, her coils of braids loose. I got the impression from the creases in her tan blouse and brown slacks that she, like me, still wore yesterday's clothes. Unlike me, the smudges under her eyes hinted she'd not taken those clothes off. Why? What had she been up to all night?

"No. Yes. Well." Ugh. "What did your consultants say?"

"That it definitely looked ritual, but they couldn't match the evidence with any popular religious practice. They said the elements—the painted bodies, the drug cocktail, the items ground up in the paints—they weren't consistent with any known symbol set. They concluded—"

"I know this one," I interrupted unhappily, "they concluded it was likely the Santeros or Magi in Shirring Point, maybe the Hermites or the Sisters of the Sea. Or some recent NuVuDoo sect not on the Register. Something like that. Am I close?"

"They didn't name names, but the general idea, yes. Should we look into those groups?"

"No!" My voice modulated poorly and the negative came out blaring.

"I know you have friends among—"

"No." I repeated more quietly. "I can't prove anything. Yet. But the Shirring priests and magi—they're just the obvious choice for a frame. I don't think they know anything, they're too shook up in the wrong way. And they're worried because they figure they'll be blamed regardless. And look, they are being blamed regardless! Something else is going on."

"But it would be a simple answer?"

"But it wouldn't be the right answer. No matter how tidy."

We paused, both of us thinking.

A few minutes later Sorreno switched gears, since neither of us could pluck a revelation from the silence. "I've also had some officers working the drug angle, the beckerwood brew and the NQ. We've been having some"—a pause for loaded meaning on the next word—"trouble there."

I took a haul from my espresso, unsurprised. The obvious meaning of Sorreno's "trouble" being that the Red City drug scene was notoriously tight-knit and difficult to penetrate. Specialty drugs, like NQ, were even tighter. And specialty drugs favored by Operators: the tightest. The second meaning to Sorreno's tactfully chosen "trouble," of course, being that drugs meant working with officers from Zi's Vice division, and, well, most of those officers were on some drug Capo's payroll. I remembered Luzzie Vai exchanging something with one of Zi's cops while I'd surveilled him at the Julia Set three days ago. It was nigh time to have that confrontation with Luzzie I'd been planning.

"Drugs are on my to do list," I peered sadly at how little espresso I had left in my mug.

Sorreno laughed at my words, but didn't comment; I wasn't sure why. "Where we've had more traction is on the victims." And she smiled for the first time since she'd arrived, albeit predatorily. "You're going to like this."

I finished my coffee and looked over my shoulder to the greenish-blue sky of Red City and the puffy high clouds of morning, trying to be patient with this slow mode of information exchange favored by normals. I longed, for the zillionth time, for Sorreno to just shove data at me instead of flattening it into endless, blunted words. So much more information can be encrypted into an image, a memory playback, a bubble sent at the speed of thought....

"The Operators in Tracking put together a beautiful report on everything Nessa Mason and Claudia Foucault did in the three days before their deaths. And they found a connection."

"A connection?" My heart beat faster.

"The last data imprint either of the victims made was entering the Integration Office."

My fast-beating heart came to a dead stop. Whether Sorreno had meant I'd "like" this information sarcastically or not didn't matter—I liked having the fact of the connection quite a lot; I disliked its implications just as much. "Great," I answered just as ambiguously, pulse returning.

"We couldn't get the same detail for Aysha Ayers obviously, but they were able to find her altered facial pattern on a few sensor recordings. Including that the last visual feed recorded of her was also entering the Integration Office. Connection on all three. I'll make the report available to you as soon as I hit the office. It's top-notch stuff."

"Good. Thanks. I'll get it sorted."

Then she put on her stern school teacher face and narrowed her eyes. "Two more things Hoshi, ones you won't like. One, what did I say about talking with Samo Oro? That man could be dangerous, and I can't tolerate you disobeying my orders when you're on consult any more than I could tolerate it when you were on staff. In fact, given your situation, I can tolerate it even less. There's half a city out there that would love to see you fail at your Integration job.

"But more importantly, Oro has access to, and intimate knowledge of, the Integration Office. He knows how to use a plaster-sealer. He found the bodies and he's a hobby artist who uses the right brand of paint. He's our number one suspect, and you need to treat him as such."

"I didn't talk to him! It was an accident! How did you know!"

"We have Oro under manual surveillance, Hoshi. What part of 'under manual surveillance' did you think meant we didn't have plainclothes watching him every moment of every day, even while he's at work?"

"Well, I didn't talk to him."

"You interacted with him. On purpose. I know you, Hoshi. We have to play everything—everything!—on the up right now; you know what could be at stake."

Yeah. Public opinion on Integration Law.

The likelihood of me keeping my apartment.

The likelihood of me preventing the next victim from becoming the next victim, and that next victim might be me—

Problem was, if I wanted solve the case, I might have to do things—like disobey Sorreno's orders—that would get me in trouble with Mai over at Integration. And even if I did solve the case, whatever the answers were might not do much good for public opinion. The media was ever-hungry for anything that would put us Ops back in the wrong. "Well, I learned something useful about Oro," I frowned sullenly. I wasn't going to apologize.

Sorreno made a frustrated noise and pressed her tired eyes with the backs of her hands, an uncharacteristically child-like gesture. Then she shifted, uncomfortable on the floor. Maybe I should buy her a chair, one of those folding things for camping. Then I could stash it in a closet when she wasn't around.

"Okay," Sorreno said wearily, "what did you learn."

"I learned from his reaction to me that Samo Oro isn't an Op-hater. Or even an Op-noticer. If he's responsible, it wasn't caste-driven. But I don't think he's responsible. I think someone else walked through the IO walls and dropped the bodies. I think Oro was on the up when he told his story. I think whoever is responsible knows Samo very well, and that's why they used the same brand of paint pigments that he uses for his hobby art. I think they were counting on him, specifically, investigating the stink from the refuse bins. I think he's also being set up, along with the Shirring magi. Maybe to take the fall for someone else. Maybe to generate a very specific effect on public perception. Maybe both."

My reward for that revelation was a dubiously arched eyebrow.

I shrugged, "Believe me or not, your manual surveillance will show that the man who helped me clean up my lunch mess barely even glanced at my forehead, and he was more concerned with doing his job than he was about my clumsiness or even his dirtied jump suit. Someone needs to start looking at Oro's circle of friends and acquaintances instead of at Oro."

Sorreno's fingers worked at her locket while she closed her eyes. Thinking or resting. Or just de-stressing. Maybe all three. "Okay. I'll think about it. That's the best I can give you for now. Resources are very limited at the moment, even for a high priority case like this one."

"Right." It was my turn to switch gears, "I'm still processing the code on the victims, sorry it's taking so long. But I should be able to start cracking it late tomorrow or early the next day. Really."

"I know how long it takes for you to process code into idio," she waved a hand at me, "and don't try to change the topic. Second thing you won't like, is about what happened to your face. And from the way you're moving, the rest of you."

"Just neighborhood stuff. Hey, you look like you were up all night, anything I could help with?" Well, two could pay the unpleasant topic game.

"Hoshi. Angel told me what happened." Unfortunately, she evaded my evasion. "Angel's worried about you, and so am I. This conversation is not negotiable. I brought you something." She dug into the inside pocket of her rumpled suit-jacket and pulled out a shocker. Matte black and about half the size of my fist, the little weapon was powerful enough to require a special permit to carry. It had four clear loops to slip one's fingers into, and nestled comfortably in the palm of a hand. The charge it channeled could reach a full two meters, and take down anything up to and including the size of a stampeding bull. It didn't kill, but anyone it shocked would think it had.

I cringed, shaking my head.

"You passed your training, you've had your permit for years, it's all on the up."

I kept shaking my head. It wasn't that. "You know I'm not comfortable with physical violence—"

"That's why I'm ordering you to take it. I've told Mai Chandra at the Integration Office that carrying the shocker is now a condition of all your contracts with RCPD. She'll be asking you about it next week."

"You wouldn't do that—"

"I just did. I don't have officers enough to protect you. You have to protect yourself."

This was as offensive as Lillie and company trying to drive me out of Shirring! Plus, I hate weapons. I don't trust myself with them. I don't trust my eyes, my aim, my coordination between eyes and brain, I don't—

"I'm as progressive as they come Hoshi, but you're as familiar with your med papers as I am. You take terrible and unnecessary risks when you're focused on a case. You also have a problem with admitting any sort of vulnerability. Those are liabilities in our line of work. They're what get people like you and me dead for no good reason. That shocker is your new best friend. Deal with it instead of something worse than cuts and bruises and scars. Stay alive. Or I swear by Hearth and Home I'll kill you myself."

CHAPTER 12

I was furious with Sorreno. We'd disagreed on points before, but never like this. Before we'd only disagreed on work points, theory points, points related to logic and cases. She had never interfered in my personal life before. I thought she was my friend. I thought she understood, at least marginally, how badly I needed to be in control of my life.

I sulked in front of my window, watching the tiny people on the streets twelve stories down, weaving through their hours. If I squinted, the colors of their clothing melted them into long rivers of pattern.

None of them were forced to carry a shocker. Or to report in to the IO. Or to be under constant threat of being displaced from everything they loved and thrown into a supervised livestock pen in a job they hate but will be imprisoned or even killed for not doing with no hope of anything better if—forbid!—they end up accidentally missing a meal two weeks in a row.

I hit my fist hard against the hard glass.

The pain giving me something namable, tangible, blamable to justify my anger.

The bitterness of my life up until two years ago broke over the surface of my consciousness and I scratched at the synthskin covering the unhealed scars.

Three years ago, I had lived in the same building as Martin. Before Integration Law, all Operators in Red City had to live together, surveilled by a house mom in the flesh and by seawalls of security Memside. In return, we were told, we'd need never worry about anything. We'd be "taken care of." With "love."

But just as technology had become both everywhere and unseen, humanity had perfected the glass cages that held their technologists. We become as ubiquitous and invisible as the environmental systems in the walls, something everyone relies on but no one wants to know about. Superficially, I had lived in my own room, tended my own things, could sail the Mem whenever I wanted—and yet, there was not a single action I took that was not filtered, assessed, judged, channeled to serve the purpose of the normals. I wasn't allowed to forego furniture back then. One misstep, one indulgence of my own true nature, and punishments were meted.

Punishments like loss of Mem privilege, like additional Socialization classes, like having an escort to and from work and no escaping between. Like having even more limited access to public places than I already did because of the "No Operators Allowed" signs that were, back then, everywhere. And, if I was bad enough, having my navis removed and being sent to a Farm—so-called because people joked that we became vegetables there, not because of any friendly plowing-the-fields type thing.

I shivered, trying to beat down the pain of perfect recall that came with the bitterness. There hadn't been enough time in three years for Integration Law to mend anything. My people—myself—were no more healed in this short time than the "K" carved into the soft flesh of my cheek three nights ago.

I took a deep breath, vision gliding toward the skyline of Central, looking down the green corridor of Lan Qui Park to the turquoise of Marcie Bay. I reminded myself that healing takes time. Change takes time. Especially for something as complicated and heavy with inertia as a city. The people trying to pass the Inclusion Act were right; if Operators were included in policy decisions, things would get better for us. I was less sure about the timing. The city didn't seem ready. Would we lose what we'd gotten so far if we asked for more too soon?

Shocker or no, Mai Chandra or no, back-alley attacks or no, things were better now. I could still get punished for a misstep and have no power to protest. But I lived in my own apartment without surveillance, in a building with all kinds of people, and no house mom. I was able to have a lifestyle that suited me, even if it didn't look exactly "normal." The Law had removed the city's ability to create segregated spaces and the "No Operators Allowed" signs had come down—and, gloriously, burned. No special seawalls were built into the communications protocols around my building. I could access anything on the Mem I wanted without more or less monitoring and repercussions than anyone else in the city. I could, if I really wanted, tell Sorreno I quit working for the RCPD for good and that she could shove her shocker hard and rough up a moist, dark place. I could.

But I wouldn't.

Because the mystery was starting to yield, and, no matter the consequences, no matter what pain the past had caused me, or how angry I was with Sorreno in the present, I had to know the Who and the Where and the How and the Why of the case. I've never been able to drop a puzzle once I'd picked it up. Even when I should.

And the picture of How and Where was filling in nicely.

Whoever had murdered the women had gotten them addled on a drug cocktail laced with Madame Bosco's stolen whiskey, painted them, sliced their foreheads, and ripped out their navi before they got sober enough to safely release their hardware. Then the bodies were taken to the tube station at Telecon Square (along with a jammer to static out the sensors), walked through the maintenance tunnels, through a hole made for just that purpose in the Integration Office foundation, and through the building's walls to the blind spot in the cafeteria. Dumped them in the dumpster. Backed out through the blind spot using a plaster-sealer to cover the mess. The bodies were then found by Samo Oro, the perfect frame. Fini.

The story, however, still had a lot of gaps.

Like, how had the whiskey been stolen from Madame Bosco at the Velvet Glove?

Where did the NQ come from?

How did the painting happen?

Where had the murders occurred, and how did the victims get there?

Which was to say nothing of the Who and the Why: Who killed the women, Who prepped the way, Who carried the bodies? And Why did they set up a crime at once so elaborate and so clumsy? Fortunately, concrete questions like these made for concrete avenues of investigation, and that meant I was closing in on some concrete conclusions.

So I climbed back into my berth and dove into the Mem to take care of my business with the Sea Witch. Which should fill in a few of the gaps.

I found Luzzie Vai Memside in the Dahlia Den, nursing a drink that simulated who knew what psycho-chemical effect and running his imaginary fingers, entranced, over the strange, dark flower petals of which the Memspace was constructed. His franca presented as a streamlined version of his physical self, smooth lines, deep, dark eyes, and bones delicately beautiful beneath the shifting of his living tattoos, angel and devil combined. He had a slender, prehensile cattish tail. He'd programmed his emotive routines into his chartreuse hair (foregoing the tiny robots that whirled through it in the flesh) so the hair moved expressively here, communicating complex moods and the subtle yet explicit cues of Mem etiquette. The ironic thing about the Sea Witch is that, unlike most of his clients, he's completely at peace with being an Operator. "Ah, Hoshi, I saw you skulking around the Julia Set three days ago."

"Ditto." I leaned my elbows on what passed for a table, grimacing at the warm skin-like feel of it. Just like a sun-warmed flower petal, only huge and thick and overlapping to form a semi-firm furniture shape. Not my choice of recreational Memspaces, but there were more than a scattering of others in the room, all Operators, few of them presenting as anything remotely humanoid-looking. Techno-Baroque music played at just the right volume for sensitive Operator perceptions. Dahlia is a thick place. The kind non-Ops can't find and wouldn't understand the allure of even if they could. It's all about particular, peculiar, synesthetic sensations that can't be created in the physical world. I tapped the fleshy table top and it hummed satin in my ears, "What do you want with Aysha Ayres?" I asked Luzzie.

His lips formed a slimy smile. "What do you want to give me for that answer?"

"Continued mumness on how the authorities can find you."

A long-suffering sigh and a sweet-seeming smile. "Ah, a bit of good old-fashioned blackmail. We using that tactic today?"

I nodded curtly. Luz and I have a long-standing and uneasy agreement stretching back over a decade: I don't unravel your life; you don't unravel mine. Sure Luzzie was a bad guy, but he was at least a bad guy whose mind worked like mine, and that was a lot more useful to me than a bad guy I didn't understand, like Inspector Zi. Luzzie opened doors for me into areas of the underworld I couldn't otherwise penetrate. And I reciprocated, despite the need to bathe repeatedly afterwards. I'd warned him of RCPD raids, kept his name off official reports, and pretended I'd never heard of him when asked point blank by RCPD officers. We shared an unhappy interdependence. Like the RCPD and the LEA. Like Operators and normals. Like the way the districts of the city fit together in their precarious balance of bids for limited urban resources and funding. Opposing agendas and enemy threats that occasionally allied for goals bigger than any single side.

Someday Luz and I would cheerfully destroy each other. But not today. Today was something bigger than us both.

"So? What can you tell me about Aysha Ayres?"

Luzzie let out a soft sigh, his emotives reading pleasure tinged slightly with regret. "She's so lovely. And so hell-bent on breaking into popularity with the dims. She deserves the wider exposure though, what can I say? I do what I can to help her out, you know."

My own emotives read dubious. "Yeah, I'm sure you help her out real good when she trades you credit for NQ."

The hair twitched in surprise. "NQ? No, that isn't Aysha at all. Drug does too much messing with the art. Have you seen her dance?" He stared at me like I'd missed something painfully obvious.

I shrugged.

Luzzie turned back to his drink. "What do you care about Aysha anyway? I haven't seen her around lately, you know. If you see her, tell her I miss her kiss."

So Aysha wasn't an NQ addict either. And Luzzie had no idea Aysha was dead. That cut a whole realm of possible perpetrators in the dark druggie circles and high-tower fraud channels Luzzie tangled with.

And why did I take the likes of Luzzie at face value? It's easy to tell when someone's turned off their emotive routines, and Luzzie's were still broadcasting. Likewise, emotives—because they're triggered by our real, chemically-based feelings—can't be faked, the same way a faked smile doesn't use the same facial muscles as a real one. No, Luzzie's surprise about supplying Aysha with NQ was genuine, and, despite being a bad guy, he's not heartless enough to act like she was alive if he knew differently. He had no clue what was going on. Which was consistent with my theorized lack of syndicate involvement, as well as my analysis of the surveillance on Luzzie at the Julia Set—Luzzie Vai was not involved, at least knowingly, in whatever was going on. But he was my only good connection to NQ, and to Aysha Ayers. I frowned and calculated the final pieces of my days-long cost-benefit analysis on whether Luzzie was currently adversary or ally, and came up marginally on the side of ally.

"When was the last time you saw Aysha?" I asked cautiously.

"She prefers Loie. That's the new ident I set up for her. Loie Ravine. I give that data for free since clever Hoshi has acquired Loie's original identity. Perhaps in exchange for the favor you will tell me how you factored?"

"Perhaps I will not. Loie it is. When was the last time you saw her?"

Luzzie traced patterns on the table and his drink refilled. "Six days ago. Exactly. Almost to the hour. It will be six days ago in exactly forty-nine minutes and thirty-eight seconds."

I took a deep breath and knotted back my imaginary hair. "What can you tell me about the last time you saw her?"

"She came like a rocket!" Luzzie grinned at me, unfriendily.

Seemed a good time to crush his smugness. "Loie's dead Luzzie. Five days now."

Luzzie's hair went limp and his emotives read shock with undercurrents of grief and a growing anger. I watched the hair twitch and flatten again as he ran through the gamut of reaction. "How? Who? Damn!"

"You two just casual fucks, or something more to it?"

"She—we—" Luzzie stood up and stomped around the room a few times, processing, before he settled back down in front of me. "Loie came to me three and a half months ago. Three months, two weeks, three days, and eight hours. She wanted the usual, you know, but she had nothing to pay. She was a fine dancer. Finest." Luzzie read with a level of sadness I didn't think a drug pusher was capable of, and I remembered why a large percentage of my people considered the infamous Sea Witch to be a hero. I was not so seduced. But then, I'd seen the uglier side effects of his work in my days at the RCPD.

"She wanted the usual? You mean your usual package of a new ident and a costly chemical dependence for the rest of her unnaturally short life?"

Luzzie actually tried to look offended, but in this case his emotives didn't support it. "Just the ident. I tell you, she was all about the art. Couldn't do what she did if she was on the pap."

And then Luzzie publicly replayed a memory of Jane-Aysha-Loie, and I—and everyone else in the Dahlia—forgot whatever else we were doing and stared as the dancer bent and swirled in shapes emerging from equal parts mathematics and divine inspiration. My imaginary mouth fell open and it took a full minute for me to recover after Luzzie had banished the playback.

I understood completely why Aysha Ayres had come here to apply for work under Red City's Integration Law.

But I didn't understand at all why she'd been turned down. If only because normals would be punching each other out for the chance to market her, package her, represent her in the performance circuits where she'd make the lucky winners of her contract vast, deep oceans of boundless credit.

Luzzie looked lost in a private memory now, hair drooping sadness, tears appearing on his cheeks as small, hard gems. Even his ever-changing tattoos had slowed, and I could fix on their unexpectedly abstract shapes. I'd always thought Luz's tattoos were of something concrete—figures or equations or something—just shifting faster than I could process. Maybe they are in the flesh. At any rate, I felt like crying too, and I didn't even know the girl. What a waste.

My thoughts twitched toward Claudia. I'd seen Aysha's level of wild talent before, in Claudia. Claudia who I didn't want to think about or I'd also end up sobbing in Memspace in front of the last person I'd want to open up to— "Wow," I said, to abort where my internal thought-train was tracking. "Why was she rejected for Integration? I'd've thought—"

Luzzie's hair jabbed indignantly as his eyes narrowed. "Unfair. Totally unfair. Integration application is a racket, darling, that's why old Luzzie is such a popular community resource."

"What'd Loie say about why she was turned down?"

"She didn't, but you know... You know a body has to know somebody. Take Hoshi Archer for example, Hoshi Archer knows somebody—a lot of somebodies—jo?"

I shrugged off the insinuation, which may be accurate but surely not pertinent, "Tell me about Loie. More."

"And what will you give me for more?"

"A killer's name?" I arched my brow at him.

Hair pricked forward, "How generous of—"

I held up a finger, "Only—and I mean only!—if what you give me helps me find the perp."

Luzzie pretended a pout but I had him hooked. He was akimbo enough over Aysha's death that he didn't notice my lack of specificity concerning exactly when I'd divulge the killer's ident. My plan was the day after the perp was safely in police custody.

"So, like I say, she came to me after those fuckers at Integration pulled their usual. She wanted a new ident so she could try again. I said, new ident sure, no prob, but you got no way to pay, and plus, that dance thing—nobody but you can do that. It's signatory. I mean, you'll be identified no matter where you go as long as you're doing that dance thing. New ident won't let you pass yourself off as a new person to the IO."

"Yeah, yeah. No need to spell out the obvious, Luzzie. I'm quicker than a dim." Sometimes I have to use derogatory terms for non-Ops, to keep up my street cred.

"She says to old Luz, baby you look tense. She was trying to play the hooker, you know," Luzzie laughed, his emotives shifting as he played back things in his memory I couldn't see. "I says, sweetie, you're not the type, don't you ever try to play that, you're better than that, how about we get you a new face and some gigs. I take eighty percent till you pay off your medical and new citizen ID. I mean, it's not like Loie didn't have a way to make the credit on the up."

After staring at me to make sure I was tracking, Luzzie continued rambling. "A little later Loie says, hey, it's not for trade, but I like you baby, I wanna do you. So then we hooked up a little. Casual-like. You know, friends with benes. We were rockets, all the way. She came like she was shooting for Sol. She liked old Luzzie's milk too, lapped it up she did."

Having a powerful visual imagination can be unfortunate at times. Luzzie knew full well I didn't sex hetero. And even if I did—Luzzie Vai, ew! "Useful details only Luzzie. Please."

"Yeah. We had to flow low, you know, because the dance was so unique. After she'd gotten everything paid off, she was gonna go somewhere new, start over, maybe see if the colony on Callisto would take her in, or maybe go to some rough-house like Nerion Station. She was too good for a place like that, but maybe some talent scout finds her, takes her on despite her genes, it's happened before, jo?"

"That was the plan?"

"That was the plan. Figured she'd implemented it when I stopped seeing her around."

"Who'd want her dead?"

Luzzie frowned. "Hey, you want a drink? I can get you a drink, my credit?"

I didn't respond to either the question or the credit dig. Luzzie made magnitudes more than me and enjoyed rubbing it in as much as he enjoyed telling me about his sex life. Unlike the sex details, the credit stuff didn't bother me. "Anyone at all you can think of who might want Loie dead? Jealous dancers? Angry family? She in trouble with the Black, the authorities, anyone? Anything?"

"Nah. We was flowing low, you know? Making no wake. Plus, she was on the up, my Loie. All the way on the up. Didn't want anything to ruin her plans to dance, she hadn't given up the dream."

"Anything else you can think of that could help me? Anything at all?"

"No. But sometimes it takes time to process. I'll let you know, jo, if I think of anything? Loss of Loie is most displeasing." Luzzie had gotten his feelings under control enough to re-don his slimy drug czar persona. "Lovely chat Hoshi, but time, time, time."

"Okay. Just one more thing." This was around when Luz heads off to the Julia to make his shady drug deals. He probably didn't want to slpit consciousness on me any more than I wanted to on him, so the pressure was on us both. "Just one more."

"Oh, Hoshi, I think we've run out of things you can offer me? Silence and Signal, you've given me both, what else is there but Noise? Unless you want to owe me a favor? Old Luz would love a favor from sweet Hoshi."

"I can think of plenty else, but whatever, a favor is fine. Not one that involves your cracking drug business though! Or sex! Kish?"

Luzzie smiled as secretively as the Mona Lisa. "Of course. What's your last question?"

"I need to know if you, or anyone you know, has ever supplied NQ to any of the following individuals." I gave him a list that included Claudia and Nessa, along with a few others of interest like Samo Oro, the crooked cop from Vice I'd recorded Luzzie with at the Julia, everyone who'd been in the morgue when the blood got swapped, and Madame Bosco at the Velvet Glove. Plus another thirty-five Red City residents selected at random from the public directory to round out to an even fifty.

I indicated I wanted an answer right away by not initiating the protocols of parting.

Luzzie didn't look happy about that, but he went through my list anyway, presentation still in concentration. I didn't feel bad about it. Luzzie gives people new identities—his ability to manipulate data is by definition as powerful as humanly possible. I waited seven minutes and seventeen seconds for animation to return to his eyes. "No, none of them," he answered. But his emotive routines flickered with anxiety before he turned them off.

"But?"

"Hey, no but!"

I let my own emotives show how much I wasn't buying it. "I saw a but."

"I haven't supplied NQ to any of the people on your list, ever, that's it, I swear it!"

"That's it?"

"That's it!"

That wasn't it, but it was all I was going to get by asking nicely.

I left the Dahlia Den and added another note to my workspace: Factor Luzzie's unspoken 'but.'

CHAPTER 13

I sat cross-legged on my berth, looking out my window. Sorreno still hadn't dumped the info on the victims into the case file for me, but that wouldn't have helped me with Aysha Ayres anyway. Sorreno's team didn't yet know that Aysha's new ident was Loie Ravine. But after parting with Luzzie, it hadn't taken me long to track down a sketchy picture of Aysha's life in the days prior to her murder.

She'd danced four gigs as Loie, two in Shirring, one in Pier, and one in Landing. She'd wowed the crowds at the new places, sold out the shows where she'd danced before, and forked all her credit into a shadowy untraceable abyss that could only have been Luzzie Vai's credit network.

As far as I could trace with sensorfeed recordings obtained via my PI license, she'd spent the rest of her time in her one room apartment in Shirring, at a gym four blocks down, or walking alone along the banks of Marcie Bay smiling oddly into the water. She'd kept people at a distance, all except Luzzie, whom she met warmly and stayed with for a full night, true to what he had told me.

Then, twelve hours before her death, she'd broken from her well-worn routine. She'd hopped the tube to Telecon Square with a tote bag and entered the Integration Office.

Just as Sorreno had described with Nessa and Claudia, she did not come out.

At least not alive. The next time anyone laid eyes on her was when Samo Oro checked the reek in the IO refuse bins.

If I had to take my best guess at what would have brought her back to the Integration Office, it would be that she thought she'd get a second chance at an Integration dancing job. Despite what Luzzie had said, the woman I tracked seemed too full of fire to have been content waiting on long-term plans if she had any other option.

When I sent my report on Aysha to Sorreno, I added a note to please have the Forensics Ops check for more static at the Telecon Station, earlier in the day. Perhaps the blind spot was serving as entrance as well as egress.

In my apartment, I looked westward toward Husson District, where Nessa had lived and run her pornware side-business. Afternoon light brought out the green in the sky, and sunlight slanted orange, coaxing the shadows to start their crawl toward dusk. I was achy and didn't feel like walking, but the city's breath licked at my memories and made me long to be on the other side of the window.

In my workspace in the Mem, I gazed toward my internal representation Marcie Bay where everything I knew so far about the victims was stored. The Aysha Ayres variables were filling in nicely, and Nessa's boxes were all unlatched, waiting for me to instantiate them with data. Claudia's boxes, however, remained locked and stuffed away, where they wouldn't remind me I had feelings.

Whatever I chose to do next, I'd have to trek out to Husson eventually.

And whatever I chose, eventually I'd have to face the fact that someone I'd once loved—maybe loved still—had died in an unnecessary, violent way.

In my personal mental dictionary beside to the phase "opposites attract," the picture of two magnets had long ago been replaced by a picture of Claudia Foucault and me.

A-meter-eighty tall, of identifiable African ancestry, and straight-laced as only an Op from French Arcadia can be, Claudia was the inverse of my petite, Asia-mutt heritage and "loose, Red City morality." Arcadians are among the few groups who have preserved their original language and culture through all the millennia, and that doesn't come from recklessly mixing with rejects like me.

I'd met Claudia in the last year of mandatory Socialization when we were both sixteen, one year after we'd turned major. Her parents had been sent to Cassiopeia Prime as part of a military contract for planetary fighters with a Cassiopeiean corp. Why the Arcadians need planetary fighters stumps me; Arcadia is the premiere vacation spot for anyone with a gross overabundance of wealth, and otherwise has no resources beyond its cultural pride. They were low-level Operators, Claudia's parents. Obviously, since those of us with greater abilities like Claudia and me are sterilized with great alacrity. And those like my parents who manage to find a way to breed anyway are executed without trial for their transgression.

Claudia's parents were sent back to Arcadia after the contract was done and I lost track of them.

Claudia stayed.

The only act of rebellion I think she'd ever done was to stay in Red City. She said she stayed because of me. But I knew she'd stayed because Markovich and Sons, Architectural Corp, is based here. Claudia's capabilities as a structural engineer gave her the coveted opportunity to choose which of three corporations owned her. And Claudia chose the very best.

She was happy with her life here, every part of it.

And she was firmly against Integration.

The riots were roaring outside the window of her home the day we broke up. "I'm scared," she'd said, hugging herself.

I stood at the window of the common room, looking out at the mass on the street, mostly our own people but others, too; non-Ops had started joining the cause. "Freedom of the Airwaves!" came a shout, that then became a chant, and I felt my heart beat fast and I yearned to join them but forced myself to stay put, torn between Claudia's world of safety and the dangerous, uncharted world of freedom.

"I'm not scared," I said quietly. I turned away from the new world outside, back in toward the artificially-normed interior of Operator housing. It looked exactly the same as the common room at my place, for Trinity's sake. How was that desirable?

"I'm not scared at all," I told Claudia again, more fiercely. "I want to join them."

"You'd be removed from the RCPD and sent to a Rehab Farm," Claudia sniffed primly. "Be happy with what you have."

"That's easy for you to say," I glared at the floor. "You love your work. It gives you everything you could ever want."

There was a silence, just long enough to be significant. "Not everything," Claudia muttered softly.

My eyes flicked up, too briefly to see her. I wouldn't go outside, I wouldn't join the rioters. I was cowardly that way, and for the reason so-very-rational Claudia had given. I may not like breaking code for work, but I did like working for the RCPD. And, more importantly, I would do anything to stay in Red City.

"This isn't going to work," I'd said, and left.

It was almost a week later when I realized what Claudia had meant by her softly spoken, "Not everything." That was when I replayed the scene in my memory and saw Claudia's tears, saw how her eyes were focused on me. But I didn't go back, try to fix it. I figured by then I was no longer on the list of things she wanted.

Would she still be alive now had I been less distracted?

I flicked the memories away, turned from Claudia's unopened boxes in my memory.

I had plenty of other problems to deal with. In my internal landscape, the pile of unfinished business with whatever Martin Ho was up to flickered along with all the case unknowns. Everything reeked like bad trash. I put my hands on my imaginary hips and glared at it.

In the physical world, a brinn gull, its blue-green feathers blending with the sky and contrasting with the skyline, flew toward Husson, disappearing behind Nu Towers.

Okay, I know as well as anybody that augury by bird flight went out of style in the Middle Ages, but Lillie insists there are modern truths behind some superstitions. Maybe the city herself was answering my question through the brinn gull's flight. And if not—well, it didn't matter since I had to do all the errands in Husson anyway.

I needed to go to Spectra-Media about the paints.

I needed to stop by the Velvet Glove and see about Nessa, the stolen bottle of whiskey, drugs in general, and Luzzie's "but" in particular.

I needed to visit Bill's Ragtime about... well, whatever that was about. Something related to the case Martin was building against me. Maybe.

I took off yesterday's clothes, showered, and dressed in my more usual black slacks and soft white blouse. I wasn't dressing for anything today but comfort.

Then I picked up the shocker Sorreno had forced on me and bared my teeth at it. Drug Capos, neurotic bartenders with deadly implants, relentless weeks of biting media and angry picketers and gangs of Op-haters—I could deal with them, no problem. But losing my cathedral window, my view of the city? It wasn't because I was afraid of Capos or madmen or Op-bashers or worse that I was taking the shocker with me. I was taking the shocker with me because I was afraid of Sorreno and Mai Chandra finding out I didn't take it.

I really wasn't so free.

I sighed and slipped the rings of the shocker over my fingers, the weapon fitting near-invisibly into the palm of my hand as I curled my fingers around it. I opened a channel on its short-wave frequency and imprinted it with the complex sensations that make up my unique identifier, locking the weapon to respond only to my commands. A new string of programming leapt from the device and I caught it unhappily: the controls for the weapon.

Resentment blurred the skyline as I took a last look out my window.

My window.

Mine.

I was still freer than I had ever dreamed of being.

◆　◆　◆

Tubing crosstown to Husson, Angel commed me. She was linked into the camera in her office, so I saw her standing in my workspace. "Hey Hoshi, got a moment?"

My presentation showed up on her vid feed, anger reading through my stance and tone. "Depends. You slopped to Sorreno about my encounter with the Op-bashers."

Angel made a stubborn face. "Damn right I did. I want Sorreno to go after your attackers even if you don't."

"She told my Integration Officer! Now I have to carry a shocker!"

Angel winced. "I wish she hadn't done that. The Integration Officer part, not the shocker part." She glared at me, defiant now. "I'm glad Sorreno gave you a shocker!"

I wanted to argue, but the ride to Husson isn't long, even on the local. "We'll discuss this later. I suspect you commed about something else."

Angel's yellow curls bounced as she nodded. "I wanted to mention something to you about motive and the thing that happened in the lab. The evidence switch."

I didn't like her tone but waited anyway, tapping my imaginary foot.

"I know you have a big blind spot about how the media likes to play you, and I know you don't like to hear anyone talk about your public reputation." She took a deep breath. "But everyone who was in the morgue that day knew—or could have known easily—that you are consulting on the case."

"Yeah, of course. So?"

"So, Hoshi." Angel sighed wearily and ran her fingers through her curls. "So you have quite a reputation for never missing a clue, both around the RCPD and to any civilians who follow the police or Integration feeds."

"So I've been told." Obviously whoever felt I was something special had never spent any time with me.

"What I mean is—please, this is important—anyone who swapped that evidence would have known you'd notice. I don't know exactly what that means for motive, but it means something."

"That they wanted their actions discovered?"

"Or that they wanted to get Sorreno or me in trouble, because I had to report it so now Internal is all over both of us."

"Maybe they thought I'd be taken off the case by now." Angel was sucking me into the puzzle even though I was still so mad at her.

"Or," Angel's voice broke with such concern I almost forgave her the rest of the way for ratting on me, "not meant for you to have walked away from that beating. How do you think the media would have spun it if you'd ended up dead in that back alley?"

"I don't know. Maybe it would encouraged someone to do something about the hate gangs."

"Maybe. Or maybe they'd use it to prove Operators shouldn't be allowed on the streets at all without a minder."

Hard to predict which way the media would swing, but given the connection of the case to the IO and the heat over the Inclusion Act, it probably wouldn't swing in a direction that was good for my people.

"What I mean is," Angel reached out a hand as though she could touch the side of my face, even though she couldn't see me, "you might want to add some variables to that beautiful crazy landscape in your head for the possibility that we either have an ally among the bad guys, or someone'd planned to get you, me, and Sorreno out of the picture early on. Or, well, some other reason that takes your talents and rep and the possible media angles into account."

I wasn't sure what to say to that, but was saved from comment by the tube sliding into Yuan Station. "I'm on my way to Husson on the local and I have to get off in two more stops so I gotta go. I'll com you later."

Angel folded her arms and gave me a long stare I couldn't interpret. "Okay. But be care—"

I cut the channel so I wouldn't have to figure how to end the transmit.

◆　◆　◆

Husson District is flatter than Hill where I live, lying to the west of Hill's ancient domes of long-extinct volcanoes. Both Husson and Hill are residential though, unremarkable, areas that serve the day-to-day lives of Red City's eighteen million permanent residents. Husson has an edgier vibe than Hill, and I walked past shimmering artworks adorning the sides of hip clubs, and around sudden gardens in the middle of walkways. A group of retro-punks slouched around an entryway, their white-painted faces glowing in the light of the holo above the door naming the place "Café No / Yes Books." By the fact that it bore no sigil, the place was likely not corporate-sanctioned. Everyone here seemed at least a decade younger than the people in my neighborhood, where everyone but me seems to be middle aged.

But Husson doesn't have the skyline views. Every u of credit I make, I use to pay for my view. I can't think of anything else I need.

Spectra-Media, like Madame Shane's, is a big interplanetary supply franchise—only Spectra-Media specializes in artistic goods instead of spiritual ones. Its corporate sigil is a hand and palette, and its storefronts sport rainbow stripes. Fifty-two Spectra-Media outlets of varying sizes exist in Red City. I chose the one on Green Street in Husson because that's where Samo Oro buys his paints.

"Hoshi Archer, PI, acting consult to the RCPD." I swiped my thumb over the credit plate at the counter so the young, scrawny girl could verify my credentials. I saw no point in an oblique approach here, and a lot of reasons to get it over with quickly and cleanly. "I could use your help."

The girl's eyes widened. Good. A lot of citizens in Red City like having a chance to help with crime-solving; it's a bit exciting for them I suspect. I know that's one of the reasons why I like it.

"Do you have anywhere we can talk private?" I asked.

"I, uh—I can't leave the counter unmanned. Let me get Deng over." The girl went still and quiet, and since she wasn't an Operator, I figured she was comming Deng. While I waited I noted she had nice skin, complicated hazel eyes, pretty bones, and short brown hair in an elfish cut. Also, that the patch on her white smock above the Spectra-Media sigil read "Ursula." While none of those details were relevant to the case, they definitely made the wait more pleasant.

A minute later an equally young, scrawny boy appeared from between the near aisles. The two looked at each other, then at me. "Either of you will do," I said, "just need some information about painting."

Deng scowled, "Aw, Ursula's the painter."

Ursula smiled brightly. "Yay!"

We sat in a break room with bad lights and rickety chairs. A holofeed set to a local station flickered against the back wall. Large as life, the Director of Operator Affairs made a statement about the need for calm and balance, while scenes from recent blows between protesters in Central played violently in the background. "Can we have that off?" I nodded to the mainfeed, "Kinda distracting for me."

"Sure." Ursula didn't seem to care I was an Operator. She seemed more caught in the wide-eyed romance of helping an RCPD rep on official business. "What do you need to know?"

I pulled the portable 3Vplate out of the pocket of my bolero and unfolded it on the long table, brushing aside some crumbs. But I didn't activate it yet. "What can you tell me about Seraphim Pigments?"

Ursula grinned, "They're real loose! Top quality!"

"Why would someone choose them over other paint?"

"Well, paint consists of two basic parts: a pigment and a medium. The pigment is the color, ground up real fine. The medium is another substance, like an oil or a paste. You mix the pigment with the medium to turn it into something spreadable with a brush or knife. Sometimes you need a third thing, called a binder, to make the pigment molecules stick to the medium molecules." Ursula made animated shapes with her hands while she described this, drawing pictures for me in the air.

"There's a fair amount of chemistry involved," Ursula shrugged. "Most painters don't like dealing with it, so they use pre-mixed paints. Seraphim is real loose, but they don't offer pre-mixes. Just top-quality pigments."

"So then why choose Seraphim? Why mix your own?"

Ursula kept drawing in the air as she spoke. I can see how the quirk might annoy some people, busy fingers distracting from her face, but I really liked it. Made her easy for me to understand with less effort from my programming. "Oh, some painters want to be in control of their pigment-to-medium ratios. Others like the process of the mixing, the chemistry of it, the feel of it in their hands. Or like to experiment. Or other stuff. It varies I suppose. Just personal preference."

"Can someone mix substances into pre-mixed paint, like say carbon powder or ground up shells?" I was thinking of what had been mixed in with the paints used on the victims.

"Depends on what you're trying to do. Like I say, paint-making is chemistry. Anything used as a pigment has to be ground up small enough and be of the correct properties to bind with the medium. I do a lot of mixing of stuff into paint myself, but I don't expect it to bind—it's just to add texture. Put sand in, say, and it gives this wonderful body and gritty effect! But that's the same whether you mix your own paints or pull a tube off the shelf in aisle six. You've got to get the pigments to bind with the medium if you want anything other than just surface texture."

"Do you work here a lot? Know your regular customers?"

"Oh, yeah! I love this place!"

"Any of them buy Seraphim pigments?" Of course I'd already run enough purchase histories to know the answer to that question, but sometimes people let slop info that can't be seen in the cold facts of data records.

"Oh yeah, I've got Serpahim regulars. But not many. That's expensive stuff, and like I say, not many mix their own. There's Keesha, and Andy, and, oh, and Samo—he's been coming here since before I started—and Trish. Um. And someone else... oh that little girl prodigy, Megan? Yeah, Megan Lee. She's like six and her paintings are already selling at the Martha Dowery."

I turned on the 3Vplate with a thought and transmitted a few highly sanitized samples of the ghastly pseudo-code. "Any of them paint like this?"

Ursula found my invisible control of the 3Vplate more impressive than the paintings. "Nah. I haven't seen Keesha's art, but the rest of them... nah. Whoever did this isn't much of a painter," she scoffed, haughty and more mature in her area of expertise.

I frowned at the colorful, twining images, the complex hashes and swirls and sprays. It looked pretty impressive to me. But then, I'd never been able to use a paint brush at all.

"I mean," Ursula tried to explain, jabbing her finger into the image so that it colored her skin, "it's all color-by-numbers. There's no articulation, no expression to the brushwork. It's the kind of painting that would come out of a machine that lacked AI, or someone who is good at staying in the lines but never developed their own style of mark-making. Like someone who paints walls, not canvas. I'd say machine though, it's too precise for a person, in my opinion."

"But if it's so..." I didn't have the vocabulary stored anywhere, so my linguistics couldn't translate my thoughts. My knowledge of painting consisted almost entirely of what Ursula had just told me.

She seemed to know what I wanted to say though. "Don't let the complexity and the beauty of the designs fool you. My guess is one person came up with the images but then someone or something else rendered them.

The designs are brilliant. The way they've been painted is not."

A machine, huh? If an Operator were suspended, visualizing code into 3Vplates, the program would display on her body, just like it had on Ursula's finger. Easy then, for a machine to trace.

"Wow, you really know paint." I was awed, and appreciative.

Ursula laughed, "I'm a at the tail end of my Master's program at Brandt Fine Arts College. I'm older than I look. Spend enough hours in crit with Madame Senji and you can't look at a painting without dissecting how it's made. I can't remember the last time I looked at a painting and just enjoyed it in my gut." She pounded her belly and rolled her eyes, but more in amusement than rue. "The enjoyment'll come back after I graduate. I hope!"

I bought her explanations. And her. I liked her. She was pretty. I grinned. "You've been really helpful. Really. Thanks so much!" I tried to find more questions, but she'd covered what I wanted to know and then twice that again, so I wondered if it would be appropriate to ask her for a date.

"I'm a fan you know," Ursula said quietly into my silence.

"Of Seraphim pigments?"

She laughed. "No silly, of you! I mean, you're.... You're Hoshi Archer! You solved the Parsons Robbery! And busted the Landing trafficking ring!"

All thoughts of dating were instantly devoured by embarrassment. "Inspector Cassandra Sorreno solved those cases," I looked at the floor and corrected her stiffly. "I was just the consult."

"And also the case with the—"

I stood too fast and my chair toppled and clattered to the hard tile floor. My buggy auditory filters failed to compensate in time; my hands moved to clap over my ears as I flinched from the sound, whimpering. Enroute to ears, the cuff of my bolero caught the edge of the table. Where ordinary fabric would have torn the indestructible nanofibers instead pulled over the entire table, crumbs and all, making a horrific clamor. Smooth moves, Hoshi! Well, Ursula certainly wouldn't want a date with me now!

"Sorry. Things to do," I squeaked. "You've been really helpful. Really. Thanks so much!"

"Hey, sorry. Didn't mean to, ah..." she was flustered now herself, fingers twining together, desperately ignoring the toppled furniture. "Hey, here, take my com addy in case you have more questions?" She handed me a thumbnail-sized wafer of digipage that I read into my memory hastily and handed back so she could re-use it. Then I felt awkward again because a normal would keep it.

"Sure. You've been helpful. Really. Thanks so much. Helpful. Really. Oh. Um. Oh, hell." I backed out of the break room, nodded to the kid behind the counter, and didn't breathe again till I hit outside air.

Angel was right; I do have a blind spot when it comes to my notoriety. They don't teach a person how to deal with fame in Socialization. I didn't understand it, and didn't like it either.

But I did know quite a few new things about the case. Like more evidence that Samo Oro didn't paint the victims (take that, Sorreno!), and that wherever the murders happened would have a lot of 3V plates and mechanical painting equipment.

And I had Ursula's com addy in case I ever got up the courage to ask her about that date.

CHAPTER 14

The Velvet Glove made no attempt to hide its function as a pleasure palace. The three stories visible above ground were sided with blackstone abraded to the texture of finest suede, its few windows lathered in a froth of red silk so thick light did not pass. The sultry crimson holo displayed the universal symbols for food, drink, drugs, sex, gambling, baths, virtual rooms, and robotics. Everything just on the edge of legal—and possibly over it. The doors themselves, slabs of solid bloodwood, were carved with the business' sigil: a slender lady's glove laid gently over an old-fashioned pistol from which curled a plume of smoke.

I'd been to the Glove a few times on case-related business. Not a lot, but enough to know who was who and what was what.

Old as humanity and adaptable as a jetty bug, organized crime has held the same traditions of family loyalty and internal justice for centuries, yet always with a uniquely modern flair. When old markets of crime run dry, the syndicate finds—or makes—new flows, like a river ever changing and ever staying the same. Depending on where you go in the inhabited universe, it might be considered a legitimate corporation with rights and legal powers, or it might be hunted and taboo. But it is always there, beneath humanity's surface, forming the backbone of the complex and varied underworld.

The syndicate in Red City—not quite legal but left alone to do its business within certain bounds—is run by Regina down in Shirring Point. Regina is a title not a name, and I'm not privy to whether Regina is male or female or something else at the moment. But some cartels are less bound to Regina than others, and the Husson syndicate is as autonomous as it gets.

Called the Carmine Market because of its headquarters here on Carmine Street and its tendency to corner city trade on illicit pleasures, the Husson syndicate, backed by a powerful city elite, won a small coup against Regina a few years ago. A handful of the most powerful corporate owners in Red City, wanting to distance themselves from the criminal without giving up those luxuries credit just can't buy on the up, had poured a lot of resources into legitimizing the Carmine Market and encouraging—with bloody, violent, and untraceable force—a break from Shirring. Regina retaliated by withdrawing protection from Husson, which made an enormous mess of the city's underbelly. But aside from the flurry of gangland killings at the center of the coup that decimated the smaller Husson faction, the city elite backing the Carmine got what they wanted. And the city's underworld settled back into its more stable patterns, with Carmine tithing to Regina in return for protection even the city elite couldn't buy.

The strained relations between Regina and the Husson syndicate made me tread more carefully than I might have otherwise; I knew Regina's rules a lot better than I knew the rules of the Carmine Market. And everyone at the Glove knew I had a lot of friends down in Shirring Point.

The slender man in the expensive suit just inside the door knew who I was of course. He looked like a decoration, fine boned and beautiful, but I knew better. He could have me out cold before I could say fuck, either by his own devices or by summoning aid.

"Ms. Archer. Good day to you. How may we be of service?" His tone was polite, and unfriendly.

"I'd like to talk with Madame Bosco about some whiskey," the well-rehearsed words came out of me. I kept my expression still with programming, not wanting anything accidentally read into it.

"Is Madame Bosco expecting you?" the youth pushed silky auburn hair from his eyes and looked down his nose at me.

"Alas, no. But I have information that may please her."

"Very well," the youth's weary tone let me know I was proceeding at my own risk.

I looked at my boots hoping the gesture read nonthreatening.

"Please, have a seat. Can I get you anything while you wait?"

"No. Thank you."

It took a lot less time than doorboy had been expecting for Bosco to want to see me. Not, however, less time than I had been expecting. I doubted the loss of the whiskey was what had Madame Bosco upset enough to enlist the aid of the RCPD, even if they were RCPD officers already on her payroll. My bet was on outrage over the fact that someone had managed to steal it from her at all, and in a way that had her own enforcers stumped. Not knowing where the chink—or leak—in her armor lay must be making her cracked.

The doorboy became deferential. "Madame Bosco will see you now. Someone is coming right away to escort you." But he did not become friendly.

I issued a mechanical smile, folded my hands in my lap, and waited for Bosco's henchman to arrive.

The descent started through an archway adorned with black velvet curtains and a simple holosign reading "Gaming House." The sub-level opened into a large space encrusted with enough card tables, slot programs, and live fighting to put Europa's Casino Row to shame. I slammed down as many sensory filters as I could, before the rush and jingle and frenzy could paralyze me. The filters helped with the sensory chaos, but not with the angry, suspicious looks directed my way. Integration Law doesn't apply to casinos. Normals are too afraid Ops will use our navi to unfair advantage, factoring odds and running dynamical-predictor models like the mirai equations to beat the system. I was never sure why that worry existed given that owned Ops monitored all gambling activities to make sure no one cheated, but society's fears often don't make logical sense. I was grateful to have escort through the open hostility, and wondered how Nessa had navigated this area. There must be an alternative way down, but my resources were too full of sensory programming to search for it.

Past the "gaming house" lay another archway and another set of stairs, though this arch was smaller, curtained with veils of glittering gems, and bore no sign to explain where it might lead. As the crush of the casino faded, I brought my awareness back into focus. Noticing sophisticated sensing devices half-hidden by soft, dark fabrics and fancy lighting fixtures, I gained new appreciation for Bosco's concern about the theft. More closed-circuit sensors lurked in these halls than the perimeter of the Barney Hill Jailhouse. But I had a pretty good idea of what had happened with the theft, and hoped I could make it through the inane pleasantries of the normals before slopping what I factored in my excitement.

The second level below the casino seemed to have something to do with booze and drugs. Or maybe drugs and robots? It was hard to tell. One open door exposed a dark cavern of whiskey-tasters with the snooty demeanors of wealthy connoisseurs. Through another door, someone smoked a pipe with half-lidded eyes next to a man hooked up to an enormous machine, a netting of electrodes covering his head of stringy gray hair. A young girl in a white lab coat with the gun-and-glove sigil of an employee hastily shut the door on my curiosity.

My guide did not engage with me or anyone else, just silently led me with the confident aura of a high-level enforcer. I remained grateful for his presence as we wove through the third sub-basement, listening to screams and clanking gears leaking from unmarked doors; and everyone we saw regarded me with expressions ranging from vague suspicion to violent paranoia.

The fourth level, though, getting closer to the heart of Bosco's web—or at least the heart of the operations here at the Velvet Glove—had a very different flavor. The decor, which had grown gradually more utilitarian, unfolded just as gradually into a level of luxury most people rarely see. The walls were paneled in Cassiopeian ebony, and the everbulbs hidden behind crystalline fixtures that twinkled so brightly I wondered if they were made of Ionian diamonds. The silent enforcer led me quickly past paintings that must have come from Earth's deep past, and I tried not to notice that a few of them were on the RCPD's stolen list. Eventually, we reached the heart.

Unlike most syndicates, the Carmine Market was run by a council, rather than a single Queen or King. Bosco was one of the council members, and her quarters showed it. The room reeked of wealth beneath a deceptively minimalist style. Intricate inlays of precious metals and semi-precious stones surfaced the otherwise-basic oval table and chairs. Against one wall, a simple, unassuming vase of flowers rested—a quick cross-reference in the Mem revealing it as an original Ming containing orchids shipped from Arcadia at great expense to last but a day. A rack of samurai swords, the only decoration on the north wall, I recognized from mainfeed coverage of the theft as once belonging to the head of 100 Worlds Music Corporation. Like the Carmine Market itself, Bosco's receiving room was luxury condensed in as small and tight a package as possible, glitter obfuscating stories best left untold.

Bosco, however, overshadowed it all.

Madame Bosco's honorific had been rightfully earned on the up, rather than being some Black-market nick-name. She'd been a Diva at the Red City Opera for over forty years before retiring into a life of crime for enigmatic reasons of her own. She wasn't pretty—never had been pretty—but carried herself with the kind of dramatic authority that made something so trivial as beauty moot. She commanded her crew like she had commanded the stage; she commanded every iota of my attention. My guess was she was closing in on around eighty years local time—nearly a century Earth-standard. The only way age had affected her was by increasing her shrewdness.

"Hoshi Archer. Nice to see you. Would you like anything, anything at all? I have Costa Rica Lourdes de Naranjo, the real stuff, from Earth."

Madame Bosco knew how to butter a girl up. Earth had maybe two inches of good soil left for growing coffee beans and those beans remained some of the best in the inhabited universe. I didn't want to say yes because I didn't want to owe Bosco a thing. On the other hand, not even an Op can resist—or risk resisting—the force of nature that is Madame Bosco's gifting. "Yes, that would be very nice," I whispered.

The espresso appeared too quickly. One demitasse, a single shot, a tiny cup of china so thin I worried I'd break it to bits in my clumsy fingers. From aroma to the aftertaste, it was pure bliss. I opened my eyes to Madame Bosco watching me with perfect satisfaction.

"Is that your vault?" I set the cup down gingerly and pointed behind her at the wall, blank save for its papering of gold and crimson lace. Though of course I already knew it was.

Bosco raised her dramatic black eyebrows high, but her red-painted lips, quirking into an even more satisfied smile, showed no surprise at all. "I believe I shall go to you instead of to Red City's Finest in the future."

I knew where the vault was because I'd been watching through the sensors as earlier today Bosco unloaded enough powdered rush-opiate into it to kill a small colony. Clever holography masked the door to the room-sized safe; it required, in addition to a code, a drop of blood to open.

"Go on, tell me more," Bosco encouraged but did not sit. She folded her slender arms over her jet-beaded business suit and watched me with bright, black, unblinking eyes.

"You gave Nessa Mason access to the vault," I stated, looking away, her eyes as painful to me as the sun.

Bosco nodded in my peripheral vision.

So I laid it out. "Firstday, three weeks ago, Nessa dropped off a set of pornware chips, which is why you gave her the vault access, right? She insisted on being the only person to touch her goods before sale, one of her Operator quirks. Not sure when you noticed the whiskey missing, but that's when she took it. If you have your people check your sensor archives carefully for tampered footage, you'll catch a spot with Nessa's citizen ID embedded in it. She could alter the feed, but not without leaving a footprint."

Bosco waited, but I didn't have anything else to say. The theft itself was as simple as a crime can get. The reason for the theft, well, that was the real mystery. Nessa had collected at least one of the items used in her own murder, and at great risk to herself. Murder it may have been, but there still seemed a willingness on the part of the victims to abet their own deaths. Maybe Nessa had been pressed into stealing that whiskey against her will, but I didn't think so. I'd had contact with her in the Mem up until two days before she was murdered, and Nessa hadn't been acting like someone who was scared.

The silence continued. I shifted, uneasy. What had I forgotten?

The hard old woman stared at me, her head up and nostrils flared, chest out as though she were preparing to belt an aria.

I cringed and didn't know what to do.

But when the Black Widow of Carmine Street finally spoke, her tone was gentle, and whatever had made the air go dangerous must not have had anything to do with me. "And where is Nessa Mason now?"

"Nessa Mason," I did my best to meet Bosco's scary eyes, "is dead. I'm consulting on the investigation of her murder. Copious amounts of that particular vintage were found in her body. Whoever murdered her has your whiskey."

She barely skipped a beat before responding, but she did skip one. "That's very interesting."

"You have thoughts as to motive?"

Widening eyes and nostrils flaring told me that was the wrong thing for me to have said, but then she softened again, and nodded, as though in answer to some internal dialogue. "Nessa Mason had a very ambitious heart. If she hadn't been one of your kind I might have considered her for... promotion. Her ambitious heart, in some ways, beat akin to my own. Unfortunately, promotion would not have been appropriate."

"You mean she'd wanted to—she asked if, for example, maybe you would be her mentor?" I wanted to just blurt out, did Nessa want to join your mob? But Bosco wasn't an Operator, so I had to play normie games.

"Something like that, yes."

"And you turned her down?"

"I reminded her she already had two excellent careers in advertising and pleasureware, and she was young enough to not need a third. I told her to check back in a decade, maybe two. That things would be different then."

"You think she might have stolen the whiskey for someone who offered her that third career?" I bit off the rest of the words, *despite her caste*. Nessa was certainly ambitious. But Operators in syndicate leadership positions in Red City were very, very rare. Bosco would have lost a lot of face if she'd taken Nessa on.

"Something like that, yes." And that was all Bosco was going to give a gal with perfect recall. It was enough; she'd told me what I needed to know. The promise of expanding her enterprises would have been enough to get Nessa to agree to almost anything, including a ritual to summon an élan vital. With enough resonance, an élan could plant thoughts right in a person's mind—at least that's what Lillie has told me about her relationship with Ogun. Not to mention the panicky stories about the aliens the mainfeeds ran in order to sell views. Nessa was the sort who always wanted more—whatever the cost.

My ascent with my enforcer-guide back to street level of the Velvet Glove went much faster than my descent; apparently Bosco had decided she could now trust me with knowledge of the elevator—or realized I would find out about it on my own anyway.

I wasn't ready to leave the Glove yet, though; I'd had a revelation that needed a bit of a follow-up to confirm. There's nothing like doing a huge favor for a crime boss to open doors few ever enter. Madame Bosco wasn't the first crime boss I'd done a huge favor for, but her gratitude had me arriving, along with my enforcer, at a cold back room where the smallest of the street dealers lurked.

"Well, well, it's Hoshi Archer, the Lame-Brain of Baker Street," a voice sneered from the shadows as the slimy-suited men and women laughed. "Look what the world's coming to, they let those sorts off their leashes. Would've been better to just kill 'em all. Be a kindness, don't you think. To have to live like that...."

Guffaw, guffaw, guffaw. Oh, please. Why can't the bigots at least come up with clever insults?

The enforcer who escorted me down must've given the pack of goons a look, because they shut up with the bigotry and shuffled their feet in lost face. The enforcer settled just inside the door, watching with lazy-lidded eyes. An extension of Bosco's power, reminding them they were at the bottom of her hierarchy. For which I was extremely grateful.

I pictured what I wanted my body to do and fed it to my motor programming, waiting the clunky, uncomfortable milliseconds to turn an empty chair around and sit on it backwards in a motion that might have looked natural. I took a deep breath, positioning myself to push.

"Hello boys and girls," I grinned, harnessing the delight of making them maximally uncomfortable to make the grin more genuine. "We're going to have a chat about your recent dealings with Luzzie Vai, a.k.a. the Sea Witch, kish?" It's the question I came to get answered, but also a reminder to them of my unique position in the underground. *Yes, I am THAT Hoshi, the one who warns Shirring Point of certain kinds of raids and protects the likes of Luzzie Vai—and perhaps you.*

Whatever intel Luzzie had withheld at the end of our conversation had been bugging me. Threads in my thinking kept breaking off to puzzle at it, mostly from the angle of why Luzzie would lie about who on my list he'd dealt to. Reasons that were—to his thinking at least—unrelated to the murder of Aysha Ayers. Because I really believed Luzzie would go out on quite a lot of limbs to help me catch Aysha's killer.

I'd stuck Nessa on the list, of course.

But also a few folks associated with the Velvet Glove: two men powerful in city politics, an enforcer I knew, and Bosco herself.

Luzzie had a niche market, for sure, and he had a cracky kind of pride about it. You couldn't even mention someone else doing the same sort of business or he'd throw a tantrum worthy of a toddler. So what might Luzzie not want to confess to me?

"Who'd Luzzie Vai have you play middle man for in the past month?" I asked the goons. "That is, if you dims can remember something besides your own names, jo?" I hoped my voice sounded as condescending as I wanted it to sound.

The spun-up woman with the blue fingernails of a tracer addict jerked forward, but the guy next to her, dirty but straight-looking, held her back. He glanced at Bosco's enforcer who feigned boredom threateningly. "Vai. Yeah."

I stuck my elbows on the pricey carved table. It looked like it had been lifted from a museum, jarring in the crudeness of the context. "Yeah?"

"Yeah." Dirty-but-straight guy swallowed. "Sometimes Vai's clients don't want to deal direct with Vai. Don't like getting near retar—Operators. So then Vai gives his pap to me with a cut for my effort and I sell to the buyer for him. Everyone's happy. Jo?"

I took a deep breath along with a prayer to Signal, Encoding, and Noise for patience, and connected a few more dots for the man. "I'm interested in anyone you sold to for Vai in the past month. That means recently. I can give you a list to look at if—"

"Cleopatra Square," the words exploded from the tracer addict.

At first I thought she was just too sapped-out to be talking sense, since people buy drugs, not places. But another guy, more a kid who clearly wasn't over major, elaborated. "We did the exchange at Cleopatra Square. Whoever it was really didn't wanna be known. They didn't just not want Vai to know 'em, they wanted nobody to know 'em. Not us either. It was on a Fifthday. Fifthday of last month, I think the third Fifthday, just before the evening rain. We showed up, picked up the credit slip that'd been left for us, and dropped the goods. That's all. In a—"

Dirty-but-straight guy slapped the kid across the face to shut him up.

Sweet.

"That's okay," I felt a flush of sympathy for the kid. Given other life circumstances, maybe he would have ended up at the police academy instead of the broom closet of a mobster's castle. Given other circumstances, could I have ended up like Luzzie Vai? "I don't need to know the details of the drop. Just the person you'd dropped to. But where and when's good too, and you just gave me that."

The woman in the very back who hadn't said a word yet shot a glance at Bosco's enforcer. "We can, um, maybe help out a little more."

"Oh?"

Dirty-but-straight gave the woman the side-eye but seemed too scared of her to slap her. Then the woman leaned forward and the others dropped back and I realized she was really in charge of the operation. "That drop was peculiar," she said as her face, skin starting to go dull with age, came into the light. She looked at me hard enough I couldn't stand it and my eyes were forced to drop. "Peculiar because someone appeared out of nowhere, took the goods, then disappeared again. Like there was some sci-fi teleport thing or something." She kept staring at me dully, then abruptly snapped her fingers and hissed, "Disappeared just like that!"

I jumped at the sound and really wished I hadn't. Programming kept my voice steady, "Anything else you can tell me? Height, weight, anything?"

The woman leaned back into the shadows. "Nah. Person was wearing a loose dress or coat or cloak or something, couldn't see nothin'. Just—appeared and disappeared just like that!" She snapped her fingers again from the darkness.

Well, it wasn't as good the citizen ID of the buyer, but it was something to go on. Once sci-fi teleporter devices were eliminated, there probably was something interesting about that particular area of Cleopatra Square. "Hey, where exactly did you see the buyer appear and disappear?"

There was a long, baleful silence from the lot of them. Then the quiet woman gave up, "Check around the Pissing Boy Fountain."

"Okay. Great. You've been real helpful. Really." I stood up. Turned away with some effort to overcome memories of being pelted in the back with hard objects. They wouldn't dare. Just before I walked out with the enforcer behind me, I turned and winked at them, "You've been real helpful—for a bunch of dims, anyway!"

CHAPTER 15

Sure there was a lot of bad happening. But the joy of fitting the pieces of a tricky puzzle into place could not be damped by anything so small as Martin's scheming or the itch of healing wounds.

The whisky was Bosco's, stolen by Nessa, for use in whatever events led to the murders.

The NQ was Luzzie's after all, just dealt by a middle-man, and now it was just a matter of tracking who'd been lurking around Cleopatra Square in the early evening on the third Fifthday of last month. I'd have Sorreno sic the forensics Ops on that; Trinity knew there was enough on my to do list already.

The paintings were rendered by a machine but imagined by a human, and I'd pre-processed enough of the ghastly pseudo-code by now to know it was true code.

The case was yielding, the clues unwinding. Whatever Gno's muttering about circuits or Blu Lou's warning about human sacrifices, élan vitals, and corruption at the heart of the city, what I had here were concrete facts. Real faces of real people and the perfume of the city and the promise of a solution that didn't require alien entities or modern gods, but just lousy human beings doing really shitty things to each other.

In fact, I felt so good that when I got home I was going to face Claudia. Finding the connection between the three murdered women needed to be my next step.

Eight blocks past the Velvet Glove, I turned off Carmine Street onto Flemming: to the blaring orange facade of Bill's Ragtime, the clue the city had given me about... well, whatever it was about. Martin's scheme?

I'd know soon enough. I was on a roll and the city had never steered me wrong. In fifteen years of sensorfeed overflow in my sleep, the only thing as certain as the nosebleeds was the importance of the intuitions. Even the bright orange facade and the swirly circus-y lettering of Bill's Ragtime screamed *IMPORTANT!*

But when I stepped inside, the only thing still screaming was my head in the slow-strobing *SALE* holo that pulsed overhead. Even the clothing was boring: plain natural fibers, "professional casual," the sort of fare someone with no imagination and modest credit would wear to their uninspired office job.

Okay, maybe I was selling the place a little short. I could see myself in some of the clothing: soft, comfortable, staple.

But the place was entirely bereft of obvious clues. There weren't even any customers.

I'd been equally disappointed by the Bill's Ragtime purchase history I'd pulled from the Citizen ID records all those days ago. No one I recognized had shopped there in the past six months. Not even Integration Officer Mai Chandra, who I'd caught red-handed with a Bill's Ragtime bag slumped against her chair yesterday. That didn't mean she'd bought anything, though. The bag was good quality, the sort a person might reuse a few times before stuffing it in the reclaimer.

But I would not be daunted by the lack of obvious clues. There had to be an un-obvious clue somewhere.

I ventured further in and poked through the clothing racks, fingering the linens and reading how they were a hundred percent locally grown fibers woven by Cassiopeian craftspeople. Maybe the city was trying to tell me I needed new clothes.

I plucked some basic black and white items off the racks and went to the rear of the store to ask for the dressing room.

The man behind the counter sneered openly, telling me with his face that my kind was not welcome. He couldn't do anything about it, though, because Integration Law was quite clear on my right to be there. Unfortunately, the

Law said nothing about attitude.

Used to *The Look*, I ignored him and walked myself to the back corner to try on clothes. And to try on whether I'd find it more satisfying to purchase something to spite the clerk, or to cast an anti-bigot vote with my credit and walk out empty handed. Since the cream-colored blouse with the frills in front fit well and felt good, I leaned toward the very loud and politically pointed purchase option.

Three buttons of the blouse of undone, I stopped, fingers frozen.

It was that feeling when someone says a person's name, and they don't hear it consciously, but their attention is drawn anyway. That I-need-to-listen feeling.

I stood still, breath held; but heard nothing.

So I dropped my audio filters completely.

SOUND

stampeding ROARING HISSING CRACKING RASPING TICKING THRUMMING SCREAMING

SOUND!

Fingers pressed to my eyes till I saw stars, sweat prickling the bridge of my nose, *focus Hoshi!* Isolate. Identify. Factor what is figure and what is ground. Find labels for all the sounds. *(Dear Trinity, please unbraid the cacophony, help me through the maelstrom, separate the Signal from the Noise...)* Information Encoding—

THERE!

The roar of the environmentals adjusting the room based on my biofeedback.

The hiss of the everbulbs above.

The crackle and pound and slam and tap of the sales clerk working beyond the dressing room door.

The rasp of my breath sucking air.

The tick-tick of high heels walking on the floor one story up, tracking across the ceiling.

The thrum-thrum of my heart pushing blood.

The sound of voices through the wall on my left—

AH-HA!

I ran a subroutine to block all frequencies but those of the voices, and most of the sonic mess went away. I kept the rest of my auditory filters off. No need to amplify or reduce; as soon as I cut all the background noise, the signal of the voices came through perfectly.

"We've got to take Archer down a few more notches." An older voice, male. Authoritative.

"It's too soon. There's three whole days till Lastday." Younger, an unpleasant whiner. Also male.

"She'd be weaker by now if you hadn't bunged dealing with her last time."

I didn't immediately recognize either voice. Splitting a thread of consciousness, I queried my memory index.

"How could I have known she could fight!" Whiner.

"She can't fight you idiot! She used to work for the RCPD! They give their pet 'tards toy self-defense programs. You would've taken her on the second swing, don't get me started again!"

"Yeah, well, I don't work for the swine like you do, so how was I supposed to know," Whiner whined.

I should have goosebumps. Instead I was enthralled. Was the City really giving me this big a present, in return for the awful headache and nosebleed the other morning? It wouldn't be the first time something I'd processed unconsciously from the sensorfeed overload had saved my life. My fingers went to my face, the swollen remains of that back alley incident. I poked into all the nearby sensors, but none observed the room to the left. That was okay; I could work with the input from my ears just fine.

Authoritative Guy continued, "Anyway, Ho's got everything set to clip Archers' wings in Phase Two. So we have cripple her more, and fast."

Martin Ho! First buddying up to Inspector Zi to get me in trouble for something that never happened, now conspiring with Op-bashers to do what? Beat me up? Slay me? Martin was an annoying snot, sure, but he wouldn't willingly work with Op-bashers, no matter how much he hated me.

Then I remembered Martin's unprecedented, uncharacteristic violence at the Rose and Thorn when I'd called him an Effram Caper. That was important, a clue too.

What was I missing about Martin?

"We shouldn't be using Ho. That fucking retard started going through Mai's records. He thinks Mai's been fudging Archer's reports."

"What?" Authoritative Guy shouted, and I wondered why that information had upset him so.

"I told you we can't trust a k-dromer to do anything right," Whiner Guy kept whining.

"Well, did you put a stop to it?"

"Not yet."

"Not yet! What, you as defective as one of them? Fuckin' idiot!"

A long pause. Not enough information to guess what was happening, if anything besides the two of them engaging in a glare-off or one of those other ape-like dominance games normies play with each other.

"Well. She is not going to be pleased," Authoritative Guy finally muttered, with emphasis on the unnamed "she."

"She—"

But Whiner was cut off by the squeak of door hinges and the pat of footsteps entering the room.

The sales clerk from Bill's Ragtime said, "You'll never guess what just walked in."

Curse it all to Noise! I'd filtered out the sounds from the clerk, not realizing they were Signal! My memory index gave a positive ID on Whiner's voice as that of my attacker, the one who'd carved my face. I needed to get out of Bill's Ragtime. Fast!

And yet, I stood motionless, listening still. Fascinated.

The clerk elaborated, "It's Archer. In dressing room three."

Then came the scraping, rustling commotion of people standing in a hurry.

"And this is exactly why she needed to be weaker by now!" Whiner exclaimed. "She's too fucking nosey!"

The sales clerk laughed, "Well, curiosity just killed our cat!"

A volley of snickers.

They moved as they spoke, sound fading and a distant door opening and then the sound looped back toward me.

I still wore the cream-colored frilled blouse, tagged with a tacking pin to prevent theft. But there was no time to avoid turning robber. What were they going to do, report me to the RCPD? I grabbed my bolero and ran like fire out of the dressing room and out the front door.

Three sets of feet pelted after me slap-pound-slap, but I couldn't take the time to turn and look. I couldn't take the time to shrug into my bolero either, but it seemed worth doing in case I needed to use it as a shield again. Running and dressing at the same time constituted a Very Complicated Maneuver, and I cursed my clumsiness and the precious seconds it cost me, but I got the jacket on.

I hit the street, crying out as I stepped into shattered splinters of sound. My auditory filters were still down from the eavesdropping. If I were a better or faster programmer, or maybe less clumsy, I'd be able to reprogram them on the fly; but all my processing cycles were consumed by moving my body over uneven pavement and around passers-by. Moving me—where?

I cut most of my linguistics so I could push my consciousness into nearby sensors, looking ahead for a clear path of flight.

With the city screaming in my ears and the double-vision streaming in my eyes through a world without boundaries or meanings, I ran. Recognition flashed at odd intervals, unexpected understandings. Then flickered out into a blind blur.

I needed to get to safety before my nervous system absorbed more than it could bear and my background programming shut down completely to recover and then that would be the end of me.

I ran.

They ran after me slap-pound-slap.

I ran down unnamed alleys and through unseen lobbies and across Serenity park, and the three thugs ran after me. Pound-slap-pound a little louder each time.

My feet hit the Serenity tube station steps and tripped down, losing ground to catch a stumble against something soft and yielding at the bottom. I ran between the disinterested bodies of commuters, straight toward the tunnel where the tube rides on its bed of sound—deadly when the tube is about to come. But I was still alive after I crossed it, so it must have been dormant. I was so lucky it seemed the city herself was watching out for me.

On the other side of the tube bed, a smudge of shades-of-gray meant nothing, but my fingers found the round coolness of a knob and I pulled my awareness out of the local sensors to open a channel to the lock. Tube stop maintenance tunnel. No time, no cycles to crack the encryption, I pulled out my unauthorized RCPD credentials and shoved them at the lock. Master key to the city's utility system.

My fingers turned the knob of the maintenance tunnel door but slap-pound-slap told me the thugs had reached the edge of the platform four meters away and stopped, hesitant to risk what could be an activated sonic track. I turned to look before I could curb my curiosity. Visuals focused, bare threads of linguistics responding to danger-patterns: the bad end of a litegun pointed straight at my unprotected belly as the people on the platform began to back away.

I put my palm up, fixed my eyes on the litegun, and commanded the shocker to release its charge.

White lightning arced over the tube bed, up to the goon with the gun.

And dissipated against an invisible barrier.

The goon bared his teeth in animal triumph and braced to fire on me.

Dissipated? What the fu—

Screams shattered the cohesion of the world and everything went blank as my nervous system overloaded.

Emergency auditory filters slammed up in automatic response to intolerable sound, and awareness of the world whooshed back hysterically. I gasped, mid-fall. The sonic tube was approaching. The bed of sound it rode on was screaming. Too high-pitched for the normies' ears, but all too audible to an Operator's naked senses. My knees impacted concrete as my nervous system lurched back from blackout.

Smoke curled from the door behind me, and an acrid smell. I looked up; the litegun's pulse had missed me by a breath only because of my sound-stunned fall.

Clawing at the maintenance tunnel door knob, I shoved the heavy steel open with the weak weight of my body as the tube rode into the station and stopped, separating me from my attackers. I fell through the opening and shoved the door closed behind me, gambling that the goons would not be able to unlock it as quickly as I had. If nothing else, they would have to wait for the tube to finish exchanging passengers.

I stood and kept running, working the unfamiliar tunnels through the sensors. I felt my background programming slipping away like sand through a sieve, and focused limited resources on running. I emerged three stops south at Xiou Avenue Station and stopped. My lungs could hold no more breath.

I tried to transfer processing cycles out of motor and back into sensory and linguistics, but I couldn't hold the images steady in my mind to activate the programming. The damage had been done. Nerves too shot to support most background programming, I rode the tube home in a blank of sound and motion and the terror of undefinable shapes, pounding my forehead against my fists to try to regain control of my perceptions.

By the time I clawed my way up the stairs to the landing outside my apartment, I had enough brain function back to remember the tracker in the stolen shirt and realize I needed to dispose of it. I also had enough brain function back to know that was all I was going to be able to do before mind and body just gave up, so I'd better be in a soft, safe place when it happened.

I opened the door to my studio with a thought and a push.

Sorreno stood within. Along with a posse of uniformed officers. She didn't look happy. They didn't look happy. I didn't have enough background programming to look like anything other than a slack-faced, dirty, exhausted Operator on the brink of collapse.

An officer I'd never seen before stepped forward with a restraint and said, "Hoshi Archer? You're under arrest for violation of Integration Law article 15b, sub-unit 6 You have the right to a non-violent arrest, do you waive that right?"

I stood stiff as a building, staring at nothing, and swayed back and forth.

The officer made a move toward me with the restraint.

Motor controls kicked in before common sense, and I turned and ran.

I ran like fire.

I did not look back.

I went straight back the way I'd come, arriving at the station just as a tube slid into view. Scrambling through bodies like a drunk, I fell toward the center of the crowd, grateful for evening rush hour, loving Red City for hiding me in the press of her people.

Looking through sensorcams I saw the officers boarding pink platforms down.

Pink?

Six, not pink. Six platforms down.

My thoughts weren't working right, as resources both meat and machine scrambled to keep proxying for too many physical and mental abilities I don't naturally possess. My lungs felt full of acid. Note to self: get more routine exercise.

Where was I?

Insufficient linguistics for identification.

Green dot on ceiling. Green means northbound, Cherry Hill to Shirring Point. Express. Red City systems and stations deep in my bones, more innate than breath.

No stops between here and Shirring, but once the tube stopped, there would be four more blocks to run to safety.

Through the sensorcams, I watched the cops search, clumsily.

Eight minutes to Shirring, two cars closer to Hoshi.

Six minutes to Shirring, three cars away.

Five minutes, one car—

The tube moved slowly into the station; the cops were zero cars away.

Just four more blocks to run.

I shut off everything but motor. Red City, help my feet to find their way.

Animal sounds. A howl, and whimpers. Impossible input. SOUND! (Is that me screaming?)

Four blocks.

It was four blocks from the tube station to the gateway of Shirring Point. Four blocks—

I ran.

I ran like fire.

Three blocks.

Two.

One.

I wasn't going to make it.

Hot speed fired past my face. Hyper-drive reflexes involuntarily turning me, like an idiot, to gaze on a mess of Noise I couldn't process. Patchwork lacerations of sound-image-texture and the scent of berries and sweat, and screaming, hard shapes and pinkness—

Linguistics pulled resources from who knows where and identified the officers less than two meters away. They did not identify anything else in the surrounding scrambled-egg world.

My palm came up, eyes fixed on the officer with the tranqgun, aiming the shocker, torqued motor controls moving me faster than I could keep up so I had no sense of my own limbs in space.

"HOSHI ARCHER!" a scream, distinct, behind me.

The officers turned toward the shout.

I swiveled instead of firing, falling through the gateway of Shirring Point, and made straight for the maze of Frontal Market as linguistics shut down again and all I had left were fragments of memory and prayer.

A foot fall.

A shout.

The edge of my cuff.

A turquoise brinn gull, pecking at the blackstone.

The bleached blue paint on the wall of a six-story building, pale, salt-weathered wood showing through in spots.

A steel door.

My experience like a holo missing scenes.

Something to do?

Six stories, all stairs.

A burnt umber lintel and the friendly smell of oil and metal and cinnamon.

Shove this mass of shapes and sounds into a door lock. Kelvin's citizen ID code.

Safe.

Safety.

The interior of Kelvin's apartment.

The hard impact of a wooden floor. Shivering so hard I tasted blood.

As overload flattened me into catatonia, I thought with surreal clarity one perfectly formed sentence made entirely of words: Isn't it ironic that the bad part of town is where I'd fled in order to be safe?

CHAPTER 16

Softness.

Warmness.

The smell of garlic and onions sautéing, and the yeasty smell of baking bread.

"Hoshi, you hungry? When was the last time you ate?"

Kelvin's voice. What—

Oh.

Right.

My head throbbed like a hangover and I checked time in a panic, calming only when I saw a mere five hours had passed since overloading. Everything hurt in the aftermath of unacceptable levels of stress on top of bruises aggravated by exertion.

"Hoshi, you hungry? When was the last time you ate?" Kelvin asked again.

"Un. Nuh. Known." I answered, eyes closed. My voice came out in halting, grinding syllables.

What was known, by the feel of it against my body, was that I was lying on the old velveteen couch in Kel's living room beneath that natty afghan of his. I mucked with my programming, hoping to make something more like communication happen.

"Night," came out of me. Yeah. Not quite what I was after. I tried again, and got a longer string of words. "Night. Last. Ate. Bouillabaisse? Last night." I paused, memories coming as slowly as everything else. "But. Plugged into berth. Last night, this morning. Maybe then. Nu-nu-nutrients. Maybe?"

A long-suffering sigh from Kelvin.

"Don't. you. start," I grumbled, but my heart wasn't in it and my tone fell flat.

I struggled toward a sit, whimpered, and lay back down again.

Kel's sounds entered the room and I cracked my eyes. Sensory was running again, and his homely pale face and washed-out straw-colored hair read more beautiful to me than an angel. He held a plate of scramble and toast in one hand and a bottle of Pain-Ez in the other. I couldn't believe how badly I wanted that food now that I saw it.

Kelvin didn't ask me what was going on. He didn't remark on my condition or on the implications of finding me in a crumpled mess on his doorstep. He let me eat and recover and get the rest of my programming back online.

But the moment I dropped my fork on my empty plate, he exploded with, "Hoshi-Moshi! What is going on! You're all over the feeds, and the story isn't good."

I wasn't happy to hear that. But I wasn't surprised.

Kelvin thumbed a button under the coffee table and the 3Vplate on its surface lit with more holicons than I could process without getting dizzy. He flicked his eyes over them quickly, fewer displaying each time, until he hit the one he wanted—a cartoony image of a spaceship in a circle—and expanded it with a blink. It wasn't a city-wide main, but it was a respectable local from Landing District.

"It's criminal how the feeds use you." Kelvin's voice held the quiet fierceness he reserved for someone he was about to punch in the mouth. "It's like watching them pull apart Marly Jones during the Marsten debates all over again, and being able to do just as little about it." His eyes hovered on the feed's spaceship-in-circle sigil, and the holicon dissolved to copy.

"...ion Law took another turn for the worse today when news leaked of Hoshi Archer's participation in gang-related crimes." The reporter was a prim, conservative woman who looked like she shopped at Bill's Ragtime.

The feed switched to a man in a blue coat blazoned with the snake-and-staff sigil of government medical. "The danger with letting Operators like

Archer have so much leeway is that they don't possess the intellectual or emotional capacity to understand when they have transgressed the social contract. I don't believe Archer understands what she is doing—no Operator would. But that doesn't make her actions right."

I watched Kel avert his eyes from the red dot at the top of the display that would invoke the dossier on the speaker. My blood boiled, but I sat still and grim as Kelvin.

"Law Enforcement authorities are refusing to comment"—flash to Sorreno evading the prim reporter, ducking into a doorway where press could not follow—"but we have confirmed an official arrest warrant exists for Archer's citizen ID at this time. We've been unable to contact Archer or her Integration Officer for comment. We were able to get comment from Larson Smith of how this development impacts the bids for an Inclusion Act, and...."

"Oh, this is not good," I whispered, programming mistaking the strength of my emotions for a desire to communicate.

"No, not good at all," Kel answered, not realizing I hadn't meant to speak.

"How long have you known?" The 'feed droned on about how my "crime" was proof Operators couldn't be trusted in administrative positions, even though that logic held about as much water as a bucket without a bottom.

Kelvin shrugged shoulders broad and hard from metalworking beneath his dark gray fisherman's sweater. "Since right after I scraped you off my doorstep and put you on the couch. I hadda find out what'd happened to you, jo?"

"What else—"

"Are they saying about you?" The anger beneath his surface hardened like diamonds and his voice almost went unsteady. "That was one of the kinder feeds."

"Kinda figured." Integration Law said nothing about respectful language, after all. But the whole thing worried me on a larger scale. The anti-Op anti-Inclusion crew would galvanize further against the obvious danger to human decency I posed. Ops had no power in the media, so no one would be spinning the feed in my—or my people's—favor.

Kelvin pressed the off switch and the nasty news flash vanished into darkness. "So what did you do?"

"Trinity, I wish I knew," I moaned. Lubricated by food and sympathy, my memory index came up with the goods quickly again, "Violation of Integration Law article 15b, sub-unit 6 apparently. Whatever that is."

"Whatever that is? Hoshi, look it up!" Kelvin's colorless blue eyes stared round in disbelief.

"What? How!"

"How? You just open a channel to the Mem and look—" And then understanding dawned and he looked even more upset than I felt. My citizen ID patterns were just as wanted in the Mem as they were in the physical world.

"I'm safe here in Shirring where most of the sensors have been smashed and there are more transmission blackout zones than uninhabited space, but that data exists in areas of the Mem way outside the local Shirring networks. I don't have any of the skills to be a signal cracker, despite the media trying to make all Operators out to be Burl Hill, Data Thief."

Kelvin was having a hard time processing. "You mean—you can't—"

"I can't enter the Mem right now. Yeah."

He kept gaping at me, stricken. Forgetting how much I do not like being gaped at.

Not that I was happy about the situation, but it didn't bother me as much as it seemed to bother Kelvin. Probably because he didn't know I could still enter the sensor networks undetected, which, while not the same, meant I wasn't trapped in my own skin. "It's okay." And then when his expression didn't change I added, "I can still use my navis just fine. Plus, there are work-arounds. But later. There's stuff I've gotta do first. Coffee?"

Shaking himself like he was trying to wake up, Kelvin smiled weakly at me. "I'll always know you're okay so long as you ask for coffee." Then he poked a calloused finger at my chest and said, "Still thieving too, I see. That time you convinced me to steal the trophy from the Blane School wasn't enough for you?"

I looked at where he pointed, bewildered, to find the anti-theft pin in the froth of ruffles of the Bill's Ragtime blouse I still wore. That dressing room felt like forty years ago. My own shirt probably still lay in a heap on the floor there. "Yeah, it's my new occupation, actually, since the warrant. Master Thief!"

"Don't worry, it hasn't been transmitting. Old Herrick on the floor below still has that selective jammer running, the one that blocks long-range citizen ID signals."

"Gotta love people with paranoid dipsomania," I sighed.

"Still," Kelvin handed me a pair of murderous shears he used for cutting sheet metal, "snip that off and I'll stick it in something corrosive for you."

I had programming give me a funny voice, slipping into my new Master Thief persona, "Ah, you shall be my henchman then! You shall be Kelly the Nose, and your first task as second to my Master Theivingness shall be to help me destroy the evidence!"

Kel's voice went nasal with sycophantic affect, "Right away Mistress Midnight, right away!"

While he was gone, I sat and frowned and thought.

Theoretically, I should com Sorreno, immediately. I should tell her everything, ask for police escort from the gates of Shirring, and sort whatever was going on via official protocols like a good little successfully Integrated Operator. I wouldn't have fled the police the first place if I'd an atom of wits about me at the time.

Realistically.... The three thugs had been carrying a current shield, and they'd had it activated when I'd fired on them. The main reason one would carry a current shield is to dissipate a shocker arc. So they'd known I was carrying a shocker. And the only people who should have known I was carrying a shocker were Sorreno, Angel, and Mai. In fact, before today, anyone scanning my records would think I carried no weapons at all. My aversion to them is well documented.

It was madness to think it, but Sorreno had been in the morgue when the blood sample evidence had been switched.

Sorreno had been the one to ensure I was carrying a shocker.

Angel had hypothesized that whoever had switched the evidence would have known I would find it—or thought I would have been taken out of the picture before I could find it. That didn't rule out Sorreno—and neither did it rule out Angel.

One of the thugs at Bill's Ragtime had been identified as working for the RCPD.

Trinity, for all I knew Sorreno or Angel was the ambiguous "she" the thugs had referred to in reverential tones!

Likewise, Mai Chandra and everyone involved with the Integration Office wasn't off the hook either. There were fewer connections there, but the murdered women were all last seen entering the IO and there was, again, the matter of who knew about the shocker.

The whole thing reeked of lies and betrayal.

I couldn't contact Sorreno or Mai—or anyone else at the station or the IO—until I knew for sure who was friend and who was foe.

So what could I do?

"Kelvin, I need espresso," I announced as he returned from destroying the tracker.

"Hoshi, you need sleep. And about two months of vacation."

"No," I shook my head. "I'm okay. As long as I don't have to stand."

Kelvin shoved his way in next to me on the sloppy couch. "Truthfully, how badly are you hurt? And don't think I've missed the fact that you still haven't told me what really happened to you."

"I am—a lot of bad is going on. Someone killed Nessa, Claudia, and a dancer you might have heard of, Loie Ravine?" To Noise with my promise to Sorreno about keeping the case quiet. The bad press about me was a million times more destructive to the city than a leak about the murders, anyway.

Kelvin stiffened beside me, his pale face draining clear to ashen. But he let me continue.

"Plus, someone's after me. Op-bashers. But that's a part of everything else too. Plus, I made the whole arrest thing worse by running because my background programs were down so I wasn't making good decisions because I'd just sprinted half the breadth of Red City to escape the Op-bashers with my sensory and linguistics programming turned off. And I've gotta factor it all before it gets worse. Caffeine, please?"

"Claudia?" Kel picked up my hand and placed his palm over mine, connecting physically in the only way I used to allow when we were kids. "Hoshi, why didn't you tell me? Why didn't you talk to me! Claudia is dead?"

"Yeah," my voice came out barely audible. "And Nessa. And Loie." My monologue had left me exhausted. Kelvin was right; I needed sleep. But sleep would cost the next murder victim too much.

"Hoshi, I'm so sorry. Claudia—I know the two of you—but—why didn't you talk to me?"

I put my other hand on top of Kel's. "Not now. Later. Coffee now."

Kelvin sighed but nodded slowly. "Guess I can't force you to let me in. If I help you out, will you use the extra time for sleeping?" Then he was gone before I could answer.

I visited the bathroom, set alarms to keep from getting buried in my head for too long, and missed my berth terribly because it would make such considerations as bathrooms and alarms moot. I was prepared to put the pieces I had so far the rest of the way together. Pieces that included Claudia. Because next to thinking about how I'd just lost my freedom and my job, rehashing failed relationships was totally delightful.

Kelvin handed me a beer mug filled with coffee darker than blackstone.

"If you want to help, look up what that Violation Code means. Find out what they think I did."

Kelvin rocked back on the heels of his work boots, hands folded over his chest. "Will you go to sleep before firsthour if I do that?"

"But—"

"Hoshi. You could stop sleeping entirely and there would still always be something else to do."

Wasn't that the truth! I mumbled unhappily, "Okay, asleep before firsthour, check."

"Promise?"

I sighed. "Promise." And shut my eyes on the physical world and re-opened them in my imagination.

◆   ◆   ◆

My workspace was a mess. I'd been pushing stuff into it nonstop, like the info from Ursula and Madame Bosco and the dealers. The lines linking the variables were knotted together like tangled yarn, and I couldn't even sit my imaginary body down in the imaginary space because it was so full of flashing, stinking, tinkling things.

I nearly fled the chaos of my own mind.

But instead, I took a deep imaginary breath, and started sorting. Ordering calmed me. I got into a rhythm. And then I started building.

Martin's scheme and the murder case no longer occupied separate spaces in my thinking. The setup and arrest, the knife attack, and the murders had become the meat on the bones of a single monster. The flesh of the facts still fit imperfectly, but it fit better than it had this morning.

As far as the original murders went, that part of the landscape was the most solid. And my to do list most concrete:

Find out who received the NQ from Bosco's dealers in Cleopatra Square.

Factor the connection between the three victims.

Pick up the trail after the victims disappeared into the IO.

And crack the ghastly painted pseudo-code. Which is what Sorreno had originally hired me to do.

Less solid was the landscape of the attacks on me. First the jump in the alley by my house, then the malicious conversation at Bill's Ragtime, then the hot fire from the litegun. An absolutely nasty illegal weapon that could have sliced me clear in two. Considering the thugs wanted to "take Archer down a few more notches" and felt "she'd be weaker by now if you hadn't bunged dealing with her last time," I felt confident that these were not random hate crimes but calculated moves designed to weaken me. On a schedule.

And Martin's case against me with the Roccini Boys—whatever I'd just been charged with—was part of this "weaken Hoshi" plan just as much as the back alley beating and the attempted shooting.

When I stopped horrifying myself by imagining Sorreno as a criminal mastermind, I remembered Martin Ho had been in the morgue too when the blood samples were switched. He'd come down on a mission from Inspector Zi. Zi who Martin had been cozying up to in the office, looking at circumstantial evidence of me sitting next to gangster Hank Roccini.

Whatever else I might think of Martin, I did not think he was a criminal mastermind. However, Inspector Zi certainly could be. He had the same politics as the bigoted thugs, and the authority of a respectable station to enforce them. There remained a number of powerful people in the city who would do anything to reverse Integration. And Zi had a lot of pawns—and a lot of benefactors.

So who had started the scheme against me? Was it really Martin's scheme? Or was it Zi's? Or the thugs'? Or the thug's unnamed "she"? And was one of them connected to the murders? Or was one of them even the murderer? The scheme had put me in a position for the media to use me against my own kind—was that the plan all along?

If there was a connection between the evidence swap and the attacks on me, then I really was in a city of trouble. Was I supposed to be solving the murders, or was I supposed to be playing a role in them? If the latter, I certainly hoped I wasn't performing correctly.

I closed my imaginary eyes and slowly pictured the peaks and domes and points of the skyline and the graceful spiral of the Arts and Culture Building, and the triple towers of the 100 Worlds Trade Union joined by their series of sky-bridges, and the prickly quills of the Red City Reporter, and—each of my 200 favorite buildings in Red City, slowly, one after another, until I felt calm.

This was all speculation.

Speculation of scenarios with non-zero probabilities.

Sorreno, who I really wanted to believe was still my friend, had that very first day said, "Three Operators your age Hoshi! Your age!" She'd warned me right then that she thought I might be on the Next Victim List.

Maybe there were two separate forces at work: one that wanted me to solve the murders, and one that wanted me to play out whatever horrific role was being prepared for me.

Or was there only one force, and my consult on the case was, itself, the role I was intended to play?

Like bile, Blu Lou's parting words to me regurgitated from my memory index in response to the associations I was forming:

"Those who attacked you—who cut your face—it was part of the shape of things to come. They cut you for a reason, a part of the attack on Red City's heart. Remember, you are a symbol in the city. Symbols, like murder, have power, are a way to call the élan vitals. In three years the public has not forgotten you were among the first to be emancipated."

And then I thought of the growing unrest in the city. Sorreno's plea to keep the case quiet so as not to light a fire. The protesters outside the IO. The tinderbox of caste tensions I'd ignored for too long from the black box of my own privilege.

Well, I'd lost that privilege now. Just like I'd never had it. Integration Law was still in a trial period, like me. Anything could upset our gains, put things back the way they were.

I swooped out in my mind to take a brinn's eye view of the landscape I'd built. Images of people, events, evidence linked together by lines of relationships. Or, in mathematical terms, nodes connected by vertices. My map of the situation looked like one of Gno's circuit diagrams. Fear dissolved the triumph of the puzzle-solving like acid.

Someone was building a situation, a structure, in which the political landscape of the city could change.

Someone was building a circuit.

All it needed were a few more connections and a zap of current.

A zap like caste-related murders at the IO. Like Hoshi Archer, one of Integration's poster children, revealed as a dangerous failure.

Which brought me back again to Blu Lou's Dragon Lines, and Blinker's fear of the Sha Chi—the bad energy. Which brought me back again to aliens living in the EM and a whole realm of stuff I'd never before needed to understand.

I needed information. Research. Data. I needed to know what had transpired in the city at the exact times and dates of the murders, the times when Blu Lou said someone had corrupted the heart of the city. I needed to connect with the mind of the city.

But I couldn't step out into the Mem, not one tendril of consciousness, because my patterns were on Cassiopeia Prime's Most Wanted list.

Which meant if I wanted to go any further into solving the murders without turning myself in—which I didn't dare do until I'd cleared Sorreno of involvement—I was going to have retreat deeper into the underworld. I was going to have to see Luzzie Vai the Sea Witch. Again.

But first, I'd promised Kelvin I'd get some sleep.

CHAPTER 17

I opened my eyes to the dawn, but all I saw were walls and doors and a slow seepage of uncertain light through shuttered blinds. No city spread before me, no skyline to light my way.

I rolled onto my back, swallowing. My right arm was numb from where I'd lain on it, and I felt hard, angry lines where the pillowcase had dug my face. Seemingly so comfortable the night before, the couch and afghan had revealed their nature as scratchy and lumpy. I missed my berth terribly, that gentle machine passively cradling me and ensuring I would never feel discomfort nor want for anything. Sure, it was meant to keep me alive during prolonged periods in the Mem, but it made a great bed also.

I could rise, cross the room, open the blinds. I could let in the light.

But all that lay on the other side of the window was the weathered gray flank of the building across the narrow street.

In my imagination, I conjured my workspace and masked out all the thoughts that filled it until I was left looking at the window to my memory. There the jagged skyline reached for faint clouds in the blue-green heavens, and Marcie Bay twinkled at the end of the leafy passage of Lan Qui Park. I'd programmed my imagination to keep time with the physical world, so the warm light of Cadmus reflecting off the shiny spires anchored me in late morning. Later than I would have liked.

Making the internal view my primary visual input, locking it in place, I cracked open my eyes. The double-vision confused my senses, then equilibrated: visual cortex successfully tricked into seeing a view instead of a wall.

I traced the skyline of Central with a fingertip. The peaks and domes and points and the graceful spiral of the Arts and Culture Building and the triple towers of the 100 Worlds Trade Union joined by their netting of sky-bridges, and the prickly quills of the Red City Reporter, and the diamond-shine off Marcie Bay with her strands of boats and piers and the incredible blue-green of the Beryl Sea all the way to the horizon—

Except the clouds didn't move. The sky was clear of birds. No wind wavered the foliage of the parks. And a thousand other tiny details that separated the physical world from the world of my imagination.

I let the image fade.

Fantasy was nice.

Feeling sorry for myself was nicer still.

But neither fantasy nor self-pity would get me back into my own apartment with its cathedral window and perfect view and my own berth. Today the cream-colored walls and rosewood floors of Kelvin's tidy-but-mismatched living room would have to do.

A digipage rested atop the afghan and I picked it up, sitting.

> *Hoshi-Moshi,*
>
> *I had to see a client about a sculpture.*
>
> *There's coffee in the drink machine in the kitchen. Just press the button it's already on the 'sludge' setting for you.*
>
> *I looked up the violation code you were arrested under. It's on the 3V in the loft.*
>
> *Be careful and I should be back by dinner. To make sure you eat.*
>
> > *Hugs,*
> > *Kel.*
>
> *P.S. Be sure to process everything around the 3V!*

I let the digipage drop back onto the afghan, took a deep breath, and limped through the morning necessities. A hot shower helped a lot. So did running my clothes through the washer. As did a second hot shower. Then, second helping of sludge in tow, I crossed the teeny-tiny three-room apartment and mounted the half-flight of stairs to Kel's workshop beneath the building's eaves.

Kel's workshop is much bigger on the inside than the outside.

Okay, not really. This is the physical world, not the Mem.

But the building is diced up into apartments as small as Kelvin's between narrow corridors of close-set doors, making it impossible to get a sense for the structure's size anywhere except the workshop. The building occupies a smallish city block. Huge panes of greenish glass, sloping sharply to shed the evening rain, form the roof and fill the space with light.

I navigated the vastness, weaving between welding devices and rolling carts of tiny drawers, some of which Kelvin used in his Frontal Market booth. Odors, metallic and acrid and salty, laid the scentscape. Something bubbled in a bath beneath humming ventilation hoods.

Right now the space was relatively empty of works-in-progress. The "clean" area I headed for in the northeast corner was stuffed with poster-sized digipages, though, flickering symbols in a mathematics so ancient I'd only worked with them in history class. Propped against the wall, reminding me uneasily of my train of thought last night, was a circuit diagram. Beside it, a floor-to-ceiling drawing of a clockwork brinn gull scrawled in charcoal on the wall. A new project, looked like. Was that the sculpture Kelvin had gone to see the man about? I wandered toward it, then remembered why I was in the loft in the first place.

I stopped and took a haul off my coffee. Repointed myself toward the 3V attached to Kel's stationary. On the bright side, I must be feeling better if I was getting sidetracked by curiosity.

I arrived amongst the blueprints to find the 3V aglow with the convoluted legalese of Integration Law. Even with linguistics taking up every spin of my navis, I've never been able to understand a word of it. By no fault of my own either; most Operators can't. It was not written for people who, as one city leader had put it, "have the natural verbal acuity of a carrot." And yes, there is something really wrong with a Law that can't be read by those it most affects, and yes, both Operators in the city and our allies protested the language, but what can we do? Requests for accessible language were twisted early on into reasons why we should be denied our freedom, so we let it drop. We'll always rely on the normies for something, just like they will always rely on us to program their quantum computers. Bitterness aside, interdependence also describes the relationship between my navis and me, between Kelvin and me, between the élans and the humans, between the brinn gulls and the brassfish and the keiffer grasses. It's not a simple thing.

Beside each line of incomprehensible bureaucratic mumbo Kelvin had added blue dots linking to annotations—the translations he knew I'd need.

I opened a connection to the 3V and activated the dot next to the proclamation "ARTICLE 15: Concerning the Assumption sar. Abetment of Extra-legal Activities, Actionable Offences, Malfeasance, Appeasement, Warbeling, and Further Syndications Thereof, inclusive, wisc."

After a half-sec, Kelvin's translation emerged in a pale pink bubble. "This section is about doing stuff that's against the regular law."

Gee. Who would've guessed?

I pushed aside metal shavings and charcoal and other objects that weren't worth my spins to identify, and planted my elbows in front of the display to read the rest of Kel's notes, not even skimming the legalese. I learned:

Article 15 is about doing stuff that's against the regular law;

Subsection 15b is about organized crime and street gangs; and,

Sub-unit 6 is about messing with data and transmission, including information theft and the manipulation of public bandwidth.

I rocked back on my heels, blinking and surprised. Not by the gang-related stuff; if Martin and Company were trying to connect me to the Roccini Boys, then that was to be expected. But I didn't understand the Sub-unit 6 part at all. My skill set didn't include data manipulation. And I don't care what less educated normies think, having once been a codebreaker for the RCPD doesn't imply one can get creative enough for data manipulation any more than being a piano tuner implies one can write a symphony. The truly perplexing bit was that with so many completely plausible things someone could pin on me, why would they go after something so implausible?

Had someone discovered my ongoing and deliberate failure to turn in Luzzie Vai? Could it be an abetting charge for my silence?

Or—I didn't want to think it—had someone discovered I could enter the city sensors unseen?

But no, those things didn't connect with organized crime or with the evidence: circumstantial footage of Hank Roccini and me at the same bar, my past shoddy work on the Roccini Gang case, Martin's quip "I know what you've been up to with the Roccini Boys"—and the charge was in a gang-related subsection of the Law. The evidence eliminated both Luzzie and the sensor bug.

What was I missing?

My thoughts remained silent on that question, but the answer was embedded in the incongruity of the situation. If I could figure out how one could come up with a plausible data manipulation charge on me, I'd have the answer to what they thought I'd done. But I wasn't likely to factor that in the next two minutes, not without more information and a connection to the Mem.

So I let it be for now, and dutifully focused instead on the area around the 3Vplate, as instructed in Kel's note. Nearly four minutes later, given the high degree of clutter, I'd sorted out a floppy hat, an ugly scarf, sunglasses, and a yellow fisherman's slicker big enough to go over my bolero. Everything a girl needs to travel semi-incognito.

I'd also sorted out the bottle of Pain-Ez, the glass of water, and the plate of scrambled eggs kept warm on the hot plate that more typically kept metals and silicates molten while Kelvin worked.

I set to breakfast with a grin. It's good to have friends.

Two hours, two more mugs of sludge, and a paranoid tromp into the center of Shirring Point later, I was thinking it was good to have enemies too.

"Well, well, it's Red City's Most Wanted," Luzzie Vai smiled evilly at me through the dim lights and fractal lace of the Julia Set Saloon as I took off Kel's enormous sunglasses. The tiny robots in Luzzie's greasy chartreuse hair clicked and spun. "I can get quite a bounty for you."

"But you won't," I sat opposite him, loosening the orange and brown ugly scarf and shoving the floppy hat out of my field of view. I folded my hands over an infinitely unfolding fractal animation that played across the surface of the table. "You're going to help me."

Luz looked at me with half-lidded eyes and waited.

"I need a new ident. Something that will let me move freely in informationspace and get around the city if I'm careful. I don't need its citizen ID patterns to last more than a week, so don't go all out. But the ident's got to last at least three days. It's got to hold till the end of Lastday."

This request did not impress Luzzie, who continued to gaze slimily at me.

"If you want who did Loie, this is what needs to happen."

Slowly Luzzie nodded, facade fading. Since there are no emotives outside the Mem, I couldn't read him easily. But I could read him enough. Beneath that oily exterior he'd been grieving, eyes rimmed red and cheeks hollow.

I'd planned to say something snide about how he couldn't collect any bounty without turning himself in too, but at the last minute I decided to be nice instead. "Look, the other day. When I said I'd give you who did Loie in return for you answering my questions. Well, I was planning to tell you who did it after I'd turned them in to the RCPD. But I'll tell you first instead. I'll give you first crack at them. Plus," I couldn't believe I was saying this, "that favor I owe you for the extra info? I'll upgrade it, same scale as this one. Big time favor. Kish?"

"So you're willing to get off your high moral soap box about Luzzie's business when it suits your personal needs, eh, Hoshi? And all this time I thought your shit really didn't stink." He wasn't going to say yes without harassing me. But he was going to say yes.

"I feel the same way I always have about your filthy drug dealing, Luzzie. But you know I've never had a problem with your forgery."

Luzzie nodded, minibots clicking and grinding in his greasy hair, facial movements obscured by the flicker of his living tattoos. Both of us were too sad for more barbs. "Deal." Then, after a brief pause, "You know there's a small surgery involved, jo?"

I rolled my eyes. "And you know I didn't just fall off the turnip cart, right?"

"You come back here in eight then, Luzzie will have what you need. Till then, here's your shopping list." He made a flicking gesture with his fingers, inviting me to open a shortwave channel.

"Shopping list?"

"Well, if you pay more, you'll get the Diamond District treatment. I could even have whoever brings you the stuff give you a massage. Care to add another favor or two on your tab?"

I shuddered and shook my head. "Shopping list is fine."

I opened a band on the infrared, and Luzzie shot me several physical addresses and an items list. I wondered who I was to become, what new person with an official citizen ID and all. I had a sinking suspicion based on the shopping list it was not the type of person I would enjoy being. I sighed, tightening Kel's hideous scarf around my neck. At least I had an option at all; not every fugitive in Red City had a personal 'in' with the region's premier identity forger.

I sunk back into Kel's enormous sunglasses and left the Julia Set, trying not to think too hard about the fact that I'd just, for the first time ever (despite what the RCPD thought), committed a very real crime. Even the smashed-out city sensors could sense my guilt, their broken lenses cold and judgmental.

My only hope now was that solving the murders would soften the punishment for this self-inflicted damage.

And hey, if it didn't, I'd have a spiffy new ident to flee the authorities with.

I scrubbed shaking, sweat-soaked hands against the ugly scarf and choked. I was up past my nose in shit much too far for glib thoughts.

Hart Street wound like a loose thread from a forgotten sweater through the worst part of the worst part of Shirring Point. Loose trash fluttered freely because people were too dejected or sapped out on substances to bother throwing it into the reclaimer ten paces away. Sea water seeped from the gutters; a pipe had been clogged for as long as I could remember. The water smelled of salt and decay, wavering between earthy and nauseating. I felt watched from every patch of darkness, knowing no disguise was enough protect me from addicts desperate for credit to hook their next fix. I stepped over refuse splayed out across the street before I realized it was a person, and felt for the hard, cool edges of Sorreno's shocker I still carried in my pocket. The street was so narrow, the buildings netted together by so many ad-hoc walkways, that the blackstone cobbles retained their twilight shadow at midday. I almost zapped a movement from the shadows before identifying it as a scavenging brinn gull, turquoise feathers oily and patchy.

Yet I loved this part of the city too. Anything else would be as absurd as loving all of a person except for their right knee cap. The original structures had been erected by the homeless decades ago, when it was unwanted ground. Then came gentrification, pushing the original architects out to edgier zones. Followed by collapse as Shirring Point became increasingly lawless, and now it was home to the destitute, the forgotten, and the hiding. All I'd ever known of the area was slippery-slick wood and the mildew-and-sea odor and feeling like my foot would punch through the floors of the buildings.

But I'd seen holos of better times. I'd read the stories these streets whispered in the mainfeed archives. She'd had beautiful days.

Guilt pressed on me. If I visited more often, this area wouldn't be so run down.

Now that was silly. I shook the feeling off.

A golden holosign blinked above the pawnshop Reconnaissance Jack, mingling with the blue of the second hand clothing store Flipz across the way. Where the spill of the signs met, they made a white light which illuminated the crossroads where Luzzie had sent me.

In the clothing store I bought the first set of items on Luzzie's list:

Baggy khaki pants.

Worn workman's tee.

Woolen fisherman's sweater two sizes too big, poor condition a plus (did Luzzie know how much I hate the feel of wool?).

Fishgutter's cap, any neutral color (I chose tan).

Fingerless work gloves with spider-grip nanocloth pads.

Pierboots, moderate condition, medium-brown.

I gazed unhappily into the dingy mirror at the back of Flipz. I liked my real identity; I didn't want to exchange it for a new one. Especially not a new one that smelled like a dock worker. I stowed my hair under the gutter's cap, a slender hat with a long visor and indestructible nanocloth netting that unfurled to keep out flies, offal, and knife fights. Letting the fine netting unwind a little hid the Operator shine of my forehead. As long as I didn't interact with anyone, I would, distressingly enough, read at a quick glance as a normie.

Which was probably the point.

But that didn't make pretending to be someone—something—else any more comfortable. I wondered what the details of this person's life would be— where did I live? Who did I work for? Did I have any family? I'd never had any family, so I hoped not. I wouldn't know what to do with them.

I yanked the sweater off and put my bolero back on. Then I pulled the sweater on over the jacket. There were funny lumps at the wrists where the triangular sleeves of the bolero bunched up, but whatever. I needed something to keep the itch of the wool away from my skin. I needed something that reminded me of myself. Plus, it was all I had in the way of body armor.

The pawnshop list was shorter:

Gutter's utility knife, midrange quality.

Rings and a necklace, conservative style, the sort of things someone with decent taste and no money would buy.

Sunglasses. Of course.

I wore my new costume to the drop point under the pier off First and Ship's Way, where I handed over my old clothes and received a set of hazel contact lenses from a sapped out tracer addict who made me feel like I was engaging in a drug deal.

I was quite sure Luzzie had orchestrated that scene specifically to bother me.

I mean, who needs that much cloak and dagger for a pair of lousy contact lenses?

Although, to his credit, Luzzie had given me a new identity with sensible shoes.

CHAPTER 18

Since I couldn't go anywhere or do anything—at least in any non-derelict part of town—until I got the final bits of my new identity from Luzzie, I decided to pass the time by spying on my colleagues. Once more I blessed that bug that let me see through the city's eyes undetected by the Memside nets that trawled for me. Migraines and nosebleeds were a small price to pay.

I sunk into the sensors at the RCPD like a sigh of relief. I had no idea how often I reached for the Mem until I couldn't anymore. My consciousness sifted through dozens of spy-eyes at once to find the patterns I sought. Patterns of five faces and voices: the people associated with the evidence swap in the morgue.

Inspector Cassandra Sorreno was meeting with Chief of Police Biyu Harrison, in Harrison's office. I couldn't see Harrison's ancient, pink, shriveled face because her back was to the lens, but her shoulders were tense below her short-cropped white hair. Sorreno, facing the sensorcam, was about to go supernova. Her brown cheeks were beet-red, her mouth an angry slash, and I saw the whites of her eyes. I wished for the nth time that the RCPD office sensorcams had sound.

Doctor Angel Smith was in the same meeting. She stood in the back corner of Chief Harrison's office, getting as small as possible. Or maybe trying to merge her spine with the crack where the two walls met. Her eyes were on Chief Harrison.

Codebreaker Martin Ho was in the lunch room, not eating a large bowl of beans and rice. Dark bags around his eyes made a mask of his pale face, and I wondered if he'd been sleeping. While his expression was lax, I knew he was brooding by the way he rubbed his palms repeatedly over his pants beneath the table. The lunch room sensors had sound, but all I heard was the mainfeed on the back wall jammering about how pro-Inclusion Act Operators and their allies had broken the windows of the Federal Housing Authority, and how the radicals from Red City Secede were trying to aid them. Which of course had the protesting Ops scattering as fast as possible because no one wants to be associated with the RCS's conspiracy-laden, nationalism-fueled, who-needs-long-term-planning approach to breaking Red City off from the Federal Banking Worlds, even from ten light years away and wearing a hazardsuit—Yeah, things weren't getting any better for the city.

Inspector Rolland Zi was in his office. He looked happy. He was reading something on his 3V that I couldn't see from my angle. I might be able to change my angle though, if I could get my mind into the sensorcam's motors and turn the device a little. The cam didn't need move a lot, not enough that Zi or the folks at Central Security who monitored the feeds would notice.

Sanitation Worker Jaali Henri was cleaning something revolting off his hands in the locker room, which was the only place in the morgue with a permanent sensorcam. I squinted my interior vision to keep my focus on Jaali without processing whatever was on his hands. The lens quality was poor, the camera out of focus, and the angle was bad. Still, despite the noise, there was something familiar about Jaali.

I split my consciousness four-way.

Chief Harrison's Office:

Sorreno leaned forward, opened her mouth as if to speak, but then closed it and shook her head. I opened a mouth-reading program and shoved as much of the situation's context as I could into its inputs: the setting, everything I knew about the people involved, the level of anxiety plain in everyone's demeanors, etc. There isn't enough information in mouth gestures alone to convert the movements into words; context is required even for skilled mouth-readers. Which didn't include me. So I'd bought this expensive program from All Eyes Corp—"Outfitting PIs Galaxy Wide!"—when I'd first set up shop. Credit well spent, that.

"I—I don't have anything to add," the program told me Angel said. Angel's body read a blind panic and she almost lost her grip on the corner of the wall.

Chief Harrison spoke then, her head bobbing, her words lost to me since her face was out of sight.

Sorreno stayed silent, hands white around that fused glass locket she fiddled with when stressing or thinking. Her short, sharp breaths changed as she modulated her breath, trying to stay calm.

Sorreno's temper was legendary in the office. It took a lot to provoke, but once someone did, it was like a levee breaking. She'd destroyed furniture with her fists, and made more than one hardened criminal piss their pants and confess.

But, for now, she remained still, the whole room suspended in tension.

RCPD Cafeteria:

Martin continued to not eat his lunch and to rub his hands along the tops of his pants, just like Socialization said he shouldn't. His eyes were unfocused and I wondered what he was seeing behind them. Was he focused mostly in his workspace in his imagination, resentful as I had once been of being dragged from codebreaking to the cafeteria? Was he in the Mem, meeting with someone, pulling data, cooking up more evidence against me? Was he just thinking deeply, or perhaps taking a break from thinking at all?

Uncertainty rattled me as I realized how little I really knew Martin. We'd worked together for almost ten years at the RCPD, but all we'd ever done was feint against each other's shields. I knew where he lived, where he worked, that he had chosen to remain owned by the RCPD rather than apply for an Integration job. But those, and the other things I knew, were just surface details, not keys to a person's heart at all. I knew people liked Martin; he was always surrounded by cronies.

But who were those cronies?

Who was Martin Ho, really?

I didn't even know what he liked to do, other than get as many accolades for as little effort as possible and attempt to get me in trouble. Did he have a hobby, an interest? Why had I never asked or investigated?

I shifted uneasily just as Martin did the same.

He lifted a fist to his face and bit it. When the hand came away, I saw little bloody toothmarks. He'd have to hide that; it would get him Socialization demerits.

Finally getting me in trouble should have made him happy. But he was in terrible distress. What had I said to Martin in the Rose and Thorn, when he'd tried to pop my imaginary head off with his imaginary hands?

Speaking of unlikely best buds, I had said to Martin in the club, *what's going on with you and Inspector Zi of 'Operators have no souls' fame? You haven't turned Effram Caper, have you Martin, turning on and turning in your own kind?*

That's when he'd tried to strangle me.

Inspector Zi's Office:

Zi continued to look happy.

I transferred my awareness on that thread into the electricity that flowed through the camera's mechanics.

Perceiving through the city's eyes and ears and gyros and infras and other sensors didn't take any effort on my part. I experienced through them, by some artifact of my buggy navis, the same way I sensed through my own eyes, ears, propioception, through my human senses, as though in some way I was the city. In fact, the senses of the city were easier to manage than organs of my own body at times, as the city's sensors weren't scrambled and cross-wired by a so-called defect of human genetics.

But flipping that relationship I had with the sensors from passive perception to physical action—manipulating the data to shoot a command through the wireless channels and make the sensor move—that took a lot of effort. No casual signal sent to the sensor through my navis, as I would have done through the Mem, this was more like a ghost trying to turn a thin leaf of paper and read the next page of an ancient text. Or like shouting the command loud enough to be heard by someone a kilometer away. I collected as much awareness as I could out of my other threads, making this one primary, and readied myself for the push.

Morgue Locker Room:

Jaali continued to wash up. And continued to look familiar.

I fed the visual of him into my memory index, gently invoking a background program to assist with the search. Something familiar meant something I had experienced, meant something recorded in my memory. Meant soon I'd have the answer.

Chief Harrison's Office:

The mouth-reading program supplied the words in expressionless deadpan, but I knew Sorreno well enough to color the tone myself. "I have enough to do without this shit," Sorreno snarled. "And you know I do too. And you know it's shit too! A steaming-fucking-pile of steaming-fucking-shit."

One of Sorreno's hands came off her locket to hit the siliplas chair so hard stress fractures formed on the chair arm.

Angel flinched, and found herself unable to achieve any more one-ness with the crack in the wall without removing her spine.

Chief Harrison's head bobbed with invisible speech.

"Then I think we're done here." Sorreno rose and stormed out, very fast, likely in an effort to avoid further damage to Harrison's furniture. I wanted to split a thread to follow her but was maxed out already on what I could handle at once and still move Zi's sensorcam.

Angel continued to cringe in the corner.

Chief Harrison's head bobbed.

"No sir, no I don't agree with the Inspector," Angel quivered.

Cafeteria:

After eating a few lackluster bites of beans and rice, Martin checked carefully to make sure no one was watching him. Then he dumped the tray into the reclaimer. He didn't go back to his cube however; he sat back down at the table and resumed rubbing his pants.

Inspector Zi's Office:

The mechanical parts of the sensorcam weren't sophisticated. Attached to the wall with a super-static field, the thing had a ball joint where the sensor's glassy eye attached to the stem of the mount. The joint could be manipulated by hand, but I couldn't do that—I wasn't there. So moving it meant sending the right signals into the sensor's little brain to ask it to rotate a few degrees on that ball joint. All the RCPD sensors were rigged to be remotely controlled by Central Security in the event of emergency. So I simply had to send the same signals that the folks at Central would have if they wanted to grab a different angle.

This would have been trivial given my RCPD access codes if I were in the Mem proper, not ghosting through the mysterious sensor bug in my head. But I wasn't in the Mem proper. So I had to gather my will.

I cut my sense of vision through the camera and waited until I felt the information moving through it like sunlight on skin. Warm. Almost subliminal. And more—a tingle, the barest hush of electricity. Electrons moving in and out, made detectable through the mystery bug in my navis. And there, beneath, a hum, a breath, that which I needed to connect with. I made the idio for the command solid so I could send it to my neurotranslator and turn it into machine language when the time was right. When I was ready to push it into that layer beneath and change the flow of those electrons signaling in and out. Green and gold rotating geometries and a coppery smell/taste/sound. A subtle prickle.

I began counting from thirty to one.

Morgue Locker Room:

Jaali changed out of his sanitary coveralls and into his street clothes.

I cut the Jaali thread entirely to focus on the more resources on the sensorcam move.

In the background, my automated memory index search continued. What was familiar about Jaali?

Chief Harrison's Office:

"I think you're wise to have us exercise caution," Angel said.

Chief Harrison's head bobbed, and her hand shot out with a digipage that went into the view of the sensor lens: a flier with my face on it. WANTED, it read. ALIVE. And included the flattened image of what my citizen ID looks like if you only experience it as a visual. Apparently my capture was worth 500c's. Well, now I knew what the topic of conversation had been.

Nice that they still wanted me alive.

Angel swallowed. And then, with skill I never knew she possessed, lied through her teeth: "I'm sorry, I can't do anything else to help you locate her. I don't know her well. I don't know anything about where she'd go for safety. I don't even know where she goes for fun. We didn't keep in touch after she left."

That was a big risk for Angel. Any search through city sensor archives, or rudimentary cross-reference of purchase histories, would instantly betray that lie. Angel and I had been going on our not-dates at least once a month since I'd left, and we'd never been secretive about it.

"Sorry. I wish I could help." Angel's big blue eyes remained steady on Chief Harrison as she lied.

Harrison's head bobbled.

Angel detached herself from the wall and fled the room.

I reallocated that thread as well to moving the camera in Zi's office. Leaving only—

Martin: Pulled something small out of his pocket and fussed with it, shooting nervous glances at the entrance to the lunch room.

Inspector Zi's sensorcam: Three. Two. One.

Translate the green-gold-coppery command to machine-speak, feel the layer, feel the signal, feel the data all around.

Zero.

PUSH

PUSH.

PUSH!

Jaali Henri walked into the lunch room, and sat down in front of Martin.

Martin: "You're late."

Jaali: "Fuck you, retard."

Martin's face twisted with hate and anger. "Here's your fucking shit." He pushed his closed fist across the table toward Jaali.

A snarl of a smile twisted Jaali's mouth. "Good thing too, k-dromer."

Martin's fist uncurled to reveal a data slip.

I added Jaali's voice patterns to my search.

Memory index hit, Jaali Henri pattern-match: yesterday, 20:26 local, Husson District. Body-shape and vocal patterns a perfect match for the authoritative-sounding goon who'd almost sliced me in half with a litegun at the Serenity tube station. Oh fuck.

Inspector Zi's stationary system: A report on data loss through the communications hubs around Cleopatra Square—right where Casidy had showed me his black holes in the Mem, right where Blu Lou's Dragon Lines crossed, and right where Bosco's dealers had dropped off Luzzie's NQ. In the top left of the report was an image of me. Beneath, my visual citizen ID again plus the flat representation of my coding patterns—those shapes and sounds as unique to an individual Operator's presence on the Mem as DNA is in the physical world.

I could see how Casidy's black holes could look like someone stealing data. Data was disappearing. It was just that no one but me seemed to have noticed the fact: it wasn't specific data missing but specific communication devices losing data. If the RCPD Ops could get their heads off me for a moment, they might realize a person stealing data, and a software or hardware malfunction in a particular hub, had the same symptoms despite their very different diseases. It was a matter of perspective.

The report showed the main beneficiary of the data syphon I'd supposedly been running to be none other than Hank Roccini and his low-level gang of thugs. So, put the circumstantial evidence of me and Hank Roccini in the bar together with my slip-up on the closed case, and then connect that with the very real missing data and—Oh. Fuck.

◆   ◆   ◆

Shock snapped the threads back into unity, then I split them again to re-locate Angel and Sorreno.

Angel had gone back to the morgue and gotten back to work. Her hands shook just a little as she picked up her sonic scalpel.

Sorreno's mouth was in full view of the dispatch office sensorcam when I found her on the chaotic first level of the RCPD. "De-prioritize the search on Hoshi Archer to theta 4," she snapped at a young man with a red beard, and my mouth-reading program translated. "Reallocate the resources to city peacekeeping. And if anyone gives you any shit, send them to me! I'm full of nothing but shit today apparently, at least according to the Chief."

The dispatch officer startled but nodded and flicked his eyes quickly across his 3V display, carrying out the orders.

"Give the poor girl a fighting chance," Sorreno muttered just as her face turned away from the cameras, and she stomped back to her office.

◆ ◆ ◆

I withdrew all my threads of consciousness from the city's sensor network, and blinked my eyes open to Kelvin's living room. The light was almost gone from behind the blinds and I needed to pee like madness.

Angel and Sorreno were taking big risks to keep me from getting caught.

And Jaali Henri was definitely more than just a morgue sanitation worker.

And I was definitely drawing closer to the center of a trap. A trap for what, though? To use me in an Operator smear campaign? Or was I part of the trap's mechanism? Or its bait?

Regardless, I now knew exactly what the RCPD thought I'd done—steal data for the Roccini Gang—and that was extremely helpful.

And regardless of all that, and the oh fuck-ness of what I'd just learned, it was time to meet Luzzie Vai again to finish establishing my new identity.

◆ ◆ ◆

Luzzie gave me a small box containing a new Citizen ID chip and a set of directions. The first of which sent me off to a black market surgery. The surgery didn't look at all like the way such places were shown in the holos. It was very modern and very clean, and had a full staff, none of whom possessed any body parts that hadn't originally belonged to them. Doctor Mike, who performed my surgery, possessed a current and legitimate medical license. He had never performed extreme biological experiments on unwilling subjects in a hidden underground lab. As far as I knew, he had never had a diabolical plan to rule the world—or at least never acted on it.

Instead, he was a kind older gentleman, semi-retired, who just happened to direct a clinic that was supported, in part, by the benevolence of Her Eminence Regina, Godmother to All Red City and Supreme Leader of Local Organized Crime.

Luzzie could have sent me almost anywhere that could keep a secret. I wondered if he'd sent me to a syndicate shop because he wanted me to have the best service—or because he wanted to maximize my level of criminal involvement. Sure, I talked to the syndicate all the time, but that wasn't the same as accepting illicit services from them.

Doctor Mike injected my face with nanobots and smart tattoos, cut the webbing of my right thumb and removed my citizen ID chip, and replaced it with the new one Luzzie had tweaked—all in less than five minutes. He'd clearly had a lot of practice.

I'd had that chip in me since they'd cut my umbilical, and even though it wasn't really a part of me, it sort of was a part of me. I stifled my horror by reassuring myself I'd saved a copy of my real citizen ID safely in both my meat and machine memories, so I hadn't really just lost who I was.

"You want this?" Doctor Mike swung a baggie too close to my eyes. I leaned back to focus on the minuscule bit of metal and the dab of my blood it contained.

"Of course I want it," I snapped and snatched my real citizen ID chip out of his fingers. "I'm not planning to be this, this, this…" I opened a shortwave channel to the new chip so I could read my own name, "Nicholas Foo person for any longer than necessary!" Then I looked in the mirror and saw what I would have looked like had I been born a man. The nanobots and tats had thinned my lips, given me an adam's apple, bushed-out my eyebrows, and otherwise subtly gender-swapped me. Somehow that was not remotely as disturbing as losing my CID.

The doctor shrugged and turned his white coat to me, meticulously cleaning his tools. "You want me to take a look at the rest of you, gratis?" he asked without turning around.

I hadn't wanted Angel to look at me, but for some reason didn't mind this anonymous gangster doing it. Thank goodness a weekly visit to a Socialization Specialist wasn't part of my Integration plan at the IO; they'd write a paper on why I felt more comfortable accepting help from strange criminals than flirtatious friends. I shrugged, forgetting that he couldn't see me.

"You want, jo?" Doctor Mike turned and repeated.

"Sure," I said. "So far I've got myself held together on self-admined first aid and spit."

The old man smiled faintly, with as much enthusiasm as my poor attempt at levity deserved. He removed the synthskin from my face and gently did stuff I couldn't see. Then he had me strip and looked me over, applying various creams and sprays and patches. Finally, after smoothing new synthskin over my cheek, he tried—and failed—to force eye contact with me. In the paternal tone of mobsters through the ages, he patted my shoulder and said, "You did a good job with your first aid and spit. No infection, healing well. But you could've used some professional work on your face there. There's gonna be a scar. Some cosmo work'll remove it for you; you want that done, you come back to Doctor Mike, you hear? Gratis for any friend of the family."

I nodded and wondered if we were done.

He narrowed his eyes and arched his brows. "Or, you could leave the scar. Scar'll make you look a little tough, jo? Tough is good for a private dick." He rocked back, very satisfied.

I didn't know when I'd become a "friend" of the Red City Syndicate—nor did I know why the appellation pleased me, given the trouble I was in—but I let it go. It was just the rules of the mob to be ever-so-polite right up until someone lost an eye, or an ear, or a life.

"Thanks," I answered simply, gingerly touching the surface of the fresh dressing. There was a lot less hurt and itch than there had been. "Thanks," I said again and meant it.

I was ten steps deeper in real trouble than I had been. But the fake trouble continued to concern me much more. I'd deal with my identity theft later.

CHAPTER 19

The first thing I did as Nicholas Foo was spend credit.

I went down to the Shirring Point docks and nervously tried to blend with the other hundred dock hands working the unfashionable end of the waterfront. The hands who were any good supposedly worked in the Pier District. Not that the people who consumed the sea's bounty deeper in the city knew or cared which end of the waterfront their fish came from, but it was a major status thing for the workers. Some bragged they were tough enough to be a Shirring Point hand and those Pier-folk were yellows. Others longed to "get outta t'guts" and explore the greener pastures a few kilos away on "t'other docks."

I'd spent a lot of time slouching around both ends of Red City's waterfront just because I loved the bustle and boats and salty air. What better way to spend a bout of early morning insomnia? Truthfully, I could find no detectable difference between Pier and Shirring Point as far as the fishing trade went, other than that the Shirring boats carted a tad more mystery-crates, especially after dark.

I went to the little market on Pier 7 because I'd been there before and had spoken with the folks who ran it, a brother and sister who'd inherited the family business. I needed to test my disguise on something other than strangers in a crowd. The little market was named "Jessie's" for reasons I'd never gotten straight—sis said it was named for their grandma; bro that it came from Jessie Mach, the oceanographer with the first settlers on the *Cleopatra*; and the dad, before he'd died, had said it was the name of a famous robber from Earth's deep past. My credit was on all three stories being the truth.

"Two whole brassfish!" I proclaimed at the counter, the nanobots in my throat making the sound come out in a hearty baritone I had not been expecting. Bonus that, though I had my escape route all picked out if the disguise failed and the sibs decided to call in the bounty.

The sister looked at me hard with a trying-to-place-you face. I took a glance toward the door already three steps down that escape route in my mind. Then she must've figured me for a dock hand who'd ventured in before, because the look turned into the polite, glassy distance of employee-customer relations.

I waved the webbing of my shaking thumb, Nicholas Foo's ident embedded in it, over the credit plate and walked out with my bag of fish.

The next thing I did as Nicholas Foo, now that I knew the ident would pass a credit scan, was something Nicholas Foo wasn't supposed to be able to do at all. I found an opening in the Shirring blackout zones, engaged the non-Op franca Luzzie had included in my fraud starter pack, and pushed my mind into the Mem with all the relief of a papper who hadn't had access to her drugs for a week. I think the only reason I hadn't cracked over not having Mem access was because I could still connect to the city through her sensors. And because I knew I could count on Luzzie for a fast and functional, if no frills, alternative route.

I didn't do anything useful, just ran a basic query to Red City Public to get a weather forecast for tomorrow (same as for today, naturally, with slight wind variations that mattered only to sailors and dock hands), purchased a few random songs from All Worlds Music just to test my credit line Memside (because Hoshi Archer never purchases music, so it seemed safe), and avoided going anywhere that anyone who knew me might be. Because as good as Luzzie's fake ID was, and as 2-D and generically-man-shaped as I looked in this normie franca that denied me full sensory on the Mem, there was no way to truly disguise my coding patterns. Anyone who knew me would, well, know me, if they just looked hard enough.

I also ran a query to Nicholas Foo's citizen ID account at the Federal

Bank to get the facts of where I lived (a boarding house on Wasco), where I'd come from (a forgettable and unpleasant area near the space port), and what my credit balance actually held (40 c's—made sense for a poor dockhand but wasn't going to get me far in real life).

My citizen ID account also told me I was out on medical after an accident with a hookcrane, injuries consistent with the more evident of my real injuries. Luzzie must've added that detail after my encounter with Doctor Mike, which was both creepy and clever. At any rate, the medical was a good thing as I didn't know the first thing about how to unload and gut fish, and I certainly didn't need Workman Corp after me, trying to chase down a rogue employee. All in all, very tidy. Unlikely to hold up for more than a week given how much I'd need to access the Mem, but a week was longer than I'd need. Hopefully.

I went back to Kel's for dinner, which is the only place I still felt marginally safe.

"Arg me matey!" I opened the door to Kel's apartment, holding the sack of brassfish up and slipping into pirate mode. "Brought ye fruits of t'briny deep!"

Kelvin came out of the kitchen drying his hands. He wore his "good" outfit, a black kilt with a faint paisley design, and a crisp white shirt with a tall collar—kept clean only by virtue of the long grey coat with the large lapels that went over the whole affair. Not the latest in fashion from the Diamond District, but with his broad shoulders and corded muscles, Kel could clean up pretty nice. He still wore the round black sunglasses and zinc face paint that protected his pallor from Cadmus' afternoon light.

"Wow," I dropped the pirate voice, "you really did go see a man about a sculpture! Landing Day best and all." Then I waved the stinky fish-sack in the air again and returned to pirate-mode, "Arg! Fishies!"

Out of proper pirate character, Kel gave me a twice-over too. "And you really did get yourself a new job, gutter's cap and sex change and all." Then with a huge grin and a pirate swagger he reached for the parcel. "Ahoy! Fishies!

Thar be feasting here tonight, me matey!"

It was at that exact moment the alarm went off in my head, freezing my nervous system entirely for a few milisecs so there was no way possible, no matter how distracted, for me to ignore it.

The pre-processing on the ghastly pseudo-code was done.

I dropped the bag of fish before Kel's hand reached it and sat down hard on the sofa. My voice came out with monotone flatness as I began rerouting resources elsewhere. "How long till dinner?"

Kel shrugged. "Why? You think of something important about your case? About an hour maybe? You got me fishies with heads and spines and stuff, so it's gonna take a bit. You know they'll fillet the fishies for free at the market, don't you?"

But my mind was already sinking into the data. "I'll come back in an hour," my mouth and throat said tonelessly from afar.

I stood in the annex to my workspace in my imagination where I'd been processing the painted pseudo-code all this long time. Shapes and sounds and textures and subtle pressures and motions slipping in all directions, and the taste of steel with peaches in the sun, and other, more ambiguous sensations enveloped me. I was experiencing the most likely reconstruction of the idioglossia of multi-dimensional quantum code, based on the flat visual representation that had been painted on the murder victims' bodies. It most certainly was true code. And I most certainly could break it.

The irony of me being an Operator is that I'm not good at programming. I mean, I can do it, obviously. But compared to others who test at my same level of ability—well, "not living up to potential" was the mantra of my educational evaluations.

What non-Ops just don't get is that we're people, like them, as varied as they are. Being a good orator does not automatically make one a capable politician, an actor, or a priest. There are a lot of factors that make up a person, too many to program even on a quantum machine; which is why there's no such thing as true AI and there never will be. And that's been proven, mathematically.

I hadn't gotten my position as senior code breaker for the RCPD because I was a good programmer or a skilled cryptographer. Trinity knows, I'm neither. It was because of what I am good at: making connections between very large quantities of disparate objects related to a particular crime. Code involved in corporate espionage had different shapes than drug running; over time I knew the "flavor" of crypto favored by one syndicate crew or another, or by a particular rone Operator and their line of protégés. Code breaking for me was all about the big picture.

Because what I really am good at is being a detective. That's why I could break code Martin couldn't, even though Martin aced his evals with glowing kudos. My breaks took four times longer than his, and my solutions were as inelegant as possible to get while still being correct. But I learned a lot about the mind that made the code, and those insights were sometimes what led to the arrest of the Op who created it. And that, too, was something Martin couldn't do.

It had taken five days for me to pre-process the ghastly pseudo-code, to take it from flat visual to full sensory. Five long days with the pre-processing running in the background whenever I'd had spare spins for it, including while I slept. Because even with the pseudo-infinite simultaneous real-time calculations a quantum processor can make, reconstructing code was on the edges of impossible.

Think of it like this: I make a two-dimensional print of my hand on a digipage. Then I give the digipage to someone else and ask them to reconstruct an exact replica of my hand in three dimensions. Even knowing in general what a hand looks like, most of the data is missing: what is the back of the hand like, exactly? Is it hairy or smooth? Wrinkly or young? How big are the pores? Does it have freckles? How thick is each knuckle, how deeply set the nails? What is the pigment of the skin? And so on.

Some of the missing information will never be recovered. But some can be calculated in other ways, by analyzing the pressure of the print, by comparing the partial information with more complete data on record, by using stochastic functions to narrow the probabilities of unknown features given the characteristics of the known, etcetera.

That's what I'd been doing to the code all these days since Sorreno and Angel showed me the bodies of the victims. I'd been trying to reconstruct what it might have been like in four-five-six-seven-N-dimensional space.

But the long wait was over, and as soon as I saw, heard, tasted, touched, smelled, experienced that reconstruction, I knew it wasn't going to take any time at all to break.

This code wasn't created by one person. Each victim must have been looped into 3V plates while their own thoughts were painted onto their flesh. They had most certainly created these programs and willingly displayed them before they'd been drugged with the NQ. The code from Nessa's body had the feel of her all through it. And I knew for a fact that Claudia's body had been covered with Claudia's programming.

♦ ♦ ♦

Memory replay, five years ago.

Flash-forward past the sex.

Rewind.... No.

Flash-forward.

"What's yours look like?" Claudia, her voice in my mind through a private channel on the infrared.

"I think you just got a good look," me, chuckling.

"No silly!" Claudia rolled over onto my belly and chest in the physical world, the weight of her comforting and exciting. The lavender in her shampoo and the fine mist of her clean sweat filled me as I laced my fingers in her short, coarse hair.

"I mean your idio," Claudia clarified, our francas sitting apart from each other in the private Memspace we shared. "This is what a *while* loop looks like to me, what about you?"

Showing someone your idio isn't forbidden. It simply isn't done. An Operator guards their idioglossia, even of basic programming constructs like a *while* loop, in the same fortress of thought as their deepest personal secrets.

"You trust..." I whispered aloud in the physical world, but all of Claudia's attention was fixed in our shared space in the aether.

Even if idio wasn't the key to modern encryption—and a reminder none of us would ever be truly understood—the shape of someone's thoughts could betray a lot about them.

Trust.

A radiation of light and gentle humming emerged in the center of our shared space; the edges curled delicately inward, creating a loose cup. Then it began to rotate with the tinkling of chimes and a cool sensation flowed over me of gold and lemons in the complex synaesthesia of the Mem's programming language. I stepped toward it, entranced, reaching out a hand to touch its soft fur.

"The *while* loop is my favorite," Claudia purred, the emotives in her cat-like franca radiating pleasure and satisfaction. "I love its symmetry, and the delicate power of recursion it contains. While X is happening, do Y. No programming language would be Turing-complete without it."

I hugged her body tightly to mine in the flesh, and she responded, nuzzling my neck and hair.

"What's *while* like to you?" Claudia prompted again in the Mem, where we sat apart.

"Not like that," I laughed nervously, as embarrassed by my own clunky conceptualization of a *while* loop as I was awed by the elegance of hers.

"Come on, show me, I'm sure it's as cute as you are!"

But I didn't show her. Was it because of envy? Embarrassment? Lack of trust? Fear she'd laugh at me?

She had rolled off of me after I'd evaded. She'd cleaned up, dressed up, and taken me out to dinner. But the incident was one of many in a long string of small things I'd done to kill our relationship.

Oh Claudia, if I had been more responsive, would you still be alive today?

I shook my head.

Focus, Hoshi.

The paintings on Claudia's corpse included a few instances of her beautiful *while* loop. Its delicate light gave a me Rosetta stone with which to untangle the program.

I transmuted Claudia's lovely *whiles* into my ugly ones and started on the rest of the crack. Claudia's code yielded to me immediately. The other two were almost as easy.

When alarm programming triggered me to stop for dinner, I found my face stiff with dried tears that must have come with the Claudia memories. And the rest of me baffled by what I'd put together.

"It doesn't make any sense," I complained as Kelvin shoveled an unreasonable amount of brassfish and vegetables onto my plate.

"Of course it makes sense, you just haven't explained it to yourself yet."

"But—"

"Tell me about it."

"But—"

"Hoshi!" Kelvin sat in front of his plate of food and half-glared at me. "You're getting lost in the minutiae and insecurity of all the programming stuff, just like you always do with code. Don't think of it as code. Think of it as clues on a case." He paused, forcing me to process all of his words. "Big-picture it for me."

I took a few breaths, waiting for linguistics to translate. "The code is exceptional. In all three cases. It's some of the most beautiful idio I've ever seen, seriously. And I saw a lot when I was owned by the RCPD."

Kelvin nodded, eating. He nodded at my plate too.

I took a small bite, having trouble concentrating on the chewing and the explaining at the same time. "But the code doesn't do anything. It doesn't, well, work. I mean, it works in the sense it doesn't produce errors, it will run. But it wouldn't do anything if I ran it."

"Have you tried to run it?"

"Trinity, no! What if I missed something or translated wrong into my idio and it went malicious in my head!"

"You can run it on the stationary in the loft."

"Thanks, but I want to know a little more before I take the risk." In a delayed reaction, I realized the brassfish was delicious. I bent over my plate.

After I'd eaten a fair amount, Kelvin prompted, "So, pretend you didn't miss anything. What would happen if you ran the code?"

I shrugged. "Nothing. Nothing would happen. Claudia's code is just a recursive framework, a series of loops and conditionals without any variables involved. There's no data to process through those loops and conditionals. They're intricate and beautiful, but..." I had nothing more to say, so I trailed off and played with my food.

Kelvin couldn't understand quantum code but his archaic programs used many of the same concepts as mine. "So that's Claudia. What about the others?"

"Aysha's code is the opposite of Claudia's in a way. Still some of the most beautiful idio I've ever experienced, but other than being syntactically correct, it doesn't have any logical structure or function at all. Like the mathematical equivalent of nonsense poetry. Like that 'Perl Poetry' stuff you tried to get me interested in when we were kids." I lost perception of Kelvin and my dinner as I focused in my workspace on the whirling, tinkling mass that held no center.

A dinging scraping screech raked my attention back to the flesh. Kelvin's fork scraped over his almost empty plate; my audio filters had dropped again.

Kel noticed my wince and stopped the scraping, squeezing my hand in apology. He pointed to my not-as-empty plate. "Might want to catch up with me."

I took some more time to eat.

After a while Kelvin asked gently, "So what about the third bit of code? Nessa's? What's it like?"

I swallowed water and glanced in my head at regimented lattices of intricately woven sensation. "Nessa's code is very different again. It's structural like Claudia's, but sensory-pattern structural." I stopped, trying and failing to find a way to describe what I was experiencing. This was the type of stuff that didn't have an analogue in the kind of programming Kelvin could understand. "Think of putting together a programmed environment, starting with the physics, the colors, what constitutes up and down, how loud sound can be played in the space, who is allowed to enter the space, stuff like that. Only about 5000 times more complicated and not amenable to being described in words." That was my best shot.

Kelvin nodded. "You mean the code to set up the allowable patterns for a Memspace?"

"Yeah. Yeah, that's a pretty good way of putting it. A little simple, but—"

"Well, what sort of patterns does it allow?"

"That's the trouble," I frowned at the head of the brassfish on my plate, its round dead eye staring up at me. "It's like it allows everything. Every kind of pattern. Like it's an attempt to encode maximal freedom while still retaining a programmable structure."

When I broke my stare with the brassfish, Kelvin was looking at me curiously. "You don't see it?"

"See what?"

"Think like a detective Hoshi, not like a programmer." Kelvin laughed, shaking his shaggy straw-colored head in disbelief. "I can't believe I just had to say that to you!"

My mouth formed a round "O" of eureka long before linguistics found a way to form it into words. In my workspace, I was overlapping the three bits of code, transmuting them into my own idio to work with them, weaving them together. The pieces fit. Of course they fit! And only a few more pieces were missing before I could tell what the program was supposed to do as a whole.

"It's not three programs, it's one!" The words came out of me in a barely intelligible explosion of sound.

Kelvin leaned back from his clean plate, smiling. "Told you you could do it."

Then my body went lax as dread washed the joy of discovery clean away. Kelvin was one step behind me this time, and I watched his mood shift toward concern. I must've gone pale as him. "It's one program. But it isn't a whole program," I finally choked out.

Kel kept looking at me.

"It needs more pieces to become whole. Variables. And, and data."

And then the full impact hit him too.

The dead eye of the brassfish stared at me, like the promise of a nightmare.

"The murderer," Kelvin voiced the really nasty bit I couldn't quite make myself say, "isn't done yet."

I'd said as much to Sorreno days ago, intuition strong that whatever pattern I'd started piecing together wasn't complete. Now I had solid reason to back up that intuition.

"No," I whispered and pushed what was left of my dinner away. "No, the murderer isn't done yet at all."

CHAPTER 20

The sensor cam on the edge of Pier District swung toward Lethe Street, and I set the timer ticking. Seventeen, sixteen, fifteen... waiting, wait for it, now—

Fourth Avenue slipped out of the sensor's eye-line; I pounded toward Third, invisible in my boot-falls.

Slipping into an alley, up a fire escape, across a rooftop, and touching down into the marshy low tide beneath the piers, the exhilaration of the sensor-evasion puzzle had me grinning through my panting.

Only to choke on the rest of my feelings as soon as I stopped moving.

I had not travelled the invisible pathway to Claudia's house in three years, but it still felt fresh as dawn and hurt ten times more than my injuries.

I spat in the mud and kept moving.

Some things were more important than my feelings.

Squishing below the docks to avoid the sensors that ran thick around the packing industry, I pulled myself onto the boardwalks again at First and doubled back around toward my destination at Lethe and Water Ave. I couldn't have been wearing a better disguise to hide from the less-avoidable human eyes; fish gutters milled the area on their way out of or onto a shift.

I crept into another alley to escape a small cam at the intersection with Lincoln, and then I was there.

Like most Operator housing, the outside of Claudia's building wasn't much to look at. Four stories, sided with coarse blackwood concrete, it sported no markings to signify its purpose. That very omission advertised "Operator housing" bright as any holo.

My hands caught the ivies and I climbed the wall through green leaves and twisted branches haunted by the scent of lavender. So many times I had stolen through the city between her sensors, climbed up these ivies, and taken an illicit, delicious laugh and kiss from Claudia.

Three stories up, I turned and looked at Pier District laid out behind me. The delicate silhouettes of the docks formed a lattice with the lights reflecting off the bay. Quaint structures perched on the boardwalks: shopping centers, museums, fishing plants, industrial moorings, the homes of the wealthy. Everything was made of native materials, pussywood, and phoenix oak, and a concrete of ornee shells and indigenous rose quartz glinting in the moonlight. Between the piers, islands of marshland shared space with the city. I knew islands far out toward the open sea where the lories would let me reach out and touch them, and feel the warmth beneath their soft, gray feathers. Shirring had been ruined by the mob, and Landing by the march of progress, but here in Pier, Red City had retained her history.

I fought my attention back around to the matter at hand. I had to deal with Claudia if I was going to solve these murders in time.

The window to Claudia's apartment was latched, but the old sliver of wire I'd stuck in the pussywood molding remained, and I used it to jimmy the latch. Like old times, I was in.

The place smelled of her. Lavender, exotic black teas, a slight soapiness. Even in the near-total dark I could tell it was perfectly tidy, perfectly clean; Claudia never could tolerate a speck of dust. But there was a coldness too, and not just from the dead nannycams, turned off because there was no one left to monitor. Even if I hadn't known Claudia was dead, I would have sensed it by the chill and the still and that undefinable line separating *out for the evening* from *gone for good.*

My fingers fumbled for the tiny, dim lamp Claudia kept by the side of her bed. Claudia had confessed to me she was still scared of the dark. I realized how, like showing me her idio, Claudia's confession had also been a question: what makes you vulnerable, Hoshi? What do you fear?

Well, vulnerability was at the top of that list. I put the little light on the floor and threw a corner of the sheet over it to better hide my silhouette from the window. I wished Claudia had asked me things flat out back then instead of hinting. I wished she'd not let me get away with silence. But I was too foolish to appreciate such questions anyway, so what did it matter.

The question that mattered now was, why had Claudia been one of the victims?

I dropped a bunch of visual filters so I could see better in the dim, and fixated slowly on all the objects in the room versus my memory index, processing both what had changed and what had stayed the same. The first thing that struck me were the architectural models covering every flat surface—tables, chairs, the stand in the bathroom that had once held a vase, everything. Tiny, delicate, most no longer than my arm and so intricate they transcended function and became art—everywhere I saw bridges. Claudia had been building bridges.

Well. That was new.

I ran a quick query to the Mem, after checking my Nicholas Foo disguise remained intact. None of Markovich and Sons' current projects involved artistic bridges.

I risked a cross-reference of Claudia Foucault intersect bridges through public Memspace, but turned up null on that as well.

Had Claudia found a hobby in the physical world?

"If Operators had been meant to be artists, we would have been given better fine motor skills," Claudia's voice proclaimed, haughtily, in my memory. Was it possible for Status Quo Claudia to change? Not by that much.

Inspecting each bridge more closely, I saw they'd been created from strips of folded paper, very expensive stuff. No glue or other means of joining had been applied—they were masterpieces of engineering. I rocked back on my heels, impressed. And even less certain Claudia had made them. I wasn't sure she could achieve that kind of skill even with impressive motor programming.

Something else was afoot.

It was by the bridge on the stand next to the bed that I found the heart and the holo. The heart was coiled up in the bed sheets, the clasp on its delicate golden chain broken. I suspected the necklace had snapped in Claudia's sleep, and she hadn't noticed. She was even more oblivious than most Ops to things in the physical world, her awareness spun fast in abstract contemplation of the mathematics supporting the structure of the world. I smiled in recall of walking through Red City's streets with her, pointing at my favorite buildings.

"How does that one work?" I would ask.

And she would tell me, alight with joy, everything there was to know about what made the building not fall down.

Now as I fingered the little golden heart, I imagined her far from home reaching up a hand to find the necklace and panicking. On its warm surface, a name had been engraved: Secelia.

The holo rested on the carved bloodwood stand beside the bed. I had missed it as an Object of Interest on my first pass because in the whole time I'd known Claudia, a holo of her parents had rested in that honored spot. Even my mind makes mistakes based on assumptions. But now, sitting on the edge of the bed with the broken heart in my hands, it penetrated that the woman in the holo didn't look anything like Claudia's parents.

Her face was beautiful, warm, and kind. Her blue eyes didn't quite go with her black hair and copper skin, but they perfectly matched the blue of her navis across her forehead, and her lips made a mischievous quirk in the five-seconds of loop over the plate.

I smiled back. I was sad Claudia was gone, sure, and regretful I couldn't tell her how sorry I was for missing the clues when we were together. I still loved her; love doesn't go away. But the acute edge I'd been expecting to shred me on entering Claudia's apartment didn't cut like I'd expected. Claudia had moved on. I was happy she'd moved on. I was glad she had found someone—Secilia—to love and who loved her back.

I arranged the necklace around the holo on the bedside table.

"She will be missed," I whispered to the little image of Secilia perpetually smiling. I gave a little bow, hands together, to the empty bed.

Then I looked back at the perfect paper bridge on the bedside table, knowing before I sent the query into the Mem that Secelia intersect bridges would hit me a jackpot.

Claudia could be self-destructive when she was upset, but not if she'd had been in love, and she certainly wasn't a risk-taker. Which told me that when Claudia had gone off to the IO with her bag of tzaddium and other ingredients, she hadn't known the nature of the risk. But why would she be interested in the alien élans? What did Claudia want that she didn't already have? This time the answer wasn't love; whenever Claudia got unhappy with me she'd smush any belongings I'd left behind into the smallest corner of the kitchen. Considering how the bridges had taken over every flat surface, Secilia wasn't on Claudia's shit-list.

I located Secilia's address Memside and sent her a sig, hoping she'd be curious enough about why a normie fishgutter would be contacting her to at least acknowledge.

"I think you have the wrong addy," Secilia started closing the channel before I could explain.

If I'd actually been a normie, that would've worked, but I wasn't and I blasted a complex gob of communication at her at the speed of thought that translated roughly as: I'm from the RCPD investigating Claudia Foucault's death and I'm under cover and I need to ask you some questions and thank you for your time don't tell anyone I was here it's a matter of Police security shhh and here are my RCPD access codes to prove it so go ahead and look them up you'll see.

"Funny way for someone from the RCPD to go undercover." Secilia's emotives read dubious, absorbing and cross-checking my information, but she left the channel open.

I'd just hammered one more nail into the coffin of Nicholas Foo's ID, but the play had worked. No one but Sorreno knew I still had the RCPD access codes. If Sorreno really was on my side, she'd overlook that they'd just dropped into the system. If not, I hoped Sorreno would keep quiet to avoid the trouble she'd be in herself for letting me keep them.

"Thank you for your understanding," I said.

Secilia nodded, emotives sad.

"What can you tell me about Claudia's relationship with the Integration Office?"

To which Secilia's franca got very red in the face and her emotives spewed exasperated, angry, and even more sad. "I told her not to get involved!"

I waited while she cooled herself down.

"Claudia was very anti-Integration, though she respected my wishes to pursue my art."

"You sell your paper sculptures at The Carver's Shoppe gallery in the Diamond District, right?"

"Yes," Secilia's tone was fierce, "and I wouldn't give it up for anything. But it's been really hard." She projected frustration, embarrassment, resolve. "I have so much trouble with the shopping and the cleaning, and it's not like I can ask for help or they'll take away my Integration papers—please don't tell anyone I just said that. Please."

"Don't worry." If only this stupid normie franca had emotives she could see my reassurance without me having to say too much. "I'm not in too dissimilar a position myself." Yeah, that was saying too much.

Secilia sighed and continued, "I told Claudia I would love to go back to Operator housing, petition to share a room with her, but still be able to work as an artist. The law went through in such a rush, no one addressed points like the fact that bonded pairs can't cohabitate if one is Integrated and the other isn't. Claudia decided that meant lobbying for a change to Integration Law."

Claudia into politics? Stranger things had happened... Well, not really.

"Claudia into politics?" Now I was glad Nicholas Foo's normie franca didn't show my feelings. They would have betrayed how well I knew Claudia, and Secilia would have no trouble deducing the rest of my identity.

"No, not really. She wanted things back the way they were. Having housemates move out—because Integration jobs mean private housing—having the house mom start expecting more from her, things she couldn't really manage to do, because these other Operators were succeeding without the extra support. Seeing me struggle with choices between my health and my job, because a lot of us really do need a little extra support. The fact that we couldn't live together because the law's a hasty mess. She didn't want to do the political stuff herself, just get the word out to the powers that Integration Law was creating these sorts of problems. It's a side of the story no one wants to tell. But the more she tried to get the Integration Office interested, the more they ignored her. She got kind of obsessed, actually, started researching how the Cantors on Callisto used their relationship with the élan vitals to sway public opinion about Operators. She thought if she could communicate with one of them she could get it to use the feedback between our species to influence the higher-ups at Integration."

It did make a sort of sense. Claudia never would have taken a risk on her own behalf, but to help someone she loved—Claudia loved with the same passion with which she programmed. And Claudia possessed the same weakness and strength as all us Operators—unrelenting focus on the object of our passion.

I said my thanks to Secilia and left the Mem. I slipped back out through Claudia's window into the night, ivy thick in my hands.

♦ ♦ ♦

Aliens had never been an interest of mine, but now that they connected with a case and the city I couldn't get back to the safety of Kel's fast enough to research. Lying on his awful afghan, I sailed into the Mem.

Callisto Relations, blinked the unassuming holicon in the corner of the "International Portals" section of Red City Public. Callisto's sigil—circles linked together in a continuity, like a three-way infinity symbol made of Borromean rings—floated over the words. Nicholas Foo's citizenship didn't come with international privileges, but I could access anything Callisto had permission to stow locally in Red City's informationsphere.

"Welcome to Callisto Relations," a recording of President Ansari welcomed me, her black hair wound in a ridiculously perfect bun.

I pushed that aside and with it all the rest of the slow normie videos meant to stimulate tourism and private funders while downplaying Callisto's role in almost destroying everything with resonance a few years ago. I made for the "Technical Reports" zone in the back of the shallow space.

Cycling fast through the index: Callisto Facts, Jupiter Facts, Embassy Contacts, Asylum Legal, International Charter Information—

"Cantors and the Ecology of Sentience - How Resonance Works. By Noa Oki, PhD, EL, Freeperson of Callisto, narrated by First Ambassador Camilla Morgan, Cantor." An awkward mouthful that, but it looked promising.

Disappointingly, the report turned out to be another annoying, dumbed-down, normie-centric video—I guess to get the good stuff one would need access to the other side of Callisto's international seawall. I forced myself to watch it because it was still more than I currently knew.

"Imagine a two-way radio tuned halfway to a station," the First Ambassador said, looking like she was twelve years old. She kind of reminded me of Angel with her golden curls, though I knew her to be a willowy meter-sixty from watching her on the mainfeeds.

An image of a quaint twentieth century ham radio tumbled into view. The sound of half-voices half-static—signal and noise—wheezed over the narration. Ambassador Morgan caught the radio in her hands.

"There's a person on the other end you're communicating with, and there's you, and there's this dial that the both of you need to tune in order to be on the same frequency as each other. The radio provides encoding and decoding of the transmission since we can't otherwise sense radio waves." The video illustrated her words in tedious detail, showing another person with another radio, the dial-twisting, the components in between that comprised a basic Shannon-Weaver model of communication: sender-message-encryption-transmission-decryption-message-receiver. And a feedback loop, as the receiver's message in return then influences what the sender says next in the circuit of exchange.

"Now we'll make a few one-to-one replacements."

The person on the other end of the radio turned into a young boy in an impossibly long, dusty coat made of metal with a cup in his hands: the way the élan vital that lived around Ganymede displayed itself to humans. The radio turned into an assortment of rocks and ice and gears and tools and a tinkling structure made of ice.

"Humans and élans communicate via radio waves and other frequencies on the long end of the electromagnetic spectrum, but we don't use a radio for encoding and decoding the signal, nor for tuning the frequency. Instead, the encoding and decoding happens through resonance—a mutual, reciprocal sharing and amplifying of the frequency at which a particular élan has the most affinity. And the way to tune that frequency is, put simply, to engage in thoughts and activities that place your own thinking in a place where it emits EM frequencies most similar to the élan's own."

Morgan stepped into the rocks and ice and gears and hit the icy sculpture with the tools, making an industrial music. The representation of Ganymede perked up, tendrils of its dusty coat radiating out in sine waves.

The animation rippled waves out from Ambassador Morgan as well, until the undulating sine waves met, mingled, mutated, and finally amplified each other until they became one strong, single wave-form between Ganymede and Morgan.

"Once resonance is established, telempathic communication becomes possible. Telempathic links can occur among groupings of humans and élans of any size, as well as between individuals, though the greater the number of entities in the link, the more difficult the resonance is to achieve."

Telempathic communication. I paused the video and sent the query out to the public encyclopedia. "Telempathic communication - The direct mind-to-mind transmission of thoughts and emotions between a human and an élan vital that occurs given sufficient resonance." Then in the fine print: "Telempathic bonds can enable humans to 'psychically' share thoughts and emotions with each other, but as there is no way to remove the élan's influence and own thoughts and feelings from the connection, it is not considered a human psychic ability, of which there remain no validated occurrences."

I hit play on the video and Ambassador Morgan continued, breezing past the oblique reminder of interstellar destruction five years ago, the last time large-scale group resonance occurred. "Facilitating resonance is why Cantors often use rituals to tune their own thinking and enhance communication with an élan vital. This is also why a Cantor does not need to be in possession of a navis—anyone who can find the frequencies and achieve resonance can have a conversation with an élan vital. Of course, the élan also has a say in the matter, and may choose whether or not to participate in conversation."

The image of Ganymede faded out, and Ambassador Morgan stood in the rock and ice and tools radiating sine waves, a sad little smile on her face. "Achieving communicative resonance is easier said than done, even for those of us who have been talking with each other for years. Like those old ham radio operators, it's not possible for either humans or élans to fully see or know who is communicating on the other end of our loop. All we have—for now anyway," she paused for drama, "—is an ever-imperfect dial tuned to a noisy station where we do our best to understand each other despite the noise."

I wished the video was interactive so I could ask questions.

And immediately realized I had another option.

It was a dangerous option, given that Nicholas Foo wouldn't know about it, let alone be able to choose it—but it was also an option that, until today, Hoshi Archer wouldn't have taken either. I hopped into a thick current and flowed to the threshold of Cantor Gno's Temple to Zaos, watching my wake behind me as it imprinted on the Mem and recorded into Nicolas Foo's Bank account. When would I have done enough uncharacteristic—or impossible— things as Nicholas Foo to trigger an alarm in the monitoring AI and rain down a hell of investigation?

"Ident's good for a week," Luzzie had promised, "no matter what you do."

The portal to the Temple shimmered in the fabric of Memspace, nearly invisible. As I passed through, soft sensations enfolded me, cool and welcoming at first. Then, more aggressively, they jutted into me, tendrils I couldn't detect in idio, sensations my flat normie presentation wasn't programmed to feel, impossible, probing, changing, filtering my core through the sieve of an invisible intelligence; I tried to cry out but had no control of my own code—

Just short of violation, the sensations withdrew, and I fell through the portal shivering, as though I'd stuck my finger in an electrical current.

The physical world has its share of temples, fortune-telling shops, and pocket altars to some minor god in the nuevo-pantheism of the modern world, more arts and culture than religion. Even my apartment building had an alcove in its blackstone siding filled with coins, rabbit statues, and a presiding statue of Tyche. Once Lillie had dragged me inside a mainstream temple to Legba, and I'd been engulfed by 3V vevés, shells, bare (and live!) electrical wiring, and hundreds of 2V screens all set on static—the most visible tech I'd ever seen outside Shirring Point or an illicit shop like the Velvet Glove.

None of these compared to Gno's Temple to the Information God Zaos.

The Mem, after all, could realize anything anyone could imagine.

And here someone had imagined information.

Not just the mediums for passing information: holofeeds, sensory inputs, binary code and mathematical symbols. But the information itself that passed through those mediums.

Endless and boundless as the Beryl Sea, information layered on information in infinite regress. Ten million mainfeed broadcasts, on top of ten million different facts about astronomy, on top of ten million ways to represent 2+2=4, on top of ten—

The layers of information were translucent, and wherever my attention fixed, I became aware of information on that layer, everything known about a single category. Ten million ways to compute pi. Ten million images of human suffering. Ten million cultures and sub-cultures, and sub-sub-genres of subcultures that had once existed on ancient Earth. Ten—

It was like seeing the city through all her sensors at once, only without the accompanying overload and nosebleeds.

I nearly derezzed then, feedback from my navis informing me I'd stopped breathing back in the physical world for so long my body had started going faint.

So I scanned the space for something stable, the same way I had focused on the whirls in the table at Rose and Thorn when I'd been trying to avoid becoming fascinated by Gno's presentation. I found, at the center of the vaulted information, Gno. She hovered over the consensual ground on a clear, dark circle, and I anchored my perception on that. The endless information faded and I started to breathe again.

"Hoshi!" Gno's pale veils brightened, waves of smiles and welcomes and Really Big Assurances that my identity was safe enfolding me in her version of an embrace. "I've been expecting you."

I'd learned from Lillie long ago not to ask anyone who talks with élans something dumb like, "Why's that?" or "How did you know it was me! Eeek!

My cover's blown!" So I merely returned the hello with what little passed for expressiveness from Nicholas Foo's presentation, and started in with the questions I'd come for. "Gno, is it possible that there's an élan living around Cassiopeia Prime? I mean, and no one would know about it?"

"Oh, I'm sure there is an élan living around Cassiopeia Prime, what makes you think no one knows about it?"

"Well, I study the city and—"

Gno cut me off with a raised finger and a surround-sound impression of laughter. "Take care your assumptions do not hide that which you need to see."

"Yeah, okay. So I just watched Callisto's normie edu-vid about resonance and is that really all there is to communicating with an élan vital?" If I'd been in my normal presentation my emotives would've been oozing skepticism. "I mean, is that all you do, set up your space here to be stuff Zaos likes, and it shows up and talks to you?"

More surround-sound tinkle-laughs. "It is a lot easier if you are a magnet—already on the frequencies the élan likes, so you don't need any ritual trappings at all. And magnet or not, there are... *other* ways to facilitate things."

"Like what?"

"You want me to give away Callisto's secrets for free?" Gno continued to emit amusement.

So I continued to press the issue. "Why yes, I do. Remember, I'm trying to factor some nasty murders before any more of our people get axed."

Gno sobered. "I know, I know. And you have done nothing to influence the completion of the circuit, have you?"

"I don't know what the circuit is, so it's been a little tricky." I hoped she sensed my anger.

"Okay." She paused, still, perhaps weighing her options and her thoughts. I held my ground, fists on my hips, trying to show I wasn't going to leave here without my answers. "Extreme events help get their attention and create resonance that wouldn't otherwise happen, like riots or murders or really good sex. Also, dramatic gestures or strong emotions from a magnet, shedding one's own blood, extremes of fear or pleasure—like a ping to someone's com, a reminder, 'hey, I'm kinda extra like you, pay attention.' Sometimes even magnets need to do something to catch their élan's attention." Her complicated veils rippled, in a lip-biting sort of way.

I nodded, but kept holding my ground until she gave me something useful.

"Also, élans can inhabit crystal matrix. It has to be cut just right, and works best attached to a navis, but it can make a kind of half-way zone between their world and ours so there's less effort to keep the 'radio' tuned." She paused to see if I was following, even though she hadn't given near enough detail for me to put the information to practical use.

"Do you have crystal matrix attached to your navis?" I asked her.

She responded by not responding.

I pursued a different thread, thinking of the program the victims had been forced to create. "Is there any way programming can influence élans?"

"Yes and no. No more or less than anything else we might do to facilitate resonance. Only less ignorable. To them, I mean. Sometimes anyway."

"Like doing the ritual closer to them?" I'm not sure where that thought came from, but it seemed right.

"Yes," Gno misted nodding sensations, "creating a hospitable environment Memside can be like calling across a room instead of shouting across a canyon. Although programming is also what we use to catch—" She caught herself. "Sorry, some things are Cantor's secrets."

"Anything else you can tell me?"

Gno dimmed and I couldn't tell if she was working with idio or expressing something beyond my ability to grasp. I had impressions of the latter, like she was signaling in a non-standard protocol, but she stopped before I could puzzle it all the way through. Gno's voice rumbled out in multi-frequency, every hair on my body back in the flesh standing on end though I didn't know how that was even possible. "Close the circuit."

"What circuit?"

"Hate or love? Segregation or union? Fear or trust? Hoshi-as-disease or Hoshi-as-cure? Public opinion has yet to swing. Complete the circuit."

"But Blu Lou said not to complete the circuit."

"Blu Lou is of the fear-faction; we are of the daring."

"What is this bloody circuit you keep going on about!"

"I can not travel your road for you," Gno/Zaos hissed and I plummeted back to my body, buzzing with electrical current.

Thanks for nothing, Gno.

I tossed and turned until sleep ate my nightmares.

CHAPTER 21

I woke the next morning at Kelvin's in a surge of adrenaline, thinking it was just another nightmare, eyes opening faster than my programming could initialize and make sense of what I saw. Then the startup subroutines kicked in and there was, not my beloved city through my window, but Lillie sitting cross-legged on the end of Kel's sofa, staring at me.

I cringed, expecting more of the "claw your eyes out" Lillie, but she put her finger to her lips, *hush*.

My mouth moved but no sounds came out; I had no words stored up yet to say. I struggled into a sit.

Lillie handed me a mug of espresso, slightly cold. She smiled weakly in apology for the less than ideal joe.

I relaxed. Seemed she wasn't going to claw my eyes out right now.

Lillie wasn't dressed in the red and blue of her god; she wore plaid pajama bottoms and a worn, over-large green t-shirt. Her frizzy brown hair stuck out as though it were encased in a constant field of static charge, like it always did. I'm not sure it's possible for her kind of hair to do anything else. Her high, full eyebrows and big brown eyes gave her tan face a perpetually surprised look. She held up her hand, showing me an egg-shaped object with prongs jutting from it.

A long wave signal jammer. I opened my mouth again as I tried to open a channel, but of course there was no signal to the Mem.

She nodded toward the coffee, reminding me to drink. Then she peered at me, trying to assess if I was awake enough for words. She frowned a little and sat back, folded her arms, and gave me another moment to pull myself together.

It was Claudia's fault Lillie and I had become friends. Claudia had wanted a Tarot reading. In Red City, people usually see a relationship counsellor when their love-nest comes undone; where Claudia was raised, Tarot readers were the cultural equivalent, and most of them had a medical license. Claudia's cluelessness about the various types of local Tarot readers, however, had resulted in us seeing Lillie, who told us quite clearly that her god Ogun was more interested in armed revolution than mending fences, and were the two of us interested in approaching our relationship from that angle?

That was back before the recent, real revolution; before Operators had rights and anyone realized Santeras like Lillie truly were in communion with non-human intelligences. Lillie had grabbed me by the arm before I could follow Claudia, who was already at the threshold in an embarrassed fluster. Claudia always took everything that didn't go perfectly as new evidence of her many flaws. Which was odd, since as far as I could tell Claudia had no flaws. But, anyway, Lillie had grabbed my arm and stopped me.

"Hoshi Archer," she'd said with deep seriousness, "will you have a cup of coffee with me? Tomorrow maybe? Are you allowed? Will they let you leave your keepers? I would very much like to talk with you about the City."

"What about the City?" I asked, suspicious, while Claudia stood in the doorway with her lips cold and unhappy.

"You love the City, Hoshi Archer. So do I. See here—" From her pocket she pulled out a token from the original tube, back before they installed the sensors to detect people's citizen ID chips. "I think we could be friends. The cards—Ogun tells me that the city thinks we should be friends."

It was the weirdest start to a friendship for even a weirdo like me, but Lillie hadn't been wrong. She was the only person I knew who loved facts about the city as much as I.

Now Lillie, sitting across from me on Kelvin's couch, decided I was awake enough for words. She looked pointedly at the jammer that was preventing me from getting a channel out into the Mem. "I'm fighting with Ogun. It's to keep him out of my mind, not you out of the Mem. Sorry."

I took another haul off the coffee and rubbed my eyes, grumpy. "Trinity, I just got my ability to go Memside back less than twelve hours ago."

And then Lillie burst into tears and threw herself at me in a fierce bear-hug, spilling precious espresso everywhere.

First I had to work through the surprise. Then motor had to figure how to handle the actions I should take. Then I threw my arms around her and held her close, all of which took four-point-five seconds. Good thing Lillie-hugs tend to be long-lasting affairs.

"Trinity!" I cursed into her shoulder, "What's with the tears?"

Lillie pushed away and stood and walked briskly around the room. Then she settled back down on the edge of the couch, sitting on her hands. "I was so worried about you, you little shit! Why didn't you get out of the city? Ogun's been riding me like the world was ending, and I almost wasn't able to rescue you from those cops day before yesterday at the Shirring gates. You're lucky I was there. You've no idea how much trouble you've been causing the city."

The memory of the end of that long flight played back; in replay it was so obviously Lillie's voice distracting the cops. "What were you doing there?" I demanded.

"Shopping! Honest! A few times a week I like to get lopé fruits from Jan Barber, and her booth was near the entrance that day. It was probably the city too, looking out for you. I wanted to do more, but there's so much empathic resonance between Ogun and me, and he keeps riding me, and Ogun—well, he's all about war, he made me come after you in Madame Shane's, he wanted me to—" Lillie started sobbing again.

I chugged the last of my espresso and waited, used to the melodrama of Lillie.

Lillie stopped sobbing. "Sometimes we disagree. Ogun and me."

"I gathered that, yes."

She wiped her face on her knees and smiled. "But enough of that. I'm here to help now. Blu Lou says you have questions. Kel let me in. I didn't want to wake you, but I can't be gone long. My shift starts in thirty minutes."

I took a deep breath, sorting the shapes of the murders in my mental landscape. I had questions indeed. "Did Kel give you any details?"

"Just that it's murders with a ritual component and that you'd say more. But I knew that already. It's what Ogun's been so upset about; someone's trying to corrupt the heart of the city."

"Uh. Sure. But there's some police stuff too." And I shared the ritually-relevant forensics.

"That whisky is really important," Lillie said a good while later. "But the beckerwood brew and the NQ, not so much."

"Not so much!" I scoffed. "Without the NQ the women wouldn't have been killed. At least not by having their navi ripped from their heads."

"No, silly, I'm not talking about important to the police stuff. I'm talking about important to the sorcery."

We had migrated to the floor. I always slip off the furniture given enough time, forcing others down to my level. Countless hours in Socialization had been wasted trying to train me out of the clearly permanent habit. Kelvin's floor was concrete, covered in old, plush carpets woven with traditional Martian designs. I traced my fingers over the semi-geometric patterns in the weaving, making them into a maze.

Lillie proceeded to educate me. "From the sorcery angle, the hallucinogenic beckerwood brew is a basic ingredient, like butter or flour in baking. It's to thin our perception between the material and the electro-magnetic, to open the senses to bandwidths beyond the visible. But your whisky, now that—that whisky is the key!"

That cracking whisky. I poked at the image of it in my internal landscape, a plain brown blown glass bottle, shaped with the no-nonsense pragmatism of the early colonial days. It cost more than 2500c's now: the price of drinking history. "Liquid history," I said aloud, my programming mistaking my thoughts for something worth communicating.

"Liquid history is right," she riffed off my verbal incontinence. "If you want to influence Red City, you've got to find the proper resonances. What better way to resonate with her than to drink her in her past, all rosy and warm?"

"Her?"

Lillie's eyes came open, her expression tired. "Oh Hoshi, don't be obtuse."

I conjured the image of the city seal in my workspace: the Valkyrie towering tall with her trident, one foot on land and one foot in the sea. The tip of her trident pointing toward Sol and the city's motto flowing beneath her: *She flies on her own wings between the stars.* She winked at me. I shivered.

Lillie shrugged, shifting mercurially to transform the uncomfortable silence back to business. "Anyway, the murders. The stuff ground up in the paint has resonant properties with Red City, just like the whisky. The shells from Broadway beach link to the indigenous life on Cassiopeia Prime. The crushed blackstone is what the city is built on and built of. And, as you informed me that first day over coffee, Red City was nearly named Blackstone." Lillie smiled showing her dimples.

In my workspace, I looked at the other things that had been mixed into the paint. "What about the bones, blood, feces, and tzaddium? None of those things have anything to do with Red City."

"No. But they have resonant purposes too. Most are basic ingredients, like the beckerwood brew. The blood and feces—you said they were from the victims themselves, right?"

"Yeah," I traced over the black lines in the warm oranges of the carpet again.

"Blood, poo, spit, bodily fluids—those kinds of things create a bond with the person they came from. In this case, it bound the victim and the paint. It 'juiced' the paint, we Santeras say." Lillie paused and I nodded, filling in information in my head. Lillie continued at my go, "The bone symbolizes the flesh. Very generic ingredient, bone."

"The flesh? As in the opposite of the Mem?" My fingers found the end of the path in the carpet and began to retrace.

Lillie's dramatic brows came together as she frowned with thought. "I hadn't considered it that way, but yeah. I mean, I was thinking of the flesh as in embodiment, mortality, on a personal and human level. But I don't see why it couldn't symbolize the world of matter and all that's in it, generally, as well."

My turn to frown with thought. I had a bit of an idea coming on, but it wasn't fully formed yet. "Let's get back to that. But go on."

"Well, that's basically it. Just need to put it all together into a story. Blackstone and beach-stuff for earth and water, just like the city seal. Whisky for the human element. Add something personal, blood and bone, to bind to a person and you've got yourself a resonance between the person and the city. Mix it in with some paint and you've got a resonance you can draw with."

"But what about the tzaddium?" I asked, fascinated by Lillie's breakdown of symbolism of my beloved city.

Lillie shifted and stretched. "Honestly, I'm not sure." She pulled Kel's nasty old afghan off the futon and wadded it up under her like a cushion.

"Well, I have a thought on that," I said tentatively, the idea formed enough now for communication. "Could it be the Mem counter-part to the bone? If the bone is our physical presence, then the tzaddium is our electronic presence. Do ritual symbols work like that?"

Lillie's demeanor took a u-turn from consideration to enlightenment, and she leaned forward exclaiming, "Yes, that fits! And yes, symbols do work like that. And your victims were all Operators and tzaddium is what makes navi and the Mem possible. The Mem, you know, is the same thing as the spirit world, just seen from the other side of technology's veil."

"So you frequently remind me," I said dryly. My thoughts were mutating with new ways to interpret old facts, and I felt like everything I'd built in my imagination was going to explode if I didn't do some sorting fast; so I tuned out Lillie's spiritualist poetry and turned my awareness inward. Shapes and sounds and textures and smells whirled as the landscape of the murders in my Memside workspace shifted, everything spinning too fast for me to get a fix. I used my navis more heavily to capture the thoughts, to pin them down and hold them in place so I could look at them. Factor which were useful, completed thoughts, and which were just the fragmented byproducts of an earlier stage at attempted understanding.

The physical evidence of the murders was all accounted for now.

The type of paint—Seraphim—was chosen simply to frame poor old Samo Oro, buying the killer time as the RCPD fumbled up the wrong tree.

The contents of the paint—the blackstone, shell, bone, blood, feces, tzaddim—each was chosen to play a ritualistic resonant role.

The drugs found in the victims—the beckerwood brew, the whisky, the NQ—each served a specific purpose too: to open the senses, to enhance resonance, and to disable the victims at the final moment.

The missing spaces of the How filled in. Each woman arrived at the ritual site with their own tzaddium and bodily fluids, paint was mixed, the rite performed. They would strip, perhaps drink the whisky and the beckerwood brew, open a channel to the 3V plates. Create some code, project the visuals out, and wait patiently, half-delirious, while a machine decorated them with their own thoughts. Then they'd take the NQ and the death—

But I was still missing why these particular women, and to what end? Was the murderer a religious fanatic, or just staging the thing in a way that would make religious fanatics take the blame? Whatever it was, I needed to factor fast, so I could have some better idea of who would be next before they actually became next. Especially if it was me.

"Lillie." My programming caused my body to make strange twitching gestures in response how much my next thought disturbed me. "Lillie, tell me a little more about the élan vital of the city."

Lillie stopped the incomprehensible monologue she had continued while my attention was elsewhere and laughed warmly. "I think that should be my question to you, Lady Hoshi of the City."

"Whatever you think I know, I really don't. So lay it out for me. Please."

Lillie sighed and looked at me sideways, half in amusement and half in exasperation. "I can't lay it out for you. I don't know. We're not able to communicate with all of the élans, and even those we can communicate with, some only resonate with certain people. It's complicated. Some can only communicate with us in dreams, in sleep, in intuitions, in revelations, while under the influence of drugs like the beckerwood brew— Hoshi? What's wrong?"

Looking down I saw my hands had gone almost white as Kelvin's. In dreams, in sleep, like the sensorfeeds that overloaded me, my ability to see through the city sensors—What if it wasn't a bug in my programming, the same bug that messed up my auditory filters, after all? "No, nah, nothing," I sputtered weakly, my voice from a distance. "Go on."

"There's nothing else to go on about. For all I love our city, she's never made contact with me. You're the one who's the magnet. I don't know anything more about her."

But I did. I knew, with a sick sensation, the Why of the murders. I knew it with an instinct as sure as the city, as sure as I'd been steered to Bill's Ragtime, as sure as the nosebleeds that plagued me the day after I'd dreamed a hundred thousand sensor feeds. "Lillie, someone who has tried and failed to seize power in the city through normal routes thinks they can get control via resonance with the city's élan. That would work, right? Then that person could draw others into the resonance, change the thinking of the whole city. It would be our own little local version of what happened during the Callisto Revolution, only with a single élan and a single world-view, instead of a bunch of élans and contending world-views so there was some hope of a positive outcome."

Lillie gave me a hard, shrewd stare that I couldn't fully interpret. She nodded once, firmly. "Jo. I think you might be right about that. Take another look at the city, look at it through symbolic eyes. You need to find a way to break that circuit. You need to stop that feedback before it starts." Then her eyes got even bigger and her brows even more surprised and she said, "Oh shit, I'm gonna be late for work," kissed me on the forehead, and ran out the door.

That cursed circuit.

Well, it's not like I didn't have clues. There were Blu Lou's Dragon Lines—and maps of the area's geomagnetism. There was the connection between the area's geomagnetism and the aesthetic of Feng Shui practiced by a lot of Red City's architects and city planners. If the killer really was trying to get the attention of a creature attracted to geomagnetism, and bits of the city like sea shells, and important bottles of whiskey, some of these things should line up.

Time for many maps.

I knew all the major city landmarks, of course. It's my city; I love her. I knew every inch of her body, every curve of her land. But I was just learning about her for the first time all over again too, the way one discovers new things about an old lover. Perhaps she whispers a secret about her past, or reveals she shares some odd interest with you; or, maybe it's finding a new special spot on the curve of her breast that makes her sigh. So I was familiar with Liu Tower's cascading fourteen-story waterfall fountains, that sometimes tempted tourists into otherwise residential Hill District. But now I knew the fountains had been built for the poetic purpose of adding "water-balance" to the otherwise dry south-east hills. And I learned that lovely Blackstone Circle, the small but solid park in the Pier District where I often enjoyed a cup of joe, had been designed to provide a stabilizing force amidst the otherwise-chaos of floating platforms, boats, and jetties. Of course I knew about the musical (and controversial) Monument to the Revolution outside Red City University in Husson. But I had not known that it had been carefully placed make use of the "overabundance of wind" that whistled across the plains to the south. And I knew, like anyone who brushes up against the underbelly of the city, that Regina and the Syndicate had carefully maintained an "eternal flame" in the heart of Shirring Point for nearly a century; but I had not realized it was for the purpose of "balancing the yin of water with the yang of power"— presumably to Regina's advantage.

And it was definitely news to me that Cleopatra Square in the center of Lan Qui Park—the dead center of both the city and the Dragon Lines—had been designed by the founders to open a flow to the element of void. I'd never even heard of the element of void. According to the public encyclopedia, "a person attuned to void can sense without senses, think without thoughts, and always perform right action, unerringly, an instrument of the flow of the Universe." I wondered what that meant for the city, if her heart was void.

The fact that Cleopatra Square was also the site for the NQ deal with the Mysterious Vanishing Buyer did not escape me. Cleopatra Square had, in fact, come up a lot over the course of this investigation. Did void allow one to also exist without being seen? Void sounded like a great power for a good guy, but for a murderer—

In my workspace I pulled up a basic map of Red City, superimposed the Dragon Lines, pulled a live-feed map of current geomagnetic activity in the city, and then marked the residences of all three murdered girls.

All three points lay within a ten meters of the Dragon Lines.

All three points also lay in different quadrants of the city. Claudia in Pier in the Northwest. Aysha in Shirring, the Northeast. And Nessa, who lived in Husson District, was near the Dragon Line to the Southwest. Which, if it were a pattern, meant we were missing someone in Hill District along the Southeast tail of the Lines. I plunked my own apartment building down on the map.

My building was near the southeast tail of the Dragon Line, but not like the others. It was about half a kilometer too far to the east.

Still, there was a pattern, and maybe half a kilometer didn't matter in terms of rituals and resonances. The human-élan psychic radio, First Ambassador Morgan had noted, was noisy.

But—back to associations and the circuit.

Four elements, four arms of the Dragon Lines, four components of a program, four quadrants of the city.

Symbolic layers.

Levels of an elemental pagoda.

Maps on top of maps.

Claudia and her structures and foundations and resistance to change. Claudia was very much a force of earth.

Then Aysha would be, what? The creative flame? Fire? Or was fire Nessa, creative in the mathematics of both corporate advertising and illicit pleasures? No, all three women were creative, impressive programmers.

I wasn't any of those things, assuming I was in fact on the next victim list. There had to be something else that gave a clue about which resonant role each woman served in the larger whole.

I shook my head, irritated by my lack of knowledge. And nervous about the vulnerable-looking little dot of my own apartment building on the plot of death.

But there were five elements, not four: earth, fire, air, water, void, typically in that order. At least they were in that order on every pagoda all over Red City.

And the code, the pieces of the program each woman had painted on naked flesh. Claudia had coded a framework; Aysha, mathematical poetry; Nessa, a Memspace environment. Variables were still needed, and also the data to instantiate them with. Were there four pieces of the program, or, like the elements, five?

The first victim had been Claudia, anti-integration Op and structural engineer, who had provided the foundation of the program. Claudia's heart's desire had been to return things to the way they were. Earth.

The second victim had been Aysha/Loie, dancer, who had provided the poetic flavor of the code. Art, heat, drive, passion, ambition, that was Aysha, driven to pay any price for a chance to professionally dance. Fire.

The third layer on a pagoda was air, which did fit Nessa: expansive, a little perverse, innovative, open and alert to anything new. Nessa had provided the environmental rules of the program. Nessa, who had blown through Red City's upper and lower worlds like a gale, only to be stopped by Bosco's prejudices. She would have participated in a ritual to open that door. Air.

So that would make me—just for the sake of keeping the thoughts flowing, no pun intended—water. Emotion, magnetism, defensiveness, flexibility? Describing me as such seemed a stretch, just as the placement of my building relative to the Dragon Lines was a stretch. I could adapt to nearly anything, true. But moody I was not, and no one ever gravitated toward me in a room of many. I could convince myself. But convince is what it would be.

Maybe I was wrong about the elemental stuff.

Or maybe I was wrong about my own placement on the murder list.

Or maybe I was right about all of it but still missing some critical detail. The symbolism of the victims and what could have enticed them into the murderer's lair felt right. Not a one of the women knew any more about how to communicate with an élan vital than I had when I'd started this investigation, so it would have been easy to trick them into thinking the ritual would get them what they wanted. It was a special kind of crazy, bred of exhaustion and fear, but I felt like the city was perking up, taking note of these details even as I did, approving my conclusions.

I took all of my crash course thinking on resonance and élans and Feng Shui, and packaged it all up and cleared my mind. I'd some other bits of more mainstream detecting to do while waiting for non-crazy insight on the rest to sort itself out.

Sticking my head into Kel's studio, I shouted over the hiss of a torch, "I need to trust you with something!"

The hiss stopped and Kel pushed off the scary lenses and masks and jumble of stuff that shielded his face, and stared hard to the left of my shoulder—his polite way of letting me know he'd be making intense eye contact if I was anyone else. He laid his tools and headgear down on a table and pulled off the nanocloth bib that protected his body from nearly everything, and came over to me. "That sounds serious, Hoshi-Moshi."

I nodded, looking up at him towering at the top of the stairs. "It is. I'm going a few places in the city. And most of them are absolutely unsafe. I want you to contact Sorreno if I don't come back. I want you to tell her where I said I was going."

Kelvin frowned and squatted down, almost even now with the top of my head.

I took a deep breath. "I know you hate Sorreno and the RCPD, but this is—"

Kel grabbed my hands and squeezed so hard with his tinker's strength that my convincing broke off with a yelp.

"I worry about you, Hoshi." Kelvin kept ahold of my hands, his big and warm around them. "You're my oldest friend. Someday, maybe, you'll understand what that means."

It was my turn to frown then. How did that relate? Motor opened my mouth, but linguistics supplied no words, as it could make no sense of my confusion of thoughts and feelings.

Kelvin looked away and scoffed, starting out harshly but ending in an amused half-laugh, "By your Trinity, Hoshi, I wish I had a curse I could use on you and have it mean something!" Then he lifted me straight up and into a scary-tight hug, muttering into the fish-smelling fabric of my gutter's cap, "Of course I'll contact Sorreno and tell her if you don't come back. But you make sure that doesn't happen, you hear? Because you know how much I hate the cops."

CHAPTER 22

Things were out of control enough to merit a list-making panic:

One - Purchase industrial-sized joe from M 'n M's Cuppa in the tube station en route to Central and think about the code.

Two - Spy on the Integration Office till closing.

Three - Replenish caffeine levels at Blue Mountain in Central.

Four - Take a stroll in Cleopatra Square, mindful of sci-fi teleportation fields, mystical Dragon Lines, and other impossible things.

Five - Return to Kelvin in Shirring for food and a good night's sleep. So he doesn't have to com Sorreno.

I thought I'd feel safe amongst the anti-Integration protesters outside the IO. Two seconds after I started wedging my way up to their front lines, I discovered there was more than one kind of feeling safe. Sure, no one would be looking for Hoshi Archer amidst her greatest critics—especially a male version of her. But if anything jostled that fishgutter's cap from my head—or one of a million other dead-giveaways I wasn't a normie—then my nanocloth bolero under that stinky sweater wouldn't be enough to protect me. So I focused on the fact that I was here as a private investigator, working undercover. I'd already cued a bunch of language and said about four thousand prayers to the Trinity of Signal, Encoding, and Noise, and another forty prayers to Red City just in case her spirit really did exist, that my audio filters wouldn't drop unexpectedly during the stake-out.

Each of the victims had last been seen entering the IO building about fifteen minutes before closing. They'd been seen going in, but they hadn't been seen going out. Unless you counted reappearing a day later as a corpse in the IO cafeteria dumpsters. So how did they disappear from the IO and why?

Obviously Samo Oro, the IO maintenance worker, was being framed.

But there had to be more to the IO than just the convenience of Oro's employment. I mean, it was the IO—the physical embodiment of Red City's controversial, clumsy, first attempts to give Operators some power over our own lives. With tensions escalating over the Inclusion Act, I couldn't dismiss the possibility of a political motive. And I couldn't dismiss factoring that motive into the murderer's plans to talk to the city, either. A feedback loop between the murderer and the spirit of the city could affect politics in the way the murderer wanted, and that's not who I wanted running things, no matter their platform.

Whatever had happened to the three women, for whatever reason, the sensorcams hadn't seen it. Replay showed each of them entering the building and going to the second floor toilet, where of course there weren't any sensors. Then...nothing. They didn't appear on any sensor footage anywhere at all ever again. Alive, anyway.

So I'd give a try at retracing their steps, see what I could find with my own senses, explore all the things that sensorcams can't pick up. After first taking advantage of my fake identity to do a little reconnaissance from behind enemy lines.

One hour before closing at the IO, I wedged my way up to the front of the omnipresent anti-Integration picket line, dodging holos of "Keep Red City REAL" and "No Crime, No Apology." As though Red City hadn't always been a home for all of us. As if enslaving Operators for five hundred years based on the worst of self-serving lies was an okay thing to do. I felt small and obvious in a sea of people who were not-like-me. I ran a simple program to pick out the familiar faces from every memory of that awful walk to and from my weekly interview with Mai, and wriggled toward a big clump of them.

"...out of work for three months," a large fellow with a big moustache was saying to a newcomer. "Been coming here every day since. Those bozos at Central City Planning don't realize their charity is putting us reals out of work."

The slender young man nodded emphatically.

"Reals"—I hadn't heard that term since the so-called "Reals Movement" was quashed during the Great Apology. These were serious bigots. I sorted through a few hundred different protocols I'd been given in Socialization for how to break into a normie conversation in a natural-seeming way. Apparently Socialization was good for something after all, just like I was hoping the picketers would be.

I wedged my smallness into the circle and boomed out in my very masculine voice and best dock-workers' drawl. "Good thing k-dromers didna take over t'docks. I'm out on medical, thought I'd come here, support t'cause." Thank the Trinity for motor programming that enabled me to say that without shuddering. On the tube ride over, I'd programmed fifty-four different ways to insult my own people without twitching a muscle.

Moustache shook my hand heartily while I hid my avoidance of eye contact behind my sunglasses. "Sorry about the medical, but glad to meet you. It's been three months, since the 'tards put me out of work. I used to run the holocams for Dirk Tsang, you know, the guy on the Pier-City mainfeed? Then this cracking 'dromer with a camera obsession comes in, steals my work. Guy can't tie his own shoes and they give him my cams!" the man scoffed.

A quick, risky scan through public records for the guy's facial pattern told me that wasn't the whole story. Seemed he'd had quite a lot of different holocam jobs—with quite a lot of gaps between them—before his recent lack of corporate affiliation, and the reason he hadn't kept any of them probably wasn't lack of opportunity. The Red City Reporter's crime pages listed him arrested seven times in the past twelve years—most-times before Integration Law, thanks—for assaulting co-workers, interviewees, and even a manager when something didn't go his way. And then there are the multiple restraining orders from past lovers. I'm sure he's got a story as to how he got so mean, but until it involves him waking up to it, I'm not interested. "Sorry t'hear, bro," I said aloud.

Everyone postured emphatically.

I counted down the average number of seconds normies spent posing before someone felt compelled to fill the silence with chatter again. Three, two, one—I blurted, "What we need's a real hit t'Integration, you know? Punch 'em in t'gut. This business with 'Inclusion?' Could go explosive with just t'right fire."

A ripple of bright ideas came on behind their dim faces. I felt the cold fist of paranoia instead, and wondered if I'd pushed to fast too hard. But no, I still had time before the evidence against me piled up. They were just having ideas about what I wanted them to have ideas about—reasons why someone might go after either me or the IO. I wanted anyone who knew anything to slop the details. A name, a confirmation of my suspicions, some more concrete plans—

"City Coordinator Corstenza," one of them suggested, "Integration's nothing without him."

Nods of agreement while another scoffed, "Fuck Corstenza. We need to burn the whole integration business down. Bomb the IO or something. You know there's plenty out there desperate enough to lob a bomb."

I had my awareness in a wide-angle, taking in a lot more than I would ordinarily so I could replay all details later in my memory. The group called out various, random ideas, caste slurs and hate speech, none of which included "let's murder a bunch of women to gain control of the local élans." Sweat prickled my nose. I was closer to the riot guards at the front than the entrance to the mob at the back. If I had to escape fast, all I'd really have to do is break past the bored RCPD riot guards and run like hell. The guards would protect me, right?

The police hadn't protected Kelvin during that riot years ago. They'd beat him near-dead, and he wasn't even an Operator.

"We should do something with the media," a woman's concrete suggestion floated up from the ocean of insults. She flipped her ashy hair out of her eye. "Bryant, you've still got ties, right, with the media?" She poked

Moustache in the ribs.

"Yeah. I got friends in the media all over town."

If circumstances were different I'd remind him he'd burned those industry bridges.

"That's when shit started going wrong for us," someone I couldn't track from the crowd said with a snarly voice. "When they paraded out their integration poster children in the media and made everyone go aw. Power of pity. What a crock of fucking shit."

"Ooo I wanted to punch those fucking retard poster children," spluttered the woman with the ashy hair.

An avalanche of agreement followed.

"Did you hear the latest with that Archer woman?" Moustache said and several others spat, as though my name were a curse that needed warding.

"I saw her on the mainfeed this morning, committed some crime, right?"

"Yeah, proof the feebles are bad news, proof right there."

Mutters of agreement and excitement spread like a rumor through the Mem, and everyone was talking about me and the potential inherent in my downfall.

"I've hated that Archer girl since day one. She's too shiny, like her shit don't stink."

"She's got friends in high places, is all."

"Good thing not all cops are tard-lovers; I've got friends that still kill the freaks, amen."

"Did you see how she was all banged up the last time she came through here? I hope someone gave her what she deserved."

I'd pushed them onto the track I'd wanted all right, and it was making me rethink my choice of destination. Not just because the more they talked about me the riskier my presence got, but because they hadn't been considering leveraging my bad press against Integration until I'd opened my stupid mouth. Curse it all to Noise!

"There's got to be something we can do with t'IO building, we're standin' right here, we're standin' here every day," I tried to push one track over to political motives for dumping the bodies at the IO.

"That Archer scum's an easier target," a beanpole of a woman in a bright red hat punched her fist into her palm. "There's already dirt on her."

"They say she was stealing data."

"I heard Archer was in with the mob."

"Reals, think about it. We could take out some poli-ads, put Archer's face on them, show that disgusting blue forehead of hers, and slogans like 'do you trust this face?'"

"Yeah! Or 'DIS-integration of Red City'!"

Everyone was talking at once, brainstorming a million ways to use my fugitive status against my people. And, still, not a one of them had slopped any of the candid insider information I'd been after when I started.

My disguise was pretty good—I was even grateful now for the fish-stink—but I couldn't imagine it was good enough to hold up against this much protracted conversation about me. Doctor Mike's gender-swap didn't hide my height or the slightness of my frame. It was time to admit I'd made a mistake. I had to get the topic changed or scram.

Could I get in one more push, one more question, before it became obvious I was probing for information? Dreadfully, I didn't know the answer to that. This wasn't like a one-on-one or small group interrogation. I didn't have any algorithms for understanding the behavior of mobs of hostile normies. And I certainly, up to now, hadn't had any experience. All I knew was this wasn't working out as planned. So I switched to asking myself: how do you plan to get out of here with your feet feeling like they're encased in blackstone? In the background, my navis gave me some panicked feedback about sustained adrenaline levels, and I crankily told it to go stimulate some melatonin production or something, forgetting that it would, and then having to belay the request. In my pocket, beneath my sweater, I fingered my shocker.

"Fuck Archer, fuck her in her fucking ass till she bleeds."

"Fuck 'em, fuck 'em all," someone yelled.

"Yeah, that's about the only thing the 'tards are good for!" a confirmation from somewhere, and laughter from everywhere.

"They don't make a sound when you do 'em either!"

"Yeah, if you make them take out that disgusting tech, they'll just lay there and let you do anything!"

"Yeah? How would you know?"

I turned off my motor functions to stop that slug I was taking at Moustache in my imagination. Then I turned them back on so I could spit a small mouthful of vomit onto the trampled grass and scarred earth.

I felt a hard jabbing sensation and looked up into a concerned expression. "Hey, you okay? You stopped moving there for a moment."

I flinched from the question but found the wit to say woodenly, "Yeah. Fine. Medical, you know?"—knowing even as I said it I'd hesitated too long before producing the response.

"The corps are against us!"

"They ain't never been with us!"

While I'd been fighting for control, the conversation about me and the media had escalated into a paranoid fervor of conspiracy theory and rape-talk and the crowd was getting hotter. I'd been as stupid as a dim not to think through the consequences of my actions. I'd come in here all smug for information about whoever was setting me up and eye witness reports about the victims—which I never even got to ask about. But crowds had momentum. Stupid Hoshi! I really was dangerous; who needed resonant feedback with an élan vital to hurt the city when you could have me and my dumb plans to rile a crowd of Op-haters into rape and murder?

"Hey," I said abruptly, loudly, off key from the tone of the rising wildfire. I shifted my weight uncomfortably and recited my extraction script. "Gotta take a piss. Y'all won't think less of me for using t'facilities at t'IO, will you?"

"Hey, piss all over the place, that's what it's good for!" someone laughed.

"Yeah! That's what we should all do!" the faceless mob picked a up new riff from my exit strategy. "We should all march right up there and take a big stinking crap on the place!"

"How do we get past the riot cops?"

The brief shift in the direction of the hate-talk from raping me to pissing on the IO (which, frankly, I'd be more than okay with) relieved enough panic so my feet could move again, and I started off with the brisk pace of someone who had to pee. Which at this point wasn't an act. Moustache muttered to the slender youth beside him after my back was turned, never suspecting I could still hear him, "There was something familiar about that gutter, don't you think?"

"Yeah, something off about him too...."

I began the litany of Red City's buildings, defense against the typhoon of panic at my back. There were the peaks and domes and points of the skyline and the graceful spiral of the Arts and Culture Building, and the triple towers of the 100 Worlds Trade Union joined by their series of sky-bridges, and the prickly quills of the Red City Reporter, and—each of my 200 favorite buildings in Red City.

Then I was, miraculously, out of the crowd, my shaking hands hidden inside the folds of my stinky sweater, walking the usual path into the IO—the path I'd taken every week for the past two years, never missing a day, to answer Mai Chandra's questions. Only now, as Nicholas Foo, non-Op, I walked between the two sets of protesters without notice. No jeers. No stares. No shouts of encouragement and solidarity. No pointing out of a hero-status that I neither deserved nor wanted. I had not been on the front lines of the Movement. I had turned away from the window that night at Claudia's, afraid of losing my position at the RCPD. I wasn't a role model for my people at all. Stupid Hoshi.

Crossing the threshold of the IO came like a nightmare. But no alarms went off; the sensor above the door read my Citizen ID as Nicholas Foo, not as Hoshi Archer.

I walked into the stark, industrial main lobby, artless and boxy. I walked though it to the east-side stairs. I walked up the east-side stairs to the toilet marked with its genderless-person-symbol on the second floor, and entered. Investigating could wait; I entered one of the ten stalls and took that terror-fueled piss.

I pulled my pants back up and sat on the toilet with my knees folded under my chin, rocking, feeling my heart pounding against my thighs. Demon-visions of the protesters outside turning to rioters, of my own stupidity fueling the very fires I'd been hoping to put out, ran my breath short and ragged. I had to get a grip, but I didn't know how. Why was I so afraid? I was never this afraid of anything!

A shriek ricocheted from the walls and my mouth went dry before linguistics identified it as simply the soft squeak of the bathroom door opening. Stupid auditory filters. I held my breath and listened to the footsteps: soft shoes with a jaunty, Operator gait. They stopped by the sinks, and then silence. Time passed and whoever-it-was breathed and shuffled.

The door squeaked open again, followed by another set of footsteps, crisp and clicking, a normie in hard, high heels. My mouth went dry again, inexplicably this time, at the sound of them.

"Hello Martin," Mai Chandra's voice, neither cold nor warm, neither welcoming nor hostile, crisp and efficient, folded me into a tiny square of terror. Mai's heels. Mai, who, if she opened the door to this stall, would catch me, Hoshi, and make sure I was never free again, even if I did manage to clear myself of my "crimes." I bit down hard on my hands, and tasted blood. But the pain cut the panic so I could think.

Wait, Martin?

"Hello." Martin Ho's return. His tone was colored with a hopeful warmth, a flavor he previously had reserved for when he thought he was going to pin something on me at the office. Not quite smug, but almost. Like the preparation for smugness.

"Are you ready?" Mai asked.

"Yeah." Some faint rustling.

"Good. I have all your paperwork filled out. We should be ready to go with it. Let me see your bag?"

More rustling.

"Follow me," Mai said.

Martin? Paperwork? Was Martin applying for an Integration job? But I thought Martin's interest in Mai was because he thought she was covering for my supposed "crimes." Martin applying for an Integration job would put a serious hole in my prior notion of reality.

Soft shoes and hard heels left the bathroom together.

I relaxed the death-bite on my fists, and as the pain faded from sharp and aware to dull and achy the panic rushed back, out of proportion to how rationally I knew I should be feeling. I found myself glad I was situated in a toilet stall.

By the time I unwound my body, reasserted a ghost of my usual self, and exited the stall, it was one minute and fifteen seconds past when the IO closed for the day. That was exactly when I realized I had completely botched something else: I hadn't followed Mai and Martin through the sensors on their way out to see where they were going and what they were up to.

Frustrated, I hit my head on the white-tiled wall hard enough to remember I still had bruises there. Well, there was still one way I could save the day.

I ran a thorough investigation of the bathroom. The toilet on the second floor had one door, ten stalls, a bank of five sonic sinks, and one window. The toilets gave off the faint earthy smell of the bacteria that kept them clean. The facilities contained nothing else; no entrances or egresses besides the door and the window. No seams in the hard-tiled walls.

I peered out through the stark glass at concrete below. The window was too small for a body to fit through, unless it was a small body like mine; plus it was on the second story and nothing friendly awaited a person at the bottom. I could see nothing to explain how the murder victims could have disappeared from here. I had found not even one useful detail to redeem the afternoon of mistakes.

I left the IO building, cold and empty now in after-hours. Outside the protesters had vanished. I kicked the empty, packed earth, annoyed, impotent, and embarrassed.

I pulled the netting of the fishgutter's cap the rest of the way over my face and put my head down. Being Nicholas Foo didn't protect me from my own stupidity.

I decided to walk the distance from the IO to Cleopatra Square. As I set out I made a bargain: I was allowed to drown in as much self-pity as I wanted on the way there, but once I reached the Square it would be all business again. Deal? Deal. I shook hands with myself.

I set off still thinking: How could I have been so stupid!

CHAPTER 23

Night had fallen and the evening rain had ended. Here in Central, the shiny-clean sides of the towers surged 150 stories and higher to create a myopic view of reality. It didn't fool me, though. In the small, narrow space between the twin Red City Reporter spires, a man hit a woman, and she threw her ring on the ground. On the bench before the impassive, windowless slab of the Federal Bank Building, an old woman sobbed; her hands trembling in the lap of her frayed, thirty-years-outdated dress jacket. Under cover of the arbor of prize-winning roses in the courthouse garden, four small boys in the red-and-gold uniforms of Red City Public School mobbed an Operator and stole her small, square backpack, the same way brinn gulls go after a mobie with a fish. I was no different than the city. A pretty story excepting all the dangerous alleys.

The wet ground glistened with moonlight as Phoenix rose over Marcie Bay, huge and reddish. Like the Dragon Lines, clues about the case and my own arrest intersected here, at the center of Cleopatra Square, in the middle of Lan Qui Park, at the core of Central District. In the heart of Red City.

Just off-center to the south, a small plaque and bit of worn metal commemorated the landing of the *Cleopatra* on Cassiopeia Prime. I ran my hands along the metal's coolness. Twisted and shiny with age and touch and evening rain, that metal had been forged on Earth. It was some part of the *Cleopatra*, but I wasn't sure what. I knew it was from something internal, because the delicate skin of the dimension ship would have deteriorated quickly in Red City's moist, temperate climate. *Cleopatra* had made a one-way trip to this tiny bit of land, rising above a planet otherwise covered with sea; a one-shot leap of faith. I started opening a channel to the Mem to look up what bit of the ship I was touching, and then realized that was the sort of thing

Hoshi Archer would do, so I stopped with a sigh and some lip-biting. Looking up that fact could wait until this was over, really.

Ignoring the plaque etched with the names of the original settlers, which I'd memorized when I was two, I closed my eyes and turned slowly 180 to the north to face the geographic center of the city. I took a deep breath, and opened my eyes on the centerpiece of the Square.

The original settlers had dragged it all the way from Earth for reasons that are lost to time. The journals and records of the "First 4000" are complete in almost every way—it wasn't that long ago the *Cleopatra* landed, relatively speaking—but aside from the fountain's listing in the ship's storage manifest, the only other note of it was that it had been salvaged by unnamed crew members from the wreckage of Eastern Metropolis for transport to Cassiopeia Prime. Someday, when there were fewer crimes, I'd have to go after that unsolved mystery myself.

It was clear to look at the thing that it had been old even before it had come here. Four tiers of basined pedestals in descending size, each supported by a slender, ornate stem, were topped by a delicate youth in bronze. Naked, he held a spear in his left hand, relaxed and non-threatening, but with a martial familiarity. His right arm arced over his head graceful as a classical dancer, a fish held easily in his fingers. Water spilled from each tier of the fountain, flowing down the slender stems into the largest, deepest basin at the base; it burbled gently, musically. Dated from early sixteenth century Italy, its baroqueness was offset by its delicacy. Buffered from the slabs of the towers of Central by grass and the graceful native greenery of the park, the Fishing Boy Fountain floated on an island of an earlier time, forever apart from the modern sea beyond.

Few people were in the square, most having taken cover during the evening rain. None of them paid any attention to me. I felt calm. According to the Feng Shui of the city, the fountain was supposed to create balance in city-center. Each of the four tiers of pools represented an element: Earth, Air,

Fire, Water. And the youth perched on top was the culmination of the five elements in Void, his easy posture and successful fishing testament to a unity with the quintessential flow of nature as a whole. It was a pagoda in essence, like all the others in the city.

I stared at the fountain, stalked around it, took it in from all angles. Consulted the maps in my head. The fountain had been placed directly above the Dragon Lines' crossing, and my imagination fancied this graceful youth as the child of Red City: avatar and emissary of the Valkyrie on the city seal, she who holds the trident pointing toward the stars.

The fishgutter's costume had protected me from getting wet in the evening rain, but I shivered anyway. Perhaps it was the slight cooling of air brought on by the growing darkness. Emissary or not, the statue didn't speak to me, and neither did the city, and I found no easy answers.

A small bustle of children skittered through the Square, trailed by sedate adults. It was still early despite the dark, which felt like it had come sooner than usual. I sat on the bench between the fountain and the twisted bit of the *Cleopatra*, facing the fountain. Closing my eyes, I cleared my thoughts. Then asked:

If I were a sci-fi disappearing invisibility device, where would I be located? How would I operate?

I shoved part of my awareness into the sensorcam eight meters away on the roof of the public latrine. The cam had been bumped by a clumsy lorrie hen months ago, so it saw a big patch of sky instead of the park; city maintenance had yet to fix it. I opened my eyes without exiting the sensorcam, and considered the sky through both the city's eyes and my own.

A bright speck of light hovered above the fish in the fountain, shining steady and brighter than any star. I was looking at the massive aerial communications hub in geosynchronous orbit above Cleopatra Square. Which lined up with where I'd sensed Casidy's "black holes" in the flow of the Mem—and where the RCPD thought I was syphoning data for the mob.

Making eye contact with the bronze youth as he spilled water perpetually into the fountain, I smiled at him. In the shadow-light of evening, it seemed he smiled back.

Pulling a 3-D map of Cleopatra Square out of my mental map-arsenal, I also grabbed a utility that let me bounce signal off of a communications receiver. Walking around the fountain and stopping three times, I calculated the com-hub's exact location. I added that to the 3-D map of the city and then did the tricky bit.

My memory of Casidy's memory of his "black holes" replayed and freeze-framed on the tiny squares of missing information. Simultaneously, I pulled up my own memory of being in the city's sensor network days later, feeling the loss of information like tiny slashes in my skin. Those vanishing threads of information had mapped to the communications network in the vicinity of Cleopatra Square, I'd gathered that much. But hadn't, at the time, had sufficient information for an exact mapping.

Now, I joined the 3-D map of the area and the com-sat above with Casidy's memory of the missing data, and also with my own. Three views of lost information, fused.

It wasn't visible to the physical eye. And it wasn't visible from within the Mem either. But in the triangulation between the two, where the worlds met, truth showed plain. The black holes in the city's data transmission network—places where information went in but no signal came out, just like the murder victims and the IO—had a location in the physical world. When the three views aligned and were adjusted to assume the missing transmission bubbles were being handled by the com-sat above the Square, the dark streaks of void converged on a single point directly to the west of the fountain, beside a sprawling keefer tree.

That would be where the monster eating the Cleopatra Square data lay.

And that would also be a match to where Madame Bosco's slimy drug dealers had described their NQ drop-off with the Mysterious Vanishing

Buyer.

Coincidence? My credit was on *not*.

My credit was on that spot marking the entrance to the murderer's lair.

I walked over casually, glad the akimbo sensorcam wasn't watching my actions, and neither were the few distracted people passing through.

When I reached the spot, I squatted in the grass. Which felt curiously like bare earth. I closed my eyes, grabbed a handful, and held it to my nose. The rich, mineral scent of soil and nothing else confirmed the presence of dirt sans grass. Opening my eyes, I held a clod of grass.

I moved a meter away. I was no longer holding a clod of grass, but a handful of soil. I tasted it. Yup, dirt.

I stepped back across the line and once more I held grass. I tasted it again. Yup, still dirt.

The grass was an illusion.

If I hadn't already been suspecting something magically weird, I would have assumed a major malfunction in the sensory processing of my navis.

But I was suspecting something magically weird, so I pulled up every map I had of Cleopatra Square—all 5,895 of them—and searched for what the magical weirdness might be hiding.

In an old blueprint from Red City's original utility planning, I found it. A manhole had once led down into the tube system, marked for sealing over after the sonic track had been laid. It didn't show up on any other maps, assumed gone, as vanished as the NQ buyer and the data and the murder victims. I crouched down again over the suspect bit of turf.

Exploring the earth with my hands, eyes closed, I found the edges of a cold plate beneath the soil. I didn't know yet what was causing the illusion, but highly adaptive programs for light-wave manipulation weren't outside the realm of the possible. The folks on Callisto sold all sorts of quasi-intelligent adaptive EM devices they claimed were joint human/élan technology—for unobtainable prices, of course. But—

There had been no disappearing here any more than there had been disappearing at the Integration Office. Whoever was behind these murders had access to some very expensive tech.

Somewhere on the other side of that forgotten hole, I'd find both the device that was sucking up those information packets from the com-sat as a side-effect of maintaining this illusion, and the murderer's lair.

I smiled, tipping my head conspiratorially at the youth atop the fountain, and began digging.

Twelve minutes and seventeen seconds later, filthy with what looked like grass stains but I knew full well was mud, I was no longer smiling. First of all, digging up clods of grass only to find beneath them more identical clods of grass was about as close to actual insanity as I hoped I'd ever get. But more importantly, I now had a good idea of what I was up against by touching it and having my navis translate the tactile sensations into a likely visual of what lay beneath the dirt. Score one for Hoshi's novel use of sensory programming! And what I was up against was a big, hard, steel-plated lock that I didn't have the key for.

As my fingertips explored cold, rectangular edges and massive, impenetrable welds, I opened a short-wave channel and tried a whole range of frequencies to connect to the electronic key-parts inside and crack the entry code. But every time I hit a frequency that the lock responded to as signal, my connection immediately fizzled out into the static hiss of noise. Whatever programming guarded the lock, it was extremely adaptive, just like the field that created the illusion of grass.

I had to get down there if I was going to stop the next murder.

I rocked back on my heels, brushed dirt/grass off my hands, and considered my options.

Which were essentially to get help or to get help.

Trinity, I hated getting help.

I glanced up at the moon Phoenix, whose relative size had shrunk as it trekked upwards off the horizon. There wasn't time to go all the way back to Shirring Point, and Kel didn't have a com.

Cursing the lousy luck and the urgent need for speed, I instead stomped away from the offending patch of earth and toward Plan B that lay a quick few kilos west in Husson District back on Bosco's turf.

◆　◆　◆

"No, I really don't think there is anything for you here, and if you don't leave, I will have security eject you," the door-boy at the entrance to the Velvet Glove informed me nasally, and flicked back his glossy mane of hair.

I closed my eyes and breathed deeply, patience at its extreme frayed end. "Please, like I said the first sixteen times, just tell her it's about the whisky. If Madame says no, I promise I'll leave or else you can stick me in a room on sub-basement level three and teach me to never come round here again."

Being Nicholas Foo: definitely not helpful when dealing with the mob.

The door-boy nickered at me and waved me away with his hand.

I weighed options versus probability of when the next murder would occur versus the remaining items on my to do list, and sighed. Realistically, if I didn't solve this thing in the next twelve hours, it would be too late. Me or someone else would turn up dead in the IO dumpsters, Sorreno wouldn't be able to suppress the case any longer, and the protesters who I stupidly gave the idea of a city scandal to would use it as an excuse to step up their belligerence. And that wasn't counting any possible feedback from an élan vital exacerbating everything. So whether or not my cover was blown really wouldn't matter at all. There wasn't time to reach Kel, there would be no help from the cops, none of my other friends had the right resources to get that manhole cover open—I was already gambling the full pot on Bosco agreeing to help me.

Casting nasty glances at the closed-circuit sensorcams in the building, really hoping none of them were tapped by law enforcement, I yanked the fishgutter's cap off my head.

After being pent up in that stinky hat for so long, what felt like a kilometer of long, straight, black hair fled out all over my shoulders. The blue of my forehead now revealed, I sent the command Dr. Mike had given me for killing the living tattoos and nanobots to return me to my female form.

The door-boy, high levels of jadedness being required for his job, did not flinch, blink, or twitch an eyebrow. His superior expression did not change at all. Perhaps people drop their shady disguises in front of him all the time.

"My identity should be displaying properly on a pattern match now?" The femininity of my voice surprised me. "Please tell Madame Bosco it's a matter of life or death. Plus, it's the only way I can catch her whisky thief."

Twenty-seven seconds later, the door-boy looked up from the 3V behind the reception desk, mouth angry. "Madame says she will see you now, please wait here."

Thirty-nine minutes later, I smiled as I started my paranoid way back toward Central, fishgutter's cap on and veil over my face, side-stepping the path of the sensors at every opportunity. Bosco would come through, I was sure of it. There was, after all, honor among some thieves. It would take a little time though, which was just as well as I didn't dare risk the sensor cams on the tubes.

Lose some; win some. There are lots of ups and downs in a city.

I was half way to Central, meditating on how cranky having a bounty on my head was making me, when I remembered my spying on Martin yesterday. He'd been sitting in the RCPD cafeteria handing a dataslip, angrily, to Jaali Henri, a.k.a. Thug #2, a.k.a. The Guy Who Switched the Evidence. That dragged with it the memory of my spying on Sorreno, her anger, she and Angel covering for me, my spying on Inspector Zi sitting smugly with the report about what I'd supposedly done—

And then the associations started flying.

Martin, querying records on Integration Officer Mai Chandra.

Martin, sitting with Inspector Zi of anti-Integration fame, pulling circumstantial evidence on me.

Martin, so upset when I accused him of cavorting with Zi and turning Effram Caper that he attacked me at the Rose and Thorn.

Martin, mentioned by the thugs at Bill's Ragtime in connection with framing me.

Martin, turning up in the IO today, making plans with Mai Chandra.

Martin, the little snot—I was willing to bet the city he was being blackmailed by the thugs who attacked me in the alley.

I couldn't contact Martin in the Mem to ask him what the fuck. It didn't matter how good Luzzie's fake ID was, channels to Martin and other people I knew well would be monitored with all the resources of Red City's Finest plus some of the folks over at the Federal Law Enforcement Agency. But a confession out of Martin could get the charges against me dropped faster than a brinn gull drops a bad clam. And fill in a few more details on the case as well, assuming the attacks on me and the murders were connected. I could dig myself out of this hole I was in—all I had to do was kiss the douche.

For a minute and a half life as a fugitive seemed the better option.

I checked time from my navis. I had a little of it still before Bosco's person was due to show up in Cleopatra Square with a way for me to open the manhole—which maybe I wouldn't need if I could get right again with the RCPD. I had a little time left, too, before Kelvin was supposed to worry. I changed direction and headed toward Martin's housing in Hill.

CHAPTER 24

As I dipped around hidden sensor plates and dodged camera lines-of-sight, I put half a thread in my workspace to make sure I had all my facts lined up. Wouldn't do to make a mistake at this stage and give Martin something real to complain about.

I rearranged my little boxes and flavors and lines linearly into "The Tale of the Crooked Cops Versus Me, so far":

Once upon a time in Red City, there was a corrupt but popular police Inspector (a.k.a. Inspector Rolland Zi) who yearned to put Operators back in their rightful place. Well, rightful according to him at any rate.

There was also a popular but corruptible young police Operator (a.k.a. Martin Ho) who yearned to destroy his arch-nemesis. Well, if there was such a thing as an arch-nemesis, anyway.

The Corrupt Inspector and the Corruptible Operator despised each other with mind, heart, and soul. They shared nothing in common, and would, in fact, cross the entire breadth of the RCPD building just to avoid the risk of taking the same lift. Except, of course, for the one thing they did share, a singular passion with the potential to bring them both together. And that one thing was this: destroy pesky, meddlesome me.

For many years, mutual loathing kept the Inspector and the Operator apart and I prevailed, for I was on the side of Truth, Justice, and the Cassiopeian Way. Plus, there was an honest, and surprisingly also popular, police Inspector (a.k.a. Inspector Cassandra Sorreno) watching my back. For all these reasons and a few more like luck, I had prevailed. Until now.

Enter: The Hate Brigade (a.k.a. the Thugs from Bill's Ragtime, including Jaali Henri of RCPD sanitation fame). The Hate Brigade also desired to bring me down.

The Corrupt Inspector had many ideals in common with the Hate Brigade, but could not be associated with such lows, lest it spoil his future chances of political advancement.

The Corruptible Operator had nothing in common with the Hate Brigade, but, being essentially a coward, would do anything to save his own skin, given relatively minimal threats.

The natural solution to everyone's problem of pesky, meddlesome me was this: Place Martin Ho as messenger-boy between the Thugs and Inspector Zi in a sloppy plot to create the major scandal involving my face being smeared across the mainfeeds—mainfeeds now projecting large on the sides of the skyscrapers along my way cross-town to where Martin lived in Hill.

I didn't tune my navis to the audio coming from the 'feeds, but I didn't need it to factor the hard-edged images flashing on the sides of buildings, the arches above tube access ramps, and the 3V displays inside store windows. Gone were the "Have You Seen This Person?" and "Wanted, Reward!" snaps of me from earlier. Gone were the thoughtful and concerned expressions of the reporters and medical experts when imagery switched to narration. Now angry faces, some recognizable as powerful opponents to Integration from politics and the media, pointed and jabbed between unflattering views of me as an angry teen and real-time footage of the mounting crowd outside the Office of Operator Affairs in Central. Guess that's where the protesters I'd angered at the IO had ended up. I was now an anti-Integration and anti-Inclusion talking point within the struggle for Operator representation in local policy. Just like I'd stupidly suggested to the anti-Op protesters.

"Operators die, the Apology is a lie!" Someone yelled from the top of the OOA's steps. "And even if it's not, they have the power to destroy us all again. Just look at Archer, turned criminal at first chance. Until Reals are in control of the code, all Operators must be back in hobbles!"

I kept the fishgutter's netting over my face in case I ended up in the eye-line of a sensorcam by accident. I kept my eyeballs up on the mainfeeds as I zigzagged cross-town. I could monitor the 'feeds with a light thread in the Mem, but seeing them projected like the ghastly pseudo-code on the city's physical body gave me a better feel of the city's mood.

I could tell from the mainfeed footage of the build-up in Central that we hadn't passed the tipping point, that place in the nonlinear dynamics of it all after which the processes of violence become irreversible. I'd witnessed enough mobs-turned-violent to know what the tipping point felt like, and I could sense it in every inch of Red City's soil, with every step of every resident through her streets and parks, with every bubble of data in her communications network streaking invisibly through her sky. The city was close to the verge, but not over it yet. There might be a lot of corruption in Red City, starting and certainly not ending with Inspector Zi and Jaali Henri. But there were enough straights in the justice system too. If Martin testified he was being threatened and coerced by thugs to Sorreno—or to any number of honest people—it could save the day for both me and opinion on Integration. And I had to convince Martin to do the right thing fast because I was due to meet Bosco's contact in Central, where the unrest was mounting, in a little over an hour. I needed to get down that manhole to stop the next murder, which for all I knew could be happening right now.

Of course Martin Ho was a liar and too slimy for even the reclaimer to want to 'cycle, but I was pretty sure I could appeal to his desire to get something for nothing. I would have about three and a half seconds to jam my argument straight into his navis on a shortwave channel, before I had to run like Noise in order to make it to Central in time for the next murder. But I might not get another chance, especially if I ended up dead myself in the IO dumpster. Dead or alive, though, my innocence could deflate what I saw projected on the walls. I could save Red City, even if I couldn't save myself. I just had to convince Martin he would be the one saving it.

The mainfeed flickering against the MAXI building at the edge of Wim

Square, ten meters tall, showed angry faces and threatening gestures. The RCPD riot guards, caught on the edges of the area trying to press the bodies back, had that edgy fight-or-flight look to their eyes I remembered from the Mayfair Riots three years ago, rage ripping through Red City like a plainsfire.

Around me on the street, traffic flowed off-beat. One set of people pounded angrily toward Central while another set walked away with quick, frightened steps. Red City had polarized, with those attracted to politics aligning in Central while those repelled fled the city's heart like animals trying to hide their panic.

Central. That wasn't just where the Office of Operator Affairs lay, but also the IO and the RCPD. And Cleopatra Square, the true Heart of the City, the place where the Dragon Lines crossed. The place where I needed to go to stop the next murder. Cleopatra Square had been so peaceful and empty such a short time ago, but now it was full of anger and spit. Would the crowds make it easier or harder for me to get myself down that manhole to where the real answers lay? I'd have to factor that when I got to it; nothing I could do about it now. Now I had to stay focused on making it to Martin without getting nabbed.

I hugged myself tightly, comforted by the familiar fabric of my bolero inside the sweater's sleeves. Cap netting down, eyes planted to the ground now instead of up into the 'feeds, I shuffled with haste, a quarter of my awareness in the area sensors trying to find the city's blind spots. Closed-circuit corporate cameras had become my enemies; anti-theft sensors and the little CID readers that floated on the outskirts of shopping towers waiting to bombard me with personalized adverts had gone from annoying to hostile. Corporate security, whether man or machine, would report me just as fast as private citizens, public servants, or law enforcement AIs.

Of course my CID still said I was Nicholas Foo, so if I was snagged by corporate CID reader it shouldn't matter. But my face was my own again, and the netting of my cap, while opaque, was not stiff enough to obscure the planes of my bones. A reflex override of an advert from my navis would spell doom, as no normie could do that.

I made a zag that forced me closer to Central than I wanted to be, and heard shouting. Looking up, I saw over a hundred flatshots slapped to the side of the Wei building, and they all flickered with a particularly unflattering 2-D of my face, tag-lined "Who Do You Trust?"

On the other side of the street, a young man jabbed at the poster with an angry finger and snapped something at the young woman beside him, but whether their shouts were pro-me or anti-me I would never learn because if I wanted to make this problem I'd created go away I needed to get to Martin yesterday. I had about twenty more blocks, and luckily all of them pointed away from Central.

I stuck my nose to the ground, my mind in the city's sensors, and my curses to the aether, and concentrated on pounding as fast as I could toward my objective.

Seven minutes and twenty-seven seconds later, Martin Ho's Operator Housing appeared before me, conspicuously anonymous, unpleasantly familiar. This building where I'd once lived had even less charm than Claudia's, made of the cheapest, ugliest tan silicate allowed by city code. The small windows made the place look like the prison it was, and the cheerful yellow and red flowers in the first story windows didn't fool me at all. I was acutely aware that I stood directly atop of the southeast tail of the Dragon Lines as I waved my thumb over the plate next to the door. I pushed the netting of the cap up a little, showing my face, my eyes, but still obscuring the blue of my forehead.

Within, I imagined the house mom having massive thick-headed confusion over why an out-of-work fishgutter from Shirring would be knocking on the door of Operator Housing all the way south in Hill. I crossed my fingers inside the wool of the oversized arms of my sweater and hoped the assumptions set up by the fake CID I carried would be enough to keep the house mom from recognizing me.

A stout woman who had never been beautiful, but compensated for it well by distracting on-lookers with exponentially more hideous make-up, peered out with watery brown eyes.

"Wadda you want?" the house mom grunted, giving me the old up-and-down.

Our minders are not to be trifled with. True, most of them are out-of-shape, insecure under-achievers who like spending time with Ops because we're the only people they can feel superior to. However, they have been given substantial training in hand-to-hand combat. Which they are also substantially trained to use on Ops should we not do as we're told. I tensed and recoiled from habit even though I wasn't doing anything that could inspire the house mom's ire. Besides, I didn't look like an Operator to her; she wasn't even the same house mom I'd had when I'd lived there. I tried not to touch my cheek where a scar was forming beneath Dr. Mike's masterfully applied synthskin.

"Um. Mar-Martin Ho. I'm, I'm here to see Martin Ho. May I come in?" I deepened my voice and swallowed, one hand nervously checking the netting of my cap to make sure it was still covering my forehead. The light was very dim in the doorway and I hoped it would keep the femininity of my features from being too obvious. I had checked through all the sensors in the area before I'd stepped up to the door, and I hadn't seen anyone as I'd paced around the building before knocking. But still, the house mom had probably been watching the 'feeds all day and—

"Martin's not here," the house mom snapped, very annoyed by this fact. Red-tipped fingernails clattered impatiently on the doorframe.

"What do you mean he's not here?" I blurted. Okay, so that's right up near the top of the list of most useless things I could have possibly said in response. I knew it was a dumb question even as I said it; I owned the inanity. But say it I did, in the disbelief that I could have come this far, with this much at stake, under so many risks to my person, my future, and the lives of others, only to find the object of my quest had stepped out for beers.

Or maybe Martin was the next victim.

The house mom was talking again, but I wasn't listening. I ducked away, turned my back to her. Out of the corner of my awareness I sensed her huffing at my rudeness as I stumbled like an eight-day-drunk to the middle of the street and into the sliver of grass and peonies at the center of the walkway. My knees gave way and I fell into the still-moist soil, landing hard enough for it to hurt, the coldness of the night time ground seeping into my thigh.

I'd gotten the connection now. By the length and breadth and heart of Red City, I had finally gotten it.

The connection between the three victims wasn't that they were all young women. Nor was it that they were all Operators; that had been simply necessary for the programming. No, the real connection between the victims was two-fold: first, as I'd already factored, was location, where they lived along the tails of the city's Dragon Lines. And second, by who they knew. Specifically, me. Claudia was my former lover, Aysha by-association to my personal ins with the underworld and the IO alike, and Nessa had been a casual friend in all the same social circles. In a city of eighteen million, the odds of me having those kinds of connections to all three victims wasn't coincidence.

Claudia had coded the program's structure.

Aysha had coded its aesthetics.

Nessa had programmed the operating environment.

And I, who was a dreadful programmer, particularly compared to the others, I wasn't going to be doing any coding at all. I was going to be running the completed program.

Claudia was Earth.

Aysha was Fire.

Nessa was Air.

And I—"Lady Hoshi of the City"—I was the element of Void, the very tippy-top of the grotesque pagoda.

But Water lay between Air and Void. And a set of variables lay between the existing components of the program and something I could run. And one more victim lay between Nessa and me, between the current state of unrest in Central and completing the ritual to generate resonance with an alien intelligence that could control the EM, manipulate people's emotions, and bring terrible harm to the city. I was on the Victim List all right, but I wasn't in the Next Victim slot at all—Martin was!

I coughed, hard, as the puzzle-box opened the rest of the way, revealing the rotten thing inside.

If Martin had entered the IO this evening, entered just before closing like Claudia, Aysha, and Nessa before him, then that meant I had—based on the forensic distance between final IO-sighting and time of death on the others—only a few hours left in which to save Martin Ho. Who, quite loudly and on more than one occasion before many witnesses in the RCPD offices, had insisted he would rather die than accept my help with anything at all.

I rather hoped he'd change his mind about that.

On the up-spin, I now knew not only who the next victim was but who the killer was as well, plus the Where, the How, and the Why. Indeed, I had the whole case figured.

I only hoped I'd be able to also figure a way out of the trap that had just closed over the top of my head—the very trap I'd walked into, willingly, every step of the way, just like all the other victims before me. Hoped I'd figure a way out in time to save us all.

CHAPTER 25

I took off through the uneasy city like a ghost terrified of itself. This time I ran toward the tinderbox. A straight shot down the tail of the Dragon Line without meandering to avoid sensorcams—speed now more important than stealth—I reached Central in seventeen minutes and fifty seconds, and crossed into Lan Qui Park three-minutes-on-the-dot later. Then I stopped, panting, on the edge of chaos.

Cleopatra Square was full of sound.

It was full of people too, sure, and motion and smells and colors and shifting forms. But it was the sound, of course, that got me. I took a step forward and threw my arms up over my head, whimpering, as yelling and breathing and stomping and shouting started to trigger the wildness of fight-or-flight. I took a step back, back over the threshold of the bearable. The rumble-and-scream of the masses made an incorporeal barrier I could not cross, as surely as a concrete wall a hundred stories high. I'd lived through plenty of riots, sure. But never had I been in the middle of one. Never had I done more than observe from a distant edge. I, who had reaped the benefits of the riots without ever having paid my dues in one.

Not that this was a full-fledged riot. It was just an attempt to provoke one. Trinity help me if I didn't make it through the mass before that happened.

I craned my eyes around, looking for anyone who might be looking for me, but the mess of bodies and colors and sweat-smells was as impenetrable—if not as painful—as the sound. There had to be ten thousand gathered, and more arriving. Grinding my teeth, I pushed my awareness into every camera I could find nearby, but all I saw through any of them was the same mud of pumping, angry, homogenized bodies I saw with my eyes. I hadn't factored something like this when I'd asked Bosco's henchman to meet me back here.

It was supposed to be just the henchman and me, two strangers passing briefly beneath the everbulb at an empty park bench, making a smooth exchange under cover of silence. Empty park bench? I couldn't even find the park benches, how was I going to find my contact? And even if I did find my contact, how would I ever make it into the crowd to reach them? And even if I got them to meet me here on the outskirts, how was I going to make it through the crowd to the very cracking center of Cleopatra Square and access that manhole and save Martin and Red City—

I slunk to the side of the Baxter Building, heart pounding from my mad dash from Hill, and hunched against the building's rough-cut lapis flank. I split my awareness between the shouting horror in front of me and my internal workspace, knocking all of my carefully arranged pieces of the case out of the way with a sweep of my arm. They didn't matter now; I needed room to work. I needed room to think. If I could create a new filter, one that compensated for this level of sensory input. Or if I could throw together an AI-assisted pattern recognition program to sift the faces of the crowd for my contact. Or if I could do something clever involving probabilities, something that would enable me to weave through the least noisy parts to get to my target.

Great ideas, all, but even as I started visualizing idio for these programs, I knew I'd fail. I wasn't fast with my code any more than I was elegant, and fear and distraction from the undulating, ever-growing crowd broke over my concentration like a storm at sea. I could sit down and pull all my threads internally, but then I'd lose awareness of the physical world completely. I could be crushed by the crowd as I wove maths, and never be wiser, only deader.

Clumsy, ugly fragments of code fell from my hands and I slammed the back of my head into the wall behind me, eyes hot with frustration. I'd never pull anything together in time. Not before I was caught by the crowd, or by the cops, or before Martin was dead.

I would have to get more help. I coughed a few times, feeling even sicker.

272 Hoshi and the Red City Circuit

I reached Luzzie Vai in the Mem at his home address; whether he was doing anything besides sitting around in his own head I didn't know and didn't care. We faced each other in the small, bare Memspace of mutual distrust he'd let me into. I hated that he was the only person I knew who could—and would—do what I needed.

"Ah, look," Luzzie greeted me with the bastard child of a smile and a sneer. "The source of all the city's trouble, right here, on my doorstep."

I couldn't tell from his emotives if he was disdaining or approving, his lively hair twisting in patterns too fast for me to read. Besides, most of my attention was on the physical world coming apart all over Central.

Asking the creep for another favor was out of the question, so I fell back on the usual threat and snapped, "If you want to continue the decadent lifestyle you've grown accustomed to, you'll patch me through to the rep from the Carmine Market who's prowling the crowd for me right now."

"And exactly how do you think I'm going to do that?" Luzzie's hair settled in a forward position, relaxed and open, with a hint of a challenge.

"Well, I thought maybe you could start by identifying who in Cleopatra Square is under the employ of Madame Bosco and connecting me up with them on a shortwave. Or, better still, simply let them know I'm waiting by the Baxter Building?"

Luzzie laughed, a sound I'd not heard before, nor hoped to hear again. His half-snickers were disturbing enough. "Hoshi gives poor Luzzie too much credit," the slime chortled. Then the laugh cut short as a flipped switch. "I'm good, but I still need data to work with. Show me what you're seeing, hearing, feeling, what's it smell like there, share sensory with me. Show me the data. Then I can point the way."

I narrowed my eyes, but the despicable unresponsive normie presentation I inhabited failed to translate the expression. Sharing sensory was, compared to Claudia's request to see my while loop, about the same magnitude as a live kidney donation was to a request for a cup of sugar. And I had refused to share the *while* loop. "No way. You do not need that much information. I know what you can do, Luzzie. You'd love access to my memories, wouldn't you? Tidbits to hold over me? Access to my idio, insight into my personality, enough so you could hack my mind later at your whim? Don't you try to play me, not now. Not when I'm this close to Loie's killer."

Luzzie shrugged. "You want to connect to your contact, you gotta show me the data."

"No."

"You want to save the city?"

I snorted, "Do you?"

A broad smile, but no awful laugh. "Does it matter to Luzzie who is in control?"

"Might if they shut down Shirring."

A scoff, "Not possible."

"Hubris."

A shrug, and finally, the truth, "If Integration Law is repealed, that just means more business for old Luzzie, jo? More Ops looking for a way to pass as dims."

We stood face to face, equal in height in our francas, arms crossed. Self-conscious of the unconscious mirroring, I uncrossed my arms and wiped my palms on my thighs. Which made me think of Martin's stress habit, and so I stopped that too. Nothing was safe anymore.

In the flesh, I pushed the heels of my hands against my temples, as though squeezing my brain might cause the juice of a better option to leak out. It didn't. I winced and glanced around. The crowd had grown, the shouting louder. Soon where I stood would be consumed too, by bodies and noise and anger and things I couldn't manage without my nervous system shutting down.

The RCPD riot guards were nearer to me now too, punching angry gestures into the air at a stand of scraggly kids wearing hats and hoods that made it impossible to tell if they were Op or normie. It was impossible to tell who in the crowd stood for what anymore; everyone was equal in their rage. The sound of a copter above meant more guards were on their way. Trinity.

"I'll give you your cracking data flow to my perception," I ground out to Luzzie in the Mem. "But that's it. There's no way you can convince me you need more than that."

Luzzie looked pleased, so I knew I'd just handed him my soul. I pulled most of my awareness back into my workspace, and pulled out some old code fragments I hadn't used since I was a child, along with the decryption pattern for my top layers of security. I began weaving them together with some new stuff that made what I was doing accessible to Luzzie's patterns. I couldn't imagine anyone, even Luzzie Vai, being good enough to crack stored memories, but paranoia is the only sane response when dealing with a leech like him, so I connected the program as far upstream of my memory index as possible. If I'd done it right, I'd just turned myself into the bio-equivalent of a full sensory holocam for Luzzie's personal use, and that was all I'd done. If I'd done it wrong, well, then who knew how deep Luzzie would be able to go into my most private memories.

I wrapped the program in the franca of a hose and dragged it through the channel I shared with Luzzie, initiating the code as I went. Luzzie took the nozzle greedily and jammed it into the side of his head.

I rolled my imaginary eyes at the theatrics while opening my physical eyes to the mess around me, and hoped that Luzzie would be able to sort it for me, even just a little bit.

"Can't do it unless you open your eyes, luv," Luzzie crooned, oily as a brassfish's holk-bladder.

"My eyes are open," I drummed my franca's fingers impatiently, compensating for the fact that Nicholas Foo's stupid normie presentation didn't have emotives to express the nuances of my displeasure.

"If that's what things look like with your eyes open, you're not one tenth the Operator I thought you were," Luzzie feigned a pout.

"I don't know why you thought I was much of an Operator in the first place. If I were any good, I'd be able to set up the filters and find the contact myself."

"You're just not opening up to me Hoshi," Luzzie tsked and wagged a finger. "Luzzie needs true sensory. Just like Teacher in first level filters class."

I just wasn't going to get out of this clean, no matter what. I had no idea if Luzzie actually needed more data or if he was playing me, but what was I going to do? Argue with him while Red City burned? Jamming the tips of my fingers into the rough flank of the Baxter Building, sighing in two worlds at once, I reminded myself of the city. I reminded myself of all the people who get hurt or worse in a riot. Of all the people I'd be forced to watch crying and bleeding and crushed when the city dumped her sensors on me in my sleep again. I reminded myself that the city was more important than any single one of her citizens, even me.

And then I dropped my sensory filters and three more levels of security, more than I ever had in my life, more than most Ops ever do in their lives, before I had a milisec in which to get spooked about the consequences of letting Luzzie in so deep.

Hot, raw roar.

Mind-splitting eye-stabbing pain.

Signal punched up so strong it was nothing but noise.

Fingernails dug into the sides of my face, next to my eyes, the sharp pain keeping me inside myself as consciousness tried to flee.

I slid to the sidewalk, knees up under my chin, rocking, eye-sting tears streaming like I'd stuck my head in a vat of freshly-sliced onions.

Luzzie Vai jammed the fingers of his mind into my internal programming like a papper who'd just been handed a kilo of his drug of choice.

Is this what the city feels like when I enter her senses like a thief? This strange invasion, this ambiguous tincture of discomfort and relief? This uneasy truce between losing control and having something more skilled than one's self take over?

When we're very young, instructors teach us how to program our sensory filters by sharing perceptual flows, just like this. That's the code I'd used, the old code from childhood. It is unpleasant enough to have someone else's foreign patterns mucking up your thinking as a kid; as an adult with so many more secrets to guard—I couldn't do it.

I needed to get in touch with my contact. I needed to be able to navigate that crowd to the manhole.

In the flesh, I sweated like I had a case of food poisoning.

In the Mem, Luzzie had my hose jammed in the side of his head. His eyes were rolled back and unseeing, but his hands worked code like a magician. Luzzie worked fast. He worked beautifully. I wouldn't have been able to follow him even if he were using franca, which he wasn't. But even his fast, incomprehensible idio made me look away in envy.

"Ah, that's more like it," Luzzie purred. "I'd always imagined Hoshi Archer had much more of a mess in her head than her crude programs and excellent skills at manipulating dims would imply."

I didn't answer the dig, too unsettled by someone's presence this close to the heart of me. Too overwhelmed by the roiling noise in which I drowned back in the physical world.

But Luzzie didn't leave the dig alone.

"I'd always wondered what happened when two class eighteens bred. That's what your parents were rated at, wasn't it? Both Operators, Class eighteen?"

Okay, that was it. I started to close my channel to the Mem and cut him off from me fast as sin. But Luzzie stuck the programmatic equivalent of a foot in a closing door, and oozed complex emotives that read equal parts condescension and apology.

Trinity, what had I done letting Luzzie in? He had me, he could do anything to me. He had—

"This is great, this is great. Got something for you to try in just a moment..."

I had to get to Martin before the city went up in riots.

The code had grown at the speed of thought, towering and intricate, full of mathematics that shivered with spider's-web delicacy. I only saw the idio of the finished program for a fraction of a second. Then it compressed and collapsed, wrapped in the franca of a steaming demitasse of espresso.

Luzzie still had the hose of my sensory feed stuck in the side of his head, but his eyes were focused back on me, and he held the cup out and nodded. The aroma of coffee curled toward me, smelling just like a cup from the Julia Set.

Once more setting the box marked "Shred of Sanity" on the shelf—easier now that sensory overload and Luzzie's tendrils in my navis had emptied that box of content—I took the espresso and swallowed.

I'd once put on one of Kelvin's creepy tinker's helmets—the one with the lenses that make his eyes big as houses—and put the lenses down over my eyes. Kel insists the lenses are great for magnifying his vision up to 500 times, but I couldn't see a cracking thing through them, and I'd chased Kel around blindly, giggling, falling all over the furniture. But I remember when I'd taken the lenses off, how the world around me had jumped into clarity. How the blind fuzzy edges of everything vanished and the sharpness of my own vision stunned me immobile.

Luzzie's program was just like that, only for all my senses. It was like I'd been wearing big fuzzy lenses that made the world impossible to bear and I'd just taken them off and could see, hear, touch, taste, smell for the first time in my life. This was the world without excess sensory input. Was this how normals perceived it? I sat stunned, immobile, speechless, and awed.

The crowd remained, still loud, still writhing. But my focus was selective. I only saw, only heard, what I paid attention to. And I was in control of what I paid attention to. A woman in a red shirt, mouse-brown hair swirling around her shoulders as she turned to yell, "Danny, I'm over here!" above the din. A riot cop, his shield pushing the crowd back, whispering, "Please, please don't turn this bad." A father and daughter, trapped by the press, working their way to escape. My senses had become a camera and a boom, able to angle anywhere—

My attention wrenched to the edge of the crowd nearest me. I wasn't in control after all.

"If you want fast, you've got to let me drive," Luzzie's voice purred in my mind, self-satisfied and unwelcome. He'd inserted a channel to himself into that insidious cup of joe, and his tendrils hadn't left my mind, they'd just dug deeper. Curse it all to Noise! "The sensory filter's for me, luv, so I can run a pattern match for your contact, though feel free to enjoy the benes."

So I was going to have a passenger for the ride. Having useful command of my senses had been an illusion. Typical. "Let's get this over with," I growled to Luzzie in the Mem and pushed myself up and away from the wall, and over the threshold of sound that had paralyzed me ten minutes before.

Moving through the crowd with new clarity, Luzzie steered my attention and my body. He was searching for my contact, at least so it seemed, and over and over I focused in on a face, or a back, or an article of clothing, and then moved on. I assumed he was looking for people he could identify as couriers for Bosco. At least I hoped. Whatever it was he was doing paid off though, as near the edge of the crowd on the southwest side my attention focused on someone and finally stayed there.

The someone didn't look like a sketchy mobster, but then sketchy mobsters don't always look like you'd expect. This one was a woman in a long black coat-dress with a tan backpack strapped to her back. She wasn't holding a sign that said, "Hoshi Archer, I'm your contact," but as I drew closer I saw her giving me an extra look-over, and then with her hands hidden from others by the folds of her coat she gave me the heart-shaped hand-signal used by the

Carmine Market. Hoping Luzzie—who'd been uncharacteristically and thankfully quiet—had gotten it right, I made my way to her through the surreal clarity.

The woman didn't say a word, just took the backpack off and handed it to me.

Luzzie gave some control of my body back but didn't leave my mind. I took the backpack and set it on the ground, wishing Luzzie wasn't watching, but grateful for his filters. Someone stumbled into my shoulder as I leaned over the bag, then cursed me and moved on. I wanted to move on too, somewhere far away from all the stomping preferably, but Luzzie had already led me two thirds of the way to the manhole cover, and I wasn't willing to give up that gained ground.

Inside the bag was a small box. I pried it open in the darkness of the backpack. My heightened filters zeroed in despite the dim and the din. A small glass bottle with a slender, curved spout rested in a cradle of foam. A wax stopper topped it. Next to the bottle was a transparent needle, hollow, perhaps glass as well. That would be the acid I needed to melt the lock on the manhole cover.

I grinned despite the mess I was in.

Rocking forward on the balls of my feet, giddy with how well my senses functioned under the influence of Luzzie, I looked up to thank the courier, but she was gone.

"One last thing Luzzie, then we're done."

No sound from the slime, but I felt him there, suckling my senses. Bosco and Luzzie Vai: how was I helping anyone by throwing my lot in with these criminals? When were the costs not worth the benefits? Did my desire for justice balance it all out? Would Sorreno's influence balance it all out? Would anything ever balance it all out?

"Luzzie?"

"Yah, luv," the saccharine purr was strained. "You got a real interesting way of seeing the world. Almost more intensity than old Luzzie can bear."

"You gotta get me to the Fishing Boy Fountain in the center of Cleopatra Square. We're already part way there." I stood and stumbled away from two men who had just started throwing fists at each other. "Luzzie, now."

CHAPTER 26

The path Luzzie led me down, puppeting my body and sorting my senses, made no logical sense. We weren't weaving through the crowd, we were randomly darting amongst it. Of course it wasn't random; Luzzie assured me he was picking a very precise path to get me where I needed to go with the least amount of impact from the crowd. Each change in angle made me a little more doubtful, however, that Luzzie was leading me anywhere I wanted to go.

Just as hope surrendered to suspicion, my body turned to face the ancient pagoda-fountain at the center of Cleopatra Square. The youth, as he had for over a thousand years across three continents and two star systems, held his fish aloft, his spear relaxed, his body graceful. I wondered if Luzzie shared my relief through his link to my senses.

I stood a still counterpoint to the Fishing Boy, the two of us the only motionless things in the Square. In the immediate area around us, people large and small, young and old, affluent and impoverished, decorated and plain, Operator and norm, pressed in toward each other as the density of the crowd increased. Those close to me however didn't shout or dart or punch the air and chant like people elsewhere. They milled a little vacantly, as though unsure what they were doing there. Something brewed beneath our feet, something that changed the flow of the crowd in this spot, just like the unseen forcefields in vorpal pool.

"Over there, Luzzie," I looked past the fountain to the northwest. He'd left me enough control that I could focus our conjoined attention on the place I knew the manhole cover to be.

Clearly Luzzie hadn't discovered the invisible hatch yet, nor come to any of the other conclusions I had about data loss in the area. He gave me highly confused and extra-cranky emotives.

"C'mon, just do it," I grumbled, cranky myself, and my body started moving again under Luzzie's direction.

I stepped into the adaptive field that made the manhole cover invisible—and fell flat on my face.

Confusion, disorientation, lack of sensation.

Had I been hit? Punched, pummeled, bumped into, pushed? Head cracked, smack! Seeing stars.

I felt the chill of steel against my cheek and smelled the must of soil, and then both sensations vanished as though a switch had been turned in my awareness.

In the sudden still quiet, I realized I was alone again in my head. Luzzie's filter program, and Luzzie as my guide through the sensory chaos of the crowd—they were gone. So were my own filters—I'd taken them down to let Luzzie in. So now I was in the center of Cleopatra Square, in the center of the rising riot, in the center of the city, in the center of a storm which had no eye—and I had no filters. The impact that had felled me hadn't been physical at all; I'd been flattened senseless by my own senses, just like when the screaming tube had felled me while I was running from the thugs. My navis had slammed a protective wall of sensory deprivation between my mind and my body.

Had Luzzie left me at this critical moment just to spite me? Just to sit back and laugh and watch me fail? He had reasons to want me to succeed, but just as many to want to see me fail. He could have intended this all along, to lure me to the center of the crowd and then drop me to die beneath the uncaring feet of the city.

Or was it the adaptive field, the one creating the illusion of grass over the breach into the city's heart, interfering with our connection? The black holes in the Mem, the data loss, sucking down into the pit of illusion. This seemed more likely, given that Luzzie's assistance had failed me the instant I'd stepped into the field.

Faint pain seeped into the corners of the sensory deprivation bubble; it would be logical, if I was prone, that I was getting stomped on. Which was bad because I doubted I'd be able to stop the murderer with a collection of broken bones.

I ran a standard routine to make my body into a sit, uncertain if it had worked because I was no longer receiving sensory input.

Okay. Well, I did know I was on top of the manhole at least given the trajectory of my fall, and that was where I wanted to be.

I also knew I should be terrified, pissing myself over the inevitable awful trampling death that could come for me while I sat utterly unaware.

But my core being had distanced itself from the enemy my body had become, my thoughts already solving the puzzle of this new predicament. Or was it the city's touch, cradling me in my panic?

Such thoughts happened on an almost subliminal thread in my consciousness. The thread of my main consciousness was too busy digging into my memory index and pulling up recall on my exploration of the manhole cover earlier, in the peace after the evening rain. I also pulled up my experience with the backpack and the box and the bottle of acid. I could cut those memories up, rearrange them, patch them back together again, and make a program to run my own body remotely from the trap of my mind. My memory of sensation could serve as proxy for the real thing.

On a third thread, the level of consciousness between the other two, I worried that if I made a mistake in any of my calculations, I'd end up eaten through with acid instead of the lock I intended to destroy.

I discarded some fragments of memory, rearranged the rest into a new sequence, and strung them all back together with basic motor programming: functions to move arms, hands, turn the torso, operate hips and legs, etc. Then I tapped into an old RCPD survival program I'd been given, one for climbing and jumping and knowing how to walk away from a long fall. I hadn't been able to find any records of how deep the manhole might go so I needed to be prepared for the worst. Luzzie might not be around anymore to puppet my body, but I could puppet myself.

On that nearly subliminal thread of my heart, I whispered to the city: please don't let me screw up my calculations.

RUN PROGRAM.

I watched myself in simulation doing the things I had coded, hoping my body in the flesh was doing them also, but really having no way to know for sure. In simulation I saw:

—myself shrug off the backpack with the acid, reach in, and pull out the pieces. Puncture the wax seal on the glass bottle with the hollow needle. Lean over the globs of welded steel attaching the lock to the manhole cover—

Though these things looked real, I'd only ever "seen" the manhole cover via the touch of my fingers, and manufactured the rest. I was seeing memories of reconstructions, simulations based on simulated memories, fictions that, hopefully, made realities.

—the glass bottle tips down over the welds and liquid flows through the hollow needle, the acid starts to hiss—

I didn't really hear anything. No acid hissing, no crowd stomping. I had no idea how long it would take for the acid to work. I had no idea how long it would remain volatile, how long I would have to wait until it was safe for my unprotected fingers to push open—hopefully—the lock-free edges of the manhole cover. I had no idea if I'd even managed any of the actions I'd programmed, if my calculations had been accurate, or if I'd just been pantomiming the motions to the air. I had no idea if I'd spilled acid all over myself and was melting into the dirt. I would just have to keep taking my best guesses, loading the odds with all that modern mathematics had to offer, and keep going.

I set a timer for three minutes. My heart beat in sync with each second, counting down. Thump-three, thump-two, thump-one—

RUN PROGRAM.

—my boots find the massive lock and push it away from the circular plate of the hatch cover, I back up on my knees now, shove the cover open, fall back on my butt, put my legs out in front of me, plunge down into the void—

Sensory perception came back to me as my feet hit concrete and I smashed down onto my knees and palms, my navis deciding I no longer needed to be protected by the bubble of sensory deprivation right at the moment of impact. I was on the ground in a pool of murky-half light and pain. Above me the rumble-stomp of the crowd shook the thin metal beams supporting the ceiling, shivering like the city herself. But the sounds in the square were dampened here, no longer a hazard to my sensitivities.

My knuckles were a mush of blood and scrapes and shoe prints, but they still moved like they were supposed to, which was more than I'd counted on. I flipped my hands over and inspected the palms. Nasty deep scrapes bled freely on the heels where I'd fallen hard through the hole, but that was all. No acid-burns. Thank Trinity for that as well.

I looked up at the slim crescent of stars, interrupted by the flickers of bodies passing overhead. I'd barely managed to push that manhole cover open at all, which on one hand was a relief because it meant the people in the Square above wouldn't fall willy-nilly into the same pit as me. On the other hand, it made me realize I'd almost failed to open it at all. The fisherman's sweater was shredded, and I'd have a much higher scrape tally if I hadn't been wearing my indestructible nanocloth bolero beneath it.

Squinting up, I had my navis calculate the distance from the parallax of my vision. Three and a half meters. I'd fallen three and a half meters. I took a deep breath in new respect for that RCPD survival program. I'd pulled the mad scheme off. But just barely. If the distance had been much further there wouldn't have been a program in the world that could have helped me take the fall.

I looked down where the broken skin of my knees had leaked dark circles into my pants. The blood hadn't leaked through the clear coating on the outside though; those fishgutter's pants were seriously waterproof.

I stood shakily and surveyed the tunnel. Small but serviceable. Bare. Very,

very old. It extended to the northeast and southwest. A rusty old door was set into the tunnel wall about three paces from where I'd landed.

I shut off a few visual filters so I could see better in the dim light of the cheap green-tint everbulb far down the bend to the northeast. The footprints in the dust led to the door, not down the corridor. Which was what I had expected.

The ground beneath my feet vibrated like I was standing on a battery; the tiny hairs on my body stood on end. The electrical tingling was the same feeling I'd had when Blu Lou'd pressed my palms to the center of Red City's map. The same sensation I'd had traveling through the portal into Gno's Temple of Zaos. I was standing in the place where the Dragon Lines crossed, standing at the city's magnetic heart. An élan vital had to be present down here, manipulating the electricity; the city's geomagentisim wasn't strong enough for human senses to feel.

I took four deep breaths. Pushed the fishgutter's cap off my head and let my hair fall free.

If there was an élan behind that door, and it didn't like me, it could kill me faster than any human murderer. All it would take was a little more electricity.

I ran my bloody, mangled fingers through the length of my hair.

If there was an élan behind that door, and it did like me, would the outcome be any better?

I was having trouble breathing. I wanted to sit.

I shed the last shreds of the fisherman's sweater, and straightened the cuffs of my bolero.

However it played, if I had to die, at least I'd look like Hoshi Archer as it happened.

I took three swift steps to the rusted door and turned the knob.

It opened easily.

After all, the other side of that door was exactly where she wanted me to be.

CHAPTER 27

Like a bug trapped beneath the curve of a bowl, I was in a circular room with a domed ceiling. The ceiling was so high I was surprised it didn't poke through the grass of Cleopatra Square above. The electricity I'd felt outside was stronger here, and reminded me of how I felt when the sensors drowned me in the city's dreams.

I opened a broadband channel, seeking anything that might come through. Ghostly impressions flickered, too vague and full of static to name but bearing the familiar edges of the sensorfeeds. Testing further, I sent out a broadcast on multiple frequencies: Red City, it's me. The energy beneath my feet rose and rippled, making the roof of my mouth buzz.

The room was stark, but not empty. Beneath full-spectrum everbulbs the curved walls gleamed with silver 3Vplates. Clustered at the far edge, three mechanical arms hovered silently, each a filigree of silver gears and pistons. Extended, each would be about twice my height. One slender mechanical hand flexed itself, displaying a nuanced articulation far superior to human fingers. Kelvin would be impressed.

In the center of the space sat a pagoda, just about my height. At first glance, it looked no different from the thousands of traditional five-element pagodas that dotted the city. Cube, sphere, pyramid, crescent, and flame—each balanced atop the other. But instead of being carved or cast from a single block, each segment of this pagoda was made of a different material. The base earth cube was of polished blackstone; the water sphere of pearly ornne shells, the kind that wash up on Broadway Beach. The air pyramid was made of grey lorrie down and the long turquoise wing-feathers of brinn gulls, and held together with copper wires. At the pyramid's point, the crescent fire bowl had been built of crystal matrix dataslips, stripped of their casings so that the ruby-colored gems made light dance on the ceiling. And, for void's flame at the very top, a tear-drop coated with pale, iridescent blue tzaddium. Tzaddium, the element that made quantum computing possible. That made me, and marked me, and shone blue beneath the skin of my forehead; that gave me my life and branded me forever other.

Then I processed what else was different about this pagoda and gagged. Attached to the cube, pyramid, and crescent were thin rectangular sheets that also shimmered with the blue of tzaddium—the navi that had been ripped from the dead girls' heads.

I looked away, up.

Above the grisly pagoda, suspended from the apex of the ceiling on wires so thin he appeared levitating, Martin Ho hung naked. Martin's eyes were closed, his face peaceful, and he gave no sign of awareness that I'd stepped into the room. I watched his chest move up and down, assuring myself I wasn't too late.

But no, he'd have to be painted before he was killed, before his navis was ripped out and slapped onto the shell-coated water sphere of the pagoda. And the painting had not yet begun. His closed eyes, his peaceful expression: Martin Ho was coding.

Movement from behind the pagoda. My eyes flicked away from Martin, watching the killer's sharp, pristine figure rise from behind the structure. Mai Chandra held a small vial aloft in her fingertips, a mockery of the Fishing Boy Fountain above. Dark blue liquid shimmered in the vial like the sinister sister of tzaddium. NQ, the drug that would sever Martin's mind from his navis as soon as his part in the program was complete. Sever it so she could rip his processor from him, silencing him forever, and then it would be my turn—

I made myself look at her, really see her. Noticed the lack of wrinkles or specks of dust on her perfect, pinstriped pantsuit. Watch her turn and place the NQ among the other items arranged on the spotless white floor. Three jars of paint brushes. Three metal trays. Seventeen jars of powdered pigments in all colors of the rainbow; three jars of oily yellow fluid to turn them into paint. A small dish of black powder; a small dish of white powder. A government issue, government controlled container of tzaddium, the kind every Operator has so we can upgrade our processors; presumably Martin's. The items were lined up and categorized with the same neat efficiency with which Mai arranged her Spartan office. And the items held the same heart-stopping threat of violence as her weekly conversations. The saw-toothed edges of her perfect hair looked like they could cut me.

"Hello Hoshi," Mai Chandra smiled at me without warmth, without coolness, just as unreadably as she'd smiled at me a hundred times over and over and over again in our weekly meetings at the Integration Office.

My hand trembled and slipped from the door to the tunnel outside. Metal clanged as it banged shut and Mai's trap sealed behind me. What else could I have done but walked into it willingly? No, not just willingly, but without regard for my future.

I'd been conned. We'd all been conned, me, Martin, Nessa, Aysha, and Claudia. Mai Chandra had conned us into lighting our own cremation fires with a smile on our faces, because we thought it was the only way to have the thing we desired most in all the world. Trinity, given the circumstances, I still thought being here was the only way to have peace for Red City. After three years of weekly interrogations, Mai Chandra knew me pretty well. She was so smart I could almost mistake her for an Operator. It was going to be hard to con her back.

If I'd made my way through the crowd without Luzzie's help, I would have been powerless by now, sinking into the same helpless catatonia of sensory overload I'd experienced at the end of my flight to Kelvin's. And Mai Chandra was counting on that to control me. But instead, Luzzie had taken the burden of managing my perceptions, protected me from overload; and my mind and senses were as sharp as ever. Mai didn't know I had that edge, and I needed to keep it hidden. So I let down the walls of programming—subroutines to

stimulate the production of endorphins and adrenaline, simulated bravado—
that protected me from my sorry condition.

A retching wave of fatigue.

A kick to the gut, the knees, the hands, stinging, torn flesh. Choking
stabbing takes-my-breath-away.

I'm going to die in here.

Electrical buzz, an alien consciousness probing at the edges of thought.

All my fault.

I'm going to die in pain.

"H-hello ma'am. Are you go. Going. Are you—will you fix it?" I pointed
my chin toward the seething square above, but motor functions overwhelmed
by pain couldn't get the movement right, and I jerked in a broken spasm.

"It's amazing, isn't it?" Mai kept smiling and pointed her own chin toward
the square, as efficient and tidy as her perfect saw-blade-edged hair and her
immaculately pressed pants. "You did that Hoshi, you got them all stirred up.
Your face on the mainfeeds. Hero turns criminal. Hero is falsely accused.
Integration fails. Integration is being *made* to fail. Your actions the tinder, the
spark, for all of the sides, for all of the city, you incite something in everyone,
Hoshi. Can you feel it beneath our feet? The city really responds to you, even
moreso than I had thought. But surpassing expectations is what you're known
for, isn't it? Such tragedy you've endured, such pain. Such an inspiration to all.
But no one can overcome that much adversity alone. Everyone needs a family.
And yes," the smile broadened but remained unreadable, "I can fix what you've
done to the city. Well, not me. Us. You and me and the city together, Hoshi,
we are all family here."

I believed her. Believed her the way millions of people in Red City
believed that the Integration Office was the answer to a host of prayers. That
belief resonated through the city beneath me and above me and a hope that
was not mine fluttered at my center, and I believed like I had believed three
years ago when I first marched up the steps to the IO with the mainfeeds all

pointed at me to proudly claim my new life, my new job, my new freedom.

Then the belief flipped and memories flashed of a knife in an alley cutting my face, a fist in the gut, of Martin being coerced with threats to turn me in—the thugs were in Mai's employ. Mai was the murderer! She had just killed three people and was in the process of killing one more. We were not a family!

And that was the opening telempathic play in our battle for communication with the élan vital that inhabited the city. With the momentum of the ritual murders and the pagoda in the center of the room, Mai had gathered enough resonance with the creature to have almost taken me at our very first move. The dangers of feedback and resonance that had spattered the mainfeeds—and justified the need for the Callisto Embassy, and Lillie's desire to chase me off-world—became, for the first time, real to me. No wonder anyone who knew anything about the élans down in Shirring Point had been scared.

"Do you understand what you have to do?" Mai's voice, emotionless, reassuring, infinitely patient.

I swallowed and jerkily nodded as I shook off a new wave of < *trust-me* > feelings from the city. I was ready for it this time, yet it still threatened to pull me under the false comfort of Mai's voice. Sheng chi. Bad energy. I said brokenly, "Program. Run."

"That's right." Mai bent and began measuring tiny, precise amounts of powdered pigment into the metal trays with a tiny spoon. She measured as slowly and patiently as she spoke, and again I felt the telempathic lull from the invisible entity in the room. Mai continued measuring and speaking, "We don't want the bad people who are against Integration to control the city, do we? Your people need access to the help they need to thrive. Even independently-living Operators like yourself could benefit from increased levels of support. I would have ensured that if I'd been appointed to the Director position. They passed me over, but I have the understanding. The vision. There are people in the city who recognize that vision, who have helped me get to where we now stand, on the brink of a stronger community. They've helped me just like I've been helping you." Then she frowned, as unreadably as she smiled. "You do realize sometimes things have to get worse before they can get better? Sacrifices always need to be made to facilitate real change." She glanced above our heads.

Trinity, she was going to let the riots happen! If the murder of three people had given Mai enough resonance with the city to have me believing she was my family, what would the murder of hundreds—maybe thousands—do? The electricity beneath my feet surged again, reminding me that the élans had a much more nuanced control of the EM than we. Reminding me of how, not-so-long-ago, angry élans had almost killed everyone on Europa and Ganymede. If the city wanted to, she could send enough current into the crowd to fry everyone. Over a hundred thousand dead, maybe more. I coughed up a "Yes" and lurched like a marionette with tangled strings toward the center of the room. If the riots did start, if people did die above, I wouldn't be able to overpower the resonance Mai was building no matter how much I loved Red City. No matter how much Lillie and Gno thought I was a magnet. I didn't think I could break Mai's resonance as it was.

I'd stiffened as I'd stood, and I moved with a million shards of hurt. A gasp came, and then a genuine stumble.

Mai didn't notice. Her gaze had turned toward Martin, her smile for the first time passing a reflection of an emotion, a soulless satisfaction and an empty bliss. I felt cold and looked at Martin too. A bliss of a warmer sort illuminated his face, the joy of coding. The expression soothed me, even on Martin's ugly mug.

I reached the pagoda at the center of the room and let my body sink painfully to the electrified floor, leaving little bloody smears as I settled. Because it no longer mattered, I slipped my consciousness out of Nicholas Foo's franca and back into my own presentation, glad to have a full range motion and expression back. And, even better, nothing in my thoughts hurt.

I flashed awareness back to Mai. She was back to mixing paints, slowly, methodically. I had a little time, but not much. I opened a channel and tuned it to a shortwave frequency so I could connect with Martin.

He was ridiculously easy to contact. And almost impossible to keep hold of. His intense concentration on his code was only half of it; his grasp of the signal slipped and toppled, like he was thumbing the dial on an ancient walkie-talkie that couldn't hold its tuning to the proper band. And there was something else too, something strange about the signal. Like I could hear scraps of other people's conversations, see bits of feed and raw data and idio flitting by; ghosts in the airwaves. They felt like my dreams tangled up in the city's. What was it Lillie had said about beckerwood brew opening the mind to transmission? The city was occupying the channel too, resonating also with Martin.

"You've drunk your beckerwood brew and whisky cocktail, huh Martin?" I projected through the noisy channel, glad our communication in the Mem could take place at the speed of thought. "You've got to concentrate. We've got to have a conversation."

"Fuck off," came Martin's reply as he identified me, and he tried to close the connection and rez me out. But I was ready with the foot-in-the-door trick Luzzie had used on me, and Martin was too woozy with signal and distracted by code to counter it.

"I promise you with every protein molecule in my DNA that I will fuck off and leave you utterly alone as soon as you finish your program. But until then, you have got to listen to me."

"Fuck off, I hate you," Martin whined, his presentation gaining animation as he pulled in a few more threads to deal with me. The edges of his ridiculous super-hero cape flickered with irritation and his hero-jaw jutted like a petulant teen.

I kept my own emotives as open and obvious as possible. No pretense, no frills. Not even trying to hide how much I loathed him back. "Did Mai tell you she'd make you a hero?"

"She made you one," Martin answered with a snarl of envy.

Thank the Trinity I didn't have to play stupid normie social fencing games with Martin as there wasn't any time. "She lied to you."

"What, you don't want the competition?"

"She lied to me too."

Emotives don't lie. And neither does the playback of perfect recall. I let him see my fear laced with silent fury every time I stepped into that Integration Office to be questioned. I replayed him my memories, unfiltered, of Mai's nerve-wracking interrogations, requests for detailed information about embarrassing things, bodily functions, forcing me to frame my existence in ways that were abhorrent because I knew if I stood up for myself she'd take away my life. "Mai told me I did this for the privilege of being in control of my life. But it was just a way for her to control me. And I bought it, bought it right up 'till earlier today. Just like you did. Just like the whole cracking city did. Just like the whole fucking world."

And then I dropped the punchline. "But last time I went to see Mai, she questioned me about my latest case for Sorreno, three women murdered, right here in this very room. She tried to get me to slop about it. Which is really funny in retrospect, because earlier today, the thing that made me realize I had never been in control, is that I factored Mai was the murderer."

Martin started in on a new whine but then went still. "The—wait, what?" He pulled all his threads in to focus on me with nearly-sober clarity.

Which meant he'd stopped coding which meant that Mai might notice and—"No, no!" My overly broadcast emotives came out all disproportionate to the panic I felt.

"Hoshi, what!" Now Martin cracked too, his cape billowing out to hide him.

"Sorry," I screwed up my face unhappily. "I'm jumpy. You have to keep coding or Mai might guess we're chatting, and she absolutely cannot know that." I checked back in with my body and found a lax, defeated posture and a half open jaw. I told myself the small amount of drool was on purpose. Mai was about half way through mixing, judging by how many paint cups were full and how many were empty. Still time, but not a lot.

Martin's franca lost some resolution as he split threads again, and I relaxed a little.

"I'll explain. Just keep coding while I do it." I pulled out my completed take on the case, including my set-up and attempted arrest, and Martin's coercion by Mai's hired thugs, and all the stuff I'd prepared to convince him to come clean to Sorreno back before I realized he'd be the one trussed up in this room. I wrapped it in the franca of a file stamped with the RCPD shield sigil.

Martin absorbed the folder. I watched his cape work its way through just about every unpleasant emotion it was possible to have. When he returned to his usual sullen glare, I poked him with a finger.

"She's going to kill you, Martin. Mai is. Just as soon as she's satisfied I have your code integrated into the larger program. Mai's behind the riot situation above our heads, and she's using us, the program, this ritual, the élan vital lurking around this region of space, the Inclusion Act lobby, all of it, to create a crisis that she can work to her advantage—and presumably to the advantage of whoever she's working for or with. She's provoking a slaughter to get it, so she can swoop in at the zero hour and come out the hero. Not you, not me, her. We both lived through the Mayfair Riots, the Epic Bombings, we know how bad things can get. Trinity, the first Mayfair Riot alone took 456 lives. We can't let that happen again. And we can't let someone with no respect for human life control city politics—especially those parts of city politics that control us Operators." I drew in an imaginary breath. "If you want to be a hero, now's your chance. You can save yourself, you can save me, you can save Cleopatra Square from another riot, you can save the whole cracking city from Mai's conception of how to make the world a better place. I'll give you all the credit, I promise. You have got to know somewhere in the pit of your black and raisin-shriveled little heart that I don't want it. But you've got to work with me for a few minutes right now. You have got to help me factor what the program you're working on actually does."

Maybe it was the whisky and beckerwood brew cocktail, but Martin's cape twitched as though he'd felt moved before he puffed out his chest and gave me his special Hoshi-glare.

"You'd better. Or I'm gonna take you down," he sneered. But there wasn't any bite behind his bark.

I nodded and yanked everything I'd figured on the program and shot it into our common space. The original paintings as they appeared on dead flesh, their multi-dimensional reconstructions, my idio, and finally a bridge into franca that Martin could quickly read. I could have deleted my clumsy idio, but I wanted Martin feeling as superior as possible, even if it meant embarrassing myself. What did it matter at this point? I was probably going to die.

Martin took one look at my ugly idio and pointed and laughed. I was embarrassed, yeah, but watching Martin's puffed-up super-hero self laughing at my ugly programming actually made me smirk a little back. That was until he banished all traces of my terribly funny idio, and began recoding to optimize the program. Martin wasn't as fast as Luzzie, but he still manipulated the code with an ease and a grace that made me snarl with envy.

Then I realized I was acting just like Martin and stopped.

"You totally korkered this," he sneered superiorly at me. "I can't believe they used to let you anywhere near code."

I stifled the urge to point out that's why I was better suited to being a PI. There were more important things than my ego for me to worry about right now. Like Martin's ego. "So you're coding the last part of this program, right?"

Martin grunted and nodded and kept fiddling with my work. He hadn't really changed anything; I'd gotten the basics right. He just was unhappy with how messily I'd done it. While he worked, I shot a glance back at Mai and her paint mixing. She was two thirds done.

"So what part of the program do you have? Data?" I prompted Martin.

He raised an eyebrow the same way an adult will to a child who asks too many pointless questions.

"So, uh," reminding myself once more that the goal no longer involved retaining a shred of dignity, "You're so much better than me at this," I groveled. And then I forced myself to grind out, even though it wasn't true, "I don't understand it."

"Well, I could just run it—"

"No!"

An evil, self-satisfied grin at my genuine horror.

"I mean, yes, soon, but not yet. Spell it out for me Martin, I'm practically a dim, remember?"

He stopped messing with the code and raised his nose into Lecture Mode. "Clearly, this program creates a new Memspace, one with some very specific parameters and a very distinct artistic flair. And something else too, something really strange. The program is intended to run in a closed circuit; it has no portals in. What's the point of creating a Memspace no one can enter? Who knows. Do I have data? No, I have variables."

"Trinity, it's a genie in a bottle!" I erupted, amazed I hadn't realized as soon as I'd seen Mai's twisted pagoda.

Martin gave me a pained expression of what-the-fuck.

I shivered in my presentation, and probably in the flesh too, unable to find words for a moment.

"Is your insane outburst relevant?"

"It's—yes. It's what the code is for, and how it all fits together with Mai's plans. Thank you, Martin."

He seemed more confused by my thank you than by my total lack of explanation, but I explained anyway. "Mai told you the point of hanging drunk and naked while robots painted your body was to get an élan to help make your dreams come true, right?"

"Yeah," Martin continued to look at me like I was a turd that had just come alive to talk crazy to him.

"She didn't lie about the ritual creating resonance with an élan, just about the part where it was going to help you. Really, it's going to help her and whoever's backing her. Did you notice the crystal matrix on the pagoda in the room? And the tzaddium flame? I talked to this Cantor the other day, and she told me élans can inhabit crystal matrix, that it makes a half-way zone between our worlds to facilitate communication. She also told me that programming facilitates communication, being another mid-way thing between us."

He rolled his eyes, emotives clarifying the meaning of the gesture as "get on with it" rather than "you're a dangerous lunatic." Good.

I continued, "Okay, so there's an élan that lives around Red City, one that hasn't made direct contact with humans yet. Did you feel her when you came down here, that buzzing under your feet, the electricity? We're sitting on top of some strong geomagnetism, the kind that attracts élans. Now think about the pagoda again—at the top is a cup of crystal matrix and a teardrop covered in tzaddium. Crystal matrix and tzaddium—it's a quantum stationary system. That's it, that's where the program runs, in that stationary with no hardware for connecting to the Mem, because an élan vital doesn't need hardware to connect to the Mem. It can manipulate signal on any wavelength it wants just naturally. You've got variables, right? But not data. Martin, the crystal matrix is for data—and that 'data' is the élan vital herself. Mai's going to have me call the creature into that matrix and trap her inside the program you're finishing. All of this, each step, the rituals, the sacrifices, they are designed to bring the city's élan into resonance with Mai. And then Mai will have her trapped there in that stationary system, trapped for her own use. She can tell the élan to fry the entire crowd above. Martin, using human-élan feedback, Mai can force Red City to become anything she—or the creepy fucks who have been supporting her—wants."

Martin's mouth made a round Ooooh, but my attention was already dragging me back toward Mai. "Okay, so here's what I need you to do. First, finish fixing all my mistakes. Then, integrate your code with the rest. But don't run it!"

"And then what?" he eyed me suspiciously, not having processed the full implications yet.

"And then you're going to save the day."

CHAPTER 28

I transferred full awareness back to the physical world. The room vibrated from above: feet stomping in rhythm in Cleopatra Square. That was never good; crowds often synchronized briefly just before they dissolved into chaos and violence. That stomping would come with chanting, but I couldn't hear it this far beneath the earth.

The crowd wasn't the only thing that had progressed in the time I'd spent convincing Martin to do the right thing. Mai had finished her paint mixing and the three robot arms had swarmed in close to her, like small, creepy children eagerly awaiting an ice-cream cone. Mai carefully doled out art supplies to each. Paint trays, brushes, rags—it reminded me of when she doled out my food in the early days of my work through the Integration Office, before I was trusted to buy my own groceries.

The élan's restless EM beneath my feet had changed too, had become... interested. Surges of electricity prickled through the concrete floor where I sat, tasting me. One surge came on too strongly and I gasped; it flinched back and withdrew, as though we had both been burned.

Mai continued equipping the robot arms in her precise, patronizing way. "When this is done, I'll see your record is made clean," she soothed me as she worked.

"Nice. Would be." I answered in the choppy, broken speech of an Operator whose linguistics were failing. "Job. Don't want. Lose."

"Of course you don't. And you won't. You're a valuable member of this community. I'll get you right back in your little PI office East of Central. Trust me."

A tug at my heart, a willingness, a belief in resonance with Mai's statement. A conviction from the city that things would be better if I followed

Mai. She had gotten me into my PI's office, had advocated for me with the landlord who didn't want to have "one of those" in his space, who said it would be "bad for business." But Mai had stood my ground for me. Said I'd be good for business. She'd given me my—

No!

I shook the feeling with a memory of anger, directing it downward at the city, though I wasn't sure if that was how the telempathic communication with the élans was supposed to work. Anger at every hostile glare I'd had to let pass, at the protesters who had plagued me for seven months straight every time I'd walked down the street to that office, at the 'feeds that sided with the landlord, bringing my people shame. Anger at Mai for reminding me of the generosity of her advocacy every time I'd balked at divulging information that crossed a boundary into the private places of my soul where she had no business questioning. Using gratitude as a key to open me up and dig around inside.

The city changed polarity beneath me, aligning with my anger now, and Mai twitched and eyed me sharply.

Mai knew. She felt the tug-of-war between us as keenly as I did.

My influence on the City, her influence on the City, aligned along some points but so, so very different. And what did the City think or feel? I was somehow sure Mai had never asked her for her input. Like the Operators assigned to her, the City was just another object to control in order to assuage some inner hurt I wasn't linked in enough yet to name.

Dizzy, I split my consciousness as only an Operator can. I shoved my anger into Thread #2 and pushed it into a more subconscious, background place. Thread #1 continued in the fore, visible to Mai and the City. I'd have to be very careful of my thoughts and feelings from now on. I had no idea if splitting threads would enable me to hide thoughts from the growing three-way link. How little I knew of the élans. How little I knew of myself. It would be a relief to give up and let Mai take control. She was so good at being in control. Yes, I should let her have control.

Mai's shoulders relaxed, and she turned away from me to address the robot arms in the same patient tone she used with me. "There, you're all set now." With a stiff gesture, she sent them to collect around Martin. She turned back to me. "You'll be all set too Hoshi, once this is over."

I began, "Thank—" but the 3Vplates turned on and the room exploded with Martin's code in the idio of his own private language.

Flashing gold streaked with bright green spun out of the white-bright, swirling into a galaxy and spinning, spilling, finally stilling. A flash of pink! Dash of violet! Then torrents of blue poured across the layers, only to be covered by translucent hashes of purple, subtle and sophisticated, overlaid with an opalescence shimmering like the inside of a perfect ornne shell. A cascade of golden means broke the surface and—

I cried out, wildly, couldn't stop myself. I couldn't stop myself even with my motor functions mostly shut down and my consciousness fragmented into multiple threads and my throat tickling with fear. It was as if all of creativity had just been splashed over the heavens for me to see.

How unprepared I was for Martin Ho's idio being so beautiful! More beautiful than Claudia's, than Nessa's, even more beautiful than Aysha's, with her artist's touch. Even flattened as it was into the purely visual dimension, Martin's code was possibly the most beautiful thing besides Red City I had ever seen. Trinity, no wonder he'd pointed and laughed at my idio. How could such an ass as Martin make something so lovely?

The City responded to my surprise, surging in half-alarm, splintering my world with a shock so powerful that as I fainted into it I wondered if she would short out my navis and kill my brain. Black terror dampened the joy then, and a thousand visions I'd had through the sensorfeeds of death and abuse and pain and anger reminded me the city wasn't safe. She was full of killers, and backs turned on back alley beatings, and people dying for want of basic human rights every hour of every day. If she—when she—decided who she wanted to resonate with, what if Red City chose neither Mai nor me? What if she eliminated us both? What if she killed us simply because she, in her alien immortality, did not recognize the vulnerability of human flesh?

Surfacing, still paralyzed from the electrical shock, I saw Mai focusing on me with pure lust—the first identifiable emotion I'd seen. It puzzled me until the wave of empathy reached me, and I felt as she felt < *eagerGreed/hungryhungry *> and thought as she thought < i am entitled to what i have worked for finally finally they pass me up and over again and again they punish they scream but i will be on top this time just waiting, waiting, all my life waiting for this moment to succeed to prove that i am worth something >

Mai was one of the dangerous things in Red City. Through the link I seeped < *fear/smallness* >

Through the link she rejoiced < no more second-place second-best mommy daddy see me now see how she hurts more than i hurt see how they hurt more than i hurt i control all things all things now >

On Thread #1, through the telempathic link I poured my < *fear* >

Through the strengthening link she sucked up my fear with < *glee* >

I poured my smallness out onto the ground at the feet of the City and my power drained into Mai, and the City swelled. The feet of the mob pounded harder, faster, harder. The walls shook with their strength and their rage. I thought/felt as the three-way resonant link became stronger < everyone was right about me i am no good a no-good stupid retard operator i had been given the world and i blew it blew it all away because i thought i was smarter than i was but i wasn't i'm operator-class stupid should have let the normals take charge stupid hoshi stupid retard hoshi >

Thread #2: (In the almost-unconscious, I lock the truth away in the small dark box where I keep the things that matter. Shh... Split out Thread #3 before I go...)

New thread, Thread #3: A practical thread of consciousness to do what must be done via machine-only software, not via link-readable wetware. Set some programing to override the numb confusion of the electrical shock. Notice the robot arms swarming over Martin, covering him with inhuman speed. Calculate the variables and the timing, set a schedule for what needs to happen between now and when Mai swoops in for the kill.

Mai picked up the vial of NQ again, its dark blue shimmering in the light of Martin's code. I continued my three threads of thought, keeping Thread #1 entangled with Mai and the City, and the others secret and close.

Thread #1: < i cannot win >

Thread #2: (I have to win.)

Thread #3: Calculating. I am going to have to be very, very fast to win.

Mai moved closer to where Martin hung above the pagoda, the NQ raised in her hand, a small, dark-blue vial of death.

Thread #1: < i need mai to help me save me be in control i just want to rest to sleep to not have to try to manage anymore >

Thread #2: (I can't let her take control.)

Thread #3: Pain control and motor ready to go back on line; clock function ready; list of actions, allocate nanoseconds to this bit, calculate milliseconds for Mai to close the distance to Martin, calculate—

Mai twitched. < how good it will be to smack this feeble down to finally have my due i am qualified *!MORETHANQUALIFIED!* to be director to be on council to be a valuable part of the community controller of the city never again will they call me a disappointment i will make them proud mommy daddy you'll be proud these operators don't know how good they have it have always had it i will save the city from its stinking self >

Thread #1: < you will save the city we will save the city we are a family >

The City responded with her own thought/feelings, < *warmth/security*

>

Thread #2: (Remember, remember, Mai Chandra is a monster.)

A final whirl and shimmer, and Martin Ho was no longer naked. He hung clothed in an exquisite suit of his own thoughts.

Thread #3: Sequence the subroutines just so, and there.

Mai nodded toward me, her communication like a knife through the link. < doU have the program? is it done? >

I thought/felt back < notyet >

I rose, stumbling as Thread #3 temporarily reallocated resources from pain control to motor. I leaned close to the pagoda and pretended to inspect Martin's code.

On Thread #1 Mai's psyche-drip fed me < *calm-and-reassurance* >

On Thread #2 (that is just the honey masking the poison below.)

Thread #3, stand by—

I stood face-to-face with Mai, between Martin and the City, above and below. The pagoda lay between us all, at the magnetic center where the Dragon Lines met. The restlessness surging from the ground subsided, as the energy beneath our feet began to focus toward me, Mai, Martin, and the pagoda at the center, spreading more < *warmth/reassurance* > in response to the feedback between us three. The sensation amplified, setting me to an uncontrollable shaking as I fell into synch with the élan's vibration. The sine wave animation in that edu-vid from First Ambassador Morgan was more literal than I'd realized. The thrum-thrum-thrum of the boots above began to syncopate with us as well, the crowd unifying as Mai and the City and I unified, pounding in the rhythm of the pulses here in the down-below.

"See, as long as you and I work together, the City is at peace," Mai remarked aloud this time, but I knew through the telempathic link that her comment was in reference to the crowd's unknowing response to the élan's broadcast. < doU have the whole program? > Mai thought/felt to me again.

I mouthed the word, but no sound came out, only the telempathic < *yes* >.

We were of one movement, one body, one mind. One thrum-thrum of the heartbeat of the City.

Mai nodded neatly and shifted forward, pulling the dropper out of the vial of NQ. The hilt of a sonic knife poked from the pocket of her pressed white blouse. Her saw-toothed hair framed her face. Her black eyes widened with < *wonder* > as she stroked Martin's jaw until it opened and I used my love of the City—which felt so natural I realized I'd been halfway to resonance with this élan my whole life—to let Mai take control.

< anything you say mai anything you want red city and i, we trust you, we'll do anything for you we are family we are community >

Thread #3: GO!

In the Mem: "Martin! Now! Run the whole program now!"

And everything else happened more or less at once from the perspective of the casual observer.

Mai dropped three drops of the dark blue liquid onto the surface of Martin's tongue. As they permeated his mucous membranes, headed straight for his bloodstream, to his heart, to his head, Martin Ho transferred the completed code into the stationary system at the top of the gruesome pagoda—and ran it well before Mai had intended for me to do the same; and without Martin's death to influence the resonance.

I shut down the self-loathing of Thread #1 as Thread #2 released the other side of my feelings, and I cried aloud with all I had left, "We do not belong to you!"

I cracked open my heart then, to Mai, to poor Martin who was too engaged in an NQ rush to know it or remember it later, and to the City above me and below me and around me and within me. I had family. I had Kelvin and Lillie and Angel and Sorreno and, like evil-bad cousins, Luzzie and Bosco and Blinker—and I had the City herself, her every street corner and sky-lift, every tree in every park, every rumbling tube beneath her crust. I loved her, even when she hurt me.

I was the magnet. Not Mai. And I didn't need to do much to flip the resonance onto my frequency.

I grasped the top of the pagoda in my damaged hands, smearing blood all over the crescent of data crystals and the shimmering blue teardrop of the tzaddium processor where Mai had meant to trap the élan, claiming it as my own.

The City manifested, unable to resist the siren-lure. She rose from the currents in the ground, pulled herself from the airwaves in the clouds, and coalesced into the room. She unfolded, a Valkyrie taller than the sky and still contained within the three-meter space, and pointed her trident toward the stars. If we'd been outside, where we could see it, she would have pointed straight at the constellation Cleopatra, straight at the star we came from, straight for Sol. She stood poised exactly like her image on the city seal.

And then she bent toward us.

And menaced us with shadows.

Tendrils of shimmering infrared probed the pagoda, exploring the cube of earth, the sphere of water, the pyramid of air, and the Memspace within the stationary system on top that was meant to contain her, irresistible in the resonance of the ritual.

Mai turned on the sonic blade, not yet having realized that dripping down her clean, precise pagoda was the salty, messy blood of Hoshi, that completely changed the tenor of the resonance building around the creature's would-be prison.

Mai moved toward Martin with the invisible blade whining.

I pulled the shocker out of my pocket and pointed it straight at the stationary system on the top of the pagoda.

All at once: Current leapt from my hand into the prison Martin had created for the city's soul, frying it useless. The Valkyrie reached for the crystalline data matrix. Mai started her plunge into Martin Ho's scalp.

As the shocker made contact with the processor, my blood, and the Valkyrie, I thought/felt < RED CITY I RELEASE YOU > The circuit closed on my terms.

I staggered away from the scorched, smoking pagoda, dazed but weirdly still alive.

The creature turned toward Mai. < uwantme? > She queried.

< !iwantyou > Mai turned, her thoughts still bared to me through the link < *confusedSurpriseQuestion?* it worked? but i thought i'd have to do more — >

Red City cupped Mai Chandra's face in her huge/small hands, and pressed her mouth to Mai's lips in a gentle kiss. < *peace* >

Mai stiffened and shook. Then she sank to the ground slowly, almost gracefully, triumph crawling across her face as consciousness drained from her eyes.

Martin looked at me, pupils enormous and blood running down the side of his head. It was a lot of blood, but the cut was small, and Mai hadn't done any real damage yet. Plus Martin wasn't likely to know or care about that cut for another eight hours or so considering his blood-alcohol level mixed with the huge dose of NQ—I've heard rumors that an NQ high alone is almost enough to get an Op hooked. NQ rush or not, Martin still looked pretty pale.

And me? I started laughing. Not the kind of laugh that comes from humor or joy, but that comes from relief so intense that the only way it can find its way out of a person is by laughter.

The élan vital of Red City turned toward me, menace fading, and cocked her head to the side, projecting < *curiosity* >. Seeing such a human expression on a creature so alien tickled my irreverence, and my sense of the ridiculous, and the hysterical edge of my relief-laugh drifted toward amusement. The mob above had stopped pounding.

< hello > I thought/felt through the now two-way link.

Red City leaned toward me, passed her arms and head through me since she was just light bent to give me something to look at. I felt her, again, inspecting me. Only this time with a lightness of touch, an understanding, however coarse, of my human frailty. She shared with me < greeting *confusion/bemusement* >.

She leaned down to kiss me too, just as she had kissed Mai—only without the brain-frying current, and for the time of that kiss, I really did feel that Red City was at peace.

"HOSHI ARCHER!" The boom of Sorreno's voice broke the spell.

I turned to see the Inspector and an impossible number of Red City's finest mob through the small door into the room. Sorreno was in full uniform and riot gear, and she wore an amplifier against her throat.

I turned back, but the Valkyrie of Red City was gone.

I straightened, shaky and bloody and entirely grinning. "Yes ma'am! I surrender!" I dropped the shocker to the ground and held up my hands. I'd never been so happy to see Sorreno. Even as one of her officers jabbed a restraint into my wrists.

CHAPTER 29

I'd only ever seen the inside of a holding cell from the outside, but it wasn't all that bad. It helped that Angel came to see me daily, with updates on my "situation." It helped even more that, despite the jammer that prevented me from accessing the Mem in any normal way, I could escape my cell—in mind anyway—any time I wanted by reaching out to the City.

"So everything's all cleared up on the crimes you didn't do," Angel told me. Her sproingy blond curls and smile would brighten anybody's day. "Sorreno's still snorting smoke about the missing thugs of course, but with Martin's evidence and all, you're no longer wanted for data thieving."

"I still can't believe the RCPD lost track of Jaali Henri," I muttered. "He'd worked here for twelve years, for Signal's Sake." Bill's Ragtime had been wiped clean as well, and no one had found any connection to the thugs in Mai's records—any connection that could be used for locating them at any rate. And Mai was dead, so there'd be no asking her.

"Well, Sorreno still insists there's something bigger behind Mai and her accomplices, that someone bad's still out there. Someone who helped the thugs go disappeary and funded her killing spree. We'll keep looking. We're also still trying to figure out where Mai got that adaptive EM field that turned the manhole in Cleopatra Square invisible. That's tightly controlled tech from Callisto, and the colony's reps haven't been forthcoming." She paused, unhappy. "Jury's still out about the crimes you did do, though." There hadn't been a jury in over 400 years, but somehow the saying hadn't died.

In between updates and smiles from Angel, I lay back on the hard tile floor, suspicious of furniture especially here, and let my mind run free.

The EM field around the holding cells that kept my navis from connecting to the Mem didn't affect the frequencies favored by the élan. It was neither through a bug in my software nor a defect in my hardware, but through a natural, partial resonance that I'd been accessing the city sensors all these years. A halfway-place between our worlds which we had, unknowingly, always shared.

Through the camera in his stationary system, I saw Kelvin working in his attic studio; through a rare unbroken cam in Frontal Market I saw him sell his tinker's crafts. Kelvin sent Lillie to the RCPD station a few times, too, to glean information about me so he wouldn't break his vow to avoid anyone in a uniform. Except for that life-saving favor he'd done for me when he'd told Sorreno where to find me. Kelvin was a good friend.

Luzzie Vai was harder for me to locate. He stayed out of the way of cameras and readers, but as I lay with nothing else to do on my prison floor, I realized I could get the City to lead me to him through the faint remainder of our telempathic bond. I couldn't see Luzzie, but I got the impression he was holding his breath, waiting to see what would happen next. If I ratted on Luzzie, I'd be out of the holding cell right here and now, and he'd be in one. He was trusting me not to make that choice. I wouldn't, of course; I was as familiar with the Prisoner's Dilemma as the next Joe who's read their game theory primer. I wondered if Luzzie was angry over Mai's death, because now I couldn't hand him Aysha's killer and fulfill my part of our bargain. He'd probably take it out of me in those two (Trinity, really two?) favors I owed him. I tried not to think about how well he knew me now. Luzzie Vai was a good enemy.

Martin Ho got a hero's reception for bringing down Mai, with my role but a minor part. His face splashed through the mainfeeds with a "Local Op Makes Good" tag that warmed the city's tenor toward my people just enough to stave off this week's near-fatal disaster. To everyone but Martin, it was clear the comic relief of his buffoonish pomposity—rather than the heroism—had done the heavy lifting.

The change in public perception was of course much more complicated.

Seemingly unconnected events had played a seemingly interconnected role: Sorreno calming the near-riot with a leadership speech that brought both sides to their knees, Martin running the program and staying alive to testify about a laundry list of crimes, Red City making a full connection with human beings for the first time, and me sorting out my own self enough to free her from Mai's clutches. They were inevitable results of each other, a completed circuit, the resonance between people and ideas.

As far as the City went, at first I'd meant to say something about her appearance and role in the matter, but there never seemed to be the right opening, or I would get cut off before I could spit it out. "Be brief," Sorreno had advised me prior to the sequence of formal questionings.

"What was Mai hoping to achieve?" an invisible questioner had asked in the pitch-black interrogation room.

"To summon the élan of the city and use it for her own agenda, Sir."

"And did she succeed?"

"No, Sir, she did not."

"Very well, that's all for now."

As time went by and the complication of the truth became increasingly awkward to spit out, I realized mum was best. Publicly exposing the élan could risk exposing my ability to enter the city's sensors. Plus I shouldn't be trusting city officials with important information anyway, Mai was proof enough of that.

In the end it was Sorreno who came up with a suitable compromise regarding the crimes I did do.

"It was a shocker malfunction," she told me first, without preamble, big and brown and voice full of boom. "That's the only way to explain how Mai Chandra's dead. The shocker wasn't tinkered with and those things can't ordinarily do lethal. Hundred percent sure, electrocution is what killed Mai Chandra."

Well, that was the end of Issue Number One, the question of whether or not Hoshi Archer had willfully taken a life.

"So there's no charge on murder 4a, subsection 16. The final ruling is an accidental 5a, with a sub-ruling L of mechanical failure in Circumstance X of personal self-defense while in an untenable situation."

I nodded slowly. Only two beings besides me knew the truth of what had killed Mai Chandra, which was that the power surge had come not from my shocker but from the City herself. Mai wasn't going to talk, and the City didn't have anyone but me to talk to.

I let out air and folded my arms around my knees. When the guards had let Sorreno into the cell with me, they'd left the door ajar behind her. I fancied that boded well, but wasn't going to count my lorries till I found out the verdict on Issue Number Two, the only real crime I had actually had committed.

"As far as the identity theft," Sorreno's mood blackened as dark as the disturbing smudges on the far wall of the cell by the latrine, "there's no doubt you did it."

I flinched from her disapproval.

"And there's no doubt that your subsequent refusal to invoke Snitch Law, cough up your contacts, and be on your merry way isn't helping your situation, either."

They wouldn't leave the door open if they planned to escort me to the hanging chamber, would they?

"But I believe this will cover it." Sorreno handed me a digipage with the RCPD seal on it.

I read the legal language 19 times before giving up. "Um. What's it say?"

"It says that if a civilian's been of Special Service to the Red City Police Department, they are granted a one-time pardon on transgressions below level 5, provided those transgressions were incurred during the time of service, were necessary to the performance of that service, and have never been entered into the public record nor publicized on any feed, local, main, or wideband."

"But there's no such thing as Special Service in the RCPD law book," I blurted, still confused. I'd been forced to read and understand the manual as part of my former indenture to the force.

Sorreno gave me a shut-the-fuck-up look and sniffed, "There wasn't until today. City Coordinator Corstenza was particularly impressed with your service to the city."

I took the clue stick and shut-the-fuck-up about the unusual nature of the thing. I kept my face serious by shutting down a bit of motor control and said with all the respect and gratitude I could express, "Thank you ma'am, and thank you to the City Coordinator."

"Not a word then."

I did smile now, letting out my joy, "Not a word."

Sorreno bent down so that the sensor in the cell couldn't see, and whispered so softly in my ear the sensor couldn't hear, "Good work PI Archer, and thank you."

Then she backed up, storms across her face again, and left me with, "See to it I never catch you buying services from known criminals again. You know better, Hoshi. There are no more get out of jail free cards for you. Or for your unsavory contacts."

I was released the following afternoon. I'd made it clear the press was not welcome; the least I could do was make sure Martin stayed in the limelight as long as possible. Plus I had something more private to take care of before getting back to my life and my new, uncomfortable understanding that, like it or not, I had influence in Red City.

◆ ◆ ◆

The Memorial wasn't on my 200 favorite buildings list, but as I looked up at it I thought maybe I should lengthen my list to 201. It was only ten stories high, and its delicate facing of carved blackstone and lapis, both beautiful and sad, made it easy to miss. But now, close up, I appreciated its lack of sharp edges, the subtle detailing on its surface, the way it swept and flowed on the corner of the block, reminding me of the prow of a ship cutting through a calm sea. Out front on a patch of native grass one of the city's characteristic pagodas sat, its top dancing with blue flame. The sight of the pagoda conjured bad memories before a warmth from outside of me pushed them away. < not all pagodas were evil > whispered the City that moved beneath my feet < not all people are dangerous >. The City's currents, too, flowed naturally now, released from the corruption Mai had placed at her heart. Given time, and enough peace, however uneasy, the City might be able to heal.

Claudia's small room in the Memorial was on the fourth floor, and as I walked through the vine-covered, sun-lit corridors to its number, I thought I saw Secilia pass me going the other way. But I didn't know for sure, and it seemed inappropriate to run after her and ask.

Within, I found the thin gold plaque etched with Claudia's name and her citizen ID. I traced the etchings below her name with a fingertip, first the dates of her birth and death, then the brief message chosen to encapsulate Claudia's life: "The Foundation of Her Loved Ones."

I smiled. She would have liked that message.

Intricate structures of folded paper had been left in the narrow space, and other things Claudia loved, the holo of her parents, the holo of Secilia, her structural engineering awards, her favorite blue robe. I pressed my fingers to my lips, and then to her name on the plaque. The scent of lavender and soap came to me briefly, and was gone.

Three hours later I was home again. Home in my apartment in Hill District, looking everywhere but my window, making myself wait as long as possible before looking, like a child too excited to unwrap the best birthday present in the universe ever. Which it was.

I knew nothing was over—that nothing was truly over because life wasn't made of beginnings and endings but of cycles and circuits and feedbacks. There was still the issue of the missing thugs, and the likelihood that their disappearance meant whatever hateful iceberg Mai had been sitting atop still had a lot of depth left unplumbed. There was still the disaster-waiting-to-happen in the form of my indebtedness to one nefarious Luzzie Vai; who knows what he learned about me while he was guiding me through Cleopatra Square. And Martin Ho—Trinity only knew how long his current hero status would sustain him before he got on my back again. Then there was the fact that I'd been reassigned to a new Integration Officer, and I'd have to report to him every week just like I'd had to report to Mai, and that the frictions between Operators and normals had yet to be resolved, and that maybe they wouldn't ever truly be resolved. There was the question of what form my relationship with the City would take, and whether I'd be able to get her to stop with the nosebleed-inducing sensorfeed dreams. There was still inequity and a lot of unrest, and the matter of the Inclusion Act remained unsettled. Operators still had no representation in the Office of Operator Affairs, at the IO, or anywhere else that made policy about our lives. And there was still the pain, both everyday and extraordinary, of the City, of her people, of the desperate and the vulnerable and the oppressed, all of whom deserved justice.

But that could wait. For today, there was peace.

For today I (and Martin Ho, and Luzzie Vai, and Inspector Cassandra Sorreno, and Lillie Redwing, and Kelvin Kovak, and Madame Bosco, and the list goes on) had saved the city.

I took off my bolero and kicked off my boots and leaned back on my berth, the only piece of furniture I had and liked and used. Then I turned over and faced my window. There were the peaks and domes and points of the skyline and the graceful spiral of the Arts and Culture Building, and the triple towers of the 100 Worlds Trade Union joined by their series of sky-bridges, and the prickly quills of the Red City Reporter, and—each of my 200 favorite buildings in Red City.

And then, for no reason at all, I thought of Ursula, the cute girl at the paint store in Husson who'd helped me unravel a pretty important piece of the case. And I thought of her smile and her elfish hair and my utter clumsiness and how I'd gotten so embarrassed I'd fled the scene just as I had almost gotten up the courage to ask her out.

I brought up Ursula's address from my memory index and looked at its pattern and smiled at her face as I watched her handing me her card.

It was definitely time to ask her about that date.

If I couldn't trust a potential girlfriend with my clumsiness, who could I trust?